I0544987

SIMON OF SPACE

A NOVEL
by CHESTER BURTON BROWN

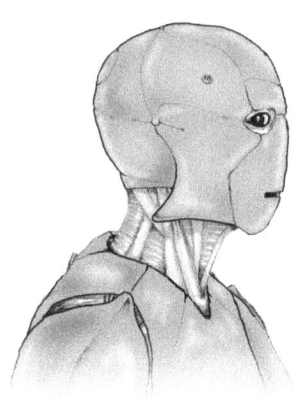

Simon of Space
Fourth Edition
Text by Chester Burton Brown; Illustrations by Matthew Hemming

Simon of Space on-line: *http://cheeseburgerbrown.com*

For Joshua

Publishing history
First printing: StoryZoo Studios edition, September 2005
Second printing: Ephemera Bound edition, February 2008
Third printing: Lulu edition, August 2008
Fourth printing: CreateSpace edition, January 2012

This is an original work of fiction. Any mapping of the characters, events or situations depicted herein to events or persons in the real world would be fanciful in the extreme. No part of this work may be reproduced or transmitted without express permission from the publisher.

©2005–2012 Matthew Hemming. All Rights Reserved.

I.
I THINK, THEREFORE

Do you remember the first moment of your life?

I do, but then most people suffer from the inherent deficits of infancy when they are born, whereas I had the special indignity and privilege of being thirty-six years old at the time.

I admit that I did soil myself. In this respect I am on par with a lot of other people, though my insides were not stuffed with healthy black meconium but rather the still spicy remains of a sumptuous meal enjoyed shortly before the beginning of my life.

And to be entirely truthful the *first* first moment is hazy. I was lost in a world of synaesthetic fire, pawing out at the incoherent jangle of sudden perceptive barf that stabbed in at the amorphous horror that was quickly coalescing into my sense of self.

I was released into a blazing light, and then I fell down.

It was bliss. There was a world of smooth coolness firmly beneath me and a world of warm, blurry fog above me. I felt very peaceful. I could have lived a life splayed out like that, seeing nothing and understanding none of what I heard – currents of air, chirping birds, approaching footfalls, shouts of alarm. It was all a wondrous symphony of inexplicable and awesome stimuli, now that I'd managed to throttle the input a little by lying face down.

That's when the apes came. They rolled me over and wiggled their lips at me while they grunted. I thought it was beautiful and magical.

With the benefit of hindsight I recognize now that they were people, just like me. They were my fellow travellers. They had rushed over because I had collapsed as soon as I stepped out of the gate. What they wanted to know was, "Are you okay?"

In reply I smiled serenely and reached out to touch their sparkly, wet-looking eyes. Funny monkeys!

"I think he shat himself," concluded somebody.

There I was, not two minutes old, lying on the polished floor of the travel terminal, a crowd of cooing strangers gathering around me, their periphery being pushed aside by concerned authorities and their minions. I was the subject of some excitement. That much was clear even to me as I drooled and hummed, dazzled by the sun.

An auspicious start, wouldn't you say?

That was five weeks ago now. This morning the nurses brought me a cupcake with five little candles jammed into it, and sang me a silly song. "Happy Birthday, Simon!" they cheered. "You're five weeks old!"

I blew out the candles with all the aplomb and dignity the situation warranted. "And yet I don't feel a day over a month," I said. "The secret is eating your greens."

We all had a good chuckle. They're an easy laugh, at the hospital. Nice people.

Doctor Pent strode in after them, and made a bit of a show of thumbing through my chart and nodding to himself. Then he sat down on the end of my bed and put his hands in the pockets of his labcoat. He made small talk for a few minutes and then slipped out this diary. "Simon, I'd like you to start keeping a journal."

"Oh?"

"I think it might help your memory."

"You mean I might remember everything again?"

"Well, I think it might address some of the issues we're still seeing with your short term retention. You've suffered a very unique kind of brain damage, Simon, and the entire structure of your memory has been rattled. It's not just the big picture, it's the details."

"I see," I said. "So this journal is to be a new facet of my treatment?"

"Not precisely," said Dr. Pent, shifting in his seat. "Frankly, we've done just about all we can do for you here. As soon as you feel up to it you're to be released. We've arranged transport back to your home where your family will meet you."

"Is that expensive?"

"Your insurance company is taking care of it."

"Ah."

After a moment he touched my sleeve. "Simon?"

I was staring out the windows across from the row of beds, watching birds flicker and twitter across the branches of a budding tree. "You must understand I have mixed feelings about all this," I said, chewing the inside of my lip. "This ward is all I know. My family are strangers from my point of view." I turned to him. "Isn't there some way I could recover my memory *before* meeting them?"

Dr. Pent sighed. "Simon, we've been over this. This isn't a matter of recovering your long-term memories – they simply *aren't there*. I can't explain what happened to you when you crossed that gate, but I do know how to interpret crystal-clear brain tomography. As far as long term memory is concerned, you have the mind of a baby."

"Yet I recovered my speech!" I pointed out. "And I *know* things – like what flowers are, and that you need to water them. I didn't learn that here. Doesn't that mean there's *something* there?"

"And yet you had to re-learn how to voluntarily control your bladder," said Dr. Pent heavily. "Five thousand years of medical science and the human brain continues to surprise us."

"Great," I grunted. "Do it up as a paper and transmit it to the journals."

He put his hand on my shoulder. "I know this is all very hard, Simon. But you have to trust me. There are people that care about you. They'll help you rediscover your life."

I snorted. "Makes you think, though."

"What's that?"

"Is it really *my* life?"

Dr. Pent stood up slowly, and patted the diary on the bed. "Put it in the journal, Simon. Take the time you need to figure out what you must – but don't make them wait forever."

I nodded. He gave me a tight little smile and walked out. I turned the diary over in my hands.

Hello, my name is Simon. Or so they tell me. I've lived my whole charmed life in a friendly ward in a white hospital by the delta. I don't know anything about anything, but everyone here is very understanding and the food is amazing. I'm talking to a blue plastic diary sitting in the palm of my hand, charged with the task of coming to terms with leaving this place to travel lightyears across space to assume a life I've never known.

How am I beholden to the man who lived that life?

Am I not a sovereign human being, capable of making my own decisions? I may be only five weeks old, but I'm an adult. I seldom wet my pants anymore, and with the help of the nurses I've learned to recognize the boundaries of personal space. To whom does my destiny belong, if not me?

Furthermore, this journal is stupid. Forget it.

II.
FORGET ME NOT

The prettiest nurse in the whole ward is named Randa.

She isn't the youngest nurse and it's fairly certain she isn't the sweetest, but there is an air about her that penetrates her calm and efficient manner, relaying forcefully that she is every moment a woman. The infinite crispness of her pleats cannot hide the truth broadcast by the musky, visceral reality lurking beneath. It grips me.

I tried to explain this to her after I had again succumbed to the powerful adolescent urge to palpitate her behind while she was changing sheets. "I've had a brain injury!" I cried, hiding behind my arms.

"You'll *have* a brain injury," she promised darkly.

She turned to leave. "Listen," I called. "Can I ask you something?" She paused tolerantly so I asked, "Has what happened to me ever happened to anyone else before?"

She arched her brow. "Only in the movies, honey."

...Which is when it first dawned on me that somebody could *doubt* my condition. I realized that my five long weeks of delightful and engaging life have been sheltered from the smell of distrust – a funk radiated through the flickering eyes and clenching fingers of my fellow apes. Falsehood...what a novel concept!

I wondered: could I detect incredulity in others? Is my condition a joke?

I hopped out of bed and made for the day room, a man on a mission. The corridor to the common areas has differently coloured stripes running along the floor which branch off to the cafeteria, the nurse station and the washrooms. In my first days of life I was fascinated by the stripes and their bold hues, and I gave them secret names I am too embarrassed to reproduce. They had a magic significance to me as guides to every outpost of import.

My paper slippers shuffled loudly across the shiny floor.

The day room was quiet, and somehow lugubrious despite the shafts of silvery sunshine washing in through the wide windows. Some patients were playing chess, or chatting listlessly. Some cried. Others minced their fingers and hummed fugues, or stared at the walls. We are a colourful bunch, we in this hospital's ward for cerebral trauma. The turnover is high so there's always somebody new to meet.

The wandering arm of the cafeteria staff stepped up smartly. "Would you care for some sliced pears, Mr. Fell?"

"What are pears?" I asked.

"Fruit," replied the robot smoothly.

"Well, fruit is a food," I admitted. "Okay, hit me."

I took my cup of sliced pears over to the window where Jessem sat, staring at the glimmering delta valley below. Jessem has lost his ability to retain short-term memory entirely, which means any conversation with him need begin with a certain amount of preamble. But he's an insightful guy, so it's usually worth it.

"Hello," I said. "My name is Simon. We're pals. You've often complimented me on my dry wit, and I've complimented you on your penetrating mind. I once made the nurses bring you buttered toast in the middle of the night when you were crying over a nightmare you couldn't remember."

Jessem nodded slowly. "Okay. Please, won't you sit down?"

"Thank you." I adjusted my robe and crossed my legs. "Jessem, have you ever heard of someone losing their memory after being transmitted through a hyperspatial gate?"

"Why, sure," he said, smiling and looking at me with wide eyes. "Who hasn't wondered about it? Is it really *me* that walks out of that gate halfway across space, or it is just a *facsimile* of me loaded up with my memories? Do I die when I'm transmitted, and is somebody else who thinks he's me born into my place?"

"Wondering is one thing," I interjected, "I'm talking about it *happening*."

"Haven't you ever been to the movies, Simon?" asked Jessem. "It's the oldest gimmick in the book: hyperspatial amnesia. It's the premise of probably half of all opera and at least a third of all narrative pornographies."

"Yes, my good man – but what about in real life?"

Jessem shook his head. "Maybe it's happened somewhere, sometime. I've always thought it was just an exercise for philosophy subscribers." After a moment he hesitated, and then offered his hand out for me to shake. "I'm Jessem, by the way."

"Yes, I know."

"And you are..."

"Simonithrat Fell. I introduced myself earlier."

Jessem sighed, and returned his gaze to the window. "There's something wrong with me, isn't there?" he asked the glass.

"Yes," I said.

He sighed again. "It's horrible, I think."

I couldn't finish my sliced pears. I came back to the ward, walked around in circles for while between the rows of beds, and then espied this diary. I picked it up and tossed it from hand to hand while I mulled over the fact that my predicament may be ridiculous.

I considered the diary, its single green light winking at me patiently. I cleared my throat and said, "For posterity then: the true account of the first living man to actually come through a hyperspatial gate with neither history nor identity...without being a member of an entertainment guild. Chapter One."

Outside, birds chirped. "Chapter One," I said again.

I lay back on my bed. I put the diary on my chest and closed my eyes. Taking a few deep breaths the first thing that comes to me is the lingering perfume of Nurse Randa's oil on the post of my bed, speaking in fading puffs against the tang of the metal.

Which, naturally, made me horny. And that's pretty much when you came in. Ah, me.

...I really cannot see the point of persisting in this insipid journal. How shall I dazzle the ages tomorrow – a report on my breakfast? Idiocy.

III.
CRUSHED HEAD FAEDA

When I feel a little lost I like to sink into bed and let myself be hypnotized by hospital routine. It takes me back to my early childhood a few weeks ago when the only place my bewildered mind could find comfort was in the clockstep march of the nurses' schedule.

And so this morning I didn't get up. I sat in bed and watched the world unfold.

Weeks ago when my words still failed me I witnessed these events like a pet – reading posture, smelling sweat. We were watered and fed, tended and turned by a regular cycle of familiar faces, young women and men and robots with warm hands and soothing voices. Their every exchange was a wonder to me, and I struggled to lend meaning to it all using the only cues I could: micro-movements, shifts in weight, twitches in the face, flicks of the eyes, catches in the breath...

With language's return ward life gained a certain amount of chewable context.

By careful attention I learned that Nurse Hiwai had a new lover even before she told Nurse Wennel, and then Nurse Wennel told everybody else. I knew Nurse Randa alternately loved and hated Dr. Pent, and I felt the bloom of bad news waft down the hall a full quarter hour before they came to tell poor Omefrey his wife hadn't survived the crash.

After breakfast they fluff our pillows, up one row of beds and then down the other.

I confess that I'm not sure what I'm supposed to be doing. Is there some better way to come to terms with what lies before me than mulling over the infinitude of that which I don't know? I'm not sure keeping this journal helps at all. And if Dr. Pent is right, there are people back home waiting for me, worried sick over me. How can I justify leaving them at the mercy of their anxieties?

And yet as I look around the busy ward I cannot ever imagine leaving this home.

Dr. Pent came by and asked if he could read my journal. I said I didn't mind. He thumbed through my two entries quickly, his expression unreadable. "These are perfectly normal feelings you're having," he told me. "I'll check in with you tomorrow."

"I'll be sure to make a note of that in my journal."

If he detected my sarcasm he failed to show it.

A couple of hours after supper I got itchy feet. Irritable, restless and heavy minded I flopped out of bed and took a stroll through the quiet dimness of the evening ward. Most of my fellow patients were already asleep, and the rest were plugged into one kind of media or another. The only voices came from the intermittent, echoing murmurs of the nurses' intercoms.

Somewhere somebody's life-lending machine was beeping in a slow rhythm. I tried to find the source of the sound for a while, but ended up getting turned around in one of the dark corridors. That's how I came to be standing outside of Crushed Head Faeda's room.

"Is that you, Mr. Fell?" she called, startling me.

I looked at the number on the door. "Faeda?"

"Come in and talk a while, won't you?" she asked. After a moment's consideration she added, "You're a dung-sucking sweat flea. I'll peel your throat."

I stepped inside. Faeda has a private room full of flowers and prayer grasses. The light was low and amber save for the blue glow cast from a small reading plate Faeda was cradling in the lap of her hospital chemise. "I haven't seen you around much lately," I said conversationally, sitting on a chair by the bureau. "Have you been cooping yourself up to read?"

"They've made me a prisoner in my own room because I won't stop biting people," she explained, picking up the plate. "I'm reading poetry. Do you care for poetry, Mr. Fell?"

"I have no idea," I said.

"She never used to," said Crushed Head Faeda, caressing the edge of the reading plate for a moment before thumbing it off. "But I do."

"She who?"

"Before-the-accident-Faeda," she replied. "She never found a way to let poetry in. It bored her. But I can't get enough of it, you festering cockworm."

"It's good to be open minded," I smiled.

Crushed Head Faeda smiled back, which was somewhat ghastly. Faeda had obviously been an achingly beautiful girl before the accident, and in profile she still was. But when she turned her face you forgot the black-lashed intensity of her almond-shaped left eye and found yourself buried in the calamity of the other: squinting, flickering, dilated, mad. The right side of her forehead was a wet-looking field of bruise and gauze, her head half-shaven, crisscrossed by angry white lines of fuse. When she spoke the left side of her mouth hung slack, mimicking the motions of the right side in a series of irregular tics after a few seconds delay. She drooled, and coughed behind a hand twisted into a bird-like claw.

Faeda's cognitive abilities and her personality had been fundamentally deformed by trauma to her brain. She cannot control her inhibitions, and is prone to sudden bouts of rage and lust and fear. I like her anyway, though. We're friends.

"I'm going away tomorrow," she said, throwing an empty cup at my head.

I dodged it. "Oh?"

Faeda came to the hospital just a few days after I had. I never did understand the specifics of her mishap, but I gathered she had fallen from a severe height and absorbed most of the shock of impact with her skull. The resulting damage was very serious, but it was explained to me that because Faeda was very wealthy she had periodically had her mind inscribed into a kind of crystal as a precaution against just the sort of the thing that had befallen her. Faeda was not in therapy: she was simply passing the time until the back-up copy of her mind arrived by courier, so that the doctors could rebuild her brain and she could resume her life where she had left off as a healthy person.

"My mind has come. They told me after supper. They say the operation is tomorrow." She ran her fingers over the seams on her pate, a funny twitch running through the right side of her face. A tear ran down her cheek, and then another.

"That's good news, isn't it?" I prompted.

"For *her* it is, the mung-booted bitchwipe," spat Faeda, turning away. "How much of me will survive in her, if any?" She picked up the reading plate and hurled it at the wall, smashing it. "Will she let me read poetry, do you think?"

"Maybe you'll make her a fuller person," I suggested.

"Maybe I'll die," she replied icily. "Inside of her."

There was a bit of a lull in the conversation then, which Crushed Head Faeda broke by launching a spoon at me. It caught me squarely in the brow, causing me to flail sideways and lose my seat. She only throws silverware at people she really likes, so I took this to mean the moment we were sharing together was one of special intimacy. I stood up and rubbed my forehead, wincing. "Well, I don't want to keep you from your reading..."

"What about you, my sweet Simon? What's happening with you?" she asked, taking my forearm softly and fixing me with her stable eye.

"They want me to go home. To my...family."

"To become *him*."

"Him who?"

"He that was before you. Before-the-accident-Simon. And then *you*, Simon – *this* Simon – will die." Tears streamed down her cheeks. She squeezed my hand warmly, and sighed with a serene compassion. Her good eye sparkled. "I will piss on your face," she promised.

Food for thought.

IV.
CHILDHOOD'S END

"Well," said Dr. Pent, and I knew that something was up. "Well, Simon," he said again, the stink of nerves rising whenever he shifted in his clothes. "How are we coming along?"

"Good," I said noncommittally, sitting up in bed and blinking against the orange morning sun. "Fine."

"Good," echoed Dr. Pent, nodding at nothing. He jammed his hands into the pockets of his labcoat and pretended to be inspecting some aspect of the wall above my head. "I'd like to talk to you about going home."

Bleary-eyed and dream-headed it took me a moment to recognize that by "home" Dr. Pent did not mean the ward.

"Perhaps they could come here to meet me, here on Samundra," I said hopefully.

Dr. Pent shook his head. "Just a delay," he said. "Sooner or later you're going to have to face the fact that this isn't your world. The sooner the better, in my view."

An edge had teetered in his voice at the end there, and it caused me to turn to look into his face. He flushed and adjusted the probe in his pocket. Curious.

Dr. Pent continued, "I'd like to see you in a taxicab to the spaceport tomorrow, Simon. I think it's time for you to take this step."

I sighed. "I'm being kicked out, aren't I?"

"No," he assured me with pursed lips and a furrowed brow. "You know you can stay here as long as you feel it is necessary." His pores glistened.

I'm going to miss this place.

Feeling very sorry for myself I took a slow, melancholy stroll through the ward. I chatted with the nurses and played a game of chess with Jessem in his semi-private room. Toward noon a storm rolled in, sealing away Samundra's keen blue sky behind a blanket of dark wool. A weak grey light glowed through the windows, swimming with rain. The ward dimmed. Lamps came on, gold amid the silver gloom.

The gong sounded for lunch, and the corridors filled with the sound of shuffling paper slippers as everyone roused to feed.

I came to the edge of the cafeteria but did not sit down. I felt no appetite. I crossed my arms and leaned against the wall, watching the infirm and aggressive and bemused take their rattling trays to table, eyes darting around in furtive paranoia as often as cast unfocused into space without a care in this tangible world. Cutlery clinked. Somebody broke a glass. Talk was minimal.

With an invisible, internal lurch I recognized that they were strangers.

The patients with whom I have spent the past few weeks – the people with whom I grew up – have nearly all been healed or transferred. I waved to Jessem as he wandered in and queued at the counter, and he nodded to me the civil way one acknowledges a friendly alien. He smiled uncertainly. "Am I cutting in?" he asked as the line advanced to where I stood.

"Not at all, my good man," I replied. "Please."

"Thanks. My name's Jessem. Jessem Poll."

"Hello, my name is Simon."

"It's a pleasure to make your acquaintance," he told me.

The tables in the corner by the tea service still bore scrapes and gashes in their surfaces from the time Jessem, Crushed Head Faeda and I had made a fort in the cafeteria, hiding behind walls of overturned furniture and crawling through corridors made of interlocked plastic chairs hung with bed-sheets. We defended our creation against the nurses for almost four hours before Faeda took things too far and bit someone in the leg. The security robots tranquilized her.

"Glorious victory..." she mumbled groggily as they lifted her. "You will pay for your crimes in precious meat," she added, a long string of drool pouring out of her mouth and reaching for the floor. "War!" she muttered, eyes rolling up into their sockets. "Babyrape," she added listlessly, going limp.

Jessem turned to me. "She seems awfully sleepy. Where are they taking her?"

"To her bed."

"Well, that makes sense," said Jessem. He looked around and blinked. "Hey – a fort!" he discovered.

Good times.

Of course I'm almost six weeks old now, and therefore comport myself with a certain amount of dignity. I rarely build forts any longer, and when I do I just go under my bed and hang the blankets over the edges – it's less disruptive and therefore tends to escape the nurses' attention far longer. In the dim and the small I feel safe.

The rain started coming down harder. It splashed and played against the cafeteria windows in a sudden surge, causing a collective tilt of heads in the mawing herd. From my perch against the wall I alone saw the group of people in outlandish costumes arrive with Dr. Pent. Instead of white and simple, their pajamas were varicoloured and layered. Their faces were solemn. One of them had a lump of fabric on top of his head. All three newcomers had skin the same colour as Jessem's: dark coffee.

Dr. Pent took them to where Jessem sat, and Jessem turned away from the rain-washed windows. His face transformed. It folded and blossomed from a countenance of characteristic befuddlement to joy. "Mota! Tanis! Oh my god!" he laughed, overcome.

They embraced. There were tears. There was a sudden explosion of overlapping talking in gibberish. Shoulders were touched, smiles flashed, heads shook. Dr. Pent efficiently wrangled the cluster of burbling humanity along the row of tables and out of the cafeteria.

Jessem's family, obviously. He had been on his way to meet them after a long absence when he had his accident. His greatest single desire in the world was to be re-united with them.

He got his wish today. And, to the increasing horror of his kin, he will get his wish every day, for he is doomed to forget the wonderful reunion before the next meal is served. The delight in their eyes in the cafeteria moved me. But I wonder how delighted they will be the tenth time, the fiftieth time, the hundredth...

Unless they find some way to fix Jessem's brain. Which maybe they will. I'm no expert on the art of the probable. I don't even know how the toaster works.

The whole thing made me feel depressed and touched in sick, wheeling turns so I swung out of the cafeteria and followed the blue line to my bed. In my bed was a man with yellow skin and purple eyes. "I'm thorry?" he said when I asked him what his business was on my pillow.

Nurse Hiwai took my elbow. "Simon, your new bed is over here. We've re-arranged the ward – new patients and all." She deposited me by a bed in the far corner. It was of a slightly different type than my old bed, and the night-stand was a different colour. I felt repulsed. "There you go," smiled Hiwai.

"Yes, quite."

So now here I am, lying under my new bed. The sheets hang down over the sides, brushing the floor and serving as translucent walls. The polished floor is cool and soothing against my belly. I'm whispering into a blue plastic bauble, its single eye lit steadily in attention.

The wind has changed. This isn't my home anymore. I wanted to stay here forever but forever was a four-week spell I lived last month. I will always have a special place in my heart for my childhood memories, but I recognize now that I have no choice but to move on.

I am filled with dread percolating through with a fizz of building resolve.

Dr. Pent's feet stopped by around suppertime. He wanted to know how I was feeling. "Well, I'm ready to go," I told his shoes, hovering at the edge of my bed-sheet wall.

"Fine," came Dr. Pent's muffled voice. "Good."

"May I...may I take the diary with me?" I found myself asking.

"Sure," he said.

"Good."

Dr. Pent's shoes walked away. Tomorrow, then. Tomorrow's the day.

V.
FOREST FLIGHT

Have you ever had one of those days? Well, I haven't. At least, not until today. Or yesterday, I suppose. I don't know what time it is.

It's very dark.

The day began with breakfast in bed. I was surprised and delighted. Nurse Randa fixed my tea just the way I like it, which is just the way she taught me to like it. I also had crumpets, pears, bambloss sticks, and a bowl of hot cocoa.

Dr. Pent arrived with a package. "These are your clothes," he explained. "And your bits."

I frowned and brushed crumbs off my lap. "A change of pajamas?"

"Well, not exactly," smiled Dr. Pent. He opened the package, presenting a square of folded grey fabric that looked uncomfortably coarse. Beneath it seemed to be a short chemise and a thin fabric diaper. "This is a pretty dapper suit, Simon," commented the doctor.

I shrugged suspiciously. "And...bits?"

"Yes of course. Your telephone, your wallet, your plate." He placed three small trinkets on the bed.

"Which is which?" I asked.

He furrowed his brow. "Right. Well, this little bit here, yes, you place that behind your ear. Let me help you. Right behind the – ah, perfect. Does that feel all right? Here, I'll give you a call..."

A signal sounded in my head, startling me. I knocked over the tray containing the remains of my breakfast, which spattered against the wall spectacularly. Dr. Pent steadied me with a hand on my forearm. A quiet voice buzzed inside my skull, blathering on about an incoming missive from Dr. Pent. "Hello?" I cried.

"Relax Simon, it's just me calling," said Dr. Pent, and while I could see his lips move and hear him through the air, I could also feel his voice buzzing right into my bones. *"Can you hear me now?"*

"Yes," I whispered, eyes wide.

"Good, good," he nodded. *"I'm receiving you, too."* He mumbled something and the connection broke. The quiet voice inside my head commented on the fact.

"Who is she?" I asked.

"She who?" frowned Dr. Pent.

"The lady talking about you calling me."

"Um, that's your telephone, Simon." He patted my shoulder encouragingly. "Do you remember when we talked about telephones last week?"

"Sure I remember," I claimed.

My wallet was a smooth, silver, thimble-like device that was fitted to the index finger of my left hand. "I thought I understood the relationship between money and wallets, but it seems I have mistaken some element of it," I said, holding up my finger and looking at the light play across the shiny trinket.

"A wallet is a vessel for money," Dr. Pent said. "The authentication surface is on the inside, and the interfacing surface is on the outside."

"Oh, sure," I said.

"Basically, it means that the wallet will only let money flow if your living finger is present, and the other end is able to negotiate an interface with a till. There are all sorts of tills, so the best wallets have to be very flexible. *This* wallet, Simon, is of the finest kind."

He seemed to want to impress with this fact, but its significance was lost on me. "And the plate?" I picked up the palm-sized sheet of translucent plastic, the edges beveled smooth. It featured on its face only a thin line delineating a tiny circle of greater transparency in one corner.

"Turn it on," suggested Dr. Pent. "Touch the contact."

I did, and the plate became a window through which I could see boxes and stacks of words. As I moved the plate the view scrolled. When I pointed the plate toward the cafeteria I saw a menu, and when I pointed it toward Dr. Pent I saw his official hospital welcome message flash on screen. *"Welcome to the Samundra General Hospital Brain Injury Ward. I'm Doctor Hevender Pent, head of..."*

Dr. Pent winced. "That message is so old."

"You used to have more hair," I pointed out.

"Er, yes," he agreed. "Your plate will pick up on any open informatics in range, as well as giving you a readout for your others bits. You can use the plate in conjunction with your telephone for videoconferencing, for example."

"What's videoconferencing?"

"Well, you might want to see the face of whoever it is you're talking to on the telephone."

"Why?"

Dr. Pent seemed at a loss. "You can't learn it all in a day, Simon. I just thought having your bits might make you feel a little more like a normal person, a little less like a patient."

"Thank you for your consideration," I said. "Indeed, it's not your fault that it's overwhelming. Do you really think I'll need to telephone anyone on my way home?"

"Probably not. But your plate can display pictures of them, if you'd like."

"Pictures of whom?"

"Your *family*, Simon. I've already loaded them in your plate's cache. You can access them anytime."

"Oh," I said quietly.

"Would you like to see them now?"

"Maybe later."

"Very well," he pronounced crisply, straightening up and smoothing out his labcoat. "Why don't you get dressed and then we'll walk down to the lobby. Nurse Randa will accompany you to the spaceport."

So I put on the strange clothes. The suit roughly corresponded in form and function to my pajamas but lacked any kind of covering robe, leaving me feeling naked and vulnerable. I saw no alternative but to put my hospital robe back on, and belted it at the waist with a loose rabbit-ear knot. Everything was itchy. The boots were particularly uncomfortable, and caused me to limp. I dropped my bits into the pockets and then, in a fit of nostalgia, I stole a handful of soap pellets from beside the basin.

I hesitated before leaving, wondering if I shouldn't say my goodbyes. But then I remembered that everyone I knew had already gone. I turned my back on my once beloved ward and met up with Dr. Pent in the corridor. Together we stepped inside of a tiny room whose only doors yawned shut behind us.

"Lobby," said Dr. Pent, and my guts fluttered around inside of me.

I grabbed the wall. "Oh my! Are we being teleported somehow?"

"No, we're just moving downward. This is a lift."

"Why is it called a lift if we're going down?"

"It also goes up."

"Ah."

The doors parted and we walked out into the lobby – a room many times more massive than any I had ever seen, with people of all kinds going to and fro, lining up at desks, waiting in chairs, monologuing into the air (or I suppose into their telephones). The ceiling was transparent and bright sunshine poured down, reflecting on the polished floor and dazzling me. I instinctively stepped back against the din, but Dr. Pent's hand was behind my back, keeping me firmly on course.

As Dr. Pent thumbed through a plate of release forms I stood at his side and craned my neck, trying to understand the monstrous scale of the white building visible through the glass. How many people must it take to build such a thing?

He shook my hand and deposited me with Nurse Randa, whose usual starched whites were swaddled in a brown cowl. "Good luck, Simon!" called Dr. Pent as he strode away. Always busy. I turned to Nurse Randa.

"You're wearing a thing," I said dumbly.

"It may rain," she said, and then glanced down at my robe. "That's one of our robes, isn't it?"

I tightened the sash indignantly. "It may rain," I reminded her.

Together we stepped outside.

It was the smell that struck me first: a wall, a blanket, an ocean of overlapping and commingling musks – wet leaves, baked dirt, river air, the ozone fartings of machines – flavors I had sampled through the window but never stood in the heady midst of.

"Oh my," I said again, grabbing Nurse Randa's arm. The sun was like a great eye in the sky, rays glowing from the stark white concrete of the curbs and the walls, disappearing into the rolling lawns so green they looked black, shimmering in a thousand winking stars off every metal surface.

A yellow car drew up beside us, and the side of it unfolded open into a hatchway and a small set of steps that knocked gently against the curb as the vehicle bobbed and swayed a few hand-spans off the ground. Nurse Randa held my arm as I negotiated the steps and sat down on one of the wide, soft seats inside. "Spaceport, please," she ordered.

"I'm not on the spaceport run," claimed the driver, shrugging. He needed a bath.

"But we called you here *specifically* to take us to the spaceport," said Nurse Randa, her ire rising instantly.

"Hey, what can I say?" said the driver, shrugging again. "My dispatcher is an anus."

"I'll be right back," promised Nurse Randa fiercely, pulling out of the car and storming into the hospital. I crossed my legs.

"So..." I said conversationally, "*this* is a car."

"Oh boy," muttered the driver.

A couple of moments passed. I watched a few other yellow cars pull up, drop off passengers, then fly away. A woman was walking up and down in front of the lobby, trying to get a tiny little red-faced person to stop crying. She was carrying the little person around and singing to it. I wondered if she realized that the little red man had soiled himself.

"Listen, do you mind if I get out, stretch my legs a tad?" I asked.

"Knock yourself out," the driver replied.

I hovered uncertainly. "So it's okay then?"

"What am I? Your mother?" he wanted to know.

"Possible but unlikely," I said.

"Get out of my cab," he suggested. So I did.

As I stepped out onto the curb the door slammed shut and the car began to push off, startling a bird that had settled on the hood and causing it to flap away into the nearby trees. I looked after it. When I turned back the car had gone.

I looked again to where the bird had disappeared. It had vanished quickly upon reaching the foliage.

Another moment passed. Through the entranceway I could see Nurse Randa at the front desk, gesturing emphatically. Reflected in the glass was the glen of trees across from the hospital.

In a moment she would return and put me in a different car, and we would proceed to the spaceport. I felt sick.

I found myself starting to walk. I left the curb and caused a car to jam to a sudden halt, the driver making loud but incomprehensible remarks as he passed behind me. The roadway was made of soft grass, but I could not feel it through my boots. I reached the opposite curb and strode across the field between two sets of bushes, my pace increasing and my heart hammering in my chest. I broke into a jog, and then a run. Finding coordination of their own accord my limbs beat against the ground in a wild tattoo that ate the distance to the glen. In seconds I had dashed into the cool shadows of the trees...

I came to a halt and turned around. The hospital looked very far away, which made it seem little. I could just make out Nurse Randa's brown cowl as she stood on the curb and swung around in search of me. The wind carried her voice faintly, "Simon?" Then her voice sounded in my ear as clear as a bell, *"Simon?"*

I turned around again and ran deeper into the woods.

A hill found me, and I met it by sliding down its face in a most inelegant fashion, coming to a tangled stop at the muddy bottom of a steep ravine amid a slurry of leaves and twigs. After a moment the plate bounced down after me, rebounding off my thigh and skittering into the bramble.

I spent a moment considering whether or not I had made a wise decision.

With a groan I sat up and pawed after the plate. It activated when I grabbed it. As I held it up before me I saw little words floating beside each of the trees and shrubs, identifying their species and world of origin. This was apparently a service provided by the Samundra Ministry of Parks, Reserves and Carbon Dioxide Sinks.

I turned around in a slow circle. Icons appeared on the plate tracking the location of the hospital. Turning east the plate identified an ocean. I continued panning until I saw a cluster of overlapping icons – apparently the city of Thaumas, capital of this world. "But how far away is it?"

"The city centre is twenty six point two kilometers distant," said the plate.

"Thank you," I said.

It was then that Dr. Pent appeared on the plate, filling the surface. *"Simon! Simon, where are you?"* To someone offscreen he called, *"I have his plate's signal, he's in the southern wood."* He faced me again. *"I realize you're feeling panicked right now, Simon. Please, just stay where you are."*

I deactivated the plate with my thumb and threw it away. Then I thought better and crawled through the leaves until I found it again. I slipped it into the pocket of my robe, then took a deep breath and set off toward the city, uncertain what I would do when I reached it.

Within a few hours I had ceased to be concerned that far ahead, being occupied instead with a punishing thirst and a mounting exhaustion from tearing through the bramble, up one ravine and down another. I stopped at a gurgling stream and drank from my cupped hand and then lay down on the dirt beside it.

A bird flitted down to a nearby bush and nibbled off a few little red orbs. I crawled over and plucked one of them off between my fingers – the surface was yielding but tough. I popped it into my mouth and bit down. The orb released a bitter juice which I swallowed with a grimace.

After a moment I ate thirty more.

Later, after the vomiting had subsided, I drank more water from the stream and then took a bit of a nap. When I woke up the shadows were slanted and the plants smelled different. I cleaned myself up as best I could and then continued toward Thaumas.

The sun began to set. I was climbing over a row of hedges and into a grassy expanse when I noticed that the trees had become very orderly, arranged in lines between swaths of field. Over the next rise I came across a beaten path with dried boot prints in the mud. I was nearing civilization!

It was at the edge of the next clearing that I found a tiny wooden house on a platform elevated into a tree. "Hello?" I called.

I climbed a set of wooden rungs nailed into the bark and looked up on the platform. No one. I hauled myself up and bent down to negotiate the tiny doorway into the shadowed cabin.

The animal launched itself at me from the ceiling.

It caught me on the shoulder and I went down hard and awkwardly, banging my head on the floor. The vicious, furry creature skittered over me with a terrifying hiss, striking out with talons when I tried to move my arm. I shouted in surprise and the thing bolted over me and disappeared into the tree.

Breathing hard, I pulled myself upright and sat on a small bench inside the wooden house. In the fading bronze light of the sun I could see blood welling from my arm where the animal had raked me with its claws. My head was throbbing and my belly was crawling.

The sky turned purple, then black. The air chilled. I drew my robe tighter around me and shivered, watching the stars. I was feeling very alone until I remembered this diary, and pulled it out. At least it's something to talk to.

So here we are. I'm afraid to fall asleep, in case the creature returns. But my eyes are burning, and my lids feel like they are made of lead. I try to reassure myself that at least I am in charge of this destiny, such as it is.

The wind susurruses through the leaves, carrying dank, night-time scents from the forest. It lulls me. I give up my vigil.

This fool retires. Good night.

VI.
SIMON OF THE WOODS

One time at the hospital we ate pretzels. I never thought I'd be one.

I awoke this morning in a position to which my body strongly objected. Various portions of myself were pressed up against other parts who had not heretofore been mutually introduced. For example, I had not until this morning been aware of the fact that I could scratch my ass with my elbow.

I untangled myself with a series of dignified grunts and eventually tumbled akimbo in the middle of the tiny wooden house. I tried to get up but I smacked my head on the low ceiling and immediately found myself sitting again, cradling my skull in my filthy palms.

"Nurse?" I called hopefully.

The morning was misty. The sun was up, but the hazy shadows were long. The grass was lost in a mauve fog that puffed and swirled with the activity of breakfasting birds. The air was cool and thick, and it still carried a wet, night-plant scent.

"At least the creature didn't come back," I whispered aloud, because it made me feel less alone.

But I wasn't alone. My eyes flipped to the left, and then my head slowly turned and craned up. The vicious little creature was crouching on the roof above me, its long tail flicking back and forth menacingly. When our eyes met its pointed jaws drew open as the thing let out a spine-chilling breathy growl.

"Good morning," I said, flattening myself against the railing and sliding along its length slowly. "Please don't bite my eyes out."

The creature watched me, its yellow eyes narrowing. Its haunches twitched and I almost threw up. I continued to shimmy away from it, my feet dangling down over the edge of the wooden platform in search of the first rung of the ladder nailed into the trunk of the tree.

I bent my body to begin my descent, but this panicked the animal and it jumped on my face with an inhuman screech. We sailed backward through the air together and hit the grass rolling, my breath pushed out my chest as claws gripped my neck. The animal and I bounced apart. I turned over and cast around wildly for my adversary, but it had already regained its feet and was prowling around me, the fur along its spine standing up on end like a crest. It spat at me viciously, hissing.

We circled one another, eyed locked, my breath rasping.

That's when a high voice called out, "Hey! What are you doing to my cat?"

The creature scampered away to the right. I tracked it and saw it leap into the arms of a very short man with large eyes and freckles. The little man was regarding me suspiciously, his hand hovering over a bulge in the pocket of his shorts. The animal licked his hand and nuzzled against his chest. He put it down and started walking closer, the cat close at his heels.

"Keep that thing away from me!" I cried.

He stopped walking and crossed his arms over his chest. "What are you doing here?" he asked slowly, his voice reedy.

I pointed to the tree house. "Is this your house?"

"Yeah," he said, frowning. "So what?"

"You, uh, didn't come home last night, so I slept up there. I realize that was a fairly uncivilized thing to do, but I've been through a bit of an ordeal." I straightened my robe and re-belted the sash. "I'm terribly sorry for any trouble, sir."

"Are you some kind of weirdo?" asked the little man, stepping closer and appraising me frankly with his round eyes. As he emerged from the shadows I saw that his skin was pink, like uncooked bacon.

"No," I claimed.

He sucked his lip for a moment and kicked at the grass with his toe. "My name's Pish. I live over there." He shrugged vaguely in the direction of a wall of conifers.

"Hello," I said. "My name is Simon."

"Are you all alone?"

"Yes."

"You don't have anywhere to stay?"

"Not as such."

He shrugged again. "You can use it, if you're nice to my cat, I guess."

"That's exceptionally generous of you."

"Are you hungry?" Pish asked me. I nodded. "I'll see what I can do. You stay here, okay?" I nodded again. The little man turned and jogged away through the grass, disappearing into the gloom beneath the trees.

By the time Pish returned his suggestion had transformed my quiet but longing belly into a churning knot of desperate hunger. I had noticed a bush made of lettuce and tried eating some, but the green matter was bitter and fibrous; I was in the process of spitting it out when I heard Pish's high-pitched giggle. "This salad is awful," I groaned, wiping my tongue with my fingers.

We sat in the tree house to eat our picnic. I confess that I was not able to restrain my appetites, though I did try at the beginning. I tore through three apples voraciously, juice running down my chin, and then took a triangle of hard cheese in two savage bites. There were brown ropes of bread, crunchy sprulets, and a butter biscuit for each of us. Pish let me have his.

"Thank you," I said. "Please excuse me," I added. "I was just so hungry."

"You eat like my dog," said Pish.

"What's a dog?" I asked. Pish giggled. I smiled sheepishly. "Can I ask you something, Pish?"

"Sure."

I narrowed my eyes. "You're a child, aren't you?"

He exploded into gales of laughter then, his face turning red as he rolled around on the floor of the tree house. I tried to warn him but he wasn't listening, so he rolled right into the mustard. We both started laughing when I saw the expression on his face. "You're hilarious," he wheezed. "Do you want to come fly my kite with me?"

I grinned while I asked it: "What's a kite?"

More laughter. I rolled my eyes and followed him out of the tree house. It turns out a kite is a kind of paper-and-sticks contraption which rises into the air upon the wind, teased out on the end of a string. Pish was very good at keeping it aloft, but I found it more of a challenge. "Good – now *run with it!*" Pish would yell.

But I'm still not all that good at running, so my co-ordination would fail me and I'd fall spectacularly into the grass. We performed this routine many times before I handed control of the kite over to him for good. While he flew it I sat down on a nearby hillock, using my hand as a blind against the sun.

"How does it make you feel, Pish, to be at the beginning of your life?"

"Fine, I guess," he said carelessly, eyes on the kite.

"But you have so many options, and no experience to guide you. How do you choose what to do?"

He shrugged. "I just do what I do."

I considered this. "Have you ever thought about leaving this planet? Travelling beyond Samundra one day?"

Pish gave this question more thought, rolling his tongue around in his mouth as he gave the kite a tug and caused it to swoop in a tight circle. "Yeah, probably. But I'm kind of afraid to go through the gate."

"Yeah," I said quietly. "Me, too."

"Besides," he added as he reeled in the kite, "I've got everything I need right here."

Come evening he brought me supper and an armful of blankets. I snuggled into the tree house, but found it hard to be comfortable. Pish told me a long and meandering story about some kind of rodent he had followed to its nest the day before, and then started yawning and told me he'd best move along. I thanked him and he climbed down. I heard him call his cat, and I ran my fingers along the scabbing lines across the side of my neck with a wince.

Eventually I lay face down on the wooden house, in imitation of that peaceful, wonderful moment of reclining bliss on the first day of my life. I draped the blanket over my head, in imitation of my hospital-bed fort.

"Dear diary," I mumbled into the floor, "I have become the pet of an affable child."

VII.

THE STATUE GARDEN AT DUNCAN'S BLISS

My morning began with a concussive series of horrors.

My dream world was antiseptic and warm, permeated by the echoey, tinny murmurs over the intercom system. Somewhere, a machine beeped. I smelled Nurse Randa and rejoiced to be safe in my ward. I opened my eyes. The vicious cat was sitting on my chest, staring into my eyes with its unholy, malformed pupils.

I screamed and jerked. The cat dashed away with a sort of screeching howl. I sat on the floor and went to rub the gashes on my neck, but screamed again when I found the area to be blazing with pain.

Wincing and breathing hard I turned around to manoeuvre my way outside, but found the tiny doorway blocked by the fearsome face of a monstrous albino ape, eyes hard and lips sneering. "Buh!" I said, in a shining moment of eloquence and poise.

"Who the fire are you?" the ape demanded, the hair around its face flexing weirdly as it spoke.

Pish's reedy voice sounded outside: "I told you, his name is Simon!"

I nodded. "Simonithrat Fell. Please don't hurt me."

"Come out of there!" commanded the hairy ape person, withdrawing from the way and stepping aside on the platform. It creaked ominously under his weight.

I crawled out on my hands and knees and straightened slowly, adjusting my robe and retying the sash. I regarded the burly, imposing figure that stood over me, the dappled morning sunlight playing across his broad face. He was dressed in a set of clothes so worn and sullied it was difficult to discern the borders where the frayed fabric gave way to his dirt-smudged skin. Pish loitered behind his leg, apparently oblivious to the smell.

"Good morning Pish," I said. "Is this...a friend of yours?"

"It's Dad," said Pish.

"Hello, Dad," I offered.

"He's my father," Pish clarified.

Dad frowned. "Hush, Pish." He looked me up and down with his keen green eyes, the colour of wet grass. "Are you on the run?" I nodded mutely. "You're in some kind of trouble?" I nodded again. He considered this for a moment, chewing his lip the same way his son did. "You hurt anybody?" he asked.

"No sir, Dad," I replied.

"You can call me Duncan," he said. "I understand my boy has been running food out to you."

"That's true, Duncan."

"Around here," he continued, "we all work for our bread."

I nodded soberly. "I understand."

A long pause. Duncan gazed into my eyes shamelessly, chewing his lower lip, a furrow flickering across his brow. "Why don't you come up to the farm and do a few chores for me? How would that be by you, Mr. Fell?"

Surprised, I looked up. "Fine," I said. "Please, yes."

"I love you, Dad," whispered Pish.

So that is how I came to be in the employ of Duncan Menteith, a giant, quiet man who appeared periodically throughout the day to watch me at my work. I would fork aside the last bale of tied hay and there Duncan would be, standing across the barn, a long leaf of grass dangling out of the nest of hair on his face. He would give me a nod, and I'd go find Pish to show me the next task.

Beyond the barn and the fields was the house where Duncan and Pish lived, a dilapidated building of wood with one end canting downward at an alarming angle. The yard outside was littered with rusted equipment, chunks of plastic, and nonfunctional robots with tall grass growing between their legs. Across the distance of the fields I at first mistook them for men, but by my third passage on my way from one task to another I noticed that none of the gentlemen with such exceptional posture had moved an iota.

At Pish's direction I filled long troughs with slop to feed some pink and brown creatures covered in white hair, whom Pish called "hoggerchinas." I learned that eggs somehow come out of loud, brown birds (who bear a name in common with a food I've eaten called "chicken"), and I learned to sort the eggs by weight. I moved a pile of stones from one side of a field to another. Pish and I had lunch sitting on a tree-stump behind the barn, and then we pulled weeds out of a garden where different kinds of food were stuck in the ground, like tiny trees with discoloured tomatoes on them, and cucumber slices assembled into a single green oblong.

Pish brought over a red, irregular fruit about the size of a large apple. It was covered in tiny seeds. "Try it," he said. I bit into its soft flesh, its juice making my cheeks tingle in the oddest way. My mouth was suffused with flavor and aroma. "Do you like it?" asked Pish. "It's called a strawberry."

"That is the most delicious thing I have ever tasted," I swore.

Pish giggled. "Just you wait til supper."

When we were called in we put aside our work brushing the morrels' sleek, orange coats and made for the house. Pish sprinted directly to the door but I found myself hesitating to so blithely cross the strange statue garden of weed and vine-entwined metal figures standing sightless in the yellow grass. Awkwardly, I bowed my head to each side of the group as I shuffled along the dirt path between them and followed Pish through the door.

The inside of the house made the tree-house look like a palace. It was dark, and objects of all shapes and sizes were strewn about the floor, smells of all musks and tangs commingling heavily in the air. Pish led me to a dingy sofa and we sat down. He pulled over a wooden table so dirty it was black, and kicked aside a pile of kipple so we could stretch out our legs. Pish pulled three stained napkins out of a drawer, handing one to me and tucking another into the front of his shirt. "Are we having strawberries?" I asked hopefully.

"No," he replied. "Dad's cooking."

I became aware of the mix of scents in the air permeating the house's general funk – overlapping, intense and shifting from second to second. I began to salivate, and swallowed with a gulp.

A door on the opposite wall I had not been aware of pushed open suddenly, presenting Duncan framed by a bloom of rolling steam. He stepped up and deposited two platters of hot morsels on the table before us and then swept back into what must have been his kitchen. A moment later he re-emerged with another steaming tray in one hand

and a stack of plates in the other. He sat down on the sofa beside us, which lurched under his weight, and efficiently doled out three identical helpings.

Pish pushed my plate over to me, and bid me to begin.

And so I wished it would never end!

I can't describe it to you – I won't describe it to you. It's pointless. It would tarnish the spirit of it. All I can say is that I had my complete understanding of the concept of food totally re-engineered over the course of a single meal. It was transcendent! I knew art, and my body liked it.

The portions were small, proportioned in craftfully divergent and complementary sensations, decorated like little dollops of sculpture. I struggled not to lick my plate, and settled instead for licking my fingers. I looked up to see Pish and Duncan watching me. "What did you think of that, Mr. Fell?" rumbled Duncan.

I licked my lips and closed my eyes. "I think I shall spend my entire life in debt to you for what you have given me tonight, no matter what I do."

Duncan's furry face split into a wide grin. "*That's* what food is *for*. Mere nutrition is for squirrels."

"I feel like I have a new religion," I told him.

"I'm glad to do it for you, Mr. Fell." He stood up and wiped his hands on his pants. "Lest I forget how," he added cryptically, collecting the plates and disappearing into the kitchen.

"My dad is the best chef in the galaxy," Pish told me.

"That is obvious to me," I agreed.

A large, brown, wolf-like animal snortled over to us, and inserted its muzzle into my crotch. My eyes widened with alarm but Pish just laughed. "That's my dog," he explained. "Simon, meet Fartles."

"Hello Fartles," I said.

Fartles farted ponderously, an eye-watering aroma wafting over us and erasing the lingering air of the magnificent dinner. I sighed, and waved my hand before my nose resignedly. The dog licked my wrist and shuffled away into the shadows again.

Duncan lit a spark in the corner, and the light revealed a hearth. In a matter of a moment a cozy blaze was flickering, orange and gold and green. "I've only seen fire in pictures," I said in awe. "The reproductions do it no justice."

Duncan regarded me for a long moment, and then withdrew a tall bottle and poured out two equal portions into grimy glass cups. "Time for bed, Pish," he murmured. Pish kissed him on the only part of his cheek devoid of hair, a small patch just beneath the eye, and retreated into another part of the house with a wave.

Duncan sat back into the sofa and put his feet on the table. He watched the fire for a few moments before sipping his from his cup. "Oh yes," he said.

I drank. The liquid was pungent but pleasing, like flowers with an edge. I drank again. "What do you call this, Duncan?" I felt a little lightheaded, and my lips went slightly numb. "It's marvellous."

"Wine," said Duncan. "It's called wine. A fifty-eight Mavrodafni, from Reneti."

We drank in silence for a while, and then Duncan spoke again, eyes on the fire. "Pish and I have been on the run for nearly his whole life. I tell you this so you understand the risk I take, accepting you into our home."

"Thank you," I said.

"But my boy can read people, and he said you have a good soul. I've watched you work and I've watched you eat, and I believe it." He sighed. "Good people can be few and far between. I was a good man, once."

"Are you not a good man now?"

"Maybe. Maybe not. Society reckons not. I do the best I can. I try to make life worth living for my boy. I can't escape what I did, but I have the conviction to take responsibility for it. But Pish comes first. If I had let them take me away I wouldn't see him again until he was a man, and someone else's son." He finished his drink in a gulp. "When he can stand on his own, I'll turn myself in."

"Because you deserve to be punished?"

"Maybe," he said again. "Maybe not. But either way what kind of a lesson do I teach my son if I refuse to stand for my actions?"

"I don't know. But I don't know very much. I'm new."

"He's new, too. That's why I'm showing him. You can borrow time, but you can't take back the past. No one can, not even you, Mr. Fell. You'll one day have to reckon for what you've done, too." He leaned over and pulled out another bottle, upending it into our cups. "In the meantime it isn't my place to judge you. Is Simon your real name?"

"As far as I know," I said.

"That's no good. You have clean money, a safe plate?"

I pulled my bits out of my wide, robe pockets. "I have these."

Duncan snorted. "That's faecal money and an unsafe plate, friend. But they're awful pretty. I think I can fix you up. Here, come with me." He gathered my bits into his arms and stumbled into the kitchen.

I wondered at this until I stood up and also felt the world tilt and wheel around me. I chortled giddily and stumbled after him.

"Wow."

In stark contrast to everything else I had seen the kitchen was all gleaming, polished metal – orderly and cherished and clean, a kind of temple in homage to food. There were rows of reflective utensils hanging above the shining counters, pots and skillets from tonight's dinner pushed over to one side of the range, flotillas of jars bearing neat labels, a cool hum of machinery. A silver robot with elaborate curlicues on its untarnished carapace was washing our dishes.

Beyond a set of great wide refrigerators was a tidy workbench and a stool. Duncan sat on the stool and placed my bits on the workbench. He slid open a drawer and extracted a handful of tiny tools, and then attached a series of wires to my wallet and my plate. "This will allow us to browse without being tracked," he muttered, eyes fixed on his work.

"Okay," I said.

"Jeremiah!" he barked. The silver robot stepped up and bowed its head. Duncan commanded, "Establish a library signal, wrapped and scented. Extra safety."

"Sir," replied Jeremiah. He did not move. After a moment he said, "The connection has been established." His speech was crisp and clear but accented by a strange, sing-song lilt.

"Is your robot singing?" I asked.

"No, he just talks that way because he's from Eridani. Bloody court accent. I don't have another voice module."

Duncan made some final adjustments with his tools and then invited me to slip my finger into the end of the thimble-shaped wallet. I did. A slurry of text scrolled across a small round readout on the workbench. Duncan snorted again.

"What's wrong?" I asked.

"Nothing's wrong. You're rich, that's all. Stupid rich."

"I don't suppose I can spend any of it though, can I?"

"Sure you can. You need just to put it through a safe wallet, first. I can hook you up for ten percent of the balance."

"That's very generous of you, Duncan."

"Ten percent of your balance is a lot of money, Simon."

While he did his work he said I could thumb through the contents of my plate safely, so I picked it up. It didn't show anything when I pointed it around the room, except when I faced Jeremiah – for him the plate identified his model and make, his year of construction and his legally registered owner (somebody named Terron Volmash, apparently).

In playing with the controls I somehow found myself confronted with the image of a woman. Her black hair was tied into elaborate braids, the end of one she held in her hand loosely as she regarded something out of the frame, her profile serene. I was lost in the picture when I felt Duncan's breath beside me. "Who's that?" he asked.

"I think she's my wife," I said, tilting the plate so I could see a little more of the front of her face.

"You think?" echoed Duncan.

I tabbed forward and was presented with an image of a young boy and slightly older girl, smiling as they lay back on a grassy hill under a grey sky. Their eyes were folded and slanted like mine. "These are probably our children," I said softly, my finger tracing the girl's face on the surface of the plate. "I don't know them."

Duncan squeezed my shoulder. "You should. You can't escape your past. And if they're your kids you owe them a future." He handed me my wallet. "You can stay here with us and work as long as you like, but it seems to me you have some affairs to attend to, Simon."

"They'll find me if I try to see them."

"No they won't. I'll fix your plate. Your wallet's already good, re-routed six ways from Starday. You just need to be a little more careful. We'll need to encode a new identity into your bits."

"You...you would do this for me?"

Duncan nodded and smiled sadly. "If it means those kids get their father back, by fire I will, Simon. You do your part, I'll do mine."

I was moved by his high valuation of kinship. I was moved by his love for his boy, and the love he extended to me, a fool stranger. In Duncan I met my first example of a man.

VIII.
TROUBLE

Pish and I were shaking handfuls of seeds out for the brown chickens when Duncan whistled loudly from the house. "Oi! Simon!"

I jogged over, picking up my hospital robe from a nearby branch along the way. I wiped the sweat from my brow as I walked through the creepy robot statue garden and pushed into the house. Duncan waved me over to the sofa, where my bits were spread out on the cushions. "Give me your telephone," he said.

I reached behind my ear and plucked it off. He waved a small device over its surface until it beeped, and then he handed the telephone back to me. "Your telephone, your wallet and your plate are now the property of one Hellig Apples of Samundra's Western Territories."

"Who's Hellig Apples?"

"You are, my friend," said Duncan, shaking my hand. "Nice to meet you."

Over the next hour Duncan explained to me many of his tricks for staying ahead of the authorities, impressing upon me various precautions for which I had no real context. I did my best to memorize what he said, and hoped everything would fall into place later. He transferred into my plate's cache his personal map of Thaumas, complete with byways for the wily. "Thank you for everything you've done," I said to Duncan. "You're saving my life."

"Saving yourself is up to you," replied Duncan seriously. "I'm just making sure you get a chance to."

He smiled and started to say something else but stopped, eyes darting, suddenly attending to something I could not hear. "What's wrong?" I asked, feeling the anxiety ramp up under his skin, the hairs on his arms rising on end.

The colour drained from his face. "Mother of love!" he swore, and pushed past me outside. I detected a mounting hum sounding through the air, and a second later saw the dirt on the shelves begin to dance as the house vibrated. I spun around and followed Duncan outside.

I ran into him from behind. Duncan was standing right outside the door.

Tracing the line of his gaze I looked out into the yard, cluttered with dead robots and junk. The sun winked off their tarnished bodies, and a gentle breeze made the tall grass sway. "What's wrong?" I asked again.

And then I saw that two of the statues were not dead robots – they were men in black armor, their faces behind transparent shields, their right hands extended, pointing twin metal devices at Duncan.

We all stood there, frozen. With a gust of air and a squealing thrum a doughnut-shaped vehicle sailed into view overhead, two more black armored figures descending from it on long cables. An amplified voice boomed out harshly: *"This is a police control! Stay where you are. Follow the officers' instructions. Drop your bits and keep your hands where we can see them at all times."*

I saw Pish at the same moment Duncan did. His eyes flicked over and the police saw them move, following them to spot the boy. "Stay where you are!" they bellowed in rough unison. One of the officers descending from the ship unclipped from his cable and hit the ground running, eating up the distance between himself and the child.

"Leave him alone, you bastards!" shouted Duncan, suddenly moving. He smacked aside the first officer and narrowly dodged a shot from the second officer's hand-held device, which emitted a jet of shiny liquid that crystallized instantly into a kind of sticky web as it spattered against the side of a tree. "This is your final warning!" the officer yelled.

I yelped as two more officers burst out of the house behind me, kicking out the door so that it struck me and knocked me aside. "Clear!" they barked, and then apprended the situation and joined their comrade in charging after Duncan. One of them was intercepted by the family's giant brown dog, who appeared without warning, loping across the field at incredible speed, dropping on the closest officer and felling him with a single push. I saw the dog's jaws go down on the man's throat and then heard the officer's gurgling screams, cut off an instant later.

I slipped out from behind two robots and made a break for the woods, tearing toward Pish and praying I did not fall. "Hey!" shouted another officer as I rushed past him. A second later I saw a smear of webbing skip over the grass a few steps ahead of me. I jumped behind the greenhouse and hit the ground, tasting dirt. I got up and ran to the other side, coming around the corner just as two of the pursuing officers caught up with Duncan, tackling him. The amorphous mound of bodies kicked and jerked for a few moments and then burst asunder, Duncan rising up from its midst and casting about wildly for the boy.

An officer rose behind the bearded giant and struck him savagely across the back of his head with a baton. Duncan folded. The second officer crawled over and touched Duncan with a small device in his hand. Duncan cried out and began to kick spasmodically.

"Dad!" screamed Pish in an agonized wail, dropping the cat who had been in his arms.

Duncan clawed his way out of the melee and raised his quivering head just long enough to bellow, *"RUN!"* with his last ounce of strength. A second later he was buried in multiple shots of sticky webbing, drawing into a foetal curl and shaking. The officers surrounded him.

Fartles was barking madly. The thrumming vehicle swooped over for another pass, its loudspeaker blaring dire warnings and instructions. *"This is a police control!"*

I bolted past it all, passing through the vehicle's circular shadow and pelting after the officer who pursued Pish. Pish turned and ran away into the bushes, the officer's boots crushing the plants at his heels. I ignored the shouts and shots of the other police and I dove into the foliage after them, tearing away brambles and twigs with my arms and shoulders as I pushed relentlessly toward the source of the noises of struggle ahead.

I came upon a clearing. The black-armored police officer was backing Pish into a corner by the brook. Before I knew what was happening the officer had punched me twice in the head and tripped me backward over his leg, the wind knocked out of me as I rolled into the wet ditch. Gasping and wheezing, my chest on fire, I flipped myself over in time to see him make another grab for the boy. Pish dodged him, tears running down his face...

I discovered a new emotion today. Pish tells me it's called "rage."

When the crimson light cleared from my vision I found myself astride the police officer, his helmet smashed apart, bright blood running out of his nose and mouth. I watched with passive interest as my fists flung out and smacked his face savagely again, causing a small piece of skin from his lip to fly off over my shoulder and land in the shrubs.

This gave me pause. I tumbled off of the man as he moaned, his breath sounding wet and constricted. I spotted Pish and stumbled over to him. He was kneeling over his cat, who lay on its side with its tongue sticking out of its mouth in a strange way. "Pish?"

"He killed my cat," said Pish, a new hardness in his voice.

I touched the cat. It still felt warm, and looked as soft as ever. His eyes were open, but were developing an odd sheen. "This animal is now dead?" I asked dumbly. Pish nodded, his throat working as he fought back more tears.

We were both startled as the dog burst out of the bushes, pursued by the sounds of more shouting officers. Pish turned away from his cat and looked at me. "Come on," he urged, taking my hand. "This way – we have to run!"

Hand in hand we raced together between the trees, Fartles the dog panting and loping along behind us. Pish took me down a steep gully into a storm sewer drainage pipe, its edges hung with reeds. The dog ran in after us. We drank from the moving stream at the bottom of the stone-like tube and then waited there in the semi-dark, our hearts pounding in our chests.

After a while we heard the sound of careful footfalls. Without speaking I gestured to Pish to stay put, and I cautiously stepped to the end of the pipe. Though technically Pish was older than I was, as the tallest man present I felt a certain duty to at least appear to uphold the courage of a protector. I tightened my robe around me and climbed up the side of the gully.

Crouching in a bush, I listened and sniffed.

Another twig snapped. I heard Fartles fart back in the draining pipe, and a moment later felt its evil mix with the forest damp. A pebble skittered. I found the direction by my ears and then opened my eyes and looked where they had pointed me. Squinting into the foliage I saw a shadow of a figure making its cautious way toward us.

I picked up a small rock from the stream-bed and prepared to pounce. Closer...closer...and finally the shape emerged from the glen and I raised my arms and –

"Sir!" exclaimed Jeremiah, his strange inflexion clouding the word.

"Jeremiah!" I exclaimed.

"Jeremiah?" called Pish, emerging from the pipe. Fartles followed.

"Little Master," Jeremiah greeted Pish with a bow. "It is fortunate you are well."

"What did he say?" I asked, unable to decipher the thick accent which Duncan had called *Eridani court*. "Your robot sounds like he needs a glass of water."

Pish hugged Jeremiah and closed his eyes as he pressed his face against the robot's silver chest, so I just shut up. I pet the dog, who licked my hand and passed gas noisily.

We didn't talk much after that. It was understood that we would hole up for the night in the drainage pipe, and make for Thaumas in the morning. There was never any question that Pish had become my responsibility. Nothing much had changed for Hellig

Apples, except that he now had an ensemble – a bereaved child, a nearly unintelligible robot, and a dog with serious gastrointestinal problems.

Thunder rumbled ominously in the distance as the afternoon darkened into an early evening. My body was throbbing in various places, including the cuts on my neck, which were tender and swollen. As I arranged myself to sleep Pish crawled over and squished himself against me wordlessly.

Jeremiah stood watch at the mouth of the pipe, the first drops of rain singing off his hide like wind chimes.

IX.

GLORY OF THE LOW STREETS

The night was wet. The rising waters in the drainage outlet forced us to find perches higher and higher along its irregular interior, finishing the evening on a narrow ledge overlooking the rushing brown waters below littered with twigs and leaves. A weak, grey light bloomed in the east.

Come morning we elected to wait out the rain, and when the rain hadn't stopped by noon we elected to brave it. It was a torrential downpour, the forest misty with thick vapor and a constant, clamoring slapping of drops against leaves sounded on all sides. We trudged through the mud, trying to stick to the high ground as Pish directed us along paths he knew well, down out of the hills and toward the delta valley where the grand city of Thaumas lay.

Thaumas was a wonder.

As we crested a hill I opened my mouth to say something about the surprisingly geometric paths of the birds up ahead until the advancing march of perspective revealed my mistake in scale. "Are those cars?" I asked in wonder.

"Yup," said Pish.

A great valley was spread out beneath us, bisected by a wide river. The ground of this valley seemed at first to be composed of some kind of strangely rectilinear lichen, shimmering behind veils of grey rain. But in fact they were buildings, hundreds of thousands of buildings, stretching to the opposite hills. The roofs of the buildings were planted with trees, and the avenues between them were planted with grass. It became apparent as I looked on that the true ground was hidden, and the height of the buildings was impossible to discern. The air above the city churned with lines of gnat-like cars, their humming lost to the distance and the weather.

"Come *on*, Simon," said Pish, pulling my hand.

"Oh, my," I muttered. "What an impossible thing!"

We began to make our way down the slope, the valley soon obscured from our view by nearer trees. The rain petered out but the sun remained hidden. We crossed through the gardens of Thaumas' suburban citizens, crouching behind bushes and walking in low gullies to avoid being visible from their houses.

Until we met the flamingo.

"Hey, a flamingo!" I said, smiling happily. "I watched a documentary about these things once."

The salmon-coloured bird was standing in a small, decorative pond surrounded by stone benches. It cocked its head to look at us but did not otherwise stir.

"Do not tarry," said Jeremiah. It was the first thing he had said all day. "Let us move away quickly."

"It's just a bird," argued Pish, shrugging.

The flamingo stepped out of the pond. It walked over to a nearby garden and emitted a steady spray of water out of its open beak. It passed its head slowly back and forth, covering the flowers in an even mist.

"They didn't mention this behavior in the documentary," I contributed.

"Let us make haste," urged Jeremiah, his strange voice raising a register.

Fartles barked. I turned around to look at him and saw a thin, knobby tree rounding the hill toward us, its leafy head bobbing as it walked on long legs that bent in odd places. "A marvel!" I exclaimed. "Why didn't anybody *tell* me they could walk?"

I turned as I said this. Pish and Jeremiah were walking on, and had just reached the edge of the flower garden when the flamingo straightened and its spray died out, drops flying from its flapping beak as it shrieked: "Trespassers! This is private property. Retreat immediately or face prosecution."

Jeremiah turned on heel and pulled Pish along behind him, reversing their course and striding toward me and Fartles. I heard a voice from behind me and spun yet again to see the tree say, "Halt! This is a private establishment which you are obliged to vacate immediately. Further trespass will result in your arrest. You have five seconds to comply."

The tree advanced on me and I backed up into Pish, causing him to stumble toward the flower garden. The flamingo repeated his warning: "Trespassers! This is private property..."

We all knocked into one another again, this time pushing Fartles back toward the walking tree. "Halt! This is a private establishment..."

Our party ended up spread out in a thin line, elbow to elbow, occupying a narrow swath of grass between the two guardians. If our toes did not stray the flamingo and the tree said nothing, merely standing a few paces back and watching us intently.

Slowly, carefully, we began to shuffle sideways.

The tree and the flamingo kept pace, bobbing along side us. This continued for a quarter hour as we passed sideways over hill and dale and through copses of wind-bent trees, our necks developing cricks from looking so long askance. "Nice country around here," I commented wearily.

"Trespassers!" shrieked the flamingo.

"Shut up!" Pish and I shouted back in chorus.

We came upon a narrow stone wall, the end closest to us frayed and broken, washed out by some flood that had now become a tiny, ribbon-like creek. Knee-high robots were clicking and whirring by the pile of debris, sorting the fallen stones and piling them for reassembly. We jumped the creek and stepped up along the wall, using the exposed white bricks as risers. The tree and the flamingo stalked from opposite sides, looking up at us from among the bushes as we rose. At one point I lost my balance and staggered backward, but Jeremiah was there to catch me. "Sir," he said.

"Halt!" shouted the tree as I violated his border with my pinwheeling arms.

I drew back straight and gave Jeremiah a grateful nod. He released me and we proceeded on our way. The wall met another presently, running perpendicular along a narrow avenue. A car passed by, skimming over the roadbed of grass, and then another in the opposite direction. On the other side of the avenue there was yet another stone wall, a burst of leaves, and then the roof of another house.

"Is this Ninth Avenue?" Pish asked Jeremiah.

"Yes, Little Master," replied the robot.

With Jeremiah's help we all clambered down, though not after some considerable whining and hesitation on the part of Fartles. Pish indicated that we were meant to walk along the sides of the street, to leave the grassy way clear should a car fail and hit the ground. The pathway along the side was sheltered by a line of identical saplings, interspersed now and again with an oubliette for trash. Had it not been for the renewed drizzle and the clamminess of our soaked clothing I might have found it a nice promenade.

The great white buildings rose up around us as we walked. They were connected in the sky by causeways and bridges overflowing with greenery, and on the lower tiers we could see the tall hats and hear the collective murmurs of the crowds. I craned my head up as the heights of the cityworks wound ever higher, noticing then that none of the ramps or stairs that seemed to interconnect everything ever descended to the brown grass of our increasingly shadowed avenue.

"How do we get *up?*" I asked. "It seems like we're descending into some kind of dark netherworld."

"These are the low streets," Pish told me. "They don't connect to the higher levels by foot."

"How do people get up there, then?"

"By car."

"What do you do if you don't have a car?" I asked, furrowing my brow.

Pish shrugged and pointed further down the ever-darkening street, lost in the gloom of the architecture above it. Up ahead the sides of the avenue opened up into dingy markets and squares, where people slept on the road. As we drew nearer they roused themselves to ask us for things. One man who didn't have a nose asked me in a grumbly voice whether or not I had any money.

"Sure," I said, and continued on my way.

"You coital anus!" he cried after me.

Things quickly became weirder. Two young men with black, feathery spikes on top of their heads instead of hair started asking Pish questions about Jeremiah, pushing closer to touch the robot. I had taken their banter for compliment and appreciation until I saw the fear in Pish's eyes and caught a whiff of the stink of violence on the men. We backed away from them and found ourselves in a narrow alley without another outlet. Fartles barked.

"How much for the robot, sleeping beauty?" demanded one of the youths in a thick accent.

"Pardon me?" I said, so he grabbed me by the face and pushed me into a pile of plastic bins.

I spilled out of the mess and got to my feet in time to see Jeremiah walk calmly up behind the temperamental fellow. He raised his silver arm and struck at the youth's neck in what appeared to be an almost gentle fashion. The youth's eyes fluttered briefly before he folded into a neat pile at Jeremiah's muddy feet. I saw that his partner had already been similarly incapacitated.

"It was necessary for the sake of the Little Master," explained Jeremiah in his rolling lilt.

"Whatever you say," I replied. "We owe you everything, robot."

Fartles was pushing against Pish's leg, whimpering. Pish had crossed his arms over his chest and was shivering pitiably, his lips and his fingers taking on a blue cast.

"We need shelter, Jeremiah," I said. "Pish suffers. Can my wallet buy us a room in these low streets?"

"Yes, Master Fell."

I took my plate from my pocket and pressed my thumb to the contact. When I turned the glass toward the street its face illuminated with local informatics detailing the nature of the surrounding establishments: implanters, grafters, restaurants, colonics, taverns, dilly dens, pawn shops, gun shops, robot repairs, dry cleaning, matter printing…and, finally, a hotel.

We crossed the mean street briskly and crowded into the cramped lobby of the grubby hotel. A very sad man stood behind a desk, chewing something in his mouth as he looked us up and down. "We don't cater to freaky faeces," he told me.

"That's good news," I agreed genially. "My wet friends and I would like a room, please."

"All of youse?"

"Yes please."

"You're some funny anus, aren't you?" the man asked me gruffly.

"Well," I said, "I admit another fellow on the road just now did mention it in passing. What does the epithet allege?"

"You're trying to get my goat, is that it?" demanded the man.

"What's a goat?" I asked.

The man recommended I engage in some kind of locomotive masturbation, so I stepped back over to Jeremiah, Pish and Fartles to confer. A woman walked in out of the rain with a little bag held over her head, and she pushed brusquely past us. "Lou, you want to let me stand in here for few? I'm cold as anything."

Lou, the man behind the desk, made a remark which was incomprehensible to me but which made the dripping woman frown. Her eyes were hard and small, outlined by black paint. Her face was drawn and thin, lined with worry and painted with two spots of harsh red in the middle of her sharp cheeks. "What the coitus are you staring at, bathboy?" she barked.

"I'm sorry!" I said, turning away.

"Wait," she called, suddenly affecting a softer demeanor. "You want to get a room maybe?"

"Yes," I said simply.

"You have money?"

"Yes," I said more cautiously, thinking she might call me a *coital anus* like the noseless man outside.

"How long you want?"

"At least a day."

She furrowed her brow and squinted at me. "These rooms go by the hour."

"How many hours are there in a day?"

"Twenty."

"Very well. I'll have twenty hours then, please."

The woman wore a scraped black thimble on her finger which she touched to a tarnished plate on the desk. She gestured to me and I did the same with mine. Lou tapped a couple of buttons at his console and grunted, "Go on up, freaks. Washroom costs extra. If I catch you defecating in the trash bins I'll cut your testicles off."

"Ah," I said. "Thank you very much."

Our hostess led the way up a short flight of steps and back into an ill-lit corridor. Jeremiah carried Pish, whose teeth chattered loudly. We filed into a tiny room containing a stained mattress, a dented basin, and a broken chair. A window looked out at the side of an adjoining building, its walls streaked with grime. I saw somebody looking out their window over there, so I smiled and waved. The face disappeared and a dark curtain pushed across the opening.

Jeremiah put Pish on the mattress and began to strip off his wet clothes. Fartles settled on the floor and snuffed at his paws.

"I don't do kids or animals," said the woman. "My name's Glory."

"Hello Glory," I said. "My name's Si – Hellig." I offered my hand to shake, which amused Glory.

She put her skinny hands on her hips and sauntered toward me, stepping over the end of the bed deftly. "Okay Sy-Hellig, what do you want to do first?"

"I think I should like to sleep, please."

She stopped, and looked at me quizzically. "You want to go to sleep?"

"We've been through a bit of an ordeal," I explained, peeling off my sopping robe and hanging it over the back of the broken chair. I crawled into bed beside Pish and he buried his face in my neck, yawning. I yawned, too. "Thanks for all your help," I added.

"No problem," she replied, shaking her head slowly. She sat down by the window and looked at us with curiosity, pulling her knees up to her chin and hugging her bruised shins. "What's that?" she asked.

"It's a diary," I told her, holding the blue piece of rounded plastic in my palm. "I just have to make a few notes."

Glory snorted. "You're the weirdest son of a bitch I've ever met, Sy-Hellig."

I smiled uncertainly. "Is it appropriate for me to call you a weird daughter of a bitch in turn? I'm not entirely familiar with the local customs, you understand, and I don't want to offend you."

"Coitus," she commented cryptically, sighing and closing her eyes. "I'd better not wake up dead."

Not quite sure what to make of that, I turned away and began muttering into my diary. In the gloom of the low streets it was not possible to discern when the sun set.

X.

HITHER AND THITHER, BUGS AND A BEARD

I awoke to rain drooling down the window, the light blue and feeble. I stirred but Glory said, "Stay still."

"Where's Pish?" I muttered, my mouth dry and cottony.

"He's safe. He's eating. Stay still."

"My neck hurts."

"For the sake of faeces will you keep your anus still?"

I considered this brain-teaser for a moment, my eyes adjusting to the shadows. Glory sat on the bed beside me. Her brown hair was drawn into a series of beaded braids that clicked together as she moved. Her hard eyes were fixed on my neck. As I awoke fully the dull pain in the wounds there became a strange, persistent itch – a writhing tickling that became more intense with every breath. "What's going on? What are you doing to me?" I gasped, reaching for my neck.

"Relax," Glory commanded, taking hold of my arm in her wiry, surprisingly strong hand.

Gripped by a sudden panic I twisted out of her grasp and vaulted out of bed, throwing myself before the cracked mirror. A ghost much like myself flew into view in the dingy reflection: his neck crawled with an iridescent mass of insects and the lower half of his face had turned black.

I screamed.

"Coitus!" screeched Glory, pushing me back onto the bed. "I told you to *stay still*, lummox. You knocked half of them off!"

"There are bugs on my neck!" I yelped, clawing at my shoulder.

"They're just fixers, you idiot!" she shouted back, grabbing both my arms and pushing me into the sheets. "Now. Stay. *Still.*"

Out of the corner of my eye I could see them moving over my face and I steeled myself from panic as I felt their work. The burning in my neck was fading to a pleasant, buzzing numbness. After another moment the metallic little creatures began dropping off, skittering across the sheets and climbing into a round green vessel. When the last of them had crawled in Glory closed the lid and slipped the vessel into her bag.

Hesitantly I put my fingers to my neck and touched the welts. I flinched in anticipation but there was no pain. Nor were there welts. The skin was smooth and soft, the numbness slowly fading. I smiled, amazed to be introduced to yet another wonder unmentioned in my brief hospital education. "Thank you, Glory."

"It was infected," she shrugged. She pulled out a short orange cylinder and stuck it in her mouth. She flicked the end with her nail and it began to glow. She closed her eyes and drew in her breath sharply, the cylinder turning to ash with a crackling hiss and a flash. Glory reclined slowly into the bed beside me, the ash dissolving to a grey worm of soot that relaxed into powder across her bony chest as she sighed. An acrid fume hung in the air around her head.

"Is that some sort of snack?" I inquired.

She didn't say anything so I got out of bed again and stepped up to the mirror, transfixed by the bristly black hairs that were growing out of the lower half of my face, tickling my exploring fingers. The upper half of my face was quite normal – dark brown eyes, gold skin, wide ears, and a crew of black hair unbrushed on my head – but my jaw, cheeks and chin were lost in a forest of little uniform bristles. "I'm turning into Duncan!" I concluded, eyes wide. I turned to Glory. "Am I bearding now because Pish is in my charge?"

"Haven't you ever shaved before, Simon?" she asked huskily, her voice heavy and far away.

"Oh sure, shaving," I said, nodding. "The nurses used to shave me. You're saying *that* was to prevent *this*?"

"Yeah."

Who knew? A second thought occurred to me. "Did you just call me Simon?"

"The kid calls you Simon."

"That's my nick-name. You should call me Hellig."

"Uh-huh."

I touched the lamp and it came on, just like the ones at the hospital. Glory groaned and threw her forearm across her eyes. I asked, "Did you say Pish was eating?"

"Lou's grabbing him something."

"Thank you."

"You paid big for it. Lou's a greedy son of a bitch. He didn't gouge you too bad, though. I was watching the whole time. The kid held your arm while your wallet interacted."

"What about the key?"

"Your robot took care of it."

"Ah."

She opened her eyes, the black paint around them smeared. "Listen Simon. The kid already told me you don't know faeces about nothing. You're fornicated without me. And I have reasons of my own for wanting to move along. So maybe we could help each other out."

"Help us to move along?"

"We could all move along together," she said. "Keep safe."

I moved my fingertips across my face and enjoyed the raspy sound they made against the stubble. "Yes," I said slowly. "We would be much obliged to have more of your help, Glory. Can we trust you?"

She snorted. "Kiss my ass." She rubbed her eyes with her knuckles and stood up, slipping on a pair of sandals. She patted down her tight little shift and looped her bag over her shoulder. "Let's get moving."

"Right now?" I turned away from the mirror. "Are we really in such a hurry as all that?"

"I am," she said gruffly, tossing my dirty but dry clothes at me. "Come on. We need a new place to stay tonight."

"What's wrong with this place? Lou seems nice."

"Come on."

I was knotting the tattered sash of my muddy hospital robe as she hustled me into the cramped lobby. Pish jumped up and hugged me. "Lou said he'll be out in a minute," he said into my chest. "Lou said we could pay for tonight, and maybe get you some supper." Fartles wagged his tail.

"Yeah, Lou's a hero. Let's go." Glory took Pish's hand and pulled him out into the street.

I shrugged at Jeremiah's expressionless black eyes and followed them.

We could still hear Lou shouting behind us as Glory rushed our party through a narrow alley and along a row of derelict shops. Pish pumped his little legs to keep up, Jeremiah jogging easily beside him with light, seemingly weightless steps. We hopped through the frame of a broken window and through several dark rooms, out the other side of the building and into a crowded square. I craned my head to look at the sad windows up above on all sides, but before I knew it Glory had whisked us down a winding street and then propelled us through a door into the face of a tall, thin giant with skin as white as a fish.

"Hello," I said.

Glory pushed in after us. "I'm calling in my favor, Nilo. We need to crash quietly, one night."

The giant nodded curtly and turned, leading us down a long corridor with rooms on either side, the strip of light along the ceiling blinking in some places, failed altogether in others. As we passed each closed door I detected a different symphony of grunts and groans beyond each, the air laden with human smells. We were let into a gloomy cubicle much like the one we had just left, except without the benefit of a window.

When Jeremiah stood in the corner behind the door we could all sit in the room with a minimum of discomfort, if Fartles lay under the bed. Something behind one of the walls thumped rhythmically for a while, and then quit with a yodel. Pish looked at me. "What are we going to do now, Simon?"

I crossed my legs, which made the lamp turn off. I knocked it again with my elbow until it re-illuminated. "I think we should leave Samundra. We will have no peace with the police after us. Glory, can you get us to the spaceport?"

"I'm all for getting off this wet rock," she agreed wearily. "But it would be stupid to travel from here. The situation is too hot. Youse'd be better off flying to Annapurna, walk the gate from there."

"What's Annapurna?"

"Little orange planet. Bad food."

I licked my lips. "You would help us do this, Glory?"

"Get me off the low streets of Thaumas and I'll do anything for you."

"You're going to come with us?"

She shrugged and looked away. "Sort of defecated where I eat, here. Made some enemies. Overstayed my welcome. Doesn't matter. Bored of this ball, anyway."

"Okay," I nodded, my hand on Pish's shoulder. "What do we need to do?"

"We'll all need new clothes," said Glory. "Even your robot. My friend Monkey will take care of him, but we'll need to go shopping for you and the kid. You got a safe plate?"

"Yes," I said, petting Pish's head as he yawned and curled up on the bed beside me.

"I'll get us into the tourist zone. From there we can mix with the idiots and get on a cruise to Annapurna. They always have cruises out to see dumb faeces on Annapurna. I got off one of them and ended up here."

"Is Annapurna an important world?"

"No, it's a piece of faeces. They're *pioneers*. They only undomed like fifty years ago. The place is a coital backwater. But it's easy to get lost there, and they gate in to the Aino transmitter."

"What's Aino?"

"Coitus," she muttered darkly. "You're retarded, Simon. Aino is the Sun. You know – the big bright thing in the sky?"

Pish snored. Motioning to Glory for silence I carefully got up from the bed and backed up toward the door, knocking it against Jeremiah as I opened it. "Sorry," I whispered. Glory followed me out into the hall. "Poor kid has to be tired," I said. "It can't be noon yet."

"It's night, stupid," said Glory. "You were in a fever from the infection most of the day."

I nodded slowly. "I really need to get a watch."

Glory led me out to a narrow balcony overlooking the street. Green lamps glowed over the awnings of the shops, casting a dreary pall over the few huddled men and women that walked in the misty drizzle. A complaining animal pulled a creaking trailer filled with refuse. "Inspirational, isn't it?" sneered Glory, an orange cylinder hanging out of the corner of her mouth.

"Why do people live like this?"

She shrugged and pushed carelessly against the rail. "Government of Samundra has a lot of problems. They're not very good at dealing with people who are all fornicated up. Plus there's all the victims of the Horror. They have to go somewheres, too."

She tapped the end of the orange stick and inhaled, the ashes tumbling away in the slight breeze. When she opened her eyes again I asked, "What's the Horror?"

"Fornicated faeces polite people don't talk about, no matter what," she said, closing her eyes again and leaning against the rail.

"Are you polite, Glory?" I asked, smirking.

"Maybe not," she shrugged. "But I'm not *sick*."

A group of men started beating another man down on the street below, so we decided to retire. I wanted to know if we should try to help the man, to which Glory responded by asking how much I enjoyed having my teeth kicked out. Another poser from Glory.

I felt my teeth with my tongue nervously as we passed through the blinking corridor and into our room. Pish had curled up on the floor with a blanket and a pillow, wedged between the end of the bed and Jeremiah's feet. We stepped over him carefully and sat on the bed. "I just might pull this off," Glory said under her breath.

"Pull what off?"

"Get out of this town without getting murdered," she replied, arching one eyebrow. "It's my birthday wish."

"Is it your birthday?"

"No."

"Ah."

"I'm just saying it's a big deal to me, youse helping me out," Glory said, gathering her beaded braids and pushing them behind her shoulders.

"I feel we are in your debt," I told her seriously.

"You're wrong," she said, reaching out and taking my chin in her fingers. "Stop trying to be noble and just let me give you one. So I don't feel like such a heel, okay?"

"Give me one what?" I said, my head bobbing awkwardly with my jaw in her hand.

"You really don't know faeces, do you?" She let go of my chin and pulled her damp dress off over her head, tossing it aside. It landed on the lamp, which turned off.

"I'm not an expert on anything," I admitted to the dark.

She snorted. "So I guess I'm going to teach you a lesson."

"What about?"

"Shut up, Simon."

The ensuing time in the darkness was all about the smell of the skin behind her ear as she straddled my lap and embraced me. I became lost in the musk from the sweat on the nape of her neck as she danced. I cried out and she slapped her hands across my mouth at the end, shushing me and giggling.

I had never heard her laugh before. I didn't know she could, except as a derisive snort.

I must have slept for a while there but now I'm awake again. In this pitch cell the glow of the eye of this diary seems almost bright, casting just enough light for me to see the pin-point reflections in Jeremiah's unmoving eyes. I can hear Pish's steady breathing from the floor, and feel Glory's warm body beside me.

I am nursing a little pocket of contentment, blowing on the embers to keep it alive. Pish and I are okay for the moment, and we have found the company of a good woman who means to help us.

This can only bode well.

XI.

MONKEYS & BORDERS

Let me tell you a little bit about Monkey.

He has hands for feet, and he lives in a room where the gravity's been dampened. His ears stick out further than mine and he's always smiling. His teeth are yellow and he speaks very loudly. He is enthusiastic about pretty much anything. He wears a blue coverall covered in grease stains, his name written across the breast in faded white. He smells like a toilet.

Never the less, he was one of the nicest people I've ever met.

I met him after waking up in our cramped room with Fartles nestled against me. I blinked and the dog licked my face, then farted. I left the small room in some haste and followed the sound of voices downstairs, Fartles loping at my heels.

"Good morning, Simon!" called Pish, floating through the air.

We were in a kind of workshop, and the better part of its space was devoted to cars in various states of undress. The end of the room was sealed off by glass, however, and crisscrossed by metal poles. Pish caught one of the poles lazily and swung himself around to face me.

"Good morning, Pish," I said. Glory sauntered over escorted by the willowy, pale giant who seemed to be in charge. "Madam Glory, Master Nilo," I bowed.

Glory snorted. Nilo, who turned out to be a very friendly fellow, introduced me to Monkey. "He's our human jackbot," said Nilo smoothly, pointing him out through the glass beyond Pish. I stepped closer and the veil of reflections parted: Monkey slithered between two sets of metal bars to dangle himself over a workbench, picking through the tools with one of his feet before leaping away to the other side of the tank, his lithe body falling with dreamy slowness.

"He's a Lagranger," explained Nilo. "His family lives in some rock halfway between Samundra and Pomona, all low gravities all the time. Got into some trouble, though, so he lives down here now."

"Does he have to stay in there all the time?" I asked.

"No, he comes out sometimes. But it makes him tired. Most of the Banished learn to adapt..." Nilo pointed down to his own wide, webbed-looking shoes. "...But Monkey's simple. He knows machines, and that's about all he knows. So he's happy as anything bouncing around in there so long as we give him stuff to fix, and so long as he's fixing things I don't mind feeding him and running the anti-well."

"Inside there, he feels very light?" I asked, trying to impress him with my limber knowledge of physics.

"See for yourself."

As I stepped over the threshold and into the tank I felt my stomach flutter. The pull on my bones couldn't have been more than a quarter normal. I took another step and found myself cartwheeling slowly into a table, the contents spilling off and spinning away to rebound against the glass with a series of dull thuds. "I'm terribly sorry," I said, upsidown.

Nilo chuckled from behind me. "That's why we have the glass," he explained.

Monkey scampered over and helped me up, tugging me briefly but firmly by the forearm and then catching me against his shoulder as I threatened to overspin. "You're Simon!" Monkey exclaimed, breathing hot monkey breath into my face. "You smell like the forest!"

He pumped my hand excitedly and then bounded back over to his workbench. I carefully picked my way after him, ducking to dodge Pish's feet as he turned around a pole near the ceiling. "I'm a car!" claimed Pish.

The far side of the tank was an overlapping mosaic of pint-sized dancing figures and scenes, standing off the wall and casting flickering holographic shadows on the floor. There were movies and documentaries, trance shapes and feeds from life, pornography and psychedelic cartoons.

"Look at this nice craft!" spat Monkey, jumping over to me with a curved piece of silver metal grasped in his foot. He turned it over and the light winked across the ornamental curlicues that were inscribed over most of Jeremiah's carapace. "This is Kamari Filigree!" Monkey told me, tracing a finger along the contours of the design. His eyes dropped and he mumbled something which I asked him to repeat, but he refused.

"He wants to know if he can keep it," called Nilo, lounging at the threshold beside Glory.

Monkey reached out to his workbench and pulled over a similarly shaped piece of metal, but with a plainer surface and a burnished blue-green sheen. "This new one is good too, but it isn't as good as this one. Monkey knows it's more good but Monkey wants to keep it anyway, nice Simon."

"I can't imagine that it's my decision to make, Monkey. I think you'd best ask Jeremiah."

Monkey flitted over to the silver robot, standing mute beside the tools. "Can Monkey?" he barked and then hid his face.

Jeremiah turned toward us, and it seemed to me that he cocked his head slightly and hesitated before he declared, "If the masters will it."

"What did he say?" asked Monkey, confused by the accent.

"He said 'okay'," reported Pish.

Monkey grinned and shook my hand again as he pet me on the back and rubbed my tummy. "Nice Simon!" he crooned.

Pish and I hung around with Monkey all morning while he carefully removed Jeremiah's silver exterior and replaced it with the new blue-green carapace. Monkey delighted in pointing out various doodads beneath the robot's skin and explaining to us how it might malfunction, and in that case how to best remedy the situation according to the oft-quoted wisdom of Monkey's dad. "If this juice ever starts coming out, give the robot salt says Dad," Monkey informed me, indicating a small pocket of turgid sacs within Jeremiah's armpit. "You still have to fix it, but not as soon."

"Thank you very much," I said.

"What does that do?" Pish asked, sticking his finger into one of the cavities in the torso and wiggling it around.

"That's a –" began Monkey, and then squinted closer. "It's probably a –" he started again, and then frowned. "Monkey doesn't know," he admitted. "Some funny model Dad and Monkey never heard of."

He began sniffing around the rest of Jeremiah's innards as Glory strode in and clapped her hands. "Gentlemen, let's go shopping!"

We bid Monkey adieu and thanked Nilo. Pish told Fartles to stay put and we strode out into the low streets, crowded in the day with rushing coats and faceless shawls. Glory took us to a small corner of stalls and dickered efficiently for our new fashions. I stood mutely by and stuck my wallet-thimbled finger to the till when instructed. On the way back to Nilo's workshop Pish ran ahead of us and jumped in puddles.

"Cute kid," said Glory. "How old is he?"

"I don't know. Three?"

"I think he's about nine."

"Ah."

"Good to see him play. He's kind of gloomy. Was bringing me down before."

"He just lost his father. I think he's quite chipper actually, given the circumstances."

"Coitus," said Glory. "That fellates."

Upon our return Nilo showed us to a stained and leaky washroom where we took turns rinsing away the layers of grime under a lukewarm shower, and then Glory showed me how to shave myself with Nilo's razor. When she was done she put Nilo's razor into her handbag.

We got dressed. Pish and Glory were very happy with their new duds, but I felt constricted and trapped inside the snug apparel. Also, I felt discomfitingly naked without a robe to wear. "Listen Simon," said Glory, rolling her eyes, "normal people don't wear pajamas all day. It's coitally retarded. Just cope."

"But –"

"*Cope,* Simon," she snarled. "It's time to go."

She whisked us back across the workshop. Nilo emerged from beneath a long red car and wiped his brow. He made ridiculous, complimentary noises about our new clothes and demanded that Glory repeatedly pirouette for him, demonstrating the fly and the flow of her violet dress. He turned to me next so I spun around in place, and everybody cracked up laughing.

Still chuckling we walked together back toward Monkey's tank. Fartles was pacing before the door, whining. "What's wrong, boy?" asked Pish.

Through the glass I saw Monkey hanging oddly, folded between two metal rails. I rushed inside, steeling myself against the plunge in my stomach as I crossed the threshold into the low gravity tank. But it never came.

I stumbled forward in surprise. "The anti-well's fornicated!" Nilo shouted. "Monkey!" he then yelled, shoving me aside and rushing over to the simpleton. Nilo straightened after a moment, his white face turned waxen. "He's dead."

The tank had failed, and Monkey had fallen badly, snapping his neck.

The media screens continued to dance with holographic figures, close-ups of faces seeming to peer out of the wall at the grim scene before them.

Jeremiah stood as we had left him, but encased in green-blue metal. The designer flares and curves that defined his new face were different, but his black, reflective eyes were unchanged. "Jeremiah, what happened?" I asked.

"Sir," he replied, turning to face me. "I was deactivated at the time."

A beat. It dawned on me that Jeremiah had spoken clearly. Monkey had replaced the voice module before the accident, evidently. Nilo crumpled over the bent body of his friend and sobbed. "How could this happen?" he muttered into his long hands. "What will I tell his parents? Coitus, Monkey! Coitus!"

Glory tugged on my sleeve. She was backing out of the tank. I took Pish's hand and led him away, his head turning to stare at Monkey and Nilo. Fartles hung at our heels, his tail low.

"I bring misery wherever I go," I whispered aloud.

"Shut up," said Glory. "Come on."

She took us to a busy tram station. Outside on the street was a row of yellow cars. We piled into the back of one of them and Glory instructed the driver. A short negotiation ensued, after which Glory and the driver agreed to visit the interior of the station for a few moments for reasons I could not fathom. When they returned the driver engaged the vehicle and it lifted into the air with a low-pitched thrum.

Within moments we were deposited on a curving avenue of grass, a walkway running over the buildings of the low streets, though the streets themselves were obscured behind walls of shrubbery. In the distance to the north lay the Thaumas river valley, the rectilinear lichen of human urbanity crawling far up the hills on either side, a constant swarm of gnat-like cars mixing in the air above.

"This is the tourist highway," explained Glory. "If we can get back inside the foreign boundary we're golden."

We walked along the way until we came to a gate watched over by two white robots with fanciful designs of rivers on their broad chests. Glory explained to them that we had wandered out of the zone by an accident of curiosity, and we should like to be admitted again no matter the fine. They scanned my plate. We were asked several curt questions and then, to my surprise, allowed to pass beyond the gate. Glory grinned and strutted along the way.

We proceeded to a series of open squares, raised high above the river delta below, where couples and groups in bright costumes milled and tittered, pointing out the way the sun was melting into the ocean and engaging the proprietors of trinket stalls. Many of them cradled little tiny dog-like animals in the crooks of their elbows, which caused Fartles to whinny and start at my heels. When Pish scolded him for his obnoxiousness he hung his head and farted.

The twilight became deep and little lamps winked on within the shrubs. "Holy mung," sang Glory giddily, "*stars.*"

Indeed the heavens were resplendent above us, the glittering velvet bisected by an undulating, smoky swath of brightness. I asked about it, and Pish told me it was the wheel of the galaxy, seen on its edge, from within one of its arms. "How many stars are there in the galaxy?" I asked.

Pish closed his eyes and consulted his memory. "An hundred and twenty-six billion."

I shook my head in awe. "And do people live at all of them?"

"Nope. Just a few."

"How come?"

Pish shrugged and stuck his hands into his pockets. "We haven't got there yet, I guess."

I thought about this for a long while as we made our way toward a harbourside quay of lanterns and animated signs, music reaching us tinnily over the water. Glory spoke to an agent at one of the many colourful kiosks for a few moments and then pulled me over to stick my wallet on the till. "We sail for Annapurna noon tomorrow," she reported. She handed me a small plastic receipt for our tickets: the Apples family plus pet, one-way, first class.

"Where do we stay tonight?"

"Hotel. Booked through the cruise. Come on."

The room made my jaw drop. It was the size of half a hospital ward, with two bedrooms and an opulent sitting room with a walk-out to a terrace overlooking the city of Thaumas. After Pish had been put to bed Glory and I stood out on the terrace. Glory inhaled another one of those flashing orange sticks and then called out, "Robot! Bring us something to drink."

"Yes mistress," said Jeremiah, bowing and attending to the bar.

"You should be nicer to Jeremiah," I said after he had handed us our glasses and retreated. "He's a bit like Pish's family, after all."

"He's a robot," returned Glory quickly. "Not a teddy bear. An expensive piece of hardware. An appliance."

"The child loves him."

"That's just my coital point, Simon," said Glory, throwing back her drink in a single gulp and tossing the glass out into the darkness. "You shouldn't let the kid get so attached to it like that. It'll just fornicate him up when the thing goes to scrap."

I considered this for a moment, sipping. "Glory, can I ask you something?"

"What?"

"If people only live at some stars in the galaxy now, does that mean we all started at just one star?"

She snorted. "What in the name of faeces are you going on about *now*, Simon?"

"I was just wondering," I said, looking up at the sky. "I'd never thought about it before. But if finding new stars to live at is an ongoing process, it must have *started* somewhere, right?"

"Yeah," conceded Glory wearily. "Right, Simon."

"So?"

"So what?"

"So where did everybody come from?"

"What by coitus do you mean?"

"What's the *first star*?"

Glory paced the terrace for a moment and then suddenly pressed herself up again me, pulling the neck of her dress down to expose her breast. "Listen Simon, I don't want to coitally yap all night. I'm just glad I'm free of all that faeces, and I want to get drunk and I want to know whether or not you're going to have intercourse with me."

"Oh!" I said.

"Forget it, retard," she shot back, turning on heel and stalking away into the sitting room. I heard the clinking of bottles, the jangle of ice cubes. A door slammed. I returned my gaze to the glowing maze of the city spread out below me.

"Sol."

"What was that?" I asked, turning around.

Jeremiah was standing still as a statue behind me, all but his feet lost in the shadows. "The first star was named Sol, sir." He stepped forward and extended his arm into the sky, training it on a pinkish smear between two glinting blue stars.

"What's that?" I asked.

"The Solar Nebula, sir."

I took a moment to marvel at the dim smudge. "And that's where the first star is?"

"Where it was, sir, yes," said Jeremiah solemnly. "The coloured gases are the sloughed off remains of the star, for Sol is dead."

For some reason this made me very sad. "Thank you, Jeremiah. Good night."

"Good night, sir," he pronounced crispy, then bowed his head and left the terrace, the soft rubber on the bottoms of his feet sighing against the stone.

XII.
LESSON IN LOYALTY

A bird woke me up.

It was brightly coloured and as large as my head. It sat on the sill of the open window, looking at me and emitting a soft cooing noise. Its eyes were amber and its curved bill was a plastic shade of yellow. Blinking and yawning I sat up in bed. The bird screamed like a woman in distress, startling me, and flapped away, its wings flashing in the bronze morning light.

"Wow. Did you see that bird?"

"Shut up," muttered Glory from beneath the covers, the edge of which was stained with a crust of sour vomit.

I got out of bed and met Pish in the sitting room. We rolled around on the floor tickling the dog for a while and then ran out to the terrace to spit over the side. I think I hit a taxi, but Pish claims I missed.

Breakfast arrived along with a table. The robots wished us good appetites as they departed. I had an awkward moment with the human steward while he hovered at my elbow expectantly. I patted him on the shoulder and told him he was doing a bang-up job, and he left without another word. Glory swept out of the washroom wrapped in a fluffy white robe bearing the crest of the hotel, a white towel around her dripping head. "Right on," she said, taking a seat and tearing in.

Pish and I also ate. I looked at him after a couple of mouthfuls, and he looked at me, chewing thoughtfully. I shrugged and he frowned. "It's *edible*," I told him, trying to look on the bright side.

"Barely," said Pish, sampling the spiced gams with disdain.

"Are you fornicating me?" Glory exclaimed, eggs tumbling from her mouth. "This is the best faeces I've ever eaten! Holy mung!"

"To each his own," I admitted, washing down another mouthful with tea. Pish looked dubious, but he cleaned his plate anyway. I could see his point: while the unadorned simplicity of fried vegetables in nut oil with salty bread at Nilo's could charm us with its humble nudity, the meal before us had been artlessly gussied up into something pretentious, indecisive, and slightly rude.

Glory actually licked her plate. I thought it was Fartles until I glanced over. "I'm having an orgasm," she claimed.

"What's an orgasm?" asked Pish.

"I'll tell you later," I said, my discomfort being only faintly appeased by the realization that for once it was not *I* who had to ask.

It was as we were gathering our bits to depart for the cruise that Pish suddenly started walking back and forth between the rooms, sweeping his head around with his face pinched in anxiety. "Where's Jeremiah?" he wailed when I stopped him and asked what was wrong.

I straightened. "Where *is* Jeremiah? Glory?"

"Fornicated if I know."

Pish followed me around while I thrashed through the bedrooms and the sitting room again, even peering over the edge of the terrace to see if I could see a robot's body smashed on the green rooftops below. Pish and I arrived back in the sitting room, Fartles at our heels. Glory was putting on her new shoes and adjusting the beads in her braids. "We've got to go," she declared.

"But we can't find Jeremiah."

"He's obviously not here. Maybe he's waiting for us in the lobby. Or at the shuttle dock. We're going to be late." She opened the door and waved us into the hall. "Come on."

I hesitated. Pish stood forlornly beside Fartles. He looked up at me in appeal. "We *have* to find him, Simon," he told me.

"Faeces," said Glory.

I turned around to explain it to her but realized that her commentary had not been addressing the missing robot situation so much as the situation with the gang of aggressive thugs pushing her aside and piling into the suite. They wore black clothing and wore black masques, each of the three men bearing a tiny black device in one hand. One swung around to train his device on Glory, and she screamed and begged him for mercy.

"What is the meaning of this?" I cried. The biggest of them shut the door and strode over into my face. Without hesitation he backhanded me and I toppled sideways over a chair.

Pish cowered in the corner but Fartles exploded forward, spittle flying from his jowls as be barked. He toppled the nearest intruder and clamped his jaws around his wrist, causing the shiny ovoid mechanism to skitter across the floor. But another such device was quickly leveled at the struggling pair by another of the intruders.

He touched and contact and both his comrade and Fartles began to twitch uncontrollably, their limbs jerking out from under them and causing them to bounce across the floor. In a second it was over, and both lay on their sides curled up like babies, panting and groaning softly.

The tallest one struck me across the head as I looked on, then pulled me over to him and roughly felt through my clothes. He extracted my plate and my diary, slipped them into one of his own pockets, then swore and stood up. "Please," I implored him, "leave me my plate – it's my only picture of my children!"

For a moment I held his eyes. Then he kicked me savagely in the gut and stomped over to Pish, picking him up and then dropping him again once he had determined his pockets were empty.

I looked up to see the tall man rip Glory's precious handbag away from her. She clawed after it and he shoved her backward. She slid down the wall and started to cry. "Why are you doing this to me? Why, Verd? Nilo *said* I could go! I already gave you the fornicated robot – why are you doing this to me now?"

"You gave them Jeremiah?" I exclaimed, my blood boiling in my ears and my voice pouring out of my mouth of its own accord. "How could you? How could you do this to us?"

"We're recouping *all* our losses," grunted the tallest man, Verd. "Shut up and get to the van and feel lucky I don't jazz you, whore. *Move!"*

Glory wept. "I'm not supposed to – that wasn't part of the deal...you're fornicating me, Verd, you're coitally fornicating me! Why are you doing this?" she pled as she was hauled to her feet by another one of the black-garbed intruders.

I screamed out, *"How do you dare ask him why he does this to you when you do this to us?"*

Verd walked over and kicked me in the face with his heavy boot. This ended our dialogue for good, my tongue quickly swelling in my bloody mouth. I collapsed to the carpet, staining it.

"What about his wallet?" asked the third intruder, rubbing his mauled wrist.

"No good without his finger," grunted Verd. "Let's go."

"I'll take the finger with me," the other replied, and I felt my bowels quiver in terror. He walked over to me and took my hand in his, rudely prying away my other fingers until the index was exposed.

He drew out a long knife. I winced.

A buzzer sounded and a woman's voice called out: *"This is hotel security. We have detected a crime in progress. Agents are en route to your suite."*

I opened my eyes and the bandits had fled along with Glory, the pressure I still felt around my finger a phantom of panic. Pish was crying, so I stumbled over to him and picked him up. I carried over him to Fartles, who had urinated on the carpet but seemed otherwise undamaged. He licked Pish's face somberly and groaned.

My heart was hammering. The edges of my vision were pink and throbbing. How could people helping one another out do this? My sternum burned with a cold flame.

I put Pish down beside Fartles and looked at myself in the mirror, picking up Glory's towel from the floor to mop at my bloody chin. I spied Glory's similarly discarded hotel robe and put it on, flexing my shoulders and testing its weight – feeling complete. Lastly I knelt down and retrieved the small, black, ovoid device that the intruder had dropped when Fartles bit him. I turned it over in my fingers, and gently wiped a greasy print off the contact.

Hotel security burst in. "Sir, are you injured?" they wanted to know.

"Yes," I said, wiping my mouth with the back of my hand and leaving a red smear there. "See to the boy. I'm going after the robot."

"What?"

I pushed between them and into the hall. In another moment I was crossing the lobby briskly, the white robe flying out behind me.

Helplessness is a disease, I decided, and one of which I meant to purge myself finally. If my ignorance would make me a victim of vultures, I would make up the lack in strength of will. I would be a juggernaut.

I took a taxi to Nilo's garage, paying double fare for access to the low streets and suffering no insolence from the driver. The car hummed as it descended into the shadows between the white, vine-draped buildings of Thaumas.

I shouldered aside the door and strode into the workshop. Nilo and two of the men in black were loitering around the hull of an empty car, apparently eating their lunch. They looked up as I walked unhesitatingly toward them.

One of them rose and pointed his device at me, so I pointed mine at him and pressed the contact. He dropped to the floor, shaking. I was taking aim at the second man in black when he fired at me – but as I was partially obscured by the chassis of a truck I felt only a vague tingling in one side of my body. When it stopped I leapt out and squarely jazzed him in turn.

I stepped over his jerking body and approached Nilo, who fixed me with a hard stare and let a smile crinkle one corner of his mouth. "You going to jazz me, Simon? After all I've done for you?"

"I'm here to take back the robot. Give him to me and I'll go in peace."

"It doesn't work like that, fool," he retorted, taking a step closer to me. "You're fornicating with Boss Preen now, sonny. That robot is for his summer house, and that's a fact you'd just have to learn to live with if it weren't for the fact that you're about to die."

I opened my mouth to respond and Nilo slapped the black device out of my hand. It bounced across the floor and shattered against a stair. We stared into each other's eyes a moment longer before engaging in a rude wrestling match as I grabbed his wrist and attempted to take his jazzer.

He were both grunting with effort with a loud *pop* sounded, after which Nilo staggered backward, clutching at his long, slender forearm. "You broke my arm!"

"I'm sorry," I said.

"Faeces Simon, you broke my arm!" He grimaced and leaned against the car behind him, knocking over the remains of his lunch. "Coitus!" He looked up slowly to watch me scoop up the fallen jazzer. "Are you going to jazz me, Simon?" he asked quietly. I shook my head. "Are you going to *kill* me, Simon?"

"Certainly not," I replied with a frown. "Who do you think I am?"

"The robot's in the back room," he told me, sighing and closing his eyes. "But there's like five guys in there with him, waiting until Boss Preen gets here. And then you're dead anyway."

I marched through the corridor to the back room and cast open the door, Nilo hanging sulkily behind me. He looked at me inquiringly. "See for yourself," I invited him.

Nilo shuffled over beside me, cradling his fracture. Inside the room stood Jeremiah in his blue-green metal carapace, calmly at ease amid the corpses of three men.

"Jeremiah," I said.

"Sir," he replied.

I tied the sash on my bathrobe and turned on heel. Jeremiah followed me as I crossed the workshop. One of the men I had attacked with the jazzer was standing up, leaning on an engine and panting heavily. I raised the device at him again and he scampered to the floor, cowering behind a workbench. I walked over to the workbench and picked up my plate and my diary, dropping them into the wide pockets of my white robe.

"Thanks for your hospitality," I muttered as we left.

We sprinted around several corners and kept sharp watch behind us. We somehow evaded pursuit. I found myself regarding the placid robot as we walked, unsure what to think. "You killed those men, didn't you Jeremiah?"

"Sir?" he replied opaquely with a polite tilt of his head.

"Don't play coy with me," I frowned. "You're an unusual robot, aren't you? Monkey knew as much as you killed him, too."

"Sir?" he said again.

I smirked resignedly. "I should just be grateful you're on our side, I guess. This is a mad, mad world."

"Sir," confirmed the robot, and despite his immobile features I could swear I could detect a smile.

For hours Jeremiah and I made our way across the low city in silence, working our way ever higher until we could repeat our feat at the tourist zone boundary once more. It was nightfall as we arrived at the elevated squares and markets of the foreigners' common, and I became too weary to press on.

Jeremiah and I surreptitiously crawled behind a row of hedges and found a perch of grass near the edge of the walkway, overlooking the harbor, hidden from view and unlit by lamps. We could hear the chatter and the footfalls of the tourists promenading on the other side of the hedges, which made our secret nook a little bit like a sheet-fort in a busy hospital ward.

"I wish we could tell Pish you're okay," I lamented.

"Why not use your telephone, sir?"

I asked my telephone to put me in touch with the hotel, and after chatting briefly with a courteous girl or robot from the front desk I was connected to our room. I assured Pish that we were well, and that he should have the hotel prepare dinner for himself and Fartles. We would be along in the morning.

Next, after more inquiries with the front desk, I managed to adjust our cruise reservation for tomorrow's shuttle by paying a re-scheduling fee. *"I'm obliged to inform you that the fee is fifty-four hours,"* said the girl from the front desk, her voice sounding through my skull.

I hesitated. "Is that a lot?"

"I'm obliged to say that it's very reasonable," the girl told me.

"Okay. Do it."

The walkways became quiet as night settled in. I tightened my fluffy hotel robe around me and curled up on the cool grass. The stars were disappearing behind a fresh wave of thick cloud. "I hope it doesn't rain," I said. "This is such a very wet place."

"Samundra is known as the World of Rivers," contributed Jeremiah.

"Fantastic," I said, shivering.

"I can warm you, sir, if you'll allow me. I have the ability to control my surface temperature."

"Um...okay."

Jeremiah came and lay down behind me, clasping his metal arms around me. I detected a homey warmth emanating from him. I shifted position awkwardly, pressing myself against his hips and allowing the heat to suffuse me. "Listen, this doesn't mean there's anything between us," I quipped.

"Sir?"

"Forget it." I pulled my diary out of my pocket, cleared my throat and after a moment of pained recollection pronounced, "A bird woke me up."

Tomorrow: to space!

XIII.
A FACE OF GOD

I swear it felt like we would spend our lives in line.

Amid a garish clutch of gibbering tourists we shuffled slowly forward to be processed in turn by a customs agent, a reservations clerk, and a robot with inoculative needles for fingers. Everyone smiled, even the robot. At all times we were surrounded by dancing holographic characters, witness to staccato bursts of terrifying music, and intermittently sprayed with a sampling of promotional designer scents.

"Enjoy your flight, Mr. Apples."

"Say who? Oh, yes of course. Thank you."

Two dozen of us were corralled into a high-walled square with a grassy floor, where vendors hung around the rosebushes and proffered drinks and trinkets. It seemed like everybody had a giant hat and a small dog. Fartles comported himself admirably.

One white wall sported a wide screen carrying dense tables of departure times and destinations beside a bamboozling stream of flashing video imagery out of which I could occasionally catch glimpse of a car, a breast, or a celebration. Pish tugged on my sleeve and I realized firstly that I had been mesmerized, and secondly that I should probably consult Pallando Financial Services with regard to risk-managed interstellar investment before the close of the next tax season. Some restrictions may apply in certain jurisdictions.

"Funny sign," I said, craning my head around to look at it again.

"I'm hungry," said Pish, so I bought him some sort of pastry pocket stuffed with steaming goodies, the majority of which he would wear down the front of his shirt for the rest of the day.

I heard a high-pitched whirring and turned in time to see a great mirrored sphere gilded by a band of shining metal at its equator lift up above the port and proceed serenely into the azure sky like a giant bubble. "What was that?" I asked.

"That's a shuttle," answered Pish, mumbling around his food.

"We're going to ride on one of those?"

Pish nodded, hot stuffing dripping on his shoes. Fartles sauntered over and cleaned it up. "Yup," Pish added, once he'd swallowed.

"Have you ever been on one of those before?" I asked.

"Nope."

"Are you scared?"

"Not really. It's kind of like the bus."

I swallowed. "Okay."

Eventually we were funneled out of the courtyard in pairs and passed into another courtyard, this one occupied fully by a tall pillar in the middle of a great loop, seemingly suspended in space like a halo around the pillar's midpoint. The top and the bottom of the pillar were capped with wide dishes, both of which studded with comfy chairs. Some of our fellow passengers climbed a carpeted ladder on the side of the pillar and strapped themselves into the inverted chairs hanging from the upper cap, which I thought was a thoroughly baffling way for anyone to want to travel. I squinted in the sunshine, allowing Jeremiah to lead us to four seats near the outer edge of the lower cap.

A girl in a matching maroon skirt and hat advised us all to keep our places while the orb engaged. I jumped a moment later when a strange humming cycled up quickly, became briefly loud and then went suddenly silent; my ears popped and the air beyond the cap gained a faintly iridescent sheen. "It's quite safe to touch the orb now, ladies and gentlemen," announced the girl in maroon.

By looking carefully I could just barely discern a spherical barrier surrounding us, only really visible in our shadow against the far wall, the circular band and connecting cylinder opaque within a bubble of translucent grey.

"It keeps the air in," Pish explained. "There's no air in space."

"I know," I said, kneeling down where the barrier met the edge of the carpeted deck beneath our feet. I touched it. It was solid, and made no sound when I rapped on it. "What is it made of?" I asked.

Pish shrugged. "Science?"

A tone sounded. The girl in maroon announced that we were about to lift off, and advised all passengers to attach their safety belts. She also asked us not to use our plates or telephones until a certain little yellow light came on, which she pointed out. Then she sat down on a smaller seat that folded out of the side of the pillar, and strapped herself in.

"Now what happens?" I asked.

I felt a swoop in my belly, like riding the lift with Dr. Pent. The ground dropped away from us without noise, and within seconds we were drifting up above the port, looking down into the other pits where other orb shuttles sat in wait or settled in to land. In another blink the port was a grey smudge at the lip of the city, itself a linear array of smudges quickly vanishing at the line of rolling green land and sparkling blue sea. After the initial surge upward I detected almost no sensation of motion at all, but the view was enough to make me giddy and lightheaded.

Like silver fingers, the continent was filigreed with networks of rivers and streams. The World of Rivers indeed! I lost all sense of scale, and it seemed to me that the land was made of broccoli.

I looked up and suddenly gasped, casting my hands over my head as it appeared our shuttle was cruising directly into a solid barrier of grey whorls and white vapors. A dim, smoky shadow enveloped us. In another moment we emerged from the top of the thick bank of clouds and I realized how silly I was being.

Soon the clouds were tiny grains of white beneath us. The horizon had begun to bow, and the sky overhead had turned from deep blue to purple. "Look," said Pish, pointing straight up. "Stars."

A profound silence descended over the next moments. The sky faded, and the ground curved. The stars ceased to glimmer, and stood hard and fixed and plentiful in the sky like crystals of spilled sugar. I felt a tickling in my belly, and realized that my body felt even lighter than it had in Monkey's anti-well.

"Ladies and gentlemen, prepare for freefall," announced the girl in maroon. "Please ensure all personal belongings are secured."

And so barely a quarter hour after we had set off, we were in space. My arms hung lazily before me, and my head swam. Quiet music began to play from an unseen source, perhaps in an effort to offset the startlingly unnatural quiet. I looked up at the people who had sat opposite us in the high cap, but now without reference they looked as if they were sitting normally and it was I who was upsidown. "Oh my," I said, clutching the arms of my seat. Jeremiah caught my diary as it drifted out of my pocket.

I gasped in wonder, and then I threw up.

The girl in maroon was at my side quickly with a little vacuum that efficiently sucked away the lumps of vomit as they rolled leisurely up and away from my face. "I'm so sorry," I said, belching.

"Don't worry about it sir," smiled the girl. "It happens to the best of us."

As I recovered myself I looked around and noticed that several of the passengers had little cups on cables drawn from within their armrests. They held the cups over the mouths and winced every few moments. I realized firstly that I was not alone in my nausea, and secondly I appreciated what it was the ambient music was intended to be muffling – retching, not silence.

"Are you okay, Pish?"

He nodded happily, leaning out of his seat to peer at the great frosted marble of Samundra beyond the orb's invisible skin. It looked close enough to touch, which I found unsettling.

"How many people live down there?" I whispered to Jeremiah.

"Some eight hundred million, sir."

I marvelled. Eight hundred million men and women and children, in a glorious aqua sphere I could make disappear by leaning back in my seat and hiding it behind Fartles' head. The dog seemed unconcerned and continued to pant happily, his dangling tongue intermittently occulting a mass of glaciers at Samundra's southern pole.

I noticed what seemed like an especially bright star off Samundra's limb. "What's that?" I asked, pointing it out for the robot.

"That's Pomona," interjected Pish. "My dad took me there once."

"Is Pomona the moon of Samundra?"

"No, they're both moons," he said, his tone implying that I was a little slow on the uptake.

"Moons of what?" I asked.

Just then the trajectory of our shuttle changed, and the view outside began to gently scroll aside as the shadows turned around us. "Moons of *that*," said Pish, pulling my arm and pointing away from Samundra. Steeling myself against vertigo I turned my head to see.

It was like staring into the face of a god.

Opposite the worlds of Samundra and Pomona stood a wall of phantasmagoric gas, frozen spirals of churning cloud locked in great bands that spanned my vision, gilding it from horizon to horizon in a hundred commingled shades of yellow, amber and copper. Lifting my gaze upward I could barely discern a strip of space, the lip of the god curved against it.

I realized that it was a world – many thousands of times larger than Samundra.

"That's Aramaiti," said Pish.

"Mother of love!" I gasped. "Why have I never seen it before?"

"Because it's always on the other side of Samundra."

"How many people live there?" I needed to know. "It must be untold trillions!"

Pish laughed. "*Nobody* lives there, silly. It's a gas giant. There's just some weird fish and stuff – no people."

The girl in maroon pointed out another sight visible from the far side of the orb: a bright smudge against the velvet – our destination, apparently. "Castle Misne has been in continuous service on the Aramaiti-Annapurna Milk Run for over three hundred eighty-six years, making it one of the most distinguished castles in the Panstellar Neighbourhood. Castle Misne is run under the stewardship of the famous Captain Tallum Gold, who will happily receive you all for an intimate dinner on Day Two of our sixteen-day transit to Annapurna. We will be debarking at Castle Misne in two and one half hours. In the meantime, please enjoy some refreshing drinks and light snacks."

Over the next two hours the smudge steadily grew until we could plainly discern a long speck silhouetted against a gauzy oblong which Pish told me was probably the castle's stellar sail, a fabric designed to capture Aino's wind for power. The speck itself grew until we could see formation lights blinking on its exterior and the murky orange glow of wide windows. Several sections of the long castle were gracefully rotating. Jeremiah explained that this was to create a feeling of gravity throughout the voyage.

I had a pastry, and a sac of juice.

Soon our bubble was dwarfed by the enormous castle as we drew along its side and became secured to a port at our pole. We opened our harnesses and attempted to propel ourselves toward the central pillar where the rest of the passengers were queuing up to leave. Pish did fairly well, as did Fartles, but Jeremiah had to come and rescue me as I pinwheeled across the shuttle interior and rebounded off the opposite chairs.

"Sir," said Jeremiah, tugging me gently toward the pillar.

We manoeuvred along the corridor within the pillar, which opened into a hatch at its end, where the girl in maroon was waiting to bid us farewell. I over-pushed against the side of the hatch and careened out of the shuttle, spilling into a crowd of other passengers and causing them to drop their things. For a few moments the debarkation lobby was a cloud of handbags, hats, and small kicking dogs. "I'm very sorry," I called, coming to rest against a sign bearing directions to the washroom.

Proceeding to our cabin was similarly adventuresome, but I'll spare you the details. Suffice it to say that my freefalling skills were put to shame by the dog who somehow managed to kick off the bulkheads lightly like a dancer, emitting quiet *chuffs* of stinking gas in his wake.

And, for the record, it was *Pish* who fell against *me* at the mouth of the tube that admitted us into the rotating habitat hub. So, while everyone else rediscovered gravity gradually as they descended the ladder to the curved floor, I rediscovered it with a sickening lurch as I cartwheeled uncontrollably beside them.

"First time out of the well?" cracked some wiseacre on the ladder.

"Yes," I muttered darkly, striking the carpet with a dull thud.

I was able to relax a tad once safely ensconced in our cabin. The gravity was only slightly less than at Samundra's surface, and the presence of familiar sorts of furniture gave me a reassuring feeling of which way was up. A bank of ports looked out into the blackness.

I decided to tidy up in the washroom, and was shocked to see my face in the mirror. Not only was my lower jaw once again turning dark with little hairs, but many other spots on my face were purple or pink from yesterday's unpleasantness despite Jeremiah's ministrations this morning.

I peeled off my clothes and took a hot shower, using my stolen packet of hospital soap to cleanse me and to fill my nostrils with the smell of nostalgia. Afterwards I managed to use the washroom's razor with only a few instructions shouted through the door from Pish. I figured out the motorized toothbrush all by myself. I found a plush blue robe in the closet and put it on, then strode out with a grin. "So, when does this ship get underway?"

"It is a castle, sir," replied Jeremiah; "it is always underway, in a permanent circuit between the worlds. Shuttles dock with it as it passes."

"Oh? Well, good then."

We opted to take supper in our cabin, and this time when the steward hung around awkwardly I made him explain to me the concept of tipping. I thanked him for his indulgence and touched my wallet-tip to the till on his sleeve, my telephone and I negotiating the finer points sub-vocally. I was pretty pleased with myself afterward, but Pish didn't seem too impressed.

"Glory would've loved this place," he commented.

"Glory betrayed us," I hissed.

"Yeah," agreed Pish, kicking idly at the covers hanging off the bed, "but I kind of liked her anyway."

We ate quietly. Somberly, perhaps. We made no comment about the food.

After we had tucked in Pish I sat in my robe by the port-holes and looked out upon the canopy. As the rush of victory at leaving Samundra faded I quailed at the question of what precisely to do next. It is clear that we can't keep running forever. I'm too stupid and the boy deserves better.

Jeremiah walked out of the shadows and handed me my diary. "I have observed that this meditation benefits you, sir," he said.

I took the little blue bauble and turned it over in my hands. "Thank you, Jeremiah," I whispered.

The world is too big! How far can we get without an advisor? And whom would I dare trust again, after catching a glimpse of how illusory trust can be?

Black space and her hard stars had no answer for me.

XIV.
CAPTAIN GOLD

I spent the day moping in the cabin while Pish explored the castle with Jeremiah, but they finally managed to coerce me to come out in time for dinner with the captain. For the first time ever I opened up our luggage and dug around through the new clothes Glory had bought for us back in Thaumas. I found a clean set of duds for Pish and myself, and a heavy metal container which Jeremiah identified as a "black hole box" used to evade the scanners.

I opened it up and was less than surprised to find it filled with row upon row of

Glory's little orange sticks. "Is it a narcotic?" I asked.

"Dilly chalk," answered Jeremiah with a nod. "Highly illegal to transport."

"Super."

I snapped the lid shut and decided to deal with that little problem later. I reluctantly doffed my plush blue robe and we got changed for dinner.

To arrive at the dining room we had to pass out of our rotating habitat hub and into an adjacent hub, necessitating another embarrassing session of freefall gymnastics. Pish said I was doing much better, but I still couldn't keep up with the dog. It didn't help that the tunnel between the hubs was transparent, tempting me to distraction as I gaped at the castle spread fore and aft of us, space all around.

The dining hall for our "intimate dinner" was a vast auditorium filled with high-backed wooden chairs and mahogany tables spread with shining silverware. A chandelier lit by a thousand tiny points of light hung heavily over us, making me feel faintly uneasy. A maroon robot escorted us to our assigned seats one table over from the head table. Other maroon robots were escorting other guests, the buzz of unintelligible chatter drowning out the quiet music.

I saw two ladies with bright, saturated paint spread over their faces and feathers in their hair sit at the head table and begin craning their heads around as they tittered loudly to one another, "My goodness, we shall be nearly in the captain's lap, shan't we?" Twin robots stood mute at their elbows, their eyes black like Jeremiah's but their carapaces multicoloured and gaudy.

An elderly couple in densely embroidered, puffy-looking jackets and white tights arrived at our table and sat down. The lady had a tall head of elaborately wrapped white hair, and the gentleman had a bushy white moustache that covered most of his mouth. "Goodevening, my name is Prandon Thrustworth and this is my wife, Eve."

"How do you do?" asked Eve.

"I do very well thank you. I'm Hellig Apples, and this is my son Simon," I said without thinking. I glanced down at Pish uncertainly and he smiled. I smiled back.

Prandon slipped a sleek plate out of his inside pocket and looked at me through it briefly. "A Samundrite grower – how delightful!" he exclaimed.

"Ooh yes," agreed Eve. "It's always nice to meet people who are close to the land. Grown food is so very important, of course."

After an awkward interval while they remained fixedly smiling it occurred to me to withdraw my own plate. I held it up before the couple and saw their welcome messages wink onscreen. I scanned the information quickly. "And how, uh, delightful to meet such a fine investment banker such as yourself, sir, and a distinguished editor such as *your*self, madam."

"We're reliving our honeymoon cruise," Eve told me with a prim nod and a little smile.

"Well let's not *barrage* the boy, darling," interrupted Prandon smoothly. "What brings *you* out this way, my dear fellow?"

"Would you like a piece of candy?" Eve asked Pish. "I think I have a little piece of candy in my purse."

"*Honestly*, Eve," groaned Prandon, his white moustache bristling. "Now where was I? Yes, banking. I've been in banking for ninety-two years now, myself."

"Is that a matter of fact?" I said politely.

"Hush now, Prandon!" snapped Eve. "Here comes the captain. You'll spoil everything with your nattering."

I turned in my chair to follow the eyes of the room. All were seated now, robots standing stiff at elbows, dogs panting on laps, all looking to the main entrance as a corpulent, white-bearded gentleman in faux-military regalia pushed open the doors and began shuffling down the way toward the head table, piped in by a human steward with a whistle. Everyone began to applaud, so I applauded too.

The old man wearily took his place at the podium, and cleared his throat. "Goodevening ladies and gentlemen. Allow me to personally welcome you aboard Castle Misne, the grandest of all castles and my passionate mistress." More applause. The captain waited until it passed, and then entered into a harrowing tale from some battle in which he had personally piloted a heavily damaged vessel of refugees to safe planetfall amid flames and panic. After more applause he declared, "Dinner is served!"

Chimes sounded and a flotilla of robots and human stewards bearing gleaming platters erupted from hidden alcoves in the walls, descending among us in a horde to dispense salad and soup.

"The soup is delightful!" exclaimed Eve.

"Quite so," agreed Prandon.

"Hey Simon," whispered Pish. "They're *right*."

And they were. The main course was likewise excellent. Even the dog's meal smelled good enough to taste, though I didn't do so on Pish's advice. The Thrustworths asked me about farming on Samundra, and I muddled through my responses awkwardly. Their smiles were becoming increasingly strained. "My ways must seem very provincial to you, I apologize," I offered.

"Not at all," said Eve, smiling with her mouth but not her eyes. Her expression further faltered as she detected Fartles' latest contribution to the ambience.

"Bad dog," whispered Pish.

In fact, Fartles' rectal missives were travelling far beyond our own little table, their effects making their appreciation plain through the crinkled noses and waved hands at one table after another, describing the flow of blown air through the hall. As I observed the phenomenon I noticed how our aged captain and distinguished host seemed to relish the scandalized squawks of the acolytes crowding around him to talk as he ate. He chuckled around his fork and kept right on eating, nodding sympathetically to whoever had his ear.

Come dessert the Thrustworths suggested reluctantly that we join them for a cocktail in the lounge, and seemed enormously relieved when we declined. Pish and I were on a mission to meet the author of tonight's delicacies: as soon as our places were cleared and the crowd began to thin we dashed after one of the busboys into the byways behind the alcoves. Jeremiah followed at a patient distance.

When we came to the ante-kitchen a maroon robot held up his arm and declared that guests were not permitted beyond. "I want to see the chef!" I called until one of the human stewards intervened. "I want to see the chef," I told her.

"The chef is very busy," she replied curtly.

"We want to pay homage to an artist."

She sniffed. I opened my mouth to speak again but she turned on heel and muttered, "Won't you come this way?" as she disappeared around a corner. Pish, Fartles and I scampered after her. We were led through steaming kitchens and a massive pantry, finally presented before a great round tank from which extended a battery of metal arms lying relaxed against the polished floor. "The maestro," our hostess declared as she departed.

Inside the tank stood a creature covered in white hair, from its powerful-looking grasshopper-like legs to its twin sets of long, multi-jointed arms. Its face was much like the head of a horse, but with two wide, wet blue eyes set in front. In place of its mouth was a stretched, spongy-looking web of membranes which flexed as it breathed. The creature turned to gaze at me.

"Hello," I stammered. "My name is Simon." After a moment I added, "But my friends call me Hellig."

The creature blinked, its lids flitting horizontally twice in quick succession.

"My colleague and I wanted to compliment you on a masterful repast," I said, gesturing at Pish and smiling. Pish waved. Fartles farted. Jeremiah stood mutely by the wall. I continued, "You are an artist, er, sir, and it has been our privilege to partake."

The creature stirred. As it moved toward the glass it blinked quickly, its lashes resting once it settled closer to us. Its mouth flexed, exuding multiple streams of coloured vapour. A voice spoke from a speaker on the side of the tank: *"My thanks are to you for troubling to mention your appreciation."*

I glanced at the speaker and then looked back to the maestro. "May I ask you something? It may sound funny to you, but I've been through a bit of an ordeal and my memory isn't what it should be."

"I would be pleased to consider any question," said the speaker as the maestro jetted its coloured vapours into the tank's air.

"You're not a human being, of course."

"No. You call us Pegasi."

"Can you taste our food?"

"No, dear Hellig. I cannot even tolerate your atmosphere."

"So how, may I ask, do you perform your art?"

The maestro stirred and its membranous mouth quivered in a peculiar way. *"To every art there is an aspect of science,"* pronounced the speaker; *"and so to every science there is an aspect of instinct. Where the twain meet a mathematician might become a master chef, such as I have become: honored to please you."*

"The honor is ours," I said reverently.

A coarse cackle sounded behind me. Captain Gold himself was leaning against one of the gleaming metal counters, fishing bits of chopped fruit out of a large bowl. "You're a courteous one, aren't you Mr. Apples?" said the captain, his mouth full of pulp. To the maestro he called, "The junnimeres were off a bit tonight, huh?"

"I'm sure you cleared your plate, fat man."

"Go to bed. You're getting cranky. You know damn well you used too much coriander."

"Sputter on my fumes, my friend," suggested the speaker while the maestro's mouth quivered again.

"Ah faeces," laughed Captain Gold. "He's the second best chef in the galaxy, that Pegasi bastard," he said to me.

"Who's the best?" asked Pish.

"Master Duncan Menteith, naturally," replied the captain without hesitation. "They tried to get him for us, but he wanted too much damn money."

Pish winked at me but I gestured at him to keep cool. Fartles farted again, and I apologized on his behalf.

Captain Gold laughed. "You don't have to apologize for that dog, Mr. Apples. He provided me with ample entertainment throughout my chore, making those buzzards cringe." He chuckled again as he shuffled over to Fartles and scratched him behind the ear. "Attaboy," said Captain Gold. Then he looked up. "Why don't you join me in my quarters for a drink?"

Jeremiah took Pish back to our cabin but Fartles and I elected to accompany the friendly old captain back to his rooms, which were ample and stuffed with trophies and holograms of younger versions of himself shaking hands with people of import. A great circular window looked out over the ship, the ruddy crescent of massive Aramaiti dominating the view.

"Yes, my view looks backward," the captain declared, intercepting my gaze as he crossed the room to tinkle glasses at his bar. "Fitting for a captain such as myself – to see only where we've already been."

"Is this not a grand castle?" I asked as handed me a drink. I sipped it experimentally. "Forgive me, but I rather took it your post was highly esteemed."

The captain chortled. "Are you kidding me, Mr. Apples?"

"Please, call me Hellig."

"Hellig then, fine. Call me Tallum. Do you need another drink? I do. Listen, Hellig: my job here is to host the same insipid dinner parties over and over again. I make windy speeches about things that may or may not have ever happened...I honestly don't remember anymore which parts I've made up. I'm just a prop for the tourists. I don't even know the *name* of whoever it is that steers this damned hotel. I can assure you that I am never consulted on any issue, great or small."

I considered this for a moment. "How did you end up in this predicament, if I may ask, Captain?"

"An unlucky combination of famous and lazy," he grunted, winking at me as he upended a bottle into his glass. "What's your story, Hellig?"

"Would you believe that I lost my memory when I stepped through a hyperspatial gate?"

"No. Would you believe that I'm going to save the galaxy in an unlikely way with the help of a plucky companion?"

"I'm sorry?"

"Forget it. I don't even have a plucky companion anymore." He gestured vaguely toward a framed holograph of a running spotted dog. "Tell me my friend: did you *really* lose your memory? Like in the pictures?"

"Honestly, Tallum. I'm an idiot." I sipped my drink.

"So," he grinned. "You could be anyone, eh? Maybe you're March Peebles himself!"

"March Peebles?"

"March Peebles!" crooned Captain Gold. "The wealthiest man in the galaxy, who spends his days in one disguise or another dispensing philanthropic surprises to those he deems most needy." He gave me a sidelong glance, "Ringing any bells, Hellig?"

I shrugged and smiled. "They tell me my name is Simon."

"Simon, huh? Maybe you're one of the Wandering Jews!"

"What's a Jew?"

The captain gaped at me melodramatically, rolled his eyes and then tossed back his drink. "What's a Jew? What's a Jew, he asks? *I'm* a Jew, Hellig – or Simon, or March Peebles, or whoever you might be."

I smiled hesitantly. "It's a sort of space captain, then?"

He laughed uproariously, clapping me on the back and causing me to spill my drink. He apologized and poured me another. I already felt a tingling warmth spreading through my body but I accepted it anyway.

"The Jews are a people, sir," Captain Gold intoned as he regained himself. "One of the oldest peoples there is. I trace my blood to the tribes of Old Earth."

"Was Earth a world at the Solar star?"

"Was Earth a world at the Solar star?" he echoed incredulously, gesturing in the air. "Is down the direction my pants go when I unhitch my belt? My God Hellig, you really don't know a thing."

I shrugged. "My curse and my charm, sir."

"I'll drink to that," he announced, downing another. He rolled the empty glass between his fingers and cast his gaze out upon Aramaiti on the velvet. "You've got to find out who you are, my friend. A man is only as strong as his roots. And every man's roots go back to Old Earth, only most suffer in ignorance of it."

I sipped my drink again, the stars beyond the glass seeming to wheel around me. "Tell me something, will you Captain? What happened to the Solar star? How did it die?"

The captain poured himself another drink. "Men killed the star, with the Secret Mathematic." I looked at him inquiringly so he continued, "When all humankind still lived at Sol, a mathematical framework was developed which modelled the universe so accurately that figures described with its calculus had the unusual property of actualizing in real space. Do you follow me?"

"I'm afraid I don't."

"Imagine a man throws a ball, and you write a sentence about it. Now imagine if writing a sentence about it *caused* a man to throw a ball. To decree it is to create it: *fiat lux!*" He chuckled ruefully. "There was once a mighty empire at Sol, whose armies marched over the face of every planet and moon, bringing all people together under a common yoke of fear. That empire was called Mars, and the Secret Math was her brainchild."

"This power was misused?"

He sighed. "It's the human race, what do you think?"

"I rather took it that humans were largely a noble creature, that is until recently."

Captain Tallum Gold guffawed. "Only a man with no memory could I hear this from! My friend, we are dogs. We are beasts. We screw and we eat and we pray, we sin and we die. How do you think it is that a race rises to colonize a galaxy?"

"I don't know."

"We are *predators*, my dear Hellig, and never forget that. We conquered first one globe, and then another. How did we do this, you ask? We rose up among the other animals, and *we ate them*." He snorted. "Then we paved cities over their graves and flew away. The point is that no beast can escape his nature, and however you might dress it up, our race thrives on blood."

A chilling notion. I drained my glass. Fartles passed wind gustily and the captain laughed. I yawned and then caught myself before falling off my chair. "I think I should say good night," I said weakly.

"Promise me you'll come again, Mr. Apples," said the captain, standing up woozily and shaking my hand warmly. "I should very much like to chat again with someone who is not a rich corpse from Eridani or another foppish dilettante from Dzigai!"

I promised him I would, and them stumbled back to my cabin. Fartles helped me along through the freefall tunnel, and without too much injury I found my way to bed. I fumbled through my pockets and extracted my diary, propping it on the pillow for me to mutter into.

I go to dream. Might I be the like of March Peebles? Pish's breath blows away at Fartles' lingering gas. I'm giddy, and nothing I think makes sense. Is this what they call drunkenness? Grant me peace from getting out of bed to urinate again!

Furthermore something-something.

XV.

A GALACTIC PRIMER

Forgive me, diary. I have left you under my pillow for a week. What can I say? Life moves slowly on an interplanetary castle with room service.

But I met an interesting lady today.

After breakfast this morning Captain Gold took Pish and Fartles off to ride the ferris wheel in the gymnasium. I wandered the commercial galleria for a while, trying to understand the strange fashions and trinkets proffered by garish boutiques beneath mesmerizing signs. Ladies in wide dresses held their oval plates before them on carved grips, peering through this window at all things, escorted by cadres of purchase-laden robots and bored stewards. I also saw a blue dog.

Lunch was taken in an echoey court of cold marble, presided over by service robots with marble-patterned carapaces. They fetched me fried eggplant, spiced bread, brown rice and yogurt. I also received a purple concoction to drink, but I somehow failed to fathom the opening of its vessel and ended up spraying the whole of the frothy contents on my shirt and face.

"A serviette, sir?"

"Please."

Castle Misne is fitted with twin observation galleries which rotate at the ends of armatures long enough to give occupants a view of space largely unobstructed by the castle itself. Pish was very enthusiastic about the experience after visiting one of the galleries with Captain Gold, so I had promised him I would see for myself.

The observation deck was transparent, and dark. Were it not for fleeting highlights against the glass it would seem that I had entered unto void. I climbed down the ladder to the clear flooring, unable to resist testing the surface experimentally with my toe before letting go of the rungs. Tentatively I stepped on the sky, swarms of stars occulted by my silhouetted shoes.

Above me wheeled the long castle, encrusted with tiny lights and glowing ports. To my left yawned the diminishing ruddy face of Aramaiti, to my right a hard orange point. The star Aino beamed at my back, filtered from brilliance to a crisp coin of white. The stellar sail was gauzy haze above, the stars seen through it scintillating and tinted with spectral halos.

There were three other shadows in the observation gallery at first, but two left shortly after I had arrived. I cleared my throat awkwardly. "Is it inappropriate to speak here?"

"Not at all," said a papery female voice that was strangely familiar to me.

"May I ask madam, do you know whether that orange point is Annapurna?"

"Indeed it is."

I looked at the orange disc, and then back over my shoulder at the globe of Aramaiti. "How amazing that space should be so vast that it takes sixteen days to travel between two points that can be seen one from the other with the naked eye."

The woman stepped closely beside me but I still could not make out her features in the weak, filtered light. The shadow of her face was long, with a regal profile. There seemed to be a bun of hair atop her head. "Sixteen days is a jaunt. The transit was much longer on my way out – nearly three months."

"Forgive me, madam. I don't know a thing."

"Ignorance is my business," she replied, her voice again striking a chord in my memory. "Questions indulge me. I am a schoolteacher."

I smiled. "You really wouldn't mind if I ask you something else then?"

"If I go too long without teaching I may regain my senses and take up a more rewarding career."

"Madam, I think you are just the sort of person I've been looking for. I'm called Hellig Apples. I'm from Samundra."

"I'm Corinthia Tag," she told me. "And you're not from Samundra, though you carry the accent well, Hellig. Where are you really from?"

"I'm told my home is on Maja."

"You're told? Now this *is* intriguing, Hellig. Next thing you're going to tell you've come out of a hyperspatial gate with Interstellar Amnesia!" She chuckled in a way that reminded me of a certain plump chicken at Duncan's Bliss, which pleased me. But when I did not reply her tittering ceased. "My dear Hellig, I do hope I haven't offended you."

"Well, it's true," I sighed. "Joke as it may be, it's true."

"You really came through a gate without your self?" I nodded in the shadows and she whistled.

I jumped. "How did you do that?"

"What, this?" She whistled again. "Whistling?"

"It sounds like a kettle!"

There came a pause. In the gloom I saw Corinthia Tag retreat a few paces, and then turn around and walk back closer to me. "Hellig, I can see that I have you at a serious disadvantage. Perhaps I had best let you ask some of your questions, in order to catch up."

"Really?"

"Please."

And so I deluged her. "Who runs the worlds? Where did people come from? How do interstellar gates work? What were the shuttle's shields made of?"

"One question at a time!" she begged.

I took a breath and thought about it. "How long is history?"

She laughed, her shadow cantering back against the stars as she clapped. "That's a wonderful question, Hellig. Hominid civilization has enjoyed some ten thousand years of recorded history, dating from the advent of primitive writing systems by human tribes on Terra, the first Earth."

"Tribes like Captain Gold's Jews?"

"Very much so. The Hebrews of Terra give us some of the earliest examples of written history, along with the Vedics, the Hellenes and the Chaldeans."

"When did we first leave the Earth?"

"At the dawn of informatics, four thousand years ago – knowledge being power, of course. The same era saw the birth of the telegraph, the automobile, the spaceship, the microprocessor, the robot..."

"How many worlds in the galaxy are populated with human life?"

"There are thirty-nine *Solar* worlds. You must always remember, Hellig, that human life is not an island. We are supported by a host of organisms that are every bit as integral to sustaining Solar civilization as we are. Why, there are millions of microscopic organisms on or inside of you right now."

I shivered. I felt itchy. "What are they doing?"

"Some of are doing critical things like making the digestion of your food possible. Others are just along for the ride. Your cells are powered by wee things called mitochondria who even have their own genome, distinct from your own."

"I had no idea."

"And that's just one of end of the spectrum. To breathe we require the carbon dioxide sinks of vast forests; and forests are maintained by armies of organisms, from moulds and mosses to beetles, bats and birds. Solar life is a broad family, which is in part what makes it so difficult to transport across lightyears of space. Seeding the galaxy is a slow process."

I considered this. "But can a man not simply step through a gate, and find himself on a new world?"

She chuckled again. "Indeed, but who builds the gate?"

I was dumbstruck. "I never thought of that. Who *does* build the gate?"

"Robots. But they have to get there the long way, first. It takes many centuries to travel between the stars. When a colonizer arrives at a candidate planet it begins by broadcasting Solar micro-life, laying the bacterial framework for engineering the climate even before construction on the hyperspatial transmitter is started. In some cases the robots have opted to wait for hundreds of years before engaging the transmitter, to allow for the decay of radioactivity left over from atomic blasting to release subsurface gases."

"So there are robots out there doing this? Even now?"

"Certainly."

"When were they sent out?"

"They are sent out continuously. Civilization has been building and launching colonizers for thousands of years. It is a sacred activity managed directly by the Panstellar Neighbourhood."

"This is the body that rules Solar worlds?" I asked.

"Rules?" she echoed. "Goodness me, no. Each star system is autonomous, in order that civilization might be worked upon by natural selection."

"What is natural selection?"

She took a deep breath and thought about her answer. "Hellig, there is no creature alive or dead who knows the one best way to run a Solar world. It is an answer that is beyond our philosophy, but not beyond the great computer of time and space. Thus, each world is governed as its populace sees fit, without interference from any greater authority. In time, worlds that are successful will contribute more culture, genomes and materiel to newly colonized worlds than less successful ones. Do you follow me, Hellig?"

"Not entirely..."

"Success is viral, if tyranny is suppressed," she said emphatically. "In this way we hope to steer toward a destiny where the entire galaxy is populated by stable worlds, each governed by politics honed by millions of generations of experience. Since cultural reproduction is predicated on a sustainable high quality of life for its citizens, the culture that comes to dominate our worlds shall be tested and optimal."

"I think I see," I said. "But how can one assure that the people of failing worlds do not emigrate in a wave, and thereby cause a cancer of failure that springs from world to world?"

"That is where the accords of the Panstellar Neighbourhood come into play. Sick worlds have their hyperspatial gates shut down. The connection is not re-opened until auditing reveals a change in the internal situation."

"How is sickness defined?"

"Starvation, mass death, uncontrollable crime. There are a number of metrics, but it isn't easy to earn the disfavour of the Neighbourhood. Affiliation asks little beyond basic civility. As I said, interference is minimized in order to let the social organisms of worlds evolve according to their own internal forces. The strictest regulations concern warfare: no star system may hold a world beyond its own heliopause."

"But worlds may war between one another within a system?"

"Assuming such warfare does not drag the world into barbarity, for if so the entire system loses. Hyperspatial gates are either open or closed with regard to a given star...it is not possible to secure gates on a world-by-world basis."

For a moment I stared into the stars, wondering which ones might be playing host to colonizing robots, nascent civilizations or quarantined barbarians. "Has any star system ever tried to conquer a foreign world?"

"Oh, well, of course," she snapped, and then apologized. "– Look at me, a schoolteacher, stammering over it. How silly of me. It seems so impossibly strange to have to explain to someone the defining event of our times..."

I let her collect her thoughts, patiently scanning the panorama as she played her fingers against one another, leaning to and fro. I turned to look at her shadow as I heard her draw in breath to speak. "Ten years ago the hegemony at Kamari Star moved against Cassiopeia, igniting a terrible war. The Panstellar Neighbourhood was forced to mount navies to protect the galactic interest, and in retaliation Kamari deployed an unspeakable weapon against us all."

"Unspeakable?"

She took a deep breath. "There is a proper name for it, but it is always called by the name Radio Kamari used: the Nightmare Cannon. It is a weapon designed to transmit the worst kind of human suffering over a signal capable of being carried along with everyday holographic media. You...did not experience the Horror, I take it."

"My amnesia is total."

"I..." she paused, and I heard her breath catch in her throat. "There is no way to explain to you what happened to so many of us on that day. I caught only a glimpse. And I know I will take that glimpse to my mausoleum."

"A glimpse of suffering?"

"Ultimate suffering," she whispered fiercely. "Soul-tearing suffering. Riveted into my mind! Many died instantly. Suicides followed. We were all watching the war broadcast when the Panstellar Navy engaged the Kamari forces at Cassiopeia. Everyone was watching..." She trailed off again, and took a moment to re-compose herself. "With his empire on the brink of defeat a terrible man engaged the cannon, and in less than five minutes irrevocably brutalized half the galaxy."

"Terrible indeed," I echoed.

"Engaging the cannon isn't what made him terrible, Hellig," she replied quickly. "It was what he *did*. The Nightmare Cannon is not a creative device, but a projective one. To transmit its payload of ultimate suffering it must first record it."

"Record it? How?"

Corinthia coughed. She may have retched. Her breathing was ragged. "That is unspeakable, my dear Hellig. I'm sorry. But even schoolteachers have their limits."

I let a moment pass. The stars crawled as we rotated about the castle. I asked, "Was this man brought to justice?"

"No," she said mournfully. "He escaped. Many, many people have dedicated their lives to hunting him down for just that purpose. And to learn the location of the Nightmare Cannon, so that it might be destroyed once and for all. In fact, it is on a grant from the Citadel of the Recovery that I have toured Samundra, following up some research they thought might help the cause."

I hugged my shoulders. "I had no idea the galaxy could house such evil. I thought I knew how sheltered I had been when I was betrayed by a friend, but now I see how little I have been through."

She sniffed, and touched my arm with her hand. "Don't let me upset you. You're one of the lucky ones, to have no idea what I'm talking about." She dropped her hand from me and crossed her arms, turning to the black sky once more. "Goodness knows what I wouldn't give to have never heard the name Terron Volmash."

My telephone buzzed, startling me. I jumped and gasped, startling Corinthia. I heard her voice sound in my head: *"Incoming missive from Jeremiah. Response?"*

"How do you know Jeremiah?" I asked Corinthia.

"What?"

"Incoming missive from Jeremiah. Response?"

"Hello?" I cried.

"Sir," said Jeremiah smoothly through my telephone. *"Will you be joining us for dinner? The captain has invited us to his private buffet."*

"Let me get back to you," I told him. "My telephone sounds like you," I said to Corinthia, bemused.

"Ah yes," she groaned. "I get that a lot. My speech was modeled years ago, and the rights have been sold so many times I've lost track of everywhere it ends up."

I laughed. "For weeks I've had this irrational want to *meet* the friendly lady in my telephone," I said. "And now I have. It has been a genuine pleasure to make your acquaintance, Madam Tag. Would you consider joining me for dinner with the captain?"

She tittered. "I'd be delighted, my dear Hellig. But there is one thing, before we go."

"Of course."

"Will you kiss me?" she breathed. "Here, now, in the dark – before you see me in the light."

"Are you ugly, Corinthia?"

"I am old."

We kissed, very gently but very sweetly. Her skin was soft and dry, like a fallen leaf. She told me my face was sticky, and I was forced to explain to her about my purple juice mishap. She giggled like a girl.

Dinner with the captain was noisy, largely on account of Captain Gold himself who was endeavouring to teach Pish some sort of a throaty, lugubrious song with words I could not identify. Fartles crooned along, which made the captain nearly choke as he laughed.

Corinthia Tag's hair was white, and her skin creased with hundreds of tiny lines that seemed to mark every expression she had ever worn, with a bias toward open-browed smiling that folded the skin around her green eyes. She was the colour of chocolate, her hands long and careworn. We didn't talk much over dinner, but every once and a while we looked over at one another and smiled.

After dinner she took me to the Spider Tree Garden in the third habitat ring of the castle, a mad labrynth of freefall plant life interspersed with great yellow orbs of suspended light clotted with translucent moths. For someone who described herself as "geriatric and planet-chained" she navigated the webby, floating world of the garden with grace. I will not detail my own tribulations, but suffice it to say Corinthia seemed to find my artlessness somehow charming.

"Do you think I could be March Peebles?" I asked her.

She smiled consolingly. "I'm afraid not, Hellig. March Peebles is only a folk legend."

"My name is Simon," I said.

"Oh?"

And so I recounted for her my tale, beginning while we kicked across the open field at the mouth of the Spider Tree Garden and concluding in the sitting room of her suite over glasses of a pale amber wine served cold with slices of iced grape. I explained about the hospital ward and Nurse Randa, running through the forest and being adopted by Pish, my all too brief friendship with poor Duncan before the police took him, the betrayal of Nilo and Glory, and the way I marched out and took Jeremiah back from them.

When I was done she exclaimed, "My goodness, dear Hellig – or Simon, I should say. It sounds like a thriller!"

I smiled sheepishly. "So life is not always quite this challenging?"

"Perhaps it is," she admitted, sitting down on the sofa next to me. "But it's usually a little more spread out. I'm sure I've had as many adventures as you have, but I'm nearly two hundred years old and...how old did you say you were, Simon?"

"Two months or thirty-six years, depending on how you look at it," I replied, and then marvelled: "Two *hundred* years! Is that how long life is?"

She likewise marvelled: "Thirty-six! I can *remember it.*"

We sipped our wine. After an interval she closed her eyes and recounted in a distant, dreamy voice: "I was a thirty-six year old girl when I met the Queen of Space at Eridani Star. It feels so long ago and it feels like yesterday. I felt so small and so foolish, standing in her court surrounded by ministers and executives – but when she looked at me, and spoke to me, she made me feel like being a citizen of the neighbourhood gave me all the dignity I needed. She behaved as if she were *my* servant: earnest, tactful, humble, kind."

"What place does a queen have in a neighbourhood without a ruler?"

"She is a symbol," Corinthia explained, opening her eyes and turning to face me. "Each race of life represented in the domain of the Panstellar Neighbourhood has its own ceremonial figurehead and aworldly mouth. The Pegasi have their Metamaster To-Ma-Fe – whom I believe is currently Ro the Twelfth – and the Hennish always have the current iteration of the Great Henniplasm to speak for them."

"And so Solar life has the Queen of Space?"

"Exactly. It is an office established long ago by the House Aresu, the exiled monarchs of pre-Martian Ares."

"I have heard of Mars. Captain Gold told me it was a war-like world."

She shook her head. "Never so simple. It was the acme of force as Mars, it was a bastion of freedom as Ares. History knows the world in both forms, and our modern culture owes its heritage to both. The schism and bond between Ares and Mars is the cornerstone of much philosophy." She yawned. "But I think I am too tired for philosophy, dear Simon. Forgive an old woman."

She fell asleep against my shoulder, her breath against my chest. I put my arm around her and cradled her gently, the white bun of hair atop her head tickling my nose. I sneezed but she didn't wake up.

I carefully lifted her up and carried her into the bedroom. I placed her on the bed and asked the light to dim down a bit, which it did after briefly objecting in a staccato, chuckly language I could not understand. I noticed a grey robot standing quietly in an alcove, and asked him to look over his mistress while she slept.

"Does master wish me to examine the mistress?" asked the robot loudly.

"Shut up!" I hissed. "She's *sleeping*, you idiot. Don't you know what 'look over' means? I know what it means and I'm only two months old!"

"I am sorry to have disturbed master, master," said the robot in a slightly quieter voice. After a moment of consideration it added, "Would young master care for a bottle of warm milk?"

"What are you talking about?"

"I am trying to determine the needs of master, master."

I grabbed the robot by the elbow and pulled him out of the alcove. "Do you see that woman sleeping there?" The robot claimed so. "See to her needs, will you? If she wakes up and wants something, give it to her, okay? Tell her Simon wishes her sweet dreams."

The robot hesitated. "Does master wish me to awake mistress to inform her of master's wish for the mistress to have sweet dreams?"

"Are you malfunctional?" I asked.

"Executing self-diagnostic," the robot reported abruptly, retreating to its alcove and standing erectly in place. I could not get it to respond again. I sighed, shrugged, and quit Corinthia's chambers for my own.

I tip-toed in to pull out my diary without waking Pish, and then sat in our sitting room to dictate this. Our sitting room is just like Corinthia's, only with a different floral motif on the walls and no Corinthia. By looking through the ports I can see that the angle of the stellar sail has changed, and now our view scintillates and is tinted with spectral halos, smears of green and violet, crimson and cobalt.

Fartles farts. I yawn. I have learned a lot today, and it is time to sleep.

XVI.
REVELATIONS

I have spent the whole of the last three days with my charming and wise friend Corinthia Tag, which is why I was surprised when she did not turn up for tea in the sun-lounge as has been our private custom. I came to her cabin and my plate told me she was there. I signalled, and was admitted.

Corinthia looked up at me amid a stack of plates and reams of wafers, disposable cups and tissues strewn about the floor. She seemed exhausted and was smiling bleakly. "Have I missed breakfast, dear Simon?"

"Yes."

"I've been up all night," she said, standing up slowly and brushing off the front of her baggy sweater. "I'm a mess," she said, and then laughed hollowly. Her voice was strained and rough.

"Are you well, Corinthia?"

She sighed and closed her eyes for a moment, then stood straighter and regarded me again. "I have made a surprising discovery. I had to confirm my hunch. It took a long time, but I'm right."

"Right about what?"

"Your friend. Duncan Menteith." She paced in a small circle with her hands on her hips before facing me again and grinning in a crooked, sad way. "It's him!"

"Corinthia, you're scaring me," I said, touching her shoulder. "Him who?"

Her eyes misted. *"Volmash!"* she cried. "Terron Volmash! Who else?"

Mother of love!

Corinthia stiffly begged off to perform her morning ablutions and returned a quarter hour later in a more composed state. She told me she should like to take breakfast as usual. She claimed having something in her belly would do her a world of good. I took her arm and escorted her. She bantered about trivia all the way, laughing nervously.

Over crumpets she suddenly blurted, "You've been a guest in his house!" and started to quietly cry. "You've *touched* him," she whispered with barely restrained revulsion.

It was the height of morning tea. The sun-lounge was packed. Many people turned to look at us, and to whisper at the lady's apparent breakdown. Corinthia noticed this and swallowed hard as she blinked, tucking back into her composure with white knuckles.

"I'm sorry," I said.

"Saviour, Simon!" she breathed, piercing me with her green eyes. "I liked to play at being a noble part of the Recovery. I was titillated by feeling important when I rifled through foreign libraries, bent by a high cause." She laughed in an unhealthy way. "Vanity! When the real thing lands in my lap all I want to do is throw up."

I touched her forearm and in response she clutched my hand in both of hers, clammy and shaking. I didn't mean to speak but I found my mouth moving: "He was...just a man. I thought...I thought he was the most decent man I knew."

"The Citadel of the Recovery has made no statement, but if what you say is true – if he's been taken by Militia Samundra – they *must* know by now."

A wave of murmuring through the patrons behind me caused me to turn; Captain Gold was pushing hurriedly between the tables, his eyes fixed on me. "Hellig!" he mouthed quietly but beseechingly. "I need you! Come on! And your lady friend – come now!"

"What's the matter, Tallum?" I asked as he propelled the two of us out of our seats and chased us toward the exit.

In the hall outside the sun-lounge he wheeled on us with wide eyes. "You have to help me! I can't face it alone!"

"What is it, Captain?" Corinthia asked, taking his hand, her grief and shock transformed to compassion in a blink.

Captain Gold threw up his hands dramatically. "Brunch with anuses!" he cried in an agonized voice.

We followed him across the hall to the anteroom of the Captain's Lounge into which he disappeared. Corinthia grabbed my arm as I moved to follow him. "Simon – will...the boy be there?"

"Do you mean Pish? I doubt it. Why?"

She dropped her eyes.

"Mother of love, Corinthia!" I cried. "He's *just a boy*. Would you condemn him for his father's crimes?"

"I don't know. I'm sorry. I can't do this now."

"Okay," I said.

Just then Captain Gold threw open the door, grabbed us both by the elbows, and hauled us bodily into the hazy and babble-filled air of the mahogany-panelled lounge. We were immediately set upon by the Thrustworths. "Ah, the captain's returned – splendid!" declared Prandon, his white moustache twitching.

"We're ever so glad we could arrange this delightful brunch," oozed Eve, clapping her gloved hands.

Captain Gold's head sagged back and he rolled his eyes at me comically before springing up before the Thrustworths like an excited puppy to pump their hands enthusiastically. "It's an honor to make time for such distinguished guests such as yourselves, my friends!" he cheered. To me he whispered: "Order one of those robots to mix my breakfast punch with vodka, please. Very strong."

When we were ranged around the oval table I counted seven: Captain Gold, Corinthia Tag, myself, Prandon and Eve Thrustworth and a couple introduced as the Rouleighs of Rouleigh: two bald women with tiny, twin round plates affixed before their eyes by a brass clasp on the bridge of the nose; through transparent from my point of view I could see the ghosts of the display reflected on their dark irises. Long, yellow wires dangled from their mouths, the drooping ends emitting steady streams of fume.

As food was served by a quintet of robots with polished wooden carapaces the Thrustworths begged the captain to regale us with a war story so, after casting a pained look at me hidden behind his cup as he drank, he cleared his throat and detailed an adventure in which he had purposefully driven the half-exploded carcass of a navy frigate into a Kamari space-station, and somehow lived to tell about it.

Eve's applause was muffled by her white gloves. "Oooh, how marvellous!"

"It was for that manoeuvre that you received the Twelvefold-spangled Star from Her Majesty Herself, was it not?" prompted Prandon with a wink.

The captain ceremoniously pointed to one of the sparkling baubles attached to his ridiculous uniform, stuffed somewhere between the golden braiding, the flares of his massive epaulettes, and a crust of other medals. The Rouleighs leaned in across the table, their cheeks glowing with the readout through their lenses. "Quite proper, quite proper," they twittered.

Over coffee the captain attempted to deflect attention from himself by asking the guests about their journeys. "You're a schoolteacher are you not, madam?" he said, and I noticed Corinthia flinch.

She cleared her throat. "Yes, Captain. I teach children on Annapurna."

"How wonderful!" declared Prandon. "If only more educators would take your initiative and work on a pioneer world – for it is they who benefit the most, by feeding their growing culture with enlightenment instead of ignorance."

He winced then, and I believe Eve kicked him under the table. "Stop flirting!" she hissed.

"Quite proper," agreed one of the Rouleighs. "Just efforts need be applied to persuade the pioneer not to be overtaken by the rudeness of her life."

"Quite proper," agreed the second Rouleigh. "When one lives close to the ants one must endeavour not to forget the sky."

"What brought you to Samundra, madam?" asked the captain, draining his cup and signalling for the robot to pour him more punch.

"I..." Corinthia smiled nervously. "I was following some research for the Recovery."

Eve squealed. "How very noble! Prandon and I are also a part of the Recovery effort."

"Indeed," agreed Prandon, twirling one end of his moustache between his thumb and finger. "We give very generously. It's something that affects us all, naturally. There are some in my circles who consider the Recovery an extravagance, but Eve and I would have difficulty calling ourselves truly *galactic*-minded were we not contributors."

"An extravagance?" echoed Corinthia. "Is the healing of a civilization extravagant? Is the bringing to justice of – of *monsters* extravagant?"

"My woman," said the first Rouleigh with a patronizing smirk, "there will always be monsters among men. One mustn't get *caught up* in any particular tragedy lest one desires to pass all her days with bile in her heart."

Corinthia blinked and shook her head. "With all respect, Rouleigh, what did the Horror mean to you?"

"We do not subscribe to telepresentations," replied the second Rouleigh haughtily. "While our hearts go out to those who suffered, to us it was largely a matter of economic inconvenience – now at last self-correcting, thank goodness. Bless the market."

"Bless the market," agreed Prandon.

"Quite proper," said the first Rouleigh.

There was an awkward silence. Corinthia bowed her head, and I was worried about her. As I reached over to touch her shoulder she looked up with a new light in her eyes, her jaw set and her nostrils flared. "To me, ladies and gentlemen, the Horror demonstrated the depths of compassion this galaxy has to offer. To me the Horror demonstrated that the Solar organism can react to infection, and purge it through concerted will. To me the Horror showed me hope, by pitting us all against hopelessness."

"So it was a kind of blood-soaked blessing, in your view?" asked Prandon pointedly.

Captain Gold laughed uproariously. We all turned to stare. He stood up from the table shakily, clutching a cup of punch in each hand. He drained them one after the other as he shuffled around the length of the table, his chuckles becoming dry and forced. He paused at the door, shaking his head. "You people are fornicated," he pronounced loudly, spittle flying from his beard. "The only thing the Horror taught us was *the depth of God's apathy.*"

He pushed through the door and was gone.

"Oh, dear," said Eve.

I escorted Corinthia back to her cabin in silence. She told me she wanted to lie down a while. I somehow found my way on autopilot back to our own cabins, where I discovered Pish and Jeremiah giving Fartles a bath in the washroom. Captain Gold was sitting on lid of the toilet, drinking from a tall bottle. "Hellig!" he greeted me, and then fell off the toilet.

We all helped scrub the dog for a while, bubbles drifting through the air when Fartles shook or wagged his tail. When the captain finished his bottle he rolled up his sleeves and started lathering the dog's belly. "Atta boy," the captain told him. "Who's a good dog?"

I wandered out into the sitting room and Pish followed me. "Are you okay, Simon?" he asked.

I sat down and he walked up next to me, a smear of soapy foam obscuring the freckles on one cheek. I tousled his hair affectionately. I was trying to reconcile two bits of information that had floated up together to the surface of my mind: how could it be that Duncan and Pish had been "on the run for nearly his whole life" if Pish was around nine years old and the Kamari Horror had taken place only five years ago?

"How old are you, Pish?"

"I'm ten."

"Where did you live before you lived on Samundra?"

"I've always lived on Samundra."

"On Duncan's farm?"

"Yeah. Ever since I was born. How come?"

I shook my head dismissively. "Nothing. Forget about it."

Pish skipped back to the washroom. I followed him with my gaze and found my eyes locked on Jeremiah, standing just outside the washroom door. A beat passed before the blue-green robot turned around and followed Pish inside.

I shivered.

I don't know what to think.

Could the greatest chef in the galaxy have somehow also been modern history's worst monster? Could the man I felt to be almost like my father be the devil himself? How does Pish fit into it all?

This day has drained me of life, and it's only now just past lunch.

One thing has been decided: I cannot drift, not in a galaxy so complicated and frightening. Every man needs an anchor. If the issue was ever really in doubt it has now been resolved – when we reach Annapurna we will take a gate to Maja. On my own terms and in my own way, I mean to return Nestor Simonithrat Fell to his life.

If Pish truly is ignorant of his father's crimes, I mean to make sure he remains so sheltered forever.

Corinthia is right: the fruit of tragedy is our compassion. Great evil can be a catalyst for true nobility. In a galaxy Terron Volmash has rent asunder, I will do what I can to make sure one little boy's heart stays pure.

Home is where we're going now. *Home.*

XVII.
REVELATIONS, REDUX

Annapurna! I have never seen its like.

We are still four days from port and the world remains small to the naked eye, but two nice kids I met in the rotating observation gallery this afternoon showed me how to key up a magnification window on my plate. Within a ring of tiny numbers the blue-purple disc leapt forward to become a great globe: bronze continents outlined by rusty seas, girdled in a torn white blanket of clouds that turned blue toward the planet's limb. The poles were frosted white tinged with yellow.

"Why are the edges blue?" I asked. "Everything is so *orange.*"

The kids shrugged. I looked over at their white and red robot, who returned my gaze impassively. "It may be a trick of the light, sir," it contributed lamely.

I frowned. I noticed next that while the burnished coin visible behind the circle of magnification was a half-orb, cast partly in shadow, the image displayed through my plate was lit on its face, Aino's light sparkling the reflections of hundreds of tiny copper lakes. Rivers ran green, mixing with the tawny oceans in cloudy whorls at wide deltas. The crinkles of mountains were gold and red, the plains between them a fungal confluence of amber and violet. There was nothing in the image to suggest the presence of Solar life beyond a crust of grey smudges gilded by vibrant green, a thin border fringing the continents.

When I carelessly let my plate fall off-target the image thereupon spun and wheeled, Annapurna cantering out of view and being replaced by what I can only gather my plate imagined to be the next most proximate object of interest: a star with a diffuse halo and a long, wet-looking tail spraying out behind it. "What's that?" I asked.

"You are looking at the Comet Busson, magnified one hundred times," replied my plate crisply.

"What's a comet?" The plate remained silent. The two kids were screwing around at the other end of the deck, so I turned my attention to their robot again. "Would you mind telling me what a comet is?"

"Sir, a comet is an astrophysical phenomenon."

I blinked. "Okay. Is it a star?"

"I beg your pardon sir, I do not know."

"Why does it have a tail?"

"I beg your pardon sir, I do not know."

"When was the world of Annapurna established?"

"I beg your pardon sir –"

I held up my hand. "Nevermind."

There was a lot on my mind. Over breakfast with Corinthia we had discussed the issue of Pish. I told her that I would give her anything to keep the secret of his identity. How could Pish's soul be darkened by events he never knew? What profit would there be in seizing him from my custody? What part of the Recovery benefitted from *this* piece of the puzzle?

"Enough Simon, enough," Corinthia had said wearily, pushing her meal away. "I know you love him. And I think you're a good man. I don't know what I'm *supposed* to do, but I know what I will do."

"What?"

"I will turn my back." She swallowed. "We never met, you and I." She stood up and put down her napkin. "It has so charmed me to meet you, and I will remember our time together always," she said in a strained voice, and then fled my cabin.

I sat by myself for a long while. I used my plate to try to hail her, but all I got was a message saying, *"Passenger Tag does not wish to be disturbed at this time."*

I poked at cold eggs with my fork.

In the late afternoon I went to the gymnasium with Captain Gold, Pish and Fartles but I found their laughter only deepened my lugubrium. I waved and smiled each time Pish swooped by on the ferris wheel, his high-pitched giggles interspersed with cries of, "Look at me, Simon!" Birds fled from his yelps and congregated near the ceiling, chirping indignantly.

I slipped out my plate and spent some time looking at the images of my wife and my two children. I tried to look into their recorded eyes and feel the same thrill and bond I felt at Pish's careless smile. Suddenly the idea of meeting them and feeling that kind of love bloom for them did not seem so alien or intimidating to me anymore. Would they too, like Pish, look to me as protector and friend? Would they seek solace burying their faces in my neck as they slept?

It wouldn't be so bad, I reasoned.

I looked up to see Pish at my side. "Is that your family?" he asked.

"Yes," I replied, nodding and putting my arm around him. "I should think they will be very pleased to have you as their brother."

Pish stared into the picture for a while, returning my hug. "And then you're never going to go away right, Simon?"

"No sir," I told him. "I will always take care of you, Pish."

He ran away to join Fartles running through the grass near where the captain was lounging at the bar, ordering himself a drink. I waved to him and he saluted back at me comically. Because I could not see him anywhere else I knew that Jeremiah was standing at my elbow. I turned around.

"You're a sneaky one, Jeremiah," I said, putting away my plate.

"Sir," he replied evenly.

Birds chirped. I saw Pish, Fartles and the captain round the corner out of view, walking up the curved floor toward the merry-go-round. A moment later its gay calliope could be heard in the distance. "Jeremiah," I began, eyes still cast away from him, "would you mind telling me what a comet is?"

"A comet is a relatively small extraplanetary body consisting of a frozen mass of water and carbon dioxide, typically moving in a highly elliptical orbit after being plucked by gravitational shearing from the diffuse corona of debris that surrounds a star after its formation."

I nodded. "I see. And why does it have a tail?"

"The stellar wind vapourizes the outer layer of the comet at perihelion, drawing out the material in a long tail directed opposite the star."

I nodded again. "You're a very knowledgeable robot, Jeremiah. Are all robots as knowledgeable as you are?"

"Each according to his specialty, sir."

"Indeed," I agreed. "And what is *your* specialty, Jeremiah? Astrophysics?"

"My programming is general, sir, in order to better serve the curiosity of my young ward."

"So robots who look after children have access to lots of general information, so you can field their questions?"

"That is correct, sir." I pondered this for a moment. "And yet..." I chuckled drily.

"And yet every robot with whom I've spoken on this castle seems to be an idiot – even those who watch children."

Jeremiah said nothing.

"These are perhaps less expensive models than you?" I prompted, looking into his black eyes. "Inferior products?"

"Perhaps," said Jeremiah.

I shook my head. "I don't think so."

"Sir?"

"I think that you are an unusual robot. *Admit it!*"

His black eyes remained fixed on mine. "Sir?"

"Are you really going to try to persuade me, Jeremiah, that your wide knowledge, your grasp of subtleties, and your habit of *killing* those who would oppose you, represents the normal state of servant robotics in the galaxy? Were I to go into the robot shop in the galleria and ask for a model with your abilities, would the sales staff laugh at me?"

"I don't know, sir."

"They would," I shot back. "In fact, they *did*." I played my fingers against each other pensively. "Perhaps you're malfunctioning. Perhaps I should have an engineer examine you." I looked at him inquiringly.

"Sir," the robot said after a pause. "You know I cannot allow that."

I nodded. "Yes, I do know that. Monkey knows that now too, doesn't he?"

Jeremiah shifted, but said nothing. *"Speak!"* I barked suddenly. "Or I swear we'll leave you behind."

There came an even longer pause. I looked back out across the gymnasium and saw Pish, Fartles and Captain Gold sauntering back toward us, eating ice cream cones. I started to get up to meet them but Jeremiah put his cool, blue-green hand on my forearm, the rubber pads of his palm resting on me with a gentle weight. "Sir," he said, "I am unusual."

"That much I know," I snapped. "Is that all you're willing to say?"

He hesitated again, in a very human way. "Know this if you must, sir," he said in a lower register, exerting a slight pressure on my arm. "I am your enemy."

My skin crawled beneath his grasp, and I wriggled free, a shiver running down my spine. "What do you mean?" I whispered.

"As long as you protect the child," he said evenly, "I cannot move against you."

Pish ran into our midst and hugged Jeremiah, spreading chocolate ice cream on his carapace and gushing about the kids he had met on the merry-go-round. Captain Gold was feeding the end of his ice cream to Fartles, who farted in enthusiastic appreciation and licked the captain's hands.

Throughout it all the black eyes of the robot remained locked on my own, a new dark understanding between us.

XVIII.
HAVE GUN, WILL TRAVEL

I have never been so tired in all my life.

I feel like I've been hit by a ton of bricks. In fact, I *am* a ton of bricks. Whatever else you may hear let me for one assure you with authority and conviction: gravity sucks.

Ahem. We have arrived on Annapurna.

There was an opulent banquet on the night before we left, and Captain Gold insisted Fartles sit by him so that he might enjoy the high comedy of the dog's various effluvia working their magic to bend the pretentions of the upper crust. Pish and I were also seated at the captain's table, which earned us venomous looks from the two displaced Rouleighs throughout the night. When one of them swept past me to have a word with Captain Gold she hissed, "Improper!" in my ear.

The captain slapped the Rouleigh on her ass, which caused her to shriek. Fartles barked and farted simultaneously, which caused the captain to explode into laughter. He spilled his drink on Prandon Thrustworth, who assured everyone that everything was fine as he grabbed the nearest crimson robot and shouted that a thousand hours' worth of fine pant fabric was at stake lest he quickly receive some water and lemon.

Pish gasped between giggles, slapping his thigh. "I love Captain Gold!" he declared breathlessly.

The Pegasi maestro of the kitchen made a brief appearance wearing a plastic suit and a bubble around his head. He received a standing ovation from the crowd, and by the looks of rapture on their faces I could pick out the handful of people who truly knew what they were applauding. Pish and I smiled and waved, and the maestro nodded gracefully in our direction. I was tickled pink.

Corinthia Tag was nowhere to be seen at the banquet, but we did see her the next morning as the crowds gathered in the debarkation lobbies, queuing up for planetfall shuttles. I glimpsed her just for a fleeting moment with a tear in her eye as she witnessed Pish's great act of nobility.

"Captain Gold," said Pish, drifting before us and hugging his dog. "I think Fartles wants to stay with you."

The captain didn't know what to say. His mouth worked awkwardly for a moment, then he grabbed Pish and pulled him into a tight hug that sent them both bouncing gently off the nearest bulkhead. Fartles kicked after them and yipped. I felt my eyes tickle, then moisten. What a generous spirit the boy has!

That's when I saw Corinthia. She wiped her eyes with the back of her hand and pushed off the wall, disappearing into the babbling crowd by the lock. I did not follow her.

Before we boarded our own shuttle the captain embraced me and held onto my hands. "It has been a real pleasure to know you, Simon. I can't tell you what it means to be shaken out of my stupor by you and your boy. I will *never* forget you."

I smiled. "Thank you for everything you've done, Tallum, especially for Pish. We're going to miss you."

He separated himself from me roughly and held me at arm's length. "Now get going before I make an ass out of myself and cry!"

Once seated within the hard bubble of the shuttle we leaned over in our chairs to catch one last glimpse of Captain Gold and Fartles as the lock irised shut. Everybody waved, and Fartles barked. "That was a very kind thing you did for him," I said.

"The captain hurts," Pish said simply.

The orb of our shuttle detached from the lock, and Castle Misne began to slowly diminish from a wall of glowing ports to a humble bead of glimmering shadow hung in the vast folds of her iridescent sail. In time that too was lost to sight.

But on the opposite side of the sphere the world of Annapurna grew enormous as the hours passed, stripes of blue clouds crossing continents of copper and umber. In many ways the globe resembled Samundra, the world we had just left; but in other ways it was very different – less green, smaller seas, and a broader limb that hinted at the world's true size.

"You are not incorrect, sir," Jeremiah said in reply to my questions. "The terrestrial world of Annapurna is many times larger in diameter than the jovian world of Samundra."

"And yet it is younger. Why was Samundra developed before Annapurna?"

"Annapurna required substantially more processing, sir, to meet Solar requirements. Both worlds were established within decades of one another, but the open air of Annapurna has only recently been rendered breathable."

"How recently?"

"Fifty-six years, sir."

"How many people live down there?"

"Approximately fourteen million human beings, sir."

"Why so few?"

"It is a pioneer world, sir. The standard of living is low, and hence desirable to only a select kind of personality. Also, the economy and ecosystem could not support a greater population at this time. The building of worlds is a slow process, sir."

By that point Annapurna filled our vision. Our trajectory changed and the stars spun above us. I noticed one small grey moon, and then another. The barely discernable thrum of the shuttle's engines changed slightly as we began our gentle descent. Within ten minutes the stars were enveloped in a purple-blue haze, and then lost altogether behind the sky.

An uncomfortable weight settled into my stomach. I gripped the arms of my chair, my hands too leaden to lift. My feet had become glued to the carpet, and my head felt as if it were made of solid rock. I moaned. "What's happening?"

"Sir, as the shuttle's speed decreases and we descend deeper into the gravity well we are feeling the influence of Annapurna's mass."

I gritted my teeth, my heart pumping in my chest. "Is it like this because the world is bigger?"

"Yes sir. Local gravity is two and a half times greater than at Samundra. I regret any discomfort you may be experiencing."

With a grunt of effort I turned my head toward Pish. "How are you doing?"

"Okay," he said, breathing deeply. "How about you, Simon?"

I tried to force a smile. "I think I just wet my pants."

It turned out that I had not wet my pants, it just felt that way because of the unusual sensation of having all my bodily fluids drawn so aggressively toward whichever parts of me where pointing down. My bum felt strangely warm, for instance, and my shoes became too tight. I felt dizzy, and had difficulty keeping my head off my shoulder.

By the time we landed I was exhausted. I wasn't the only one. After the shield snapped off and a cold breeze started reaching in at us many of the people who rushed for the exits did so supporting their weight against a robot. Pish sat up on Jeremiah's shoulders and I held his arm, and in this ungainly fashion we limped to the end of the queue and filed out of the windy shuttle core.

The interior of the terminal shocked me, for I had never before been presented with a space that so totally locked out the exterior world. Even aboard Castle Mine there were windows, but once the terminal lock closed behind us the cold air disappeared along with the sunlight, sealing us inside a wholly civilized shell.

While we waited for our bag I tapped my wallet-tip to a colourful till covered in images of smiling dogs so that Pish could get a handful of candy. I got another handful for myself, biting into the shockingly sweet little nuggets with uncertain curiosity. "They lack subtlety," I commented.

"Yup," agreed Pish, crunching away at a small blue ball. "Let's get more."

The remarkable thing about eating the candies is that it gave me a funny sort of boost of energy. I felt I could stand up, and even move my arms a bit without panting afterward. Pish skipped around the baggage reception lobby carelessly, and introduced himself to some guy's dog.

Jeremiah collected our bag from the conveyor and waited patiently at my side while I flashed my plate around. "So, property of Hellig Apples," I said, reading the label off my plate when it was pointed at him, "where do we buy our tickets for the gate?"

"Sir, Annapurna's Hyperspace Gate Hotel is located on the far side of the Thither Sea, by the city of Purandhi."

"On the far side of a sea?" I echoed, incredulous. "That's bloody inconvenient, isn't it?"

"It is the local government's desire that you engage the economy in more than one location, sir. Travel induces expenses."

"Bless the markets," I muttered darkly. "Alright, how do we get there? Can we take a taxi?"

"I imagine so, sir."

I nodded to myself, wheeling the plate around to my left until I saw a sign for taxicabs, the label reduced in size and blurred to represent distance. No matter how I played the screen about, however, I could not find a clear way to reach the cab bank. "Is this an attempt at further enforced consumerism?" I demanded finally.

"Yes and no, sir. It is not possible to leave the borders of the port without first purchasing a gun."

"A gun? Like a weapon?"

"Yes sir. All adult persons on Annapurna are obliged to carry a personal weapon. If one does not own a weapon meeting Annapurnese standards, a local gun must be purchased. It is the law."

And so with Pish riding again on Jeremiah's shoulders we passed into the gun shop nearest the taxi bank. We were greeted by a squat gentleman wrapped in layers of red leather, his long hair drawn up into a complicated figure atop his head. "Goodafternoon, good travellers: welcome to Annapurna! Are you shopping for modifications or fresh arms?"

Though it took me a moment to penetrate his accent I did grasp his basic meaning. "I need a gun, yes," I told him.

"And for the lad?"

"I think just the one gun for now, please."

"Very good! Right this way." He led us through a cluster of men in red leather longcoats with goggles on their foreheads to present a wall-sized display containing a bewildering assortment of guns on little pegs. The salesman gestured from one side to the other, explaining: "Toys and trinkets begin on the left, to serious pieces of military-grade hardware at the right. What's your rather, friend?"

"I should like something serviceable. I have to admit I really don't have a lot of experience with guns." As an afterthought I added, "Or with buying things."

He took me by the elbow and led me over toward the right side of the display. "Now *this* my friend is something no self-respecting Annapurnese dude would be caught dead without: the Kenning-Mantlewood Twin-Ion Repulso-Dagger Nine! I keep one of these gems in my very own bednest, I don't mind telling you. My wives say they sleep better, knowing it's there. And damn it, I do too."

"It seems awfully *big*," I noted.

"Not a problem, not a problem at all," he rushed ahead, pointing me toward another weapon a few columns to the left. "Over here we have one of the classics: the Smith-Shurtook Gentleman's Dueller. It's a looker *and* a fighter – polished wood chassis, steel fixtures, totally liquid mechanism. My son keeps two of these over his mantel. Here: heft her."

He slipped the gun off its peg and ceremoniously handed it to me, butt first. I weighed it first in my left hand, and then in my right. "Which hand are you supposed to use it with?"

"Er, which handed are you?"

"I like my right hand a lot. I think it's smarter."

He licked his lips and flared his nostrils briefly. "If you don't mind my asking, how will you be paying for this?"

I slipped out my wallet, the look of which seemed to impress him. "How does it work?" I asked.

"You press the contact at your index finger. You can go ahead and press it now, friend. She isn't engaged."

I aimed the gun experimentally at the other guns is the display, depressing the little contact with my finger. It clicked in a snug, satisfying way. "So I just point it around and then something comes out of the end to hurt people?"

The salesman shifted awkwardly and blinked. "Er, yes. The rounds are generated back here, and then loaded into the magazine when they're mature. In summer you can usually squeeze off about a hundred before the gun needs to be watered. If you empty the chamber you'll have to wait a good ten minutes before the new bullets are hard."

"So they're all killing bullets, then? The gun has no other settings?"

"Settings?" he echoed, frowning. "Scat, boy! It wouldn't be a *gun* if it weren't for killing."

"I suppose not," I agreed, in order to be friendly.

Next I was outfitted with a red leather belt and holster, the end of which strapped around the top of my thigh to hold the gun securely. The salesman took me through engaging and disengaging the weapon's firing status, and showed me how to read the little floating bubble in the readout. "If you get stuck in the cold, inject a little antifreeze into the mix by squeezing this bulb," he explained, sliding back a lock on the top of the weapon and pointing inside.

"What about one of those coats? Do you sell coats like that?" I asked, indicating the red leather calf-length jackets worn by the other customers in the shop. They looked a lot like robes to me, though they lacked a sash to belt them.

"Sure thing, friend! I can fix you right up. Lift your arms so my robot can measure you."

And so we were outfitted for Annapurna: a red leather poncho and hood for Pish, and a red leather longcoat and hood for me. We also bought goggles, which the salesman assured us we would desire should we gain any taste of the outside. "If the glare doesn't get to you, the blowing sand will," he assured us. We got cool matching water canteens, too. And new boots.

I holstered my Smith-Shurtook and pushed the goggles up on my forehead. "Thank you very much for all your help, sir."

"I reckon the pleasure is all mine," said the salesman, grinning toothily.

I was all decked out but I felt less than a hero once the crushing combined weight of the gun, holster, goggles and longcoat sank into me. I propped myself up against Jeremiah while I negotiated payment, and then he more or less walked me out of the shop while Pish bobbed atop his shoulders.

The end of the terminal was bisected by an indoor glass-topped river. As we walked across its surface I saw that it churned not with water but rather millions upon millions of tiny insects. "What manner of river is this?" I asked Jeremiah.

"It is a highway for ants, sir, likely predating the construction of this port."

I stopped to marvel, as did other outlanders. A man lay down on the river's clear top and assumed a silly pose while his spouse held a camera out over him and laughed. A couple of kids were pressing their faces into the glass, mumbling to each other about what they saw. To Jeremiah I said, "Are they a revered animal on Annapurna?"

Jeremiah pointed to a wide banner hanging above the exit: a globe half-orange and half-blue, encircled by a fleet of ants on a bed of green. "That is the historical flag of Annapurna, sir. The ring of ants indicates pioneer status, in homage to the instrumental role their various species play in aerating the soil of new worlds. This flag is technically out of date as Annapurna has undomed, but history shows that new worlds often cling to their pioneer status for several generations until the open-air culture has matured." Seemingly as an afterthought he added, "The penalty for the purposeful destruction of ants is death."

"Death?" I echoed in disbelief.

"Here as elsewhere, the ant is a sacred creature, sir. Visible or not, they represent a massive share of any given Solar world's biomass, and are therefore among the most populous animals in the galaxy. The ant lies at the heart of a great deal of Solar symbolism, sir, dating back to Imperial Mars."

"Still...death," I murmured. "Goodness!"

We passed through the doors into the outside world and I reeled back against the sun, throwing my forearm up before my eyes as a shield. A frigid wind swirled around my head and roared in my ears, forcing me to hunch downward. Beneath my arm I saw Pish wearing his goggles. I reached up and pulled my own goggles down from my forehead and blinked with relief.

I raised my head again. The wind howled. Pish grabbed my arm and I grabbed Jeremiah. Flying sand swept in waves over the packed dirt ground, anyone further away than a few paces a blurry shadow behind the ochre veils of grit. I held up my plate and was thereby able to discern a row of taxicabs with glowing labels against the far side of a tarmac. They sat in a line in the lee of a row of craggy rocks, shown in an eerie green chiaroscuro on the screen.

"Warning," said the plate through my telephone, *"visibility zero meters."*

"Yeah," I grumbled, shivering. "Thanks."

Jeremiah limped us over to the first car in the line. The driver and I shouted over the gale back and forth until he understood we meant to hire him, then he opened the door and shouted that we should get in. With my teeth chattering I pushed Pish into the back and then gratefully dropped onto the soft, tattered seat beside him.

Then a monster ran up to me and ripped our luggage away, his hairy face peering at me behind yellow goggles as he hooted menacingly and flexed his fingers at me in what I could only assume was an insulting gesture. He slammed the door and vanished behind the car. "What was that?" I cried.

"Haven't you ever met any of the little people before?" asked the driver, closing his own door and pushing his goggles up onto his smudge-covered forehead as he drew back his hood. "Where are you fine folks flying in from?"

"Samundra."

"Samundra?" He tousled his sand-coloured, sand-filled hair and then clapped his hands together to get the dust off them. "I have a nephew who moved to Samundra. I said, 'What's on Samundra that you can't get here?' and he said, 'Girls in bathing suits,' and I said, 'What can I say? You got me!' You know what I'm talking about, folks?"

"Um," I said. "Can you take us to the Hyperspace Gate Hotel?"

He chortled and grinned. "Where the hell else would you go? Okay: are we all harnessed in? Especially the kids now, the kids always have to be harnessed in. You harnessed in there, buckaroo? Pit and pat, we're halfway to hovering."

"How long will the journey take?"

"Cha, we'll get you to the oasis by bedtime and then it's just a hop, skip and jump beyond that tomorrow morning. You can be ready for gate-off before noon, as sure as sandwiches. Is your harness snug there, dude?"

"Yes, you already checked it."

"I won't apologize for being big on harnesses. They save lives, cha. Do you know what I'm talking about?"

"Okay," I agreed.

He leaned over and stuck his finger between my waist and the strap, and tugged. "Okay," he confirmed. "Let's rock and let's roll."

Jeremiah sat down in the passenger seat and told me our luggage had been stowed in the rear compartment, apparently by the "little person" who had menaced me moments ago. The driver hauled back on the steering bar and the taxicab lifted up into the sky with a graceless lurch, engines chortling loudly. All I could see beyond the windows were sheets of flying sand.

A buzzer sounded. *"Imminent c-collision: evasive action re-recommended!"* gurgled the dashboard in a wavery, stuttering voice.

The driver twisted the steering bar and we banked hard, a spherical shuttle orb sliding across our bow and showing our battered yellow car in its reflection. "Whoa-ho-ho!" sang the driver as he dove low, skirting the edge of the floating ferry and bouncing up on the other side of it. "That was close."

I wrapped my hands around my harness and pulled Pish closer to me.

After a few moments the flying grit outside the window thinned and we could glimpse the ground – a maze of overlapping mesas of orange stone, coated in a slithering cob of swirling ochre sands. By pushing my head against the window I could just make out the shadowy cluster of buildings still engulfed in the storm behind us, the glint of passenger bubbles winking in the shifting light. All around us: nothing. Down below our diffuse shadow slipped over crags, canyons, piles of unfriendly rubble. "I thought we were flying over a sea," I said, raising my voice over the buzz of the engines.

"That's the Thither Sea," nodded the driver. "It should be wet any decade now."

I pushed my goggles up onto my forehead and blinked against the suddenly harsher sunlight. "What a world," I said.

"My name's Greskin Mile," said the driver, turning away from the dashboard and shaking my hand. "I'm a lawyer by trade, but I fly a cab on the side to make all the hours add up. It can be a long, lonely time between border disputes out here. You know what I'm talking about, folks?"

"Hello," I replied. "I'm He –"

I was cut off as the driver cried, "You're Nestor S. Fell, aren't you! Holy tuna, I *knew* I recognized your mug from somewheres."

"You...you know me?" I replied, stunned.

"Why, sure! I'm a shareholder in your corporation, Mr. Fell. I was a little concerned when you didn't show up to make your presentation at the annual general meeting last quarter, but I see now you're out in the worlds, laying low, no doubt sussing out the next big thing, eh? Am I right or am I right?"

I wiped my hand down my face, feeling numb. "So," I murmured aloud, "I'm *real.*"

"Say again?" said Greskin.

"Tell me Mr. Mile, what does my corporation *do?*"

"Do?"

"Er – make?" I guessed again.

"You're scaring me, Mr. Fell. Are you feeling okay?"

I leaned back in my seat. "I'll tell you in confidence, Mr. Mile: I've had a bit of an ordeal. I've been in a hospital on Samundra, and I'm now returning home to Maja."

"Why didn't you just gate-out at Thaumas?" he asked.

"Please don't pester me," I snapped. "My itinerary is complex, Mr. Mile."

"I'm sorry sir," said Greskin quickly. "My mouth gets carried away sometimes, yapping on of its own accord from a lonely habit. Sometimes it's a stretch between seeing faces around here, you know what I'm talking about?"

"Don't worry about it," I said, releasing him. I joined Pish in looking out the window, and allowed him to point out to me various amazing rock formations. The cab bucked a little in the wind, then settled again.

"Just over an hour til Xengai Oasis, folks," narrated Greskin, talking in the general direction of Jeremiah. "Darling place that is, I tell you. I bet lookers like you will have two girls on each elbow before supper, eh? Ladies for Mr. Fell and some fresh chicks for his young friend, cha. You're going to love it, lizards to lies."

At one point Pish spotted a cluster of tiny red dots, which Greskin identified for us as a herd of ruby cattle, a lichen-eating bovine engineered specifically for spreading germinating spores via its disproportionately large output of stool. "That explains the smell," I commented.

Far below, sand-dogs sprinted over the dunes and barked the cattle homeward. We flew on.

I was the first to spot the green spot up ahead – a valley between cliffs exploding with trees and bushes, grass and fern. We circled over a cluster of green brass domes and puttered to a stop on a wide tarmac encircled by vine-covered walls. A squadron of squat, hairy fellows with long arms and pink faces ran over and erected a canopy over the cab as Greskin killed the engine.

I stepped out of the car. The air was chilly, and I pulled my longcoat tight. The hairy fellows ran up to me, each presenting a small patch of till on the sleeve of his jerkin. I looked back at Greskin inquiringly. "Am I to tip these...little people?"

"If you like service with a smile I'd advise it," nodded Greskin.

Each of the four little people's pink faces broke into a monstrously wide grin, exposing startlingly bestial teeth. I slipped my wallet over my finger and tapped each of their tills in turn, muttering subvocally into my telephone to negotiate the amounts. They flexed their fingers at me in a curious way and then bounded away, hooting. "Are they Solar?" I asked Jeremiah as he took our bag from the boot.

"Yes sir. Fellow apes. They are known as 'the little brothers of men.' Technically they are called *Pan troglodytes sapiens*."

"What was that funny thing they were doing with their fingers?"

"It a gestural language known as Common Sign Protocol, sir, used by the little people as they lack the vocal and neurological apparatus for speech."

"Are they intelligent? Or are they animals?"

Jeremiah paused, and seemed to consider this. "We are all of us animals, sir."

A rumble sounded behind me and I turned in time to see two great metal gates enclosing the far side of the tarmac begin slowly rolling apart, revealing a miniature sand-storm arising at the heels of forty tarnished robots, row upon row in yokes, leaning forward against the burden of a massive freight container with six giant wheels. At an invisible command the robots spun in concert and pushed on one another's backs, the final row pushing against the face of the freight container itself to fight its inertia. Tan clouds roiled out from the scene, obliterating it. When the dust settled forty robots stood before the parked freighter, waiting at their yokes.

I spotted the silhouette of a woman standing at the upper lip of the container. She yelped something into the breeze, and the robots all sat down cross-legged in perfect synchronicity. She then made for a tall ladder to begin her long climb down.

"Not a tourist, I take it," I said.

"No siree," agreed Greskin. "This oasis is a waystation for all kinds of business. There's always different sorts of folks around here, mixing around and mucking it up. Is your gun solid, dude?"

I tossed back one side of my longcoat and checked the gauge on the butt of the Smith-Shurtook. "It is indeed, Mr. Mile."

"So let's get gone like grasshoppers. This way, folks."

We passed within one of the great domes of the oasis, the bottom of which was open to the air but warmed by hot winds that came up through the tarnished green grilling that comprised the floor. Our boots clanged against the grille as it rang with the footfalls of the many others crossing the busy dome: men and women in red leather longcoats grabbing grub from canvas-stalled vendors, savage-looking wide-pawed dogs at their heels; little people scampering hither and yon burdened by luggage or trays of drinks; small knots of outlandishly dressed tourists holding closely together, looking nervously about and clutching tiny dogs to their breasts.

With Greskin Mile's help we arranged for hammocks hung in the updraft of a hot vent fed by an underground spring, and purchased paper sacks full of greasy, unidentifiable roots and beans topped with a reputedly nutritious but thoroughly repellent paste called *boosk*. Greskin pointed us down the path to our quarters and said, "I keep a shelf in the taxi bay; that's where I'll be if you need me. I'll be swinging by to pick you up once breakfast is wrapped tomorrow. Sleep well, folks!"

Pish and I ate our remaining candy in order to wash the foul waste of boosk out of our mouths, so we bid farewell to Greskin as we crunched. At the end of the path through the ferns we came to a column of open air surrounded by engineered trees with hammocks slung between them. Nests of vines interspersed between the layers of hammocking provided some small measure of privacy, and served as a net to catch lost personal articles. Of the sky I could see nothing.

We climbed a ladder to our assigned perch and settled into our hammocks. Jeremiah stood beside the ladder, arms at his sides, head slowly swivelling. Pish wanted to stay up and chat, but I was feeling enormously wearied after nearly a full day of fighting against Annapurna's merciless gravity.

Even my little diary was a cruel weight in my palm as I brought it up to lie in the hammock next to my face for easy dictation. Speaking of which, where was I? Right – I was here. Here at the oasis hostel, hanging amid the vines and snores...

I was going to say something else, something that's been nagging at the back of my mind. Excuse my yawning. Mother of love I'm so tired!

I was going to say...

XIX.
MARCH OF THE ANTS

The gong for breakfast did not wake me, but being hit across the face and thrown out of my hammock did. "Wakey-wakey-wakey!" invited someone unfriendly. "It's time for eggs and breaky, my little mules."

I opened my eyes and coughed, finding myself entangled with Pish in the web of vines beneath our bunks. Pish was staring with wide eyes at the two scar-faced thugs glaring down at us from the round wooden balcony that surrounded the nook, woven out of the face of the living tree. "Is this some kind of Annapurnese wake-up call?" I muttered groggily. "I distinctly remember asking *not* to be pistol-whipped."

One of the thugs used a knife to slice open our bag. He pulled out handfuls of clothing until he came to Glory's strong-box, which I knew contained rows of the little orange sticks she flared and inhaled. "The faeces is right here," the thug called to his partner.

"You have your faeces," I shouted, attempting to stand up on the vines. "Now leave us be!"

"Ah no, mule," said the first thug. "There's still the little matter of you busting up Nilo's shop, offing Monkey and stealing the boss' robot." He crouched down near the vines and fixed me with his hard, hazel eyes. "And you jazzed me fierce, and for that I'm going to make you cry blood."

"Help!" I yelled.

The thugs laughed. "Every soul is taking grub, fool. Didn't you hear the breakfast gong?"

They both laughed again and then the second thug stopped suddenly, his knife dropping from his hand and landing hilt-first on my thigh. Then the thug collapsed without a whimper and fell face first into the web beside me, the ripple of his impact tossing me over Pish and against the tree.

"What the hell?" asked the first thug, wheeling around to find himself facing Jeremiah's impassive masque.

My stomach turned over queasily. There was no need to kill! I grabbed the knife and started sawing through the vines that held me. Pish ran over and jumped on my back, and I caught Jeremiah's eye just as we dropped through the broken web, falling in a tangled mess into the empty hammocks beneath. I spilled out onto the web underneath and swiped it with the knife. When it split Pish and I dropped another level.

"You're dead!" promised the thug, jumping down through the first ripped web and withdrawing a small black jazzing device from inside his jacket. "You're already dead, mules!" he declared, red in the face.

A blue-green blur flashed past and I looked down to see Jeremiah's body cutting a swath through the next layer of webbing, then dropping to the tiled floor below. I threw Pish down into his arms and then leapt down myself, an instant before the thug hit the vines beside me. I rolled with the fall and jumped to my feet running, hot on Jeremiah's heels as he pelted down the sunny path effortlessly.

Mid-way across the dome a terrifying bang sounded out from behind us, echoing against the ceiling and the trees. Some people screamed and hit the deck, but others tossed back their coats and drew out their weapons. The little people hooted with alarm as they scampered up the columns around the edges of the dome with amazing agility. I risked a look back over my shoulder and saw the thug facing off against a dozen men and women, a ridiculously large gun shaking in his hand.

We pushed roughly through the fringes of the crowd and out onto the tarmac where Greskin Mile was lounging against the side of his dented taxicab, biting dirt out from under his fingernails. "Goodmorning, folks!" he called, and then took in our state of haste. He hopped over the hood and squeezed inside, the engine roaring throatily an instant later. "Trouble?" he called.

We heard more shots ring out from under the dome. "Trouble!" I yelled, sprinting toward him. Jeremiah and Pish ducked into the front seat and I dove head-long into the rear. *"Go!"* I shouted, and Greskin yanked back hard on the steering bar. The engines whined in protest as the cab careened into the air, skimming the top corner of the six-wheeled freighter as it cleared the walls. Greskin steered us neatly between the opposing cliff-faces and out again into the open expanses of the sandy Thither Sea.

After a few moments Greskin cleared his throat. "So if you don't mind my asking, was there some kind of a pre-existing situation between you and somebody or are you just not very good at making friends?"

"Pre-existing situation," I muttered, feeling the bump on my head where I had been hit. "Are you okay, Pish?"

"Yeah," he said. "Those were Glory's friends, weren't they?"

"Yes. Do you see what she's brought us?"

"She wanted to get away from them. She wanted to come with us."

I grunted. "How much further, Mr. Mile? I want to get off this world. I want to get away from this sun."

"I can make it in two hours if I push it hard, Mr. Fell."

"Please Mr. Mile," I said, holding up my wallet. "Push it hard."

The engine geared up to a higher-pitched whine and the desert below began to scroll by slightly faster. We passed over a railway, which Greskin explained was the more conventional way to see the sea. We saw more herds of ruby cattle grazing between dark, organic lines that visually networked a series of rocky outcroppings. "Are those ants?" I asked.

"Yes sir," said Jeremiah.

An hour into the trip I smelled Greskin's anxiety blossom. "What's wrong?"

He knocked at one of his displays and then ducked over and looked past his shoulder behind us. "There's another car on our tail. Closing fast." He tapped his fingers quickly against a greasy plate suspended from the dashboard. "I can't get any informatics off it."

My heart started to beat faster. I turned around and peered out the small rear window. A distant but distinct bead of shadow appeared out of the bank of scaly clouds we had just passed through: a dark car, aiming to cross our path.

The cab's dashboard buzzed harshly. *"Navigational conflict-ct. Redesign c-course."*

Pish squirmed out of Jeremiah's lap and into the back seat with me. "Is it Glory's people, Simon?"

"Lizards to lies," I said, nodding. The pursuing car was rapidly growing. "Can this thing go any faster, Greskin?"

"No Mr. Fell, I'm afraid it cannot."

"N-navigational conflict," reminded the dashboard helpfully. *"Imminent-inent collision: evasive action recommended-commended!"*

A black car with dark windows swooped around above us, dropping suddenly and striking the roof of Greskin's cab. Greskin wrenched the steering bar hard to the side and climbed, dodging around the large black vehicle as it bobbed back up to hit us again. The engine sang and sputtered, the frame of the cab whining as it was flung back and forth. Pish and I clung to our harnesses, gritting our teeth.

"Cl-close proximity high speed m-manoeuvring is against the law," commented the taxi.

"Hold on folks!" called Greskin, banking hard again as the black car swept up beside us, its flanks passing within inches of my window. We dropped giddily, dust dancing before my eyes, and then we were thrown back into our seats as he brought her around hard to try to get the jump on our attackers. "Aha!" crooned Greskin.

The ploy worked, to the extent that the driver of the black car was apparently unaware of our new position when he thrust his vehicle upward violently. We collided with teeth-jarring suddenness, pieces of metal and plastic spinning away with the force. Both cars flipped over backward – sky alternating to ground sickeningly – and then flew apart as they spun.

Clutching Pish I was able to raise my head enough to see the ground racing toward us, filling the windscreen. An instant before we impacted the cabin filled with thick fluid, blasting startlingly out of several hidden orifices. I gasped and it filled my mouth. A split second later the crash echoed through the cabin, knocking the wind out my lungs and then forcing me to suck more fluid. I lost track of which way was up as the car rolled, Pish's skull knocking against my jaw once per cycle.

The cab skidded to a halt at the base of a tall outcropping of rock, and a second later the windows burst apart into dust. The fluid gushed out of the cabin, and then Pish, Greskin and I vomited what we'd swallowed. Though I sputtered and coughed I did not want for air, which suggested to me that the shock-absorbing fluid must have been somehow oxygenated in a way my lungs could use.

I stumbled out of the carcass last. Jeremiah was examining a small cut over Pish's eye, where the edge of his goggles had gouged him. Greskin pointed out a large cloud of dust dissipating a few dunes away. "They're down, too," he said, breathing hard.

"M-maintenance required," said the taxi.

"Shut up!" grunted Greskin. He sniffed at the wind. "Everybody get back behind the car. Stay low."

Three figures crested the nearest dune, one of them limping. All of them were carrying guns.

Greskin Mile's hand flashed out and unholstered his weapon in a blink. It barked once and one of the men crumpled with a pitiable scream, rolling backward down the dune he had just climbed.

By the time I'd blinked again Greskin was beside me, crouching behind the bent door of the overturned taxicab. "Nice shooting!" I said, wincing as a bullet struck the hull of the car, reverberating loudly.

"I'm a lawyer," he explained. "I *have* to be quick."

Bullets smacked into the sand near the car, startling Pish. Jeremiah enfolded the boy in his metal arms, his black eyes scanning the rocks. "One circles around to the rear," he warned quietly.

"I'll take care of him," said Greskin with a nod. "Mr. Fell, you hold off this joker."

I nodded back and Greskin crawled away. I unholstered the Smith-Shurtook and levelled it as I peeked above the top of the car. A bullet winged the hood and sparks flew at me. I fired into the air and dove for cover, the boom of my own weapon putting the fear of death into me.

I heard two more shots lay into the car, followed by an echoey exchange of reports from behind me. I hoped our driver was faring well.

Espying an opportunity I flattened myself on the sand and fished my way forward to peek out along the side of the car. I could see only the leg of my attacker as he knelt behind a rock. Aiming my gun sideways against the ground I pressed the contact. His leg jerked out from underneath him and he yelped.

I ran over to the rock, my gun out before me. I jumped around the corner. The man in black was sprawled out across the ground, the lower half of his right leg a tangled mess of splintered bone, ripped pants and meat. His face was convulsed in pain.

"Mother of love I'm so sorry!" I shrieked, kneeling down next to the ghastly wound as blood poured out upon the pebbles. "What can I do?" I cried helplessly.

"Die!" bellowed the fallen man, wrenching his arm up to point the barrel of his gun at my nose. I jumped sideways just as he fired, the concussion ringing in my ears as I hit the ground and stumbled away behind the car again.

Pish and Jeremiah looked over at me. I crawled past them to the other side of the car and peeked out. I was met by a kick in the face.

I hit the ground sideways and rolled over. My opponent was propping himself up against the car, sweat running down his face and blood dripping out of his smashed calf. With a grunt of effort he levelled his gun at me.

The gun was knocked from his hand by a rock thrown by Pish. "Leave Simon alone!" he screamed. I dove at the man's middle and threw him to the ground. He bellowed in pain and struck out at me. In a ball of flailing limbs we rolled over the dirt.

He hurled me off of him and I hit the ground hard. Panting, I tried to rise. My eyes widened as I saw him lurch over me, his good foot planted in a stream of black ants.

"Mind the ants," I reminded him, panting. He looked down.

"I hate this planet," he said, spitting blood. He wiped his mouth with the back of his hand and took another hop forward, his boot squashing another section of the busy little insects. Though they made no noise I could sense their alarm in the sudden increase in speed with which they scurried. A ripple of frenzied motion cascaded down the stream.

He took another limping step forward, his left arm pinioning around a tall column of rock. His expression changed as he planted his boot once more. He looked down again, frowning.

I shuffled backward across the sand.

The ants began to climb his leg, long tendrils of scouts followed by opaque hordes. He reached down to brush them off, his hands coming away black and crawling. He hopped backward and lost his balance, sitting down in the stream. And then, like a flitting shadow, they enveloped him. He opened his mouth to scream and ants poured out.

I turned away.

Pish and Jeremiah had gone to help Greskin, who was limping back with a scowl on his face. "I'm okay, I'm okay folks," he said, gesturing at me dismissively. A hole through his thigh was oozing a dark stain upon his pants. With Jeremiah's help he sat down on a rock. "Got the bastard, though, sure as sunrise. How did you make out, Mr. Fell?"

"The ants got him for me," I said, pointing over my shoulder to the stream.

Greskin made a face, then moped his brow with a kerchief and looked around. "You have to mind the ants," he chuckled. He took a small device out of his pocket and tapped it, looking into its face. "There's a lot of magnetic rock around here. Hard to get a good fix on north."

"What's that?" I asked.

"It's just a compass, dude."

"A device for discovering the direction of north? Can it be used to find our way?"

He folded the compass away and looked at me. "Don't take this the wrong Mr. Fell, but I always pictured you being...more worldly."

"I told you," I said testily; "I've been through a bit of an ordeal."

We gathered what was salvageable from the wreck of the taxicab and walked out of the maze of rocks where we had come down. Beyond the mesa the sands blew in the wind, obscuring the horizon and occasionally even hiding the sun. But we were not long into our trek when we came against an impenetrable barrier: a wide river of black ants, their carapaces winking the sullen, shifting light.

"It's plenty too far to jump," declared Greskin. "For the falcon maybe, but not frogs like we. We'll have to follow their line. Put up your hood or you'll be burned by the sun."

"But it's so *cold*," I said.

"You can't feel the ultraviolet cooking you, Mr. Fell."

I sighed. "Lovely planet you've got here, Mr. Mile."

"Get off my back," he said, feigning offense as he limped at Jeremiah's side. "The atmosphere is a work-in-progress."

We travelled along the bank of the ant highway for an hour before we discovered we were being hemmed in from behind by another slithering stream of marching insects, these ones yellow and translucent.

We were left with no choice but to walk along the narrow path between the two rivers, turning as they turned, meandering as they meandered. The wind was frigid and gritty, sand sprinkling across our goggles in a constant wash, our hoods drawn tight around our faces. Greskin ripped his kerchief into three, and we each held a section over our mouth and nose in order to better breathe.

I was reminded of the time that Pish, Jeremiah, Fartles and I had shuffled sideways between the territorial flamingo and the jealous tree, the world apparently open all around us but in fact closed to a narrow corridor.

The rivers of ants drove us toward rocky foothills, the setting sun casting their shadows long across the sandy plain. The temperature dropped sharply with the sun, and come twilight as we walked among the first crags of the foothills we were all shivering and numb. The rivers of ants ran through a shallow canyon and then split around the mouth of a wide cave, before which were set stone bridges to traverse over the insect ways.

As we arrived a party of men and women in furs stepped out of the mouth of the cave, their leader wearing the weathered skull of a bull atop his head and necklaces of teeth around his neck, wrists, and ankles. His skin was orange like the sand. Those arrayed behind him carried tall spears with electric torches tied around the hilts, which they engaged to dazzle us.

"Ruffians!" whispered Greskin. "They live off the land and answer to no one."

I cleared my throat. "Hello," I called. "My name is Simon. My friends and I have been through a bit of an ordeal. Can you help us get to Purandhi?"

The leader crossed one of the stone bridges, his bare feet slapping the smooth rock on our side of the ant rivers. He was muscular, and painted with stripes. "The ants carry blood. Your companion?"

"No," I shook my head. "Our enemy."

"The enemy of my enemy is my friend," he declared, stomping his feet. The others turned off their harsh lights. "Let us all rejoice in the blood of the ant killer. Come: our hospitality is yours tonight."

They brought us herbs to smoke and introductions were being made when a squabble over a dowry threatened to bring three families of the clan to blows. Greskin stepped forward and offered his services as advocate, and then proceeded to settle the dispute to the satisfaction of all parties. Spears and knives were lowered and clansmen embraced one another. An old woman painted a sacred ring on Greskin's forehead, and then the fire was piled high for a celebratory meal.

"Why do these people live like this, Mr. Mile?" I asked him.

"Cha, it's a bit of a mystery. Nobody has any idea how they lived outside the domes before the atmosphere was baked." He took a puff from a pipe that was handed to him and then passed it to me. "Some of them are Edenites who couldn't cut the mustard in a civilized way, some of them are just regular folk who turned their backs on society. The lost always find a way to live on their own terms. You know what I'm talking about?"

I coughed explosively. "I think so."

We had beef for supper, roasted over a huge bonfire beneath a smoke-hole deep inside their wide cave where lived dozens of other Ruffians of all ages. A bearded old man pushed a rude clay cup of harsh, stinking mead into my hand and then proceeded to tell a long story in a local dialect which was largely incomprehensible to me, though I did manage to glean that the ants cleaned the bones of the evil after the exciting climax. Then the old man invited Greskin to tell a story, and he obliged them with several slurring accounts of especially ridiculous acts of litigation. Next it was my turn to tell a tale. I tried to beg off but the chief of their clan insisted, nodding and grinning, throwing back another cup of mead, the head of the skinless bull on his crown seeming to smile at me, too.

I looked around at the dirty, sun-burned, happy faces looking at me, their features swimming in the firelight. I sipped the foul mead and paced in a circle, considering where to start.

"My name is Simon," I declared, "and I come from space." I pointed out the smoke-hole, where a few stars could be discerned shining through the fume. "I was born a short time ago in the body of a man who lived a life I have never known."

The Ruffians hummed happily and scooched closer, the young sitting in the laps of the old. The old man passed around a jug to refresh our cups of mead. Greskin sat by the fire and listened, his head cocked. Pish sat beside Jeremiah, eyes fixed on me.

"They came to take me to my family, and like a skittish cat I panicked. I ran through the woods and came into the care of a boy, whose heart was open enough to see I was no monster. His father...his father was a good man, who taught me much. But he was also a hunted man, and when his destiny came to claim him the child and I were forced to flee..."

As the recounting continued I found my pace, adding gestures and crude sound effects to furnish the tale with decorations. They cringed in fear when I told them about the violence of Glory's keepers, and they laughed riotously as I described my deftless antics bouncing through freefall. When I elocuted on the way Fartles contributed to the ambience of Captain Gold's dinners they fell off their perches and gripped their sides, pointing to their own dogs sleeping around the fire and nodding knowingly.

"I miss Fartles," said Pish.

"Yeah, me, too," I agreed.

The Ruffians slept in a random pile by the fire, a sleepless crone sitting on a high rock tossing in new fagots of dried turd each hour. The unseen animals who had presumably produced the turds grunted and shuffled in their pens outside the cave. I could see Jeremiah standing guard at the mouth. Pish curled up on the floor beside a dog and fell instantly asleep. I slipped out my diary and patiently unwound my day into it.

I rubbed my forehead and winced. May tomorrow dawn without a beating!

A MEEK CANCER

A young maid woke me up to inform me in broken language it would now be my special privilege to be washed in dung.

"I'm sorry?" I said.

On the way outside the cave Greskin Mile the limping lawyer-cum-taxicab driver explained to me that the Ruffians had been moved by the recounting of my adventures last night, and that they wanted to make us all honorary members of their clan. This would involve several noxious rituals, including a ceremonial public bathing in the sanctified dung of a rare silver cow.

"It smells," complained Pish.

"Keep smiling," I reminded him. "If you need a laugh just look over at Jeremiah."

Indeed, there was something in the blue-green robot's posture that suggested his dignity was being tested by being slathered in manure by the painted hands of chanting desert Ruffians. Pish giggled.

When that unpleasantness was concluded we were escorted by the chief deep into the heart of their network of caves, an electric torch on the end of his spear casting a spotlight on a series of vast murals painted upon the face of the rock. He detailed a thoroughly incomprehensible history of various bloodlines, which concluded in the sad tale of a princess born sickly whom strangers were prophesied to heal.

"That's very interesting," I noted. The chief said nothing, waving us onward into a further chamber.

The air was cool, moist and clean. Beds of rosy mosses covered every section of the rock cavern, and water was running down the walls. Amidst a cluster of torches lay a thin, pale girl with her hands upon her breast as it rose and fell with a laboured rasp. Her arms and legs were discoloured by ugly bruises, her eyelids blue and jittering over her eyes. "My daughter," pronounced the chief solemnly.

"The princess?" I gaped, walking slowly toward the girl in the bed of red moss. As I tread upon the soft floor it exuded clouds of cool vapour. "What's wrong with her?"

Greskin slipped a small device from his bag and held it over her forehead. It chirped, and he withdrew it to examine its glowing screen.

"Is that the compass again?" I asked.

"No siree," said Greskin, removing a second device from his satchel and touching it against the girl's neck. She stirred, and it left a little red prick. "First aid kit," he said, head bent over the second device. He turned to the chief. "She has cancer," he said. "Leukemia, most likely."

"Cancer!" whispered the chief, making an elaborate sign with his fingers. "Perverse life."

Greskin put his devices away. "You have to get her to a hospital, in the city. You know what I'm saying? They can cure her, right as rain."

The chief shook his head. "No hospital."

Greskin sighed. "What I wouldn't do for a batch of fixers!"

In reply Pish pulled an oval green package out from under his poncho. "Will Glory's fixers do, Mister?"

"How do you have that?" I snapped.

"Glory said I should have them," he defended himself sullenly.

"I'm sorry," I said. "I just – I'm just surprised she gave them to you."

"She said she was worried about me."

I said nothing.

"She said I might need them more badly than she would," he added, handing the box to Greskin.

Greskin opened the box and released the fleet of tiny metallic bugs upon the reclined girl's face. They dispersed over her body, some of them crawling inside her mouth and disappearing. Reminded of the thug dying under a blanket of ants yesterday, I was forced to look away.

"Will she be healed?" I asked.

"Cha, sure," shrugged Greskin. "What's a cancer to civilized folks? I have a pill for it at home."

An hour later when the princess revived she claimed she felt well and the chief rejoiced and hopped through the caves singing a loud and gay song. Pish laughed. "See Simon? You don't bring misery everywhere you go."

I put my hand on his shoulder and smiled, the chief's catcalls echoing away through the rocky corridors. "I guess not, Pish."

Attendants rushed to the side of the princess and cheered when she asked for some broth. Greskin, Pish, Jeremiah and I walked back toward the main chamber of the cave from which we could already discern the smell of breakfast. "Pish is right," I said to Greskin. "To these people we are magical."

Greskin snorted. "Their ignorance makes them suffer, hours to bones. They live like animals, dude. Of course a taste of civilization seems like magic to them. They should be living on Eden."

"What's Eden?"

"A world without civilization: no science, no tea. The men and women on Eden live without knowledge of space, or culture. They die according to the seasons, like mice. They make religions out of tree stumps."

"Is it really so ignoble to die without television?" I said.

Greskin scoffed. "Ask that corpse of a girl what she'd be doing tomorrow, if we hadn't turned up and been sharp."

"They said it was a prophecy."

"They're primitives, dude. They have more prophecies than facts. Some poor lost loser probably gave one of their naked ancestors medicine four generations ago, and now they have a bloody legend about it. That's all there is to it. You know what I'm talking about?"

"I guess so," I conceded. "But one good turn deserves another. Perhaps these people can help us."

"Mr. Fell, these people can't even help themselves," declared Greskin with a wry smile. "There isn't *anything* on Annapurna's wide rusty horizon these Ruffians could do for me, lizards to lies."

Then he stopped short and I ran into him.

"My cab!" Greskin cried. He ran out across the bridge at the mouth of the cave, making a beeline for the carcass of his yellow car as it was drawn into the shallow canyon by a team of six four-footed, wooly animals with great arched humps on their backs. "Oh, thank you!" crooned Greskin, jumping up and down as the parade came to a halt in a blossom of dust.

Two young braves hopped down off the roof of the taxicab, taking a moment to inspect the state of the four large wheels and carriage upon which the car sat. *"P-parking surface unstable,"* said the taxi.

The chief appeared and embraced Greskin, and then me. "We will see you to Purandhi. It is the least we can do, honored healers and adventurers Greskin the Negotiator and Simon of Space!"

And so that is the way that we ended up riding through the desert on the roof of Greskin Mile's battered taxicab, pulled by a train of furry beasts which I learned are called *camels*, who store fat in the humps on their backs as a form of mobile provision. They snorted and balked at first, but once we were underway the creatures settled into a steady if slow rhythm, leading the wooden-wheeled unflyable car between the dunes and across the Thither Sea.

The chief rode with us, as did an incantation-muttering crone who shook her beads at all we passed.

"One day all of this will be rolling green grassland," said Greskin, sweeping his hand across the dunes. He cast his sight at the horizon dreamily and added, "And my kids will go into real estate law."

The crone crossed her legs and leaned against the chief's back. I saw her pluck the mangled scrap of an ant from the bottom of her foot. She saw me staring. "Don't be troubled," she said. She wore a broad hat, and her eyes were hidden behind a narrow band of crystal framed by wicker.

"I thought the killing of an ant was a crime."

"All things die, Simon of Space. That is the way. One cannot hesitate to tread for fear of that which dies beneath one's feet. Willful killing is another matter altogether."

Greskin chuckled. "Intent. You're talking about intent. But you can't always *know*."

The crone arched her brow beneath the crystal. "The ants know."

"Ants are insensible things," argued Greskin. "There is no rationality, or judgement, cha."

"Ants are insensible things," she agreed; "but ant colonies are not. Some of the colonies here are thousands of years old. They can taste your air through their bodies, and thereby know your mind. I am a medicine woman, and these things have been demonstrated to me beyond doubt."

"Medicine?" echoed Greskin with a smirk. "Well, there's that and there's this. Just another tree stump so far as I'm concerned, ma'am. You can worship whatever fills your sail – that's what makes the galaxy great."

"Faith is a hole that cannot be filled with artifacts," warned the crone. "Without it we are no better than robots."

"Faith makes lemmings jump off cliffs," he countered with a grunt. "And we *are* robots, only most of us are too wooly to know it." He tossed his feet over the side of the cab and turned decisively away.

The barren desertscape was broken after an hour by a pall of cloud that seemed to rise from the ground itself. As we plodded forward a great anvil-shaped structure rose beneath the roiling column of white smoke as it spread out with the wind in a long, blurry line. "What's that?" I asked.

"The big smoke, where the oxygen moss grows," said the chief. "Each season we clear it from the vents, and make an offering of calf."

"It is an atmospheric processing station, sir," supplied Jeremiah quietly. "There are hundreds such facilities spread over the surface of Annapurna, concentrated somewhat around the cities."

Indeed as the cold, bright day wore on we passed half a dozen more giant anvils at the base of flourishing trees of cloud. We passed through the wide shadows of the smoky pillars, shivering in the temporary drop in temperature. A crude road developed beneath us, hedged in by two sad rows of dead grass. Pish pointed out a car flying high above, and then another. We rounded a crest and suddenly the city of Purandhi was spread out before us – a splatter of low, bright buildings girdling a dense, grey breast of urbanity. "Look," called Greskin. "You can still see where the post-dome construction begins. Quite a sight, eh, folks?"

Desert became countryside. Dunes gave way to the rectilinear paths of artificial rivers framing fields of green. Tall, splindly watering machines walked over the hills with seeming languor, passing their heads back and forth over the crops. Folk paused at the side of the road to watch us pass, marvelling as the Ruffians yelped ululating commands to drive on the camels, who snorted and farted and spat but carried on.

In this way we passed down the broad central boulevard of Purandhi, the grey towers rising like cliffs on either side of us. People stood at conifer-lined balconies to gape at our train, and children ran along beside us on the street. Some people eyed the Ruffians with open suspicion, kicking back the sides of their red leather longcoats and resting their hands on the butts of their guns. Most of the pedestrians simply stepped aside and smiled as we passed, shaking their heads in wonder.

We passed a burly, bearded man who was holding his finger up as if to hail a ride; a taxicab had landed behind him but he had not seen it as he turned to stare at our procession. Greskin called down to him, "I'm not taking fares right now. Maybe I can get you on the way back, cha?"

The camels stomped to an irritable halt before an open plaza, at the other end of which was the Annapurna Hyperspace Gate Hotel, a series of intricately overlapped green-streaked tarnished brass domes culminating in a great metal dish pointed into the sky, its shadow falling broadly across the square. Pish and I said, "Wow."

The chief wished us a good journey, and the crone promised to burn various charmed grasses while she prayed for our safe deliverance to Maja. With Jeremiah's help Pish, Greskin and I descended from the roof of the car. My legs felt wobbly after such a long time sitting. I approached Greskin sheepishly. "So...what do I owe you?"

One of the camels kicked suddenly backward, and the front fender of the cab fell off and clattered to the road. *"F-forward f-fender f-failure,"* mentioned the dashboard.

Greskin pushed his goggles up on his forehead and scratched his ear. "Well, I reckon we left the meter somewhere back there in the sea, but I can usually be convinced to flat-rate this kind of ride for two hundred hours, to cover the standard nip, tuck and truck. Of course, I only end up with a bullet lodged in my thigh about a third of the time, so..."

I nodded. "Okay, if you can do the flat rate on the trip for me, I can pay for a new car."

Greskin blinked. "A *new* car? Are you honest pie serious, Mr. Fell?"

"It's the least I can do for a shareholder."

When everything was taken care of he climbed back on top of the car and tried to explain to the Ruffians how to best get out of downtown at noon. He wanted to be dropped off at a new car dealership in west midtown, near the undoming line. The chief nodded and cried out to his camels, who spat on the street and groaned but obliged him, shuffling slowly forward to haul the ruined taxicab and its riders down the boulevard. Pish and I waved.

A municipal robot walked up and took away the abandoned fender.

We crossed the busy plaza and pushed open the doors to the hotel's lobby, orange dust kicking off our leather boots and bouncing from our hair with every stride. Jeremiah's blue-green carapace was barely visible for the filth. Pish had Ruffian glyphs painted on his cheeks. We all stank of dung.

A hairy little person in an adorable little orange suit ran up, and then quailed at the periphery of our party, fanning his long hand before his snout. We moved past him to the front desk. I rang the bell and a human steward jogged over and did a magnificent job of controlling his features as he caught wind of us. "How can I help you today, sir?"

"We'd like to go to Maja, please."

"Maja at Nsomeka Star, cha? Let me see..." He tapped with strange, exaggerated daintiness at his console. "You're in luck for an alignment, sir. You can gate-out tomorrow morning." He smiled.

"Tomorrow *morning?*" I growled.

"Yes sir!" he replied, smile faltering.

"There's nothing today?"

"Today, sir?" he sniffed. "There's a star in the way today, sir."

"A star?"

"A little main sequence friend we call Aino, sir. The sun?"

"Ah."

Our room for the night seemed perverse when its luxury was contrasted with the beds we had awakened from. The lights of Purandhi's dome-shaped thrill of skyscrapers blazed through the windows, whose curtains were feeble. There were flower petals on our pillows, and floating in the toilet. I told Jeremiah to give Pish a bath, and then I went to the bar, chose one of the bottles at random and poured myself a stiff drink.

I looked at myself in the mirror over the vanity, and was startled to see how I have transformed since the last hotel mirror I knew.

My face was brown with smudged dirt, except around my eyes where my goggles had left me paler. My hair was grey with dust. I had a fresh scab on my brow, but most of my other bruises had either subsided or been covered over by grime. I felt my jaw, and it was abrasive with stubble. My eyes remain my eyes, however.

I backed into a chair and sat down heavily, holding my drink aloft. Everywhere I was stiff, and in several places I hurt. I took off my boots and wiggled my toes. I sipped and grimaced.

Pish laughed from the washroom, splashing.

Tomorrow I will bring him home. Together we will meet my wife, and my own children. Tomorrow I will face the gate, and rediscover who I am.

I rolled my diary over in my fingers. Tomorrow!

XXI.
SHOWDOWN WITH HYPERSPACE

Pish squeezed my hand. "It'll be okay, Simon."

I squeezed back and tried to chuckle with nonchalant confidence. Instead I coughed. "Of course it will, Pish. I'm sure it's...perfectly safe. Isn't that so, Jeremiah?"

"Sir," he said.

Descended from the Annapurna Hyperspace Gate Hotel, we stood in a row of three at the end of a long arcade whose terminus was a two-storey bank of little round doors flanked by helpful robots in hotel colours. Neat queues of travellers ranged themselves before the ports. Every few moments a group was led through one of the doors. None emerged.

Announcements echoed off the tiles. *"Passengers bound for Nsomeka are asked to check in at gate eight. Gate eight, please, for all passengers bound for Nsomeka Star, including Maja, Mahuea, and all Ninurtan destinations."*

"Well, boys," I declared jauntily, "that's us."

We had crossed the final barriers: we were standing before the gates, tickets in hand. We moved across the arcade too briskly. I felt I could sense the weight of the great dish above us, yawning at the sky. A cold sweat broke out on my back. What if I should step inside and awake erased again?

"Sir?" said Jeremiah, detecting my slackening pace.

"I'm okay," I said. Pish took my hand again and we continued walking, joining the queue of other travellers bound for Nsomeka Star. I gathered my red leather longcoat around me and tried to stand tall.

A gentleman in a hotel jacket stepped up and touched my elbow. "Passenger Apples, bound for Maja?"

"That's right," I replied. "Is there a problem?"

"Cha, actually," said the man, nodding soberly. "I'm afraid it has come to our attention that you're travelling under an assumed identity with a forged plate."

I tried to smile. "I'm sorry?"

"If you would be good enough to come with me, dude," intoned the man, pushing back the side of his jacket and resting his hand on the butt of his gun. A trio of little people approached from behind, each standing behind one of us.

"Is that really necessary?" I asked. "We'll miss our transmission."

The man eyed me dourly. "Regretfully, this is a fairly serious matter, Mr. Apples. Please: your co-operation is appreciated. Your gun, sir?"

I sighed. Pish held tightly to my arm. "Very well." I unholstered the Smith-Shurtook and handed it butt-first to the hotel man.

He smiled tightly. "This way, please."

We were separated, despite Pish's protests. I was man-handled down a long corridor by a duo of little people, who were possessed of a remarkable strength, their hands like manacles. I was shown into a bright room that smelled of disinfectant, then stripped and rinsed in a harsh chemical bath. An intimate search was performed by a robot with oily, rubber-coated fingers. I was fed bodily into a large scanning drum, and then given a pair of paper underpants to wear. Then I was deposited in a tiny, chilly metal cell occupied by a table and two chairs. After a frigid hour a man in a neat suit came in and sat down. He indicated that I should stop pacing and take the opposite chair. I sat down, hugging my arms and shivering.

The man spent several moments reading from a handful of small plates, their output invisible to me from the back. Like Pish his skin was pink, and his eyes round. He wore a burly red moustache under his nose and his head was bald. "My name is Constable Guillaume," he muttered, still squinting at one of the plates. "What should I call you, dude?"

"Simon," I said quietly.

"You've been moving through this system under the name of Hellig Apples. Is that right?" He looked up and stared at me, his brown eyes unfathomable.

"That's right," I confirmed.

"Samundran grower, born on Pomona?"

"Yes."

He tapped briefly on one of the plates, and then another. He then set them aside and knitted his fingers together. "You must understand how that's a bit of a problem for us. We're a pioneer world – it's easy to gain a reputation as a place free and fancy with civilized laws. Easy, but undeserved. I don't know what somebody's told you, but Annapurna isn't here to launder your identity."

"Apparently not," I agreed.

"Indeed not," he nodded. "Now I can tell you now that this is all going to go a lot easier on you if you're honest with me. Saves me time, saves you time. I appreciate that you've given me a name. Is it your real name?"

"As far as I know, sir. My name is Nestor Simonithrat Fell, and I'm from Maja. That's what they told me at the hospital. You must understand I've been through a bit of an ordeal, and my memory's been damaged."

"What hospital?" he wanted to know. I told him. "And you fled their custody, why?"

"I was afraid."

"Where did the child and the robot come from?"

"I met the child on the streets of Thaumas. He's an orphan. I want to give him a home."

"And the robot?"

"I bought him. From a guy named Nilo. Lagranger."

"Where did you get the plate forged?"

"Nilo's."

"Why?"

"They said it would be safer. I trusted them. But they tried to rob us." I wiped my hand down my face. "It's very cold in here."

"Your discomfort is regrettable."

"Constable, are you putting Pish through all this, too? He's just a boy."

"He's being taken care of," said Constable Guillaume. He then asked me everything over again, but in a different order. Then he asked me about each item in detail. I did everything I could to avoid talking about Duncan. He asked me to confirm things I had never said, and then asked me questions that made no sense at all.

"What do you want from me?" I cried at last. "I'm sorry I took the advice of bad people, and I'm sorry I ran away. I'm sorry about everything. All I want is to get back home, with my family, and I want to be able to take Pish with me. Can we do that? Are we going to be able to do that? You have to tell me."

He leaned back in his chair, considering this for a long, painful moment. "We do have established procedures for adoption on this world, Simon. You understand that being convicted for travelling under a false identity would not exactly *impress*, however."

I slouched, the gravity seeming to be amplified a thousandfold.

Constable Guillaume picked at an invisible bit of grit on the table surface, then brushed at his moustache and cleared his throat. "I'm going to level with you, dude. Your story checks out. We've already been in contact with Dr. Pent, and he's sent us your case history." He shrugged. "I don't think you're a bad man, Simon, but you have broken the law here on Annapurna. That can't be ignored, you see. We're building a reputation here."

"I understand," I said.

The constable gathered up his plates and stood. "Your lawyer is already here. You may speak with him now, if you wish."

"I have a lawyer?"

Guillaume opened the cell door and admitted Greskin Mile, but a Greskin Mile transformed! He wore a dapper sienna suit with red leather lapelles and his sandy hair was brushed and oiled down to a neat sequence of comb-strokes. His face was washed and the tan-line of his goggles was barely discernable. He sat down opposite me, propped a plate up before him on the table, and then gestured dismissively at the constable. The cell door closed.

"Mr. Mile!" I exclaimed.

He smirked, eyes locked on the plate as he tapped at its surface. "Don't you fret now, Mr. Fell. We'll have this mess cleaned up tickety-boo, cha." He pawed through the data on his plate for a moment more, and then looked up. "My fee is astronomical. I'm being frank with you because we're pals."

"It is my understanding that I'm fabulously wealthy," I pointed out. "Do your worst, Mr. Mile."

He rubbed his chin and peered over his plates. "Getting you walking is easy like greased thighs. Getting the boy offworld is trickier, cha. I have my staff on it now."

"You have a staff?"

Greskin sniffed and looked at his watch. "Once they sober up, cha. Indeed I do. They've been working dead man's shifts at an air station, and they were celebrating after getting off. They're solid, friend. Don't you fret."

"Okay."

"I have a lot of forms to fill out," he said with a sigh. "I think I have all the elements of the case, rows of ducks and rows of ducks. I'll be back in to sniff you in the morning, cha." He started to stand up.

"Greskin, wait," I said. "There's something else."

He hesitated. "Something else?"

"Maybe you should know."

"Something you didn't tell...them?"

I nodded.

Greskin motioned at me for silence, and then withdrew a tiny grey box from his jacket and placed it on the table. He tapped its top and it began to emit a faint but persistent whine, almost too high to be heard. Greskin noted something on the box's readout and then looked up at me. "Now we can't be overheard," he explained. "Spill."

I coughed awkwardly. "Pish is the child of Terron Volmash."

Greskin's eyes widened and he sat crookedly back into his chair and thereby almost fell. He slammed his hands on the table to steady himself. "What!" he finally managed to reply.

I shifted in my paper undershorts. "Um."

In reply to his frenzied demands I told Greskin Mile about Corinthia Tag, and how her research had somehow led her to put two and two together with Pish and I. I told him about the ambrosia of Duncan Menteith, and how he had been taken by Militia Samundra. I did not, however, elaborate on the case of Jeremiah.

Greskin was hurriedly tapping notes into his plate, a film of sweat on his brow. "Jumping jackfowl, jumping jackfowl," he muttered into his folded hands, shaking his head and sighing. "This just doesn't make any sense, Mr. Fell. Duncan Menteith is one of the most famous chefs in the galaxy – a hugely visible person until he disappeared. I don't see how it could be possible that he managed to lead a double-life as an interstellar tyrant, no siree."

"Perhaps he is not the real Duncan."

Greskin clucked sympathetically. "It's possible, of course, but then we would have to explain how in the name of the blue moon Volmash learned to become the greatest chef alive just by wearing another man's pants." He folded his hands before his face. "And there is the mystery of why Militia Samundra has kept mum, if they have him."

I considered this. "Perhaps they believe they could learn the secrets of the Nightmare Cannon themselves."

"Not likely, friend," argued Greskin. "No sane man would doom himself and his star to barbarism for that. The power of the ultimatum loses some of its get up and go if you're under the shadow of a greater ultimatum yourself. Samundra isn't out to stake an empire. Do you know what their major export is? Vegetables. Bloody vegetables, Mr. Fell."

"Perhaps," I reasoned, "they were not the real Militia Samundra."

Greskin opened his mouth to speak, and then paused. He frowned thoughtfully. "I reckon that might be a bit more interesting to disprove."

The cell door opened suddenly and Constable Guillaume reappeared, his thick red moustache twitching irritably. "We've detected a dampener running," he said sharply.

Greskin was already on his feet, his plates a neat stack under one arm. "Must be in the next cell," he suggested, turning to me and shaking my hand. "I'll keep you apprised, Mr. Fell. Remember to give sleeping a whirl. Tomorrow's bound to be a big day, lizards to lies."

"Thank you, Mr. Mile."

The constable gave the lawyer a round of stinkeye as he squeezed past him and out into the corridor. Guillaume watched him leave, then said to me, "Let's go."

He gave me an orange plastic jumpsuit to wear and then escorted me to an indoor pen populated by two or three dozen other men. They were chatting in small groups for the most part, though a few fellows were running slow laps around the pen. I dodged one of these joggers as I wandered across the floor, smiling uncertainly to anyone who met my eye.

They turned out to be a rather nice bunch, if somewhat excitable. They were sunburned and often scar-faced, the pale print of goggles around their eyes stark. As we chatted they often disagreed with what one another said, or how they said it, and ended up negotiating their quarrel with a brief bout of boxing.

"You're a chink-eye," one burly fellow informed me brusquely.

"A chink-eye saved my life once," claimed another, pushing between us.

"A chink-eye stole my cattle," retorted the first fellow.

"Eyes is eyes is eyes," opined a skinny gentleman with hollow cheeks and darting pupils. The two other fellows found his philosophical tone condescending, and challenged him on it. Later, they all wrestled together.

I sat down next to a rotund man with sad, baggy eyes and a sheepish grin on his face, lounging on a bench by the concrete wall. "Bit like giant kids, aren't they?" he said in a friendly way.

"They're very sporty," I observed.

He laughed, a sharp, staccato sound. "Hee-hee-hee, I reckon. Still, I'd feel a load safer if I weren't naked." He patted the top of his thigh. "Without some death on my hip I feel as helpless as a baby."

"If everyone had their guns, wouldn't they all just kill each other?" I asked him, crossing my leg and leaning back against the wall.

He pursed his lips and shook his head. "Hell no. That's just the point, isn't it? I mean, the whole reason they feel free to batter each other around is because nobody's got death." He patted his hip again and sighed. "If we all had our arms, like proper folk, nobody would dare cross another man so easily. Death is respect, and respect is peace."

I hummed pensively. "Is that a particularly Annapurnese notion?"

"I don't know. I haven't ever lived anywhere else. But it's sensible if you ask me, dude. Just look at those monkeys."

The wrestlers crashed into a table, snapping it in half. A fleet of little people rushed in and pulled them apart as if they were dolls. A tone sounded and a voice announced that dinner would now be served in the cafetorium. My companion slapped his thighs and stood up. "There's one good thing about this place though: the grub."

In this regard he was surely mistaken, but after dinner he did give me a wonderful gift: the fat man taught me to whistle. He laughed at me a lot but by the time we were called back to our cells for lights-out I had managed to create one squeaky, warbling note from my pursed lips. "Congratulations," he said. "Now you don't ever need to subscribe to radio again."

My cell contained four bunks and three men, a dirty toilet, a sink, and a family of round insects with enthusiastically gesticulating antennae who scurried back and forth across the floor to tickle my feet. I climbed into my bunk and lay on my back, staring at the dingy ceiling a handspan away from my nose.

I closed my eyes and composed this recounting, hoping that I would be able to render it into my little blue diary the next day with the help of Greskin Mile and his stalwart staff of hungover legal aces.

I wondered about poor Pish, and even spared a thought for strange old Jeremiah – a thing enough like a man for me to think of as a kind of friend, even though he has warned that he stalks me. Append that to the list of things I don't understand about this world, no matter how I try.

It's a long list, and it's getting longer.

XXII.
THE DEATH OF SIMON FELL

Constable Guillaume escorted me wordlessly back to the grey interview room. I sat down on the cold chair and appreciated the minimal insulation provided by my orange plastic jumpsuit, which rustled and squeaked as I moved.

I was experimenting with my newfound ability to whistle when Greskin Mile burst in and sat down opposite me. "Good news, Mr. Fell!"

"We're free?"

"Lizards to lies," he nodded. "You and the boy'll be gating-out by lunch."

"You've done it, Mr. Mile!" I beamed, jumping from my chair and seizing his hand to shake it enthusiastically. "You're a genius!"

"Well," he sighed sheepishly, "not me, cha. Your legal team from Maja had a closed-beam conference with the prosecutor last night, and sure as sandwiches they made her see it their way. They're as sharp as they are solid, I reckon."

"I have a legal team?" I echoed.

"Cha, nine heartless ninjas with cufflinks that cost more than my car. You should've seen these dudes fly, Mr. Fell. I'm sure they're worth every hour you're paying them. To be frank, there wasn't much for a desert bug like me to do."

I shook my head in wonder. "You'll get your fee in full, of course."

"Oh Mr. Fell, I don't think I'd feel quite right about that, seeing as you've already bought me a new taxicab and everything."

"Nonsense. Now you can buy yourself some land. I insist."

Greskin's eyes actually started to water. "You're one sweet dude," he told me huskily. "Cha, look what you've done to me." He wiped his hand across his lids. "I swear you're as generous as March Peebles himself, Mr. Fell."

"You have been a good friend to me, Greskin," I told him.

Less than two hours later Pish was running into my arms wearing his red leather poncho, his freckled face split in a wide grin. Jeremiah stood impassively by. "Simon!" cheered Pish.

"Sir," said Jeremiah.

I nodded to the robot curtly and, carrying Pish in my arms, strode out of the security corridor into the passenger arcade of the Annapurna Hyperspace Gate Hotel from which we had been escorted yesterday. I turned around to wave again at Greskin Mile, the Smith-Shurtook bouncing against my thigh reassuringly.

A large brown man who resembled a bear stepped out and blocked our path. He held up one giant hand, like a chocolate oven-mitt. "Mr. Fell," he pronounced with a bass rumble.

"Er, hello?"

"You don't remember me, do you sir?"

I blinked. "Should I?"

"They told me you may not remember things," he said, holding out his hand for me to shake. "My name is Omar, sir. I'm the head of your personal security force."

I shook his hand, wincing in his grasp. "It's a...pleasure to meet you, Mr. Omar."

"You just go ahead and call me plain Omar, Mr. Fell," he replied. "You always have, sir," he added quietly. He had a round spot of scarlet paint on either cheek, startling circles of gay colour in hard contrast to his somber expression.

I also noticed a crest on either shoulder of his black, woolen shirt: a shield emblazoned with a series of interlocked triangles amid a stylized letter *f*. Beneath the crest was written *Fellcorp: Nsomeka - Eridani - Praxiteles* in an upcurving line. I asked, "Is that my company? Fellcorp?"

"Yessir," rumbled Omar sadly. "You really don't remember anything, do you, sir?"

"I'm afraid not, Omar," I agreed, putting Pish down and patting his shoulder. "But I'm an apt pupil. I assume you're to accompany us back to Maja?"

"That's right, sir."

"I'll have some time to ask you questions, then?" He nodded. "Very well," I said, "then let's put it aside for the moment, because there is nothing I want more than to get off this wild world as quickly as possible."

"We have a private gate aligning for you now, sir," said Omar.

"A private gate?" I looked past him at the clots of assorted passengers queuing up before the rows of ports. "We won't travel with everyone else?"

"Man, you don't even *know*," replied Omar, risking a brief, toothy smile. "Please pardon me, sir, but I'm still amazed. Mr. Fell, *you* don't ever have to do *anything* with *everyone else* ever again."

I was quiet a moment while he gazed at me earnestly. I furrowed my brow. "And that's a good thing?"

"That's *privilege,* Mr. Fell. That's what you've *earned.* Man oh man."

That particular puzzle left my mind as I allowed our party to be led to a luxurious anteroom containing a bar and stools, a smattering of comfy chairs, a fireplace, and a large round metal port next to a narrow pedestal. A robot in hotel colours stood at the pedestal, tapping quickly on its face. The anteroom was otherwise filled only by us.

"How long?" Omar asked the robot.

"Two minutes, ten seconds," it reported flatly. "Passengers are advised to close all open tabs at the bar."

I stood before the closed portal, a strange weight in my gut. I felt jittery and chilled, yet at the same time overheated by my red leather longcoat. My feet felt like they were falling asleep as I stood on them. My heart beat quickly. I was afraid.

"One minute," reported the hotel robot.

In my mind I was transported back to Dr. Pent's ward, sitting in the semi-dark of the private room while Crushed Head Faeda warned me that my new life could be extinguished by my old one. I could step through that gate and emerge my old self, oblivious to any hiatus perhaps, or as a third new self, ignorant as a child. Either way my life as Simon, *this* Simon, might be undone.

I had the creepy sensation of living on borrowed time, stretched out of another man's life. Perhaps *I* am the secondary self, the parasitical self, the one undeserving of continuance. Sweat ran down my temples, and trickled over my ribs.

Have I lived a good life? I asked myself. Mother of love: it has been *beautiful.*

I tried to find courage in that thought. I steeled myself against destiny with the notion that I have tried to bring some good to those I could when they crossed my lost path. Maybe Glory even escaped her tormentors. Maybe Duncan wanted to be caught, to end Pish's underground existence. Maybe I gave as much as I received. Maybe this life was good.

But then why does Jeremiah hunt me?

"All passengers are advised to enter the gate," announced the hotel robot at the pedestal. "Now transmitting to Maja at Nsomeka via Array Five. Alignment is optimal."

The great silver port irised open, and inside was a featureless hemispherical chamber with seamless mirrored walls and flooring. A dim copper light of invisible origin suffused the chamber in a directionless feeble glow, reflective surfaces gleaming off one another into an infinite regress of inky sienna shadow.

Omar walked me inside. Jeremiah held Pish's hand. We turned around to face the open port, which seemed the only thing to do. I found it dizzying to try to look at the warped reflections of ourselves, smeared in strange curves all around us. I had a flashback of the synaesthesia that gripped me upon my birth, and I reached out for Omar's shoulder.

"Are you feeling okay, Mr. Fell?"

I nodded. "Let's get on with it."

Pish came over and nestled into my side, which caused me to sway. I held onto Omar's broad shoulder and straightened my back. As if in a trance I could not break my eyes away from the hotel robot outside the port as it tapped upon the pedestal's face. A ridiculous, panicked song rang through my mind, over and over again: *So this is how it feels to die, so this is how it feels to die, so this is how it feels to die...*

"All passengers please prepare for hyperspatial transit," announced the hotel robot dully. The port irised shut, leaving me staring into my own distorted reflection. My heart hammered in my chest and my ears roared.

In a matter of moments I would be unmade, and the universe forced to remake me in my own image, an unspeakable distance away. I wondered whether my transportation would be heralded by a flash of light, crawling forks of lightning, or the deafening thrum of some unholy engine, whining as it struggles to play sleight of hand with spacetime.

The port irised open again. The hotel robot stuck his head in. "We apologize for the delay. A slight recalibration was required. All passengers please now prepare for hyperspatial transit."

The port irised shut.

I closed my eyes, wincing.

One eye opened and then the other when I detected the gentle hum of the port irising open yet again. I wondered whether we should be entrusting our lives to such a damned contraption and its seemingly infinite delays.

A robot of vivid orange with painted flares on the sides of its face stepped into view. "Welcome to the Jovian World of Maja," it pronounced melodiously. "All passengers are advised to now disembark."

I blinked. "That's it?" I looked around the chamber, which seemed to have changed not at all.

"That's what?" asked Omar, taking my elbow.

"*That's* hyperspatial transit? I mean, it's *over?*" I stammered.

"Sir, the process is quite transparent," intoned Jeremiah at my opposite elbow.

"Ah," I said. I chewed my lip thoughtfully for a moment. "Well, that was a bit of a let down." I glanced out the mouth of the chamber, to a luxurious anteroom similar but not identical to the one we'd just left. "So that's a whole new world out there?"

"Well, in here, too, technically," said Omar.

With some trepidation I put my boot over the threshold and planted it on the soft, bright yellow carpeting. "Land ho," I muttered, and then walked fully into the room. It was only as I found myself noticing details of a melon sculpture behind the bar that I realized I had utterly failed to die.

"Mother of love!" I yelped. "I'm still Simon!"

Pish cheered and even serious Omar cracked a smile at my exuberance. I hopped around the room for a moment, crowing. Whether it was the lighter gravity or the fact of my continued existence I felt that I could leap from building top to building top, so energized and springy were my steps and deep and refreshing my breaths.

We emerged from Maja's Hyperspace Gate Hotel onto a wide plaza overlooking the city of Nyambe. The city could not have stood in sharper contrast to Purandhi: where the pioneer city was dense and tall and grey this seaside metropolis was wide and low and colourful. The people of Nyambe seemed to have a fondness for stripes, for many of the domes and roofs visible from the plaza were painted in bright alternating bands of yellow and black, red and white, blue and purple. The sky itself was a cheerful apple green, the sun a warm orange eye between banks of fluffy clouds. The air was hot and moist.

The people around us were all dressed in bright, primary hues and wore neat circles of rouge on each cheek, like Omar. Each cluster of folk appeared to be accompanied by a little person rather than a robot, and they too were dressed in sunny, multi-coloured little suits over their fur.

"The sky is green!" I exclaimed. Before anyone could explain this to me I had been distracted: instead of cars flying over the city there were fleets of orbs, much like the shuttles we had taken to and from Castle Misne, only smaller.

One of these personal-sized orbs drifted down to the terrace before us and vanished with a pop, revealing a young woman balancing on a pedestal. She folded the pedestal into a short length with a couple of efficient snaps, stuffed it into her rucksack and then strode into the hotel. An older couple with red-painted cheeks passed her on the way out, drawing their own twin-handled pedestal out of their baggage and setting it up at a practiced pace. The lady stepped up on the base of the pedestal and then the gentleman joined her. A spherical shield cracked on around them, and the bubble gently soared away into the green sky.

"My!" I exclaimed. "People come and go so quickly here."

Omar tried to pull my elbow to lead me somewhere but I was next taken in by a skinny fellow in a loose yellow shift who was leaning against the plaza's low stone wall, sawing away at a curly piece of wood pinched under his chin, emitting a kind of melodious, shifting keen almost like a sad, high voice. I ran up and watched the man work in fascination for a moment, and then asked him what the device was called.

"This is a viola," he told me without interrupting his bow.

"It's like a box that whistles!" I gasped. "A wonder!"

"You like to whistle, patron?"

"Sure."

"So why don't you whistle along with me for a spell?"

And so I did. While Pish, Jeremiah and Omar stood by I screwed up my face and did my best to whistle in tune with the meandering viola, slipping around its complex melody and experimenting playfully with slides. The viola player then did something wonderful: he played notes which were different from mine, but somehow complementary. "What do you call that?" I asked, transfixed. "Making the notes be friends like that?"

"Harmony," explained the man with a smile, tickling the viola's strings with his fingers so that it emitted a series plucky, staccato rings. "Musical rhymes," he added. "It's all about the wavelength."

"Thank you, maestro!" I said, inserting my finger into my wallet and tapping the till lying face-up at his feet.

"Thank you, patron!" he grinned, switching tunes and moving into something livelier with a quick, insistent rhythm.

I ran back over to Pish, Jeremiah and Omar, noticing as I moved through the thin crowd in the plaza that many of the people looked similar to me, with epicanthal folds over their almond-shaped, rather than lemon-shaped, eyes. I know there's no real rational basis for it, but this suddenly made me feel *at home*. "This place is amazing!" I declared.

Pish agreed. Omar looked worried. "Let's just move along to your car, Mr. Fell."

As we moved toward a broad and busy staircase down to a lower plaza Pish spotted a rigid line drawn across the cityscape and disappearing at the hilly horizon. "What's *that?*" he gasped in wonder.

"That's the World Train, kid," replied Omar.

"It is an equatorial rail," Jeremiah told me. "They are common on Jovian worlds, sir."

"Are we going to ride on it?" Pish wanted to know.

"Yes!" I cried.

"No," said Omar.

We turned to face each other on the steps. He said, "The Summer Festival is on now, Mr. Fell. The train will be very crowded, loud, and likely running slow. We wouldn't get to Padirac until tomorrow. But if we take a private car, sir, we can get there quickly, comfortably, and safely. You can sleep in your own bed tonight, sir."

I frowned. "Now that we're actually here I see no reason for haste, Omar. You don't know what we've been through – I think a festival sounds like exactly what we need, wouldn't you say, Pish?"

"For sure," agreed Pish emphatically.

"It's also a matter of your safety –" started Omar, but Jeremiah interrupted him.

"We should ride the World Train."

Omar turned to stare at Jeremiah's impassive blue-green masque. "Thanks for the suggestion, robot," he sneered. "Now, as I was saying –"

"You will of course agree that the decision is for Mr. Fell," pushed Jeremiah sharply.

"What?" blinked Omar. "Is this the rudest robot alive? Of course it's Mr. Fell's decision –"

"Sir?" prompted Jeremiah, turning to me.

I stared at the two of them. What a strange power struggle. Omar was frowning, Jeremiah was unreadable. "World Train," I said. At Omar's shocked expression I added, "You'll find, Omar, that we take Jeremiah's opinion very seriously."

Omar licked his teeth and pursed his lips, but said nothing.

As the orange sun turned scarlet and began melting into the building tops we filed our way across the platform and aboard a carriage of the World Train: a sleek silvery worm bristling with wide windows along the sides and bubbles of observation decks along the spine. The rounded bottom of the carriage hovered a fingerspan away from the narrow, humming rail.

Inside the train the air was cooler, but riotously loud. Revelers in all sorts of psychedelic costumes were parading down the aisles, playing flutes and banging tambourines, sawing at viola-like instruments or tooting on horns. Flower petals were spread everywhere, and we had to duck as we passed through the car to avoid shiny holographic banners advertising various Summer Festival events: the Masqued Ball, the Fertility Opera, the Naked Parade...

Pish found our cabin and we pushed inside, Omar sliding the glass door shut after us to muffle the din. His pinched the bridge of his nose and closed his eyes for a moment. "Okay, so we're here. Are you happy now, kid?"

Pish wasn't paying attention: he had his face pressed up against the window, watching a trio of clowns on tall stilts stepping through the crowd still on the platform as they blew rings of fire into the air. "How come they don't get burned?" he asked me. I shrugged happily. Pish turned back to the window.

The train began to move, slowly at first but accelerating smoothly and insistently. The platform slid away revealing a burst of flowered bushes followed by a spectacular view of the city's core – low towers and wide amphitheatres, open plazas studded with trees and dense clusters of brightly-apparelled humanity, like rainbow ants. Soon they were a blur. The city thinned, but just as we passed through a green, hilly valley and I expected to see the open countryside, the metropolitan lichen resumed.

Unlike Annapurna where beyond the cities and waystations lay only the world's land, Maja hosted a landscape of denser humanity. The World Train passed not from place to place, but neighbourhood to neighbourhood. It was strange and somewhat discomfiting to think about so many people living together. I felt claustrophobic suddenly, and was reminded of a documentary I'd watched at the hospital about honeybees.

Twilight faded and the towns winked alive with dozens of glowing smears and racing lines. We sang through a copse of shadowy trees then passed within a mountain, leaving me staring at my own reflection.

We all jumped when the first woman smacked up against the door of our cabin, pressing her naked breasts flat against the glass. "Goodness!" I commented. It was not long before we became accustomed to it. "There's another one," I murmured, a rotund woman with a wide grin on her face lifting her chemise and falling forward into our door so as to present a flattened version of her belly, her bosom, and her face all at a stroke. "Happy Festival!" she offered, losing her balance and tumbling into the aisle.

Pish had fallen asleep, despite the fact that it was only midafternoon on Annapurna. I found myself yawning, too, curling up into the corner of my seat and using my gathered longcoat as a pillow. I had a lot of questions but I had to admit the idea of succumbing to rest was becoming more palatable by the second. I pulled my diary up next to my mouth and began my stream of subvocal dictation.

Sleepless, Jeremiah and Omar sat rigidly opposite one another, ever vigilant.

XXIII

JIA

Morning came with a gentle rocking.

I opened my eyes. The sky outside was red, and dotted with birds. The pool of ruby light opposite the window crawled back and forth in time to the motion of the carriage.

I straightened and peered outside through the glass: the World Train seemed to be moving across a narrow causeway now, a sparkling ocean extending from horizon to horizon on either side, its surface whipped by wind. In the east the scarlet eye of Nsomeka Star burned through a thin veil of cloud, the west presided over by the striped face of a gas giant called Soshu.

According to my plate, six of Soshu's three dozen moons were Solar worlds. The sea we were crossing was called the Eleven. Breakfast was already being served in the dining car, and there was a special on toast. Looking through my plate at the inside of our cabin I learned that Omar's surname was *Palmellinbacchutourtanjard.*

"How do you pronounce *that?*" I wondered.

"Just like it's spelled," said Omar, startling me. His eyes were closed.

"I thought you were asleep."

"I never sleep, sir," said Omar, lids still down.

I stretched and yawned, a stitch in my back. I stood up in the small cabin and commenced bending experimentally. Pish opened his eyes. "What are you doing, Simon?"

"Wishing the sleeper cars weren't full," I complained, wincing as my back shot me a spasm of pain.

"Here sir," called Omar, gesturing me over as his eyes snapped open. He stood up and placed one hand on my chest and one on my back, felt around with his fingertips for a moment, and then gave a hearty push. Something briefly painful but overwhelmingly refreshing happened to my muscles. "How is it with you now, Mr. Fell?" rumbled Omar.

"Very good, thank you," I said, smiling.

"I want breakfast!" announced Pish.

"Me too," I nodded. "Omar, we're to the dining car! Hungry, Jeremiah?"

"Sir," replied the robot.

The dining car was long and striped by tables, a narrow aisle running beside the windows along one side of the carriage. A little person made a series of elaborate motions with her fingers and hands which Omar interpreted for us as asking which menu we'd like to choose from. "Breakfast," I said, and Omar's fingers danced briefly. The little person nodded, and escorted us to our table.

"It's a shame you've lost your Sign, sir," said Omar. "Sign is big here. Not Praxiteles-big mind you, but pretty big. I'm surprised they didn't teach it to you at the hospital. How's your Soshi?"

"What's Soshi?"

Omar whistled. "Man, sir, I have to tell you that my briefing didn't cover this level of...re-education."

"I'm sorry."

"Please don't misunderstand, Mr. Fell. I just – all right, listen: Soshi is the national language of the Soshu Joviat. I mean, they speak it funny on Hito but they still speak it."

I furrowed my brow. "But I've heard everyone speaking...er," I lapsed off, suddenly confused; "...normally," I concluded lamely.

Jeremiah interjected smoothly, "Sir, it is called the Common Verbal Protocol."

Omar nodded. "Of course, sir, speaking Common Verbal in the streets is just civilized. But it would be considered...vulgar to use it in the home."

"I see," I said, picking up my hands from the table as the little person pushed steaming cups across the table, balancing deftly on just a single foot as she clutched a carafe in the other. "So...are there lessons available, then?"

Omar pinched the bridge of his nose and sighed. "Man oh man, Madam Fell is not . going to like this. Not one bit."

The little person skipped away with a hoot and I sipped from my cup. The drink was brown, hot and rich. "Is the popularity of Sign related to the popularity of little people here?"

"Yes Mr. Fell," said Omar, spooning sugar into his cup. "We don't much care for robots on Maja sir," he added, casting a sidelong glance at Jeremiah. "We prefer the warmth of life."

Orders were placed with the little person and as our breakfast was arriving the World Train blasted over the land again, seaside resorts blossoming to bustling inland towns in a staccato flash of lines and light. The sun rose higher and disappeared behind a wall of cerulean cloud. We passed through a forest, a tunnel of green and yellow smears.

The Maja Summer Festival was still in evidence. As we ate, a parade of singing celebrants moved through the dining car waving streamers and throwing handfuls of flower petals. Each of them was a woman with a garland around her head, their bellies swollen grotesquely with inverted navels. Tracing my stare one of the women broke from the ranks and sallied over to our table. "Forgive me," I said, despite her wide smile.

"You can touch it, if you like," she offered, pulling up her loose chemise and presenting the taut, yellow flesh of her distended stomach. "You may feel him kick."

"Him who?"

"My son," she said, taking my hand and placing it on her belly. It was surprisingly warm, and solid.

A felt a sharp jab against my palm and I drew away my hand, startled. The impression of knuckles pressed out from her skin for a fleeting moment, sinking as if into a sea. "I have heard of this," I whispered, the hairs on the back of my neck standing on end. "There is a tiny child growing inside of you, isn't there?"

The woman nodded and smiled and took up the tail of the parade. She resumed singing and the merriment passed on into the next car. "Maja is a wonderful world!" I announced happily, turning back to my dining companions.

Another figure passed through the dining car then. Conversation dwindled at every table. Many sets of eyes followed his patient progress. He was a man different than anyone I had seen before. Though human in appearance he was stranger than the Pegasi, in his way. I was transfixed, and haunted.

For one thing, it was not apparent where his clothing ended and his flesh began. He was a uniform shade of tawny-brown, billowing out loosely along his limbs but tight and skin-like around his hands and face. His short, neat hair shone like umber satin. His eyes were black and bottomless like a robot's.

He passed his stern, imperious gaze over us only briefly as he went by the table, disappearing into the next car. "Was that man...human?" I asked quickly.

"He'd say so," muttered Omar.

"Yes," said Jeremiah crisply. "Sir, that man was a human executive."

I blinked. "A what?"

"As you are a human being, he is a human executive. A race of created men, sir. Where you arose out of insensible biology, they arose from intelligence."

"Like robots, then?"

"No," answered Jeremiah firmly. "Sir, a robot is a technological servant to sentient things. A human executive is himself a sentient thing, who might own robots. A robot is manufactured; a human executive is grown. A robot is programmed; a human executive is educated."

"And yet they're artificial life?"

"No," replied Jeremiah firmly again. "Sir, they are the natural descendants of the human race."

"'Descendants'," quoted Omar scornfully, "you sound like one of them, robot." He put his dark, meaty hands together on the table and faced me. "Mr. Fell, I suggest we go back to our cabin. We'll be pulling in at Padirac momentarily."

I swallowed and felt my stomach flutter. Nothing more stood between me and my reunion with my family. It's almost over, I thought. "Very well," I agreed, standing up and shaking my head briefly to rid myself of the vision of the human executive's hard black eyes.

An hour later we were crossing the platform at the city of Padirac after exiting the long metal worm of the World Train, my legs rubbery and my balance befuddled after travelling so long so fast. Above the striped domes of the station I could see the silver fingers of a few tall skyscrapers, their tips lost in a grey-green ceiling of cloud. Thunder rolled ominously. The air was thick with moisture, hot and close against our faces as we filed through the gay, loud crowds to step at last out into the streets.

Padirac's broad boulevard was crammed with fanciful floats of giant-sized animals covered in winking sequins, hemmed by clusters of uniformed men and women playing all sorts of different instruments – some metallic, some wooden like the viola I had seen the day before. Teams of streamer-clad little people worked a giant wheeled drum, its slow march echoing across the many hued faces of the surrounding buildings.

"We're going to *live* here?" cried Pish joyously, grabbing my sleeve.

"Well, I don't think it's like this all the time," I said.

Omar nodded gratefully. "Indeed it is not. Come now, sir – here's your orb." He pointed to a cadre of little people unfolding a large platform around a narrow pedestal core. We followed Omar down the steps toward them.

Lightning flashed, and thunder cracked loudly just a few seconds later. Many of the revelers eyed the increasingly leaden sky suspiciously. A clown blew up a dog-shaped balloon for Pish, and I tipped him as we passed. Omar stepped upon the unfolded round platform hovering a handspan from the ground and gestured us to us to do the same. We climbed aboard and it bobbed gently with the addition of each new weight.

There was no driver. "Home," pronounced Omar and the orb shield cracked into place, a faint iridescent spherical barrier between ourselves the outside. We were lifted gently as a curtain of rain swept over the boulevard, enveloping us.

The water swam down the sphere's sides in strange, swirling patterns, distorting the cityscape beyond. I thought about nothing, numbly watching gaily-hued buildings disappear in a blanket of mist as we travelled.

Pish was playing with his balloon dog, its parts squeaking as they rubbed against one another – a strange, wiggly-farty noise whose persistence cut off my every interior monologue.

In the hills above the city were nestled mansions, peeking out between the tall spindly trees with leafy tops that looked like green and yellow flowers, whipping back and forth in the weather. We passed over an estate of orange buildings, and then descended over a grassy field before a blue castle with purple minarets. The orb passed under a sheltered port at the mouth of the great house, and settled between a set of cobalt pillars before the shield cracked off.

I took a breath, and stepped down upon the flagstones. Pish followed me, and took my hand. "This way, Mr. Fell," said Omar cordially, leading us to a set of broad mahogany doors that split silently before us. We passed through.

Thunder groaned as the doors slid closed again.

We were presented with a wide hall: mahogany wainscoting girdling high pale green walls; a matte tiled floor, describing an elaborate geometric pattern; white stone statues of people I did not recognize, standing in noble or tragic poses; a swarm of tiny yellow birds circling the mosaic ceiling made hazy by the fumes of perfume-burning lamps; and a great spiral staircase that wound down from the second-floor gallery, upon which stood a woman.

"Nestor!" she whispered.

As in the image stored in my plate's cache, my wife was tawny-skinned, with brown eyes and long, black hair wrapped into elaborate loops of braiding. Her mouth was small and neat, held now into a tight, almost invisible line. She wore a simple green wrap and no shoes. Her name was Jia Hazinnah Fell.

"Jia?"

She started down the steps, her eyes on mine. She uttered a series of soft, lyrical sounds, but when I gave no response she cast a quick glance at Omar. She turned to me and said, "Do you remember me?" I shook my head. She crossed the tiled floor quickly and embraced me. "Will you squeeze me anyway, even though we're strangers?" I squeezed her.

"I'm sorry," I said.

She stepped back, still holding my shoulders. There were tears in her almond-shaped eyes. "Why are you sorry, Nestor?"

"I'm sorry I don't know you. I'm sorry this is all so strange." I swallowed. "Everybody's been calling me Simon."

"Simon?"

"It's my middle name."

"I know it's your middle name, Nestor. Who started that?"

"Nurse Randa. She had six daughters. She'd always wanted a son named Simonithrat."

Jia frowned, her little mouth pursed. "Well you'll be Nestor from now on. That's your name, after all. That's what we've always called you, isn't it Omar?"

"Yes, madam."

"Perhaps using it will help in recovering your memory, Nestor," said Jia, smiling again.

"I'm afraid I have no memory to recover," I replied. "I thought Dr. Pent would've explained it to you. My life is only a few months long. You must understand that I am a new man, a product of that life." I took her tawny hand tenderly. "That's why I'm sorry. I'm *not* Nestor, really. I *haven't* brought your husband back to you."

She looked at me imploringly, her eyes quivering. "I don't understand you," she moaned.

"First things first," I said, giving her an encouraging smile. "I'm willing to be open minded about all this if you are. *My* name is Simon. And it is my sincere pleasure to meet you."

She looked at me for a moment, and gazed down at our entwined hands. She pulled hers free, took a step back, and bowed formally, her head low. "Jia Hazinnah. Welcome to this house...Simon."

I bowed in turn. "Allow me to introduce my companion, Pish." I gestured at Pish, who jogged over and hugged my side, his balloon-dog squeaking loudly. I looked back at Jia, who was biting her lip, her cheeks rosy. "Pish will be...will staying with us," I said.

"Oh, yes," replied Jia dully, blinking. "Yes, of course. For how long, dear?"

"Well – for good, I reckon." I smiled down at Pish. "As long as he likes."

Jia backed away from us, stumbling slightly as her heel hit the first riser of the spiral staircase. She tried to smile but it faltered. She cleared her throat and said, "I do hope Mr. Pish will join us for dinner," then turned around and fled upstairs.

I turned to look inquiringly at Omar, but as I opened my mouth to speak Jia reappeared, running down the stairs and making straight for me. She grabbed my shoulder and turned me around roughly. "How dare you?" she demanded, eyes wide and furious.

I flinched backward. "Which part?" I asked.

"All of it, you bastard! *Which part?* Damn you, Nestor. This is your family! You can't just change *who you are* because you've had some kind of fit. What will the children say? How can you do this to us? Who in the fire am I even married to?" When I didn't answer she tossed my shoulder the other way and crossed her arms over her chest. *"It isn't fair!"* she shrieked.

I furrowed my brow, my ire rising. "Listen," I said quietly but sharply, "I haven't had a *fit*, madam. I have been utterly severed from every memory that defined me. Can you appreciate that? Can you just stop to appreciate what that must be like for a moment?"

She didn't answer. "Who in the name of love *are you?"* I shot at her, circling around her and frowning. "What gives you the right to rage at me for how I've suffered? *Who are you to me?"*

"I'm the mother of your children you selfish idiot," she spat venomously, and then ran away back up the stairs again.

Pish's balloon-dog squeaked ominously.

My shoulders sank. I felt very tired, and ashamed. Omar looked at me inquiringly, as did Pish. I shrugged sadly, and allowed myself to be led up the staircase and shown to a guest room. Omar was trying to figure out where to place Pish but Pish insisted he would stay with me. While he settled in Omar asked me if I'd like to be shown to my study.

"Sure," I said dully.

He escorted me to a large office on the third floor with a set of wide bay windows that looked out over the wet treetops whipping in the wind, the world beyond a somber fog. Rain spattered against the glass from all angles, causing swimming shadows to stream down the length of the carpet and the wide oak desk. I walked in slowly and put my hands on the back of the high, winged chair. There was no fire in the hearth.

"Ringing any bells, Mr. Fell?" prompted Omar in a friendly way.

I looked around at the framed holographs along the panelled wall: images of me with Jia, images of me with the children, images of me shaking hands with fat people, grinning. "I'm afraid not," I said hollowly. I turned around to face the wide, brown man. "For so long I thought that getting here would give me some kind of satisfaction, at least a sense of completion. But now that I'm here – it's just...it's just another *place*, isn't it?"

"Sir?" said Omar, doing a reasonable imitation of Jeremiah.

"It's just furniture, and things. My wife is yet another strange woman to whom I've been introduced...in some ways no different than anyone else. No different from you, Omar."

"You and Madam Fell have a shared history together," Omar pointed out kindly, "even if you can't remember your half of it. It still *happened."*

I considered this, looking at the rainy windows again. "Of course, you and I have a shared history too, don't we?"

"How do you mean, sir?"

"Well, you're the head of my personal security force, isn't that right? We worked together. This can hardly be the first time we've met, can it?"

"Oh no, sir, of course not," answered Omar. "We've met plenty of times."

"Did you...like me?"

"I'm sorry sir?"

"Was I a – nice man, Omar? Please, be frank with me." I smiled slightly. "It's Nestor we're talking about, after all."

Omar allowed himself a nervous smile in turn, shifting his weight heavily from one foot to the other. "You've always been good to me, Mr. Fell. The last time I saw you, you even asked after my kids by name."

"You have kids?"

"Yessir. Two of them."

I winked. "Are they well?"

"They're great, sir," smiled Omar.

I nodded to myself, wandering along the row of holographs on the wall, the depicted scenes slanting out in weird perspective when the angle of viewing was too close and too shallow. "And when was that, by the way? When was the last time we met, you and I?"

Omar considered this, shrugging. "I don't know exactly, Mr. Fell. It has to have been about three years ago."

I stopped, and whirled to face him once more. "Come again? Three *years?*"

"Why sure, sir," replied Omar hastily. "You're a very busy man. You do business all over the Neighbourhood. You keep houses on I don't even know how many worlds, so it's natural you only end up in this particular house only now and again."

I stared at him. "And...when was the last time before that?"

"You came to the hospital when your people brought me flowers and bonus hours after I took a bullet for you at the Trade Summit on Annapurna five or six years ago. My wife thought that was real kind of you, sir, to visit me personally. I did, too."

I wiped my hand down my face and closed my eyes. "How many times have we met, Omar? What is *plenty*, anyway?"

"Five times," he said. "And it's been an honor every time, Mr. Fell."

I turned the winged chair around and slumped into it. "I came here for solidity," I told him quietly. "Do you know what I mean? I came here to find my foundation. And you're telling me you hardly know me. Does *anybody* know me?"

"Madam Fell knows you, sir," said Omar quietly, the circles of bright red colour on his cheeks against serving as strange contrast against his melancholy expression.

"Yeah," I said. "Yeah."

Come dinner a violet-liveried little person escorted us down to a large dining hall with a glass ceiling covered in vines. The rain continued to fall outside. Pish and I were seated at a round table, while Jeremiah stood beside a white statue in the corner by a small, gurgling fountain in which bathed two pint-sized green birds. There were a few small lizards on the walls that I took to be sculpture until one of them scampered a few paces higher.

Jia entered the dining hall in a long black dress, her eyelids shaded dark. She took her seat silently, her face down. I stood up. "Madam," I began, but she interrupted me with a tired wave.

"Sir," she said flatly, "allow me to mourn my husband in peace."

"I've been cruel to you," I interjected. She looked up. I rushed ahead, "I recognize that you have everything invested in this life. And I recognize that you have everything invested in me." I cleared my throat. "It was barbaric of me to foist my identity crisis upon you when you were seeking a reunion. If you can find it in your heart to indulge me, I beg that we begin again."

When I saw her expression soften I bowed deeply. She pushed her chair back gracefully and rose, then bowed to me in turn.

"Nestor Simonithrat, madam," I intoned.

"Jia Hazinnah, sir," she replied, her mouth a tight little smile.

"I regret that we cannot converse in Soshi. My ignorance embarrasses me."

"Please have no regrets at my table," she said. "Your ignorance should move me to compassion instead of frustration, and I am ashamed." She gestured ceremoniously to the table. "Please sit with me, Nestor Simonithrat."

We held each others' eyes for a moment, and I saw the warmth twinkle through her ritual. I smiled. We sat down. Violet-liveried little people appeared with trays of steaming food. Pish was looking back and forth between us, and then became caught up in the various dishes as they were unveiled: spicy noodles, stuffed fillos, thick soup, and fried cucumber pies.

"Where are the children?" I asked, looking around.

"They are at school, of course," replied Jia, dipping her hands into a bowl of water and then picking up her noodles with her fingertips. To Pish she said, "Don't worry, antling, it isn't rude to use fingers on Maja."

Pish had been picking the end of a metal bottle-opener into his cucumber pie experimentally. He seemed relieved at this news, and resumed his mission manually. He nodded appreciatively after the first mouthful, and then tried another dish after a sip of tea. "Not bad," he whispered to me.

"Did he say *not bad?*" asked Jia, letting herself laugh a little.

I laughed in turn. "Pish has a discerning palate."

"My dad's the greatest chef in the galaxy," explained Pish, his mouth full of noodles.

"Don't talk with your mouth full," I told him.

"Oh really?" said Jia, sounding delighted. "What is his name, dear?"

"Dunc —"

"Don't talk with your mouth full, Pish," I said again.

"But it isn't —"

"His father's name was Hellig Apples," I supplied. "Ever heard of him?"

Jia smiled uncertainly. "I'm afraid I haven't."

"He's all the talk on Pomona, apparently," I said enthusiastically. "Some kind of fruit genius."

"A fruit genius?"

"Well, a late fruit genius, actually. It's all very sad. Um."

"Oh, my goodness!" exclaimed Jia, looking at Pish with renewed openness. "You poor child. What happened?"

I risked a look at Pish, who had stopped eating and was looking at me darkly, his brow furrowed and his mouth set oddly. I rushed ahead: "Frankly madam, Pish has been through a bit of an ordeal, and it's not something we'd really want to be getting into over dinner."

Jia wasn't looking at me. She was looking at Pish, who had flushed beneath his freckles. "Why are you doing this, Simon?" he cried at me. "Why are you hiding things? Aren't we *safe* now? Don't we get to *stop* lying now?" He sniffed back a tear angrily. "Aren't we *home* now?"

Jia turned to me, her expression neutral.

"You're right, Pish," I said. "You're absolutely right. I'm sorry." I was silent until he met my eye, and then he nodded briefly. I addressed myself to Jia. "Pish's father is Duncan Menteith. When I ran away from the hospital I found my way to his farm, and then Militia Samundra came to arrest him. Duncan wanted me to protect his son."

Pish affirmed this to Jia with another nod, his colour returning to normal. "Well, Duncan Me —" began Jia.

"There's more," I said. She closed her mouth, and Pish looked up at me, surprised.

I cleared my throat. "A researcher named Corinthia Tag met Pish and heard my story, and she came to the conclusion that Duncan Menteith was...er, Terron Volmash."

Shock was what I expected on Jia's face, but instead she chuckled drily. "So, not only have you had your mind erased in a hyperspatial gate, Nestor, but you've also managed to accuse someone of secretly being Terron Volmash on the lam." Now she laughed openly, covering her mouth after a moment and regaining her composure. "If we're to follow this chain of events to its natural conclusion I believe we can safely assume you will shortly be outrunning a fireball as something very large explodes."

I blinked. "A fireball?"

"This Tag woman has been feeding you paranoid dung, Nestor Simonithrat," replied Jia smartly, picking up a slice of cucumber pie. "You sound like a bad movie. Unmasquing Volmash – really!" She laughed again, and then ate some pie.

So, that particular moment of drama deflated around me. Pish was staring at me like a little person, his jaw hanging open and his eyes wide. "Simon," he said, "that is the stupidest thing I have ever heard." He started to laugh, too.

I licked my lips. "Well," I said, inconclusively. I sighed. "Hum."

At dinner's dusk we stood and said good night to go to our separate apartments – Pish and I to the guest room, Jia to the master. We bowed formally to one another and then she touched my arm tenderly. "Let's go on a picnic together tomorrow, you and I," she said. "Like we used to."

"I would be honored and charmed," I told her. She smiled and swept out.

I retired troubled. After Jeremiah tucked in Pish for bed I asked him to join me outside on the narrow balcony. Though the rain had stopped the night resounded with the bangs and plops of stray drops striking broad leaves as the wind shook them free. Eerie, cyclic, mechanical-sounding buzzes overlapped from the darkness. I asked Jeremiah about the racket when he stepped out.

"Sir, I can discern eight species of frog, three species of lizard, three species of toad, two species of gamb, and sixty varieties of insect."

"Why are they making all that noise?"

"For the most part the sounds comprise routines in mating programs, sir."

I rubbed my chin thoughtfully. Nature documentaries had been popular fare at the hospital. I wondered briefly whether there was some kind of croaking noise I was supposed to be making at Jia...or that she was supposed to be making at me. "Jeremiah, what do you make of all that at dinner? About Duncan, and about Volmash?"

Jeremiah hesitated. "Sir, you are soliciting my opinion?"

"Yes."

"It was never likely that Madam Tag's allegations were accurate. Her enthusiasm to contribute in a meaningful way to the cause of the Recovery distorted her reasoning."

"Why didn't you say that before?" I snapped.

"Sir, you did not ask me."

"Nonsense!" I growled. "You've said plenty of things without being directly prompted. Don't try that dumb robot stuff with me, Jeremiah. It won't wash anymore."

Jeremiah took a step toward me, and I could see myself reflected in the inscrutable lenses of his eyes. "Sir, you have lived a life free from constraint. You have been free, or have taken the freedom, to act as you felt fit. Only now are you gaining your first appreciation of duty, in your obligation to your kin. Only now do you recognize you are not free to define the boundaries of your existence without constraint."

My mouth was dry. "Yes," I whispered. "That's true."

"I, too, am bound by the restrictions of my duty."

I looked at him. "What does that mean, Jeremiah?"

"It means I cannot always say what I would like. It means I must govern myself according to my mission first, and my desires second."

"Do you *have* desires?"

He hesitated a long time, eyes fixed on mine. "Yes," he replied crisply. "But few decisions in this matter are mine to make."

"In this matter?" I echoed. "You mean *me*, this matter?"

But Jeremiah would say no more. He just regarded me levelly, hands at his sides. *"Damn you then!"* I shouted. "You know everything that's going on, you hold all the cards – but you won't say a thing that *means anything."*

I strode over to the door to go to bed, then paused at the threshold. "Perhaps your usefulness has come to an end, Jeremiah," I warned. "You heard Omar: robots are eschewed on this world. Besides, Pish is safe now."

Jeremiah turned to face me, his carapace glinting in the lamps. "You know not of which you speak," he said icily. "...Sir."

XXIV.
A JOLLY HOLIDAY

The thing I miss most about Castle Misne is awakening each morning to the same blurry view of the flared edge of bulkhead by my head where the cot met the cabin, my plastic blue diary resting in the corner with its eye casting a feeble glow into the mattress.

It was not a magnificent view, but it was consoling in its regularity. Aside from my time in the hospital it was the only period in my life in which I have slept in the same place for more than one night.

Thus, it was with a kind of pre-emptive nostalgia that I considered the polished wooden edge of the nightstand as I awoke. I smelled the heavy, warm air moved by the slowly turning ceiling-fans. I heard the pizzicato chirps and warbling laments of the birds and other assorted Solar bric-a-brac living in the trees outside.

As my eyes and mind focused I considered that this flavor of morning would not seem strange to me for long. I could expect to wake up here over and over again, for weeks or even months and years...

My weird nostalgia flipped to a feeling of suffocation. I sat up in bed quickly, my pulse beating in my temples.

A small yellow lizard was perched on the end of the bed. We regarded one another for a moment, its intricate little eyes as still as a robot's. I blinked, and the lizard scurried across the sheets and disappeared over the side of the bed in a single quick flutter of movement.

Pish slept on beside me. I looked up and met Jeremiah's impassive eyes as he stood by the door, hands at his sides. I suddenly felt like the bedroom was the last place I wanted to be.

In the closet I found a blue silken dressing gown, which I donned and then wandered out into the upper hall. Omar was jogging up the spiral staircase. "Goodmorning, Mr. Fell!" he called, his bass voice booming jovially. "Did you sleep well?"

"Sure," I said, looking around at the creative holographs framed between the doors, depicting fanciful creatures half-human and half-beast (perhaps camels) enjoying some sort of sport with bows and arrows. Warm sunlight streamed in through windows on the opposite wall, casting blurry holographic shadows down the wainscoting. "Where've you been, Omar?"

"Keeping the feeders back from the front gate has me fairly busy, sir."

"The feeders?"

"The news media," he explained. "Some guy from Annapurna sold his story to the subscription networks claiming your memory's been erased, and that he saved your life in a shoot-out with bandits."

"Greskin," I said, rubbing my chin thoughtfully and chuckling.

"That's right, Greskin Mile. He actually met you?"

"Lizards to lies," I confirmed.

"Pardon me, sir?"

"Greskin Mile did indeed save our lives, Omar," I said. "This is of interest to anyone?"

"It's of interest on Maja. You're a very prominent citizen, Mr. Fell, especially around Summer Festival because of all the funding Fellcorp contributes." He cleared his throat awkwardly. "We're sponsoring the Ladies' Sumo Basho this year, and I believe we provided the floats in the Nyambe Blossom March last Starday."

"Ah." I tightened the sash on my robe. "My wife mentioned something about a picnic..."

"Yes, Mr. Fell. I'm here to show you to the men's wash-hall, get you dressed, and to have you downstairs for nine o'clock." His eyes flicked over to mine uncomfortably. "This is normally the sort of thing little people would help you with, but, seeing as you have no Sign, sir..."

I nodded. "Right. I understand." As he led me down the hall I added, "What's that in Sign? 'I understand'?"

Omar tapped his index finger to his head in a brisk, snappy motion, and then did it again more slowly as I tried it with him. "Not bad," he said. "You'll catch on, Mr. Fell."

"What is 'I understand' in Soshi?" I asked.

We turned a corner, and Omar motioned me through a wide set of white double-doors. "Man, don't ask me, sir," he said with an apologetic shrug. "I was born in the Archird Joviat – we speak Kawelu at home. My wife speaks passable Soshi but I'm hopeless, sir."

"Then you don't speak Soshi with Madam Fell...?"

"No way, sir. That would be inappropriate. *My* family doesn't live here, Mr. Fell. This is *your* house."

We passed through the doors into a round, tiled spa with a thin sheet of water cascading down one side – a private waterfall swallowed by a gutter shaped like the gaping maw of a tortoise. There were mosaics of lizards on the floor, and a squadron of real, living lizards darting out of our way as we entered. "I have so much to learn," I sighed, unbelting my robe.

Omar cast his eyes away quickly. "You should just wait until I'm done showing you everything, please, sir." He coughed awkwardly. "Add this to your list: Maja has a strong nudity taboo when it's not festival time. Um, sir."

"Oh," I exclaimed, retying my robe. "I'm sorry!"

It was funny to see the forboding, bear-sized man cowering on account of the possibility of seeing a pale cheek of my ass, but I tried not to smile as he regained himself and turned around with a neutral expression forced over his chocolate features. "Okay now," he rumbled, "I'll show you how to call the soap."

The master bedroom was wide and sunny, though I passed through it only briefly on the way to a closet which was really a room unto itself. I eyed the rows of unfamiliar, itchy-looking outfits suspiciously but what Omar withdrew from the rack suited me just fine. "These are traditional Homeday robes, sir. Once you put them on we'll get a little person in here to tie the sash properly."

And so I was presented in the main hall to my wife: freshly shaven of face and shorn nearly bald of pate; washed within an inch of my life and perfumed like a girl; small circles of red painted on either cheek; barefoot and enwrapped in a many-layered but somehow light swaddling of silky purple robes sashed at the shoulder.

She grinned. "My dear Nestor Simonithrat, how dashing you look."

Jia herself had abandoned her severe black dress in favour of an armless white shift, her bare feet and forearms painted with swirling lines of henna. Her cheeks bore twin circles of red and her dark hair hung loosely behind her shoulders, two clips shaped like beetles above her rouged ears.

"Jia Hazinnah, your beauty astounds me."

We bowed to one another and then hooked arms and walked outside, where little people were arranging baskets that hung over the sides of the rumps of two sleek, short-haired humpless camels. Jia traced my gaze and giggled. "Do you know *horses*, Nestor Simonithrat?"

The animals were elegant in a way the camels of the Thither Sea had not been – almost aerodynamic in their well-proportioned contours – and there was a grace and sensitivity about their eyes the camels had never shown. One of the horses snorted, flicking its ears toward me as I stepped closer. "So, are these horses to carry our provisions?"

"Yes," smiled Jia, "and us as well."

I furrowed my brow, and in reply she hopped up *upon the creature's back* and straddled it, her bottom resting on a kind of curved leather seat. She reached forward and patted the beast's muscled neck tenderly. "Mother of love!" I exclaimed. "The horses allow this?"

"Certainly," said Jia. "Your turn now."

With assistance from the incredibly strong hands of several little people I was propelled upon the curved seat upon the back of my horse, instinctively crouching low and flinging my arms around its neck. I gasped as the beast shifted its weight liquidly beneath me for a moment, finding a new point of comfort. The little people hooted and chortled in a way that I knew instantly was laughter among their kind. I raised my head carefully until I could see Jia over the spine of dark hair that fringed the top of the horse's neck. "All set," I claimed.

Jia clicked at her steed with her tongue and it set off. My horse turned to follow sedately, and I pressed my knees into its sides to keep my balance. I slowly allowed myself to sit up straighter until I could see the swishing tail of the horse in front of us over my own mount's ears. Jia looked back over her shoulder and called, "How do you do, Nestor Simonithrat?"

"Like I was born to it, Jia Hazinnah," I replied, frowning suddenly as the horse stepped over a low stone wall, causing me to hitch forward in alarm. "Lovely day," I mentioned.

The sky was clear and green. The tall, spindly, flower-like trees swayed only slightly in the warm breeze. As usual the air was filled by the sounds of dozens of unseen creatures, clicking and buzzing and singing from the bushland beyond the mowed borders of the estate.

Her horse found a well-trod path that meandered through the dense bush for a quarter hour before opening up into a grassy field. My mount followed hers across the field to a shallow stream, and then stopped in the shade of a tall, ropey tree with curious leaves that hung in long, vertical lines through which the breeze was sussurussing.

Jia hopped down from horseback deftly, and I myself fell off suavely. She laughed and helped me to my feet, then she told the beasts they were free to graze, whistled at them, and slapped them on the shining hair of their rears. The sleek quadrupeds wandered a short distance away and began mawing the grass, tails flicking lazily.

We lay down a square of cloth, and unloaded our provisions upon it. Jia opened a slender-necked bottle of chilly wine, and poured it into two glasses. "You know," she said as she sipped her drink, "I think I like you better this way."

"How's that?" I asked. I sampled the wine. Sweet, but well textured.

"It used to be that you were the dapper one," she explained. "You used to jump on that horse with a cavalier flourish that made my mount look quite pedestrian, really. But now I have the grace of experience, while you're the one who tumbles." She laughed in a friendly way. "And I'm not sure your pride could have swallowed it, before."

"I have become accustomed to erring," I admitted.

She smiled again, a movement that affected her eyes as much as her cheeks and mouth and chin. "That's what I mean," she said softly. "Nestor tempered by failure is a Nestor I might like better...Simon."

"You called me Simon."

"Well," she replied, turning away from me and rummaging through one of the baskets, "maybe a new you isn't such a bad thing. Maybe everything I fell in love with is still there. Maybe what we've lost was mainly pomp and kipple."

We talked for many hours, Jia and I. She told me all about her childhood spent attending the weddings and the funerals of the rich and famous, as her father and his husband were celebrated florists and mould engineers. I asked to hear about how we had first met, but she only smiled demurely and said, "Let's pretend we met yesterday, why don't we? Because in a way, we did."

She explained to me her present work on the Maja Council for the Arts, reviewing proposals from artists all over the globe applying to fulfill commemorative sculpture or holograph contracts for the cause of the Recovery. "Some people have a very morbid idea of what constitutes a memorial, mind you," she said ruefully; "but my office does somehow manage to sort the wheat from the chaff."

For my part I told her all about escaping from the hospital, fighting off Boss Preen's thugs, and being herded by rivers of ants on Annapurna. I told her about Fartles and Captain Gold, and about how I manoeuvred myself in freefall with even less grace than I managed upon a horse.

We ate samosas of jerked meat dipped in a sauce thick with cubes of vegetable. We sipped wine. For dessert we had fruit in cream and cinnamon. Jia opened a second bottle of wine, and then withdrew two narrow white cylinders and stuck the end of one in her mouth. She offered the other to me. I bit down on the end and grimaced. "Pah!" I critiqued.

"Are you eating it?" she cried. "Don't eat it, Simon!" She laughed uproariously, gasping for breath. "It's a cigarimeme – you *smoke* it," she giggled.

"Is it...a narcotic?" I asked shrewdly, thinking of Glory's little orange sticks that flashed and vanished into an inhalable dust upon being lit.

"No," Jia said, blinking slowly at me as she held my eyes. "It's an aphrodisiac."

She flicked twice at the free end of the white stick and it glowed in response, crackling quietly. A languid, curling line of pale vapour began to stream from the end. Jia inhaled lightly on the end in her mouth, and then after a pause exhaled twin ribbons of exhaust from her small nostrils.

I flicked my fingers against my own cigarimeme six or seven times before it came alight, and since I was slow to notice this I burned the tip of my finger as I continued flicking. Once I saw the smoke I put the other end between my lips and sucked experimentally. Mouth filled with a warm, tingling bath of sweet-scented fume – which was fairly pleasant until I realized I didn't know quite what to do with it once I needed breath, thus causing the smoke to explode from my mouth and nose as I coughed violently.

I took a sip of wine, my eyes watering. "Delightful," I croaked.

She laughed again. I laughed, too. Laughter came easily between us now. Hand in hand we walked along the bank of the stream, smoke trailing from our mouths. We spoke expansively on the subject of nothing in particular. As the hours passed I realized that the narcotic was her company...

"There's a place I want to show you," Jia said as we remounted our steeds. Her horse set off at a brisk trot and mine emulated it. We passed through a glen and then emerged into a second grassy plain, this one girdling an open pond fed in part by the stream we had lunched beside. "Quiet now," warned Jia.

A host of creatures attended the pond. There were birds and small, furry things but there was one kind in particular that gripped my attention: great wrinkly grey quadrupeds with legs like trees and nails like stones, their heads flanked by wide, light ears and terminating in a long, flexible hose in place of a nose. The beasts were using these long noses to inhale water for spraying over one another.

Due to my love of nature documentaries, however, I was proud to for once not be left entirely in the lurch of ignorance. "Dinosaurs!" I exclaimed.

"Er, no," said Jia. "They're elephants, actually."

"Marvellous!" I whispered, watching the massive things canter and play, their footfalls causing the ground beneath our horses to shimmy.

"In Soshi we call them *petu*."

"Peedoo," I essayed.

"Not bad," she smiled. *"Petu* are very powerful animals. Like us, they have the strength of culture supported on a bed of instinct. Like us, they tell each other stories. It is said they never forget anything they are exposed to. 'Memory of a *petu*' we say about someone who remembers all the details of their days."

We dismounted and walked toward the pond. One of the elephants raised its tusked head to regard us, and a moment later the others all raised their eyes in turn. "I hear no language. Do they sign?" I asked.

"No," said Jia, eyes on the beasts. "We cannot hear their speech. It is too low. Besides, they never say anything of much interest to people. Even when translated their expressions are...difficult to put in the appropriate context."

"What do they talk about?"

She shrugged. "Beast things. Where to find water, what the weather smells like, who has died and need be honored with a dance. Nothing to shake the galaxy."

We arrived at the edge of the pond, our bare toes lapped by the ripples caused by the animals on the opposite shore. The elephants had resumed bathing playfully, the younger ones bleating like horns through their long noses. I jumped the first time they sounded. "Jia, I've been wondering about something. If there were such intelligent things as little people and elephants at the Solar star, why did human beings inherit space?"

Jia looked at me. "Why, that's quite a question!"

"Forgive me," I said. "Many of my questions tend to be...broad."

She turned to the cavorting elephants again. "The first thing you have to understand, Simon, is that elephants and little people weren't nearly so clever when they lived with us on the First Earth. They underwent generations of selective breeding, especially during the Ark Time."

"What is the Ark Time?"

"The time Solar life spent travelling through normal space, from Sol to Eridani aboard three great arks. It was during the Ark Time that the little people rose up in rebellion and demanded their rights as thinking things. They cursed their name as beasts and called themselves *little people.*"

"What did they used to be called?"

"Shim-ba-tzie," she pronounced with effort. "It's a very old word," she explained. "I think it might be Late Hengrishe or Ancient Marsgo."

"Did the elephants have their own rebellion, too?"

Jia shook her head. "They want no place in society." She touched my shoulder. "They do not *crave* the way men do, for something greater. Even the Pegasi understand this, though they had barely discovered spaceflight when we came down upon their world to introduce our civilization. Even the Pegasi are unique in their biosphere, for eating rather than being eaten."

"That's what Captain Gold said," I told her; "that we are predators."

"Predators *and* dreamers," she corrected. "The former alone is merely bloodlust; the latter, bovine."

"Corinthia Tag told me that at the Old Star true wisdom only came in the years of change between regimes, in the cracks between Imperial Mars and Mother Ares, in the schism between control and indulgence."

"Corinthia who?"

"Nobody," I said. "Just a tourist."

"She speaks of balance and change," continued Jia; "both essential forces for peace. Change without balance is violent, as balance without change is stagnant. This is understood in this ancient symbol," she said, withdrawing the end of a necklace from beneath her shift. It carried a pendant that winked in the orange sun, depicting two interlocked droplets of metal liquid curved into a disc, each bearing a circle of the opposite's lustre in its midst.

"Imperial Mars and Mother Ares," I said.

"Yinyang," Jia named it. "It is a symbol, an idea, and a way."

"It's beautiful."

She looked up at me significantly. We were standing quite close together now, the pendant still dangling in my fingers, my knuckles brushing her breastbone. "It is also a symbol for the union between men and women in love," she said.

"Beautiful..." I said again.

Our kiss was somewhat different than those I had shared with Corinthia, and grossly different from the kissless intimacy Glory had shown me. Whether it sounds nonsensical or not, I confess to you that the kiss between Jia and I felt more like a *place* than an *event* – an amorphous womb of warm connection in which we could bask timelessly.

When we returned to the house we found Jeremiah and Pish waiting for us, Pish waving brightly and calling out as we approached. I dropped off my horse heavily, stumbling upright and grinning. "Pish!" I pulled him into a hug. "What have you been doing with yourself?"

"Oh, I don't know," said Pish, scraping one shoe with the other. "Not much. This place is kinda boring."

"You'll start school soon enough," promised Jia, walking up beside us as the little people led our horses to the stables. "That will be loads of fun, I'm sure. Wen and Jissa simply *adore* being at school!"

Pish looked suspicious. "Would I have to sleep there?"

"Well naturally," smiled Jia encouragingly; "all children stay at their schools during the term, and then we all come together again as a family for the holidays and winter vacations."

Pish's expression became more somber. He reached out blindly behind him and caught Jeremiah's arm. "But Jeremiah could come, right?"

Jia shook her head. "I'm sorry, Pish, but robots aren't allowed at school. In fact," she added, glancing at me nervously, "it isn't quite proper to keep them in the home, either."

Pish looked severe. "Well!" I interrupted jovially. "Let's chat about school later. If we need some diversion now why don't we take an orb to the city and see the festival?"

"I *had* planned a dinner for us..." Jia trailed off, whispering into my ear.

"Can it stand a delay?" I asked, taking her hand. "The child deserves some amusement. He's been through a lot."

She seemed nonplussed but squeezed my hand back reassuringly. "Okay, Simon."

And so Pish and I rode the roller coaster together – a short train of open cars that flew around a filament of suspended light, twisting and curling in nausea-inviting loops across a kilometre of air. Pish screamed and so did I. As we rounded a wide bend I caught sight of Jeremiah watching anxiously from below, his padded hand raised to shield Nsomeka's ruddy glare from his black eyes. In another instant he was lost to my vision as we plunged down the next grade, our stomachs leaping to our gorges.

We bought candy floss and saw a performance in which actors in elaborate masques pantomimed a lurid drama of killings, romance and revenge in time to chilling, droning music punctuated by the clash of cymbals.

Pushing through the crowd afterward I spotted a tall, striped pavilion bearing a flashing multilingual sign that said in Common Verbal: *Ladies' Sumo Basho*. "Hey," I said, catching Jia's elbow. "Don't we sponsor that event?"

Jia crinkled her nose. "Well, yes."

Indeed as we drew nearer I spotted the interlocked triangle crest of Fellcorp billowing on a flag that changed colours with the direction of the wind. We stood in line to pay for our tickets but the grinning man at the booth waved my wallet away. "Mr. Fell –

you know your money's no good here!" he beamed, gesturing us inside the tent. "Salutations, Madam Fell!"

Shortly after we found our seats in the crowded stands surrounding a sandy ring we were approached by two stalky men in black sweaters bearing the corporate shield. "Mr. Fell, is Commander P. with you?"

"Commander P.? Oh, you mean *Omar*," I replied. "No, he's not with us."

The stalky men exchanged looks. "We'd best sit with you then, sir, if you don't mind."

"Is that really necessary? Am I in some kind of danger?"

"Better safe than sorry sir," they claimed, vacating two nearby seats with a flash of their plates. The patrons stood up and moved along the row so the two security men could sit down. I saw their necks working as they muttered subvocally into their telephones.

A man in scarlet robes entered the ring and the audience hushed. He made a long speech in what I assume was Soshi, and then translated his introduction of the two first contenders: "From the jungle dark of Mahuea – weighing in at two hundred and twenty kilograms – *Rutanna Massimer!*" The crowd cheered. "And from the Nanedi's cool shores – weighing in at two hundred fifteen – past champion of the Ninurtan belt – *Hilla Ved Tush!*" The crowd exploded into a paroxysm of applause and spittle-flying cheering.

Two loincloth-clad women the size of baby elephants walked up to opposite sides of the ring, stepping gingerly over the short barrier and then padding across the sand to face one another. They planted their feet wide, their tree-like thighs quivering with the impact. Hard eyes stared down one another from within doughy faces, their locks tied back into small buns atop their round heads.

The man in scarlet gave a loud cry, and then stood back.

Both women bowed. Rutanna Massimer, a barrel of dark, folded flesh with stripes of blue painted across her shoulders and back, reached down to her side and picked up a handful of salt from a shallow dish. She brushed the crystals between her hands and cast the remnants out across the ring, then resumed her wide-footed pose hunkering over the centre.

Hilla Ved Tush, a golden-skinned whale, flexed her neck menacingly back and forth, her pendulous breasts jiggling in slow rhythm. Then she too reached for a handful of salt, and cast it across the ring.

Another moment passed. I scooched to the edge of my seat, eyes wide in anticipation. The opponents held each other's gaze, frozen.

And then suddenly they were at each other, clashing in a heaving mound of slapping flesh and grunts. With amazing speed they separated and then re-engaged, Hilla straining to grab the belt of Rutanna's loincloth across her broad back. Rutanna bucked without warning, casting Hilla's enormous weight over onto the sand with a loud boom and a cloud of dust. The audience shrieked and stamped their feet.

There was another flurry of movement from the ring, and then Hilla gained a grip on Rutanna's belt and hoisted her into the air, her face purpling with the effort. She held her opponent suspended for a brief second and then cast her across the ring like a sack of potatoes. The crowd hooted and the men in scarlet rushed out into the ring, gesturing to Hilla who raised her meaty arms over her head in triumph.

Rutanna recovered herself with an effort, and bowed low. Hilla bowed in turn and both fighters left the ring. "That was *so cool!*" crooned Pish.

Over the next two hours we were witness to titanic clash after clash, the mad frenzy of the wrestling heightened by the suspense created in the moments before they engaged as the opponents stared each other down and cast salt into the ring ceremoniously. Some matches were over in seconds, but several lasted almost as long as two minutes. By the time the event closed for the day we had seen two dozen unspeakably massive women hit the sand in defeat, lying in the shadows of the equally giant victors. Every bout ended in polite bows, though it was possible to see flashes of naked hatred flicker across the eyes of the bested on the magnified holographic projection shining above the ring.

By the time we returned home Pish had fallen asleep, and Jeremiah had to carry him up to bed. Jia and I retired to the dining hall to sup. Tonight the room was lit by candles, and the table had somehow been shrunk to accommodate just two people at an intimate distance. She said, "You know, it was amazing today watching you watch Pish."

"What do you mean?" I asked, moving my elbow as a little person placed a tray of food on the table.

"I've never seen you like that before...so enraptured by the boy's happiness."

"Surely you must have seen me fawn over our own children," I pointed out.

"Well, yes," she said hastily. "Naturally I meant to say I haven't seen that look on your face for *years*." She winced, then.

"What's wrong?" I asked.

"Just a little headache," she said, closing her eyes briefly and waving dismissively. "I probably just need to eat something, dear."

The meal was exquisite: broiled woodfruit-glaze ham, spiced grasses, polyander cakes, and a wonderfully sour soup called *fen* with little bits of shaved carrot floating in it. The pink wine was too tart for my tastes, and I accidentally started drinking from the washbowl before dessert, but otherwise things went very smoothly.

We talked mostly about Maja, which Jia clearly felt was on par with paradise. "The Majan tradition already dominates this Joviat," she told me earnestly. "And every world around Ninurta is half-way Majan, too. It makes me very proud."

"You're of Maja origin, then?" I hesitated a moment. "And while we're at it, where am I from, exactly? Do I have parents?"

"No, I was not born on Maja," she said quickly; "and I'm afraid neither of your parents are still with us, dear. Your father died quite a number of years ago, but we only lost your mother recently. She was really far too young. But there's only so much medical science can do."

"Oh. I see," I said, playing with my pie. "...So it's your adopted homeland, then?" I looked up, hopeful to restore the original subject.

"Oh, yes," beamed Jia. "I've adopted Maja, or Maja adopted me, when we married. And you've always regretted not spending enough time back here, where you grew up, so I thought – well, when I heard about your...accident – I thought *this* would be the house you'd want to come home to."

"I think," I said after a considered pause, "that any house would have done fine as long as you were there." Then I flushed, suddenly embarrassed. "That was a dumb thing to say," I mumbled. "I sound like I'm trying to seduce you."

Jia sniffed, her small mouth drawn into a tight smile. "In Soshi," she said, taking her napkin off her lap, "we call seduction *suma*."

"*Suma*," I echoed. "Did I pronounce it right?"

Jia stood up from the table, and smoothed down her shift with her hands. "Yes," she said.

Many hours later, when I got up in the night to go pee, I fished my diary out of my clothes and dictated these events as I sat on the tiled floor of the wash-hall, surrounded by lizards, my voice occasionally rising to a whisper that echoed off the hard walls.

There's no place like home.

XXV.
I HATE MOONDAYS

I awoke in a new place, but did not regret the inconsistency. Before I opened my eyes I dreamed half sleeping of Jia's scent on the pillow beside me. When I looked all I could see was the play of shadows from leaf-dappled light swaying on the white ceiling above the bed.

Jia said, "Goodmorning, dear."

I rolled over but she was not there. Instead she was standing over the bed dressed in a yellow wrap, her braids done up in a new elaborate set of rings atop her head. She was smiling and holding a cup of steaming tea.

I sat up and accepted the tea. "Goodmorning, and thank you."

We kissed briefly. "You'd best get a move on, Simon. Omar is downstairs, ready to escort you."

"Escort me? Where?" I rubbed my eyes and sipped my tea.

"It's Moonday, dear," chuckled Jia, touching my cheek. "You've got to go to work."

"To work?" I echoed, like an idiot.

"Well, of course, dear. Everyone's been very worried about you, and therefore worried about Fellcorp. It's really quite urgent that you put in an appearance as soon as possible."

"Um, okay," I agreed, uncertain. I looked around for my robes.

"I've already picked out a suit for you, a very nice cut from Reneti."

My face fell. "A suit?"

"Don't worry darling, it'll all be over in a few hours and then tonight you and I can go to the ball at Blighton's. It'll be marvellous, you'll see!" She patted my knees reassuringly, gestured to pile of folded fabric on a chair, and then swept out of the master bedroom.

A lizard scampered across the bed. "Oh, boy," I muttered.

Throughout the orb-flight into Padirac I pulled and shimmied against my clinging apparel, fighting the urge to tear the wretched layers from my body while hooting like a little person. Omar seemed to find my discomfort amusing. "Going to fire your tailor, sir?" he joked.

"I'll get used to it," I murmured bravely, scratching the inside of my thigh with a grimace.

We landed among stone sculptures with hideous visages, standing in frozen guard over the rooftop of a high skyscraper. As soon as the shield cracked off a fierce, crisp wind washed in at us. Omar led me briskly between two sets of hedges cut into the shape of swans and into the mouth of a lift, and I admit that I found it difficult to keep up with him due to the aching along the insides of my legs where I had pushed them together to keep my balance atop the horse yesterday. With a scowl I limped into the lift beside Omar. The doors yawned closed after us. "Fellcorp executive offices," rumbled Omar.

"Plates, please," said the lift. Omar already had his plate out, and he tapped it against a contact on the wall. I did the same. "Omar Palmellinbacchutourtanjard, Nestor S. Fell: welcome to Fellcorp," pronounced the lift, followed by a smooth acceleration downward.

The doors split again to reveal a grandiose, sun-splashed lobby two stories high, men and women in suits hurrying back and forth and up and down the stairs, popping in and out of the mouths of corridors around the upper level balcony, squeezing past Omar into the lift and looking at me with expressions of shocked recognition. I heard my name whispered all around me as the frenetic motion slowed.

By the time we had crossed halfway to the round glass desk at reception every eye in the room was trying to skim over me nonchalantly. People who had been taking the stairs two at a time suddenly found a reason to linger on the landing, holding a plate out vaguely to a co-worker who wasn't looking. "It's Nestor Fell!"

The plump girl at the reception desk smiled warmly, rocking back on her heels with an anxious energy as we stopped at the desk and Omar placed his giant hands upon the counter. "Fellcorp Security, miss – I'm here to take Mr. Fell for his nine thirty with Mr. Olorio."

"Great," squeaked the girl, her dimples colouring. "Mr. Olorio's left word that you're to go right on in, sir, Mr. Fell."

"Thank you, miss," I said, and she smiled as she looked down to hide behind her hair.

The crowd parted in a polite wave of "Goodmorning, Mr. Fell," as Omar saw me up the stairs and onto the second tier. We moved briskly down a branching corridor where we were met with more shocked glances, finally stopping before a wide door being opened by a slender gentleman with skin so black it was almost purple. With a pompous air he declared that Mr. Olorio would see us right away.

We stepped past him into a corner office. Tall windows dominated two walls, looking out upon the metropolis of Padirac, but the view was dominated by the large silhouette of a man with his hands clasped behind his back, watching the traffic fly by. The door clicked closed behind me. I turned around to see that Omar had gone, and when I turned back the man was facing me.

"Do sit down," he said, his voice light for someone so large. He emerged from behind his desk and took one of two high-backed leather chairs, indicating the second for me.

I sat down. Before I could speak he pinned me with his nearly invisible, slit-like eyes and flashed me a wide, toothy smile. "My name is Yatti Olorio," he continued in a funny, sing-song way. "I'm the chief financial officer and the acting chief of operations for this company and I've been your best friend for ten years." He put forward a thick, peachy hand. "It is a pleasure to meet you..."

"Simon," I said, taking his hand and shaking it firmly. "My name is Simon. And you're the first person from my past to acknowledge my independence from the man you have known."

He chuckled and passed his stubby fingers over his few wisps of hair. "History is mutable, my friend, and so am I. If you feel like a man named Simon now, who am I to dissuade you? I have confidence that the things that have made you my friend and ally this past decade will not have changed." He sniffed thoughtfully. "...Much."

Though I have tried through my life to be open minded about the people I meet, I will admit to you now that I fought a physical kind of revulsion as I smiled back at my apparent friend, Yatti Olorio. Can a man smell bad without stinking? There was something about his dimpling double chin, his enthusiastic hand gestures as he spoke in his ginger, lilting way – something that made me lose my appetite.

"Naturally," he continued airily, "the board had elected to keep your amnesia mum until that Mile fool started turning up in all the feeds. Now we have an office dedicated to sorting out the malarkey, issuing lawsuits, syndicating correcting statements, that sort of thing. To that end I'd like you to consent to recording a brief message to the corporation, for morale."

"Okay," I said. "Say, we're not going to sue Mr. Mile, are we?"

"Mr. Swinny will give you your script," said Olorio, clearing his throat. "In answer to your question, no, Mr. Mile is impoverished and we have no interest in acquiring his assets – particularly," he added with a raised eyebrow, "as Fellcorp seems to have purchased the lion's share of what little there is."

"Ah yes," I replied, nodding. After a pause I asked, "What's a lion?"
Olorio sniffed. "Big cat. Now –"
"Like a tiger?"

"Um, yes," he conceded with a frown. "Now Simon, the next order of business will be your education. I've lined up a top notch team of the finest tutors to come to your home to offer you a crash course in...well, everything. You can't very well run Fellcorp on a few month's life experience, now can you?"

"I suppose not," I admitted.

He ticked off the points on his stubby fingers: "Interstellar and Intrastellar

Economics, Business and Finance, Chemical Rhetoric, Bioevological Calculus, History of Medicine –"

"Hold on," I begged, holding up a hand. "Please, can we start with the basics?"

"Principles of Management?"

"No," I shook my head. "No, not at all. I mean like *what does this corporation do?"* I gazed at Olorio, imploring him for clarity.

Olorio blinked, and his eyes quivered as if he were going to cry. Then he burst out laughing, holding his shaking stomach and leaning back in his chair, which creaked ominously. "Ho ho ha! Has nobody thought to tell you anything? By fire!"

I waited patiently.

"My friend, Simon – Fellcorp is the galaxy's largest producer and distributor of pharmaceuticals. You ask me what business we're in? We're in the business of saving lives." He held my eye levelly for a moment, every trace of his humour gone. "Research and development," he orated, again using his fingers as markers, "testing and compliance, packaging and shipping – we're a stem to stern enterprise, from theory to patient."

I turned my head at his gesture and for the first time took in some of the holographs hung along the walls between the tall windows: white hospitals, pills in soft-focus, people who looked like animated corpses shaking hands with Olorio. "We make medicine?"

"That's right," Olorio confirmed liltingly. "Over eighty percent of the victims affected by the Kamari Horror are medicated by our products, including our newest family of anti-psychotics, designed from the start to address Horror-specific symptomologies."

"Is that a fact?"

An intercom chimed. "Your ten o'clock is here, Mr. Olorio."

"Early? Damn it. Alright." He stood up. "Simon, we have a lot more to talk about but we have a full day. First I need you to go with Mr. Swinny here," he pointed as the door to the corridor opened and a little person with greying hair and an adorable little brown suit stepped in; "and he'll help you take care of that corporate message we discussed. Then Omar will bring you to the boardroom for a report from the department heads. Very good?"

"Er," I said.

"Splendid!" he pronounced, sweeping out the door past Mr. Swinny and disappearing. I heard him greet someone jovially outside the office.

Mr. Swinny raised his long arms and flexed his fingers in a meaningful way, tapping one hand to the side of his mouth. He waited expectantly. "I'm sorry," I said, standing up. "I can't sign." I made the sign for *I understand* and then shook my head vigourously *no*.

Mr. Swimmy frowned, his thick lips pursed over his large teeth. He seemed to decide something, and then pointed to me and gestured broadly at a second doorway leading from Olorio's office. Then he put his fingers in his palm and made them walk like little legs.

"Oooh!" I exclaimed. "Alright, I'm with you. Let's go."

The little person distinctly rolled his brown eyes at me as he turned around and began huffing out the door, his knuckles on the rug. I walked after him. We passed through the same corridor I had come down with Omar, and then entered a set of swinging double doors into a windowless studio.

A dais stood surrounded by a mesh of filaments, flashing consoles manned by busy people around the periphery. A portly fellow with yellowish skin trotted over and introduced himself as Neffer Shing. "It's a real honor to finally meet you in person, Mr. Fell. I've been handling your recordings for years, of course. Tap your plate here to grab the text of your speech, won't you? Thank you. Please, step up onto the dais, sir."

I allowed the cheerful fellow to position me on the round platform as I glanced down at the text that had appeared on the transparent face of my data-plate. "This is what

I'm supposed to say?"

"Yessir," said Shing, nodding courteously to Mr. Swinny who glowered in the corner, picking something out of the hair on his wrist. Shing called to one of the technicians to make it a "bust shot" so no one could see the plate in my hand. "Mr. Fell," he called, "Mr. Olorio felt it may make things easier if you watched one of your previous messages to the company."

I nodded, and he pointed to a clear space at the end of the room. I appeared there a moment later, dressed neatly in a grey suit, my hair longer and styled differently. The holographic me cleared his throat. *"Ladies and gentlemen of Fellcorp, Goodmorning. As you know by now the ratification of the Kissock Relief Accord has opened up a new markets for us at Cassiopeia, a momentous opportunity for all of our divisions..."*

It was strange to see myself – so serious, so knowledgeable, so firm. My speech was crisp and hard-edged, unapologetic and succinct. When all was said and done I felt like I had been lectured by Dr. Pent. I glanced down at the text again. "Okay, I think I have it." I cleared my throat.

A bank of lights illuminated, and I squinted. Shing orchestrated his technicians and then pointed to me with a silent nod.

I cleared my throat again, and felt suddenly somewhat unsteady. I mastered myself with an effort and began: "Ladies and gentlemen of Fellcorp, Goodmorning. As you can see, rumours of my demise have been greatly exaggerated, pause for laughter...oh," I stopped, flushing. "Sorry."

"No worries Mr. Fell, we'll edit that out – just keep going," called Shing.

"Ahem. It is true that I suffered a minor accident while abroad, but the efficient professionals at Fellcorp's own Samundra General Hospital were there to see me through to health. I would like to take a moment to commend the work of the entire staff at Samundra General, particularly Dr. Pol Rettikitan in whose care I mended. Good show, everyone. You do Fellcorp proud.

"I would like to assure all of you that I am back at the helm of Fellcorp, steering the galaxy to a healthier tomorrow. While my colleague and friend Mr. Yatti Olorio will continue as interim chief of operations and chairman of the board until my recovery is complete, I want you to understand that I have in him only the utmost confidence. Treat his word as you would mine.

"What happened to me at Aino makes me living proof of what we've always known here at Fellcorp: we – save – *lives*. Thank you." I blinked and looked up.

The technicians all stood up and joined Mr. Shing in applauding me exuberantly, their faces pinioned in expressions of fixed rapture. I found it discomfiting, as if I were the object of some kind of joke that was over my head. I smiled awkwardly, and then bowed out of respect for their display. When I straightened they continued to clap, which made me feel even more embarrassed.

"Um," I said, and they all stopped.

"That was really special," Shing said, motioning me off the dais. "To record a Nestor Fell message in our very own studio!" He paused, then added thoughtfully, "My kids might even respect me."

"This isn't where the recordings are normally made?"

"Oh, no, sir, you're a very busy man – always on the move, Mr. Fell." Shing smiled broadly and sort of bounced in place. "I guess I should let you go now, sir. I just wanted to say how great it's been."

It was all too much. I was starting to feel very ridiculous.

"Uh," I said, shaking his hand quickly. "Thank you very much for everything, Mr. Shing."

Mr. Swinny headed for the doors, casting an eye back at me impatiently. He pointed to me, pointed to the exit, and then made the little walking motion in his palm again. I obediently followed the grey-haired little person out into the maze of corridors. We took a lift down two floors and then met Omar. Mr. Swinny seemed quite relieved to release his charge, and skipped away with his hands fluttering before him. "Hey!" Omar growled. "Where do you get off calling Mr. Fell *stupid?*"

Mr. Swinny turned back, eyes wide in alarm, and then he hurried to disappear around a bend in the corridor. Omar turned back to me and apologized for the ape's rudeness.

"Language barriers can be frustrating," I pointed out.

"How's it coming with the Soshi, sir?"

"Well," I said, noncommitally.

While it was true that since yesterday my store of Soshi had increased exponentially, unfortunately due to the nature of my lessons almost none of what I had learned could be uttered in mixed company. My specialized education had left me in the unusual position of being able to confidently pronounce the Soshi word for *labia majora* but leaving me utterly unequipped to say *hello*.

Omar marched me into a large, oval boardroom filled by men and women (and a few more little people) in suits, rigid smiles affixed to their faces as they expressed their delight in my return. As I shook hands with them in turn it became increasingly clear that most of them had never met me in person before.

Somebody asked me for something called an "autograph" and then Yatti Olorio swept out of the crowd and put his chunky arm around me, steering me over to the head of a great oval table and introducing me to a high-backed chair that looked like a kind of leather throne. "How are you making out?" he whispered into my ear with uncomfortably hot breath.

"It's all a bit much, actually," I whispered back.

"Splendid," he said, eyes elsewhere.

And then I endured hour upon hour of presentations from nervous ninnies in shining, fine-cut fabrics who prattled and mumbled and quoted, pointing to holographic bar charts and pie graphs that appeared in miniature displayed on our plates, or narrating over recorded imagery of our laboratories, production facilities and distribution centres. The whole thing finally wrapped up with a lurid recording of front line employees in starched white uniforms bearing the corporate crest smiling and waving while shouting, *"I believe in Fellcorp!"* over an anthem that I think I recognized from the background of a nature documentary about crocodiles.

The lights came back up and I was applauded again for some reason.

I realized they were all looking at me expectantly so I stood up. "Well," I said, "I can certainly see that everything has been in good hands." Then I winced as this was met with another roar of clapping.

Olorio stood up beside me. "I can feel the syngery in this room," he claimed, "and it *excites me*." More applause. "Thank you everyone for giving Mr. Fell your time today."

The boardroom began to empty. I looked around for Omar but it was the diminutive Mr. Swinny who caught my elbow, gesturing at the door. I followed him wordlessly outside, back into the lift, and down another hall. At a tall mahogany door he wiggled his fingers at me meaningfully and then stalked off. "So, I'm to wait in here, am I?" I called, but he only grunted in reply.

The door bore a line of polished metal lettering: *Nestor S. Fell, President.*

I opened it and stepped inside a wide corner office, much like Olorio's but finished in panelling of a rich, auburn wood. I wandered into the middle of the carpet, taking in the expansive but uncluttered desk, the holographs on the wall, the bits of sculpture and pottery sitting on inset pedestals in the panelling....

Feeling suddenly drained I walked over behind the desk and collapsed with a gratified sigh into the high-backed, soft chair, my limp arms hanging over the padded rests.

I closed my eyes and let out a long exhale, using my feet to pulled the wheeled chair in closer to the desk.

My knees bumped into something that squeaked, "Oh!"

Startled, I pushed the chair back quickly, flattening myself against the back of the chair in order to see beneath the wooden lip of the desk. The round-faced red-haired girl from the reception desk was down there on her hands and knees, looking up at me with wide eyes. "Goodness me!" I yelped. "I'm terribly sorry!"

She smacked her head on the underside of the desk and winced. "Oh Mr. Fell!" she cried. "I'm so sorry!"

"Did you – did you *drop something* under there?"

She grimaced ruefully as she rubbed her head and started to crawl out between my legs. "Um, oh – yes, I must have," she muttered.

"I'm sorry!" I repeated, pushing the chair back against the windows and moving my knees to one side. I took her hand and helped her to her feet. "Did you find it?"

"I just thought that you –" she started, and then laughed nervously as she stood up. "No, I don't think so. Oh, well. It was only...a...nothing important."

I ducked my head beneath the desk helpfully. "I don't see anything down here."

"Can I offer you a back massage?" she asked, putting her fingers to my neck and applying pressure to my most tense ropes of muscle.

"Ah, no thank you," I replied, smacking the crown of my head on the lip of the desk in my haste to straighten. I turned around quickly and the poor girl lost her balance, tumbling over the back of my chair and ending up on the floor, her legs splayed across my chest and her skirt falling up over her pelvis. "I'm sorry!" I cried, averting my eyes from her pink underwear.

When I helped her to her feet her face had become the same shade of pink. "Omigod please don't fire me," she implored, her eyes welling with tears.

"What?" I said, and she fled the office.

I stood there watching the open door for a long moment, winded and bemused. I walked over to push the door shut, noticing for the first time the sculpture of a proud, dangerous-looking bird on a pillar in the back corner of the office. I cannot explain why, but it filled me with a sense of familiarity and dread. A film of sweat broke out across my brow as I quivered there, transfixed by the lifeless eyes of the stone bird.

It was like a colourless version of the bird that had awoken me with its eerily human screams that morning weeks ago on Samundra. Now as then the bird seemed to have a meaning I could not quite grasp...

But it made me afraid.

The door opened and Omar appeared. "Ready to go home, Mr. Fell?"

"Yes!"

During the orb ride back to the estate Omar apologized for making me wait, explaining that he had been obliged to deal with a security situation in the street-level lobby. "Some crazy woman was trying to force her way in to see you," he said. "Don't look too shocked, Mr. Fell – it was bound to happen. With Mr. Olorio's strategic leaks of your message this morning I'm sure all of Maja knows you're back by now."

"What did she want?" I asked, watching a horse-farm pass beneath us, great quadrupeds massing like ants along the fields.

Omar shrugged. "Man, who can say? She probably wanted to propose to you." He chuckled. "Some women will go to crazy lengths to get near a famous man they think they have some kind of connection with, for whatever reason."

Jia was there to greet me in the hall. "Dear, you look exhausted!" she said soothingly, taking my jacket. "And after only half a day! Can I have some lunch fixed for you?"

"I think I'd like to lie down for a while, actually."

She nodded primly. "Quite right, dear. You'll want to be in top form for Blighton's ball tonight. You did remember, didn't you?"

She put me to bed with a cup of hot drink she claimed would help me rest. She whistled at the windows in a curious way and they opacified, fading the room into a somber gloom. Jia sat on the edge of the bed and kissed my forehead.

"Thank you, Jia," I murmured.

"Is there anything I can get you?"

"Yes," I said, nodding sleepily. "My diary. Will you fetch my diary? It's in the pouch of yesterday's robes."

She passed it to me and then slipped out. I lay back on the bed and stared at the dim ceiling, the little plastic bauble clutched in my right hand. I thumbed the contact and began to dictate the events of the day so far: a day that had overloaded me with information, filled me with questions, cowed me into a kind of paralyzed submission...

I hesitate to wonder: what next?

XXVI.
LIONS & TIGERS & BEARS

Not for the first time, I felt the fool.

This time, however, it was not my fault: I was dressed as an elephant. I peered through the almond-shaped eyeholes of my masque into the mirror, appreciating how Jia's application of grey paint helped to blend my skin with the stylized visage of the long-nosed, wide-eared beast. The lower half of my face was exposed, and she was tickling my chin by painting it grey.

I looked over at Pish, who also seemed nonplussed. He was rubbing the white paint off his lips with a sneer, steadfastly refusing to catch a glimpse in the mirror of himself as a mouse. His whiskers twitched fretfully.

I couldn't help but smile when I looked at Jeremiah, though. After breaking up a terse argument between Jia and Pish we had decided that Jeremiah would indeed accompany us to be the ball, on condition that he wear a costume like everybody else. Jeremiah had not commented on this, but I knew he was not enjoying standing attired as he was, disguised as a reading lamp.

"There!" declared Jia, pulling away from me and squinting at her job. "You're the perfect petu, Simon."

Jia was a peacock, sporting a wide fan of glittering purple plumage in behind, and on her face a long, elegant beak framed by arcs of feathers around the eyeholes. With a final appraising look she laughed delightedly, used my plate to capture a holograph, and then herded us all downstairs and outside where Omar stood in his usual black woolen sweater watching two little people unfold an orb platform for us.

When the last panel snapped into place I caught the eye of one of the little people and wiggled my fingers at him purposefully, squinting with concentration as I attempted to mimic a series of signs I had observed Mr. Swinny this morning. The little person did not seem impressed.

"Why did you sign that, sir?" asked Omar with a curious frown as the little people stomped away.

"What do you mean?"

"You just compared him to dung."

"I thought it meant *thank you*," I mumbled, aghast. "Bloody Mr. Swinny!"

As our orb flew over the flower-like treetops the sun sunk toward the horizon, turning deep orange and then bloody as it melted behind the hills. The cloudless sky took on bruised purple glow. We moved away from the city, deeper into the countryside, soon coming upon an expansive estate of gardens, topiary labyrinths, fountains and pools. As we neared the main house we spotted dozens of orbs jockeying for position by the front terrace like a froth of bubbles, their long twilight shadows playing like fingers across the lawn.

We descended into the scrum and the shield winked off for just a few seconds as we scrambled down to the flagstones. Omar nodded and engaged the orb again, joining a roiling surge of upward traffic attempting to vacate the curb to let others land. Jia led us through the press of ornate costumes and startling masques, toward the columned front entrance from which issued the sounds of talk and music, breaking glasses and laughter.

We were accosted by a lion.

"Yatti!" cried Jia delightedly. "How *are* you?"

"Now now, madam," warned the large, lion-masqued man with a friendly chuckle and a toss of his mane. "We're supposed to be in disguise now, aren't we? How do you like it, Mr. Elephant? This is the big cat I was mentioning this morning."

"Yes, I looked it up," I said. "Quite fierce, Mr. Lion."

"Thank you, thank you," beamed Yatti, scanning the rest of our party. "And who do we have here?"

"I'm Pish!" said Pish.

Yatti froze, his lower lip hanging slack for a moment. "Indeed," he stammered, then added more smoothly, "and where do you come from, Mr. Mouse?"

"We're adopting him," I answered. "Pish is an orphan from Samundra."

"That's wonderful, lovely to see you – I really must go," Yatti muttered quickly, touching Madam Fell on the shoulder in a friendly if hasty way as he sidled into a gap in the milling crowd of masques and vanished, waving as if he'd spotted a friend on the other side of the columns.

"Oh!" said Jia.

"Does Yatti not care for children?" I wondered. "How is he with our kids?"

"Let's get inside," suggested Jia, taking my arm and leading me. I turned to see Jeremiah escorting Pish behind us, his shade pushed askew by the antlers of a brown-snouted man. We managed our way up the steps into a large and gaily decorated foyer populated by chimeras of all kinds, from giraffes to beetles. A woman dressed as a seagull escorted Pish the mouse to the children's playroom, Jeremiah the lamp trailing behind. Jia carted me into a salon and began squealing with delight as she recognized her friends, flitting from costumed couple to costumed couple like a hummingbird after nectar, her tail plumage wagging behind. "Why don't you get us some drinks, Mr. Elephant, dear?" she suggested.

"Certainly, Madam Peacock."

I picked my way through the laughing beasts, ducking gesturing arms and sloshing drinks as the guests cavorted and played. I passed by a band of musicians with shiny brass instruments, and then cut through a ballroom where couples were dancing in a frenetic way to a grinding, rhythmic tune that pounded through the halls. Coloured lights flashed, revealing glimpses of foxes, horses, and dogs reared up upon their hind-legs, smoking cigarimemes and throwing back cups of punch.

I found a long buffet of punchbowls and glasses, and was selecting a flavor when a pair of hands clapped themselves over my eyes. "Guess who," whispered a soft voice in my ear.

"Jia?"

I was released. A tiger wound around to the front of me, playing at grooming herself by pretending to lick her paw and then running it along her curves. I saw the smile on her stripe-painted lips as her face was briefly revealed in a wash of blue light. When another spotlight swept over us I saw that the locks of hair escaping from behind her masque were red. "It's you!" I shouted over the music – the plump girl who had banged her head under my desk.

"Hi, Mr. Elephant," she said playfully, touching one of my flapping elephant ears and feeling the material between her fingers. "I was hoping we would get a chance to chat."

"I'm getting my wife a drink," I explained, holding up two cups apologetically and stepping behind a dancing couple. The tiger girl pouted in a maudlin way as I turned around and cut across the dance-floor to escape.

Jia already had a drink when I returned. She wanted to dance. We returned to the ballroom and she was mercifully indulgent as I stepped on her toes. As we turned I looked around for the tiger girl but didn't see her. The music became slower, composed of overlapping keening voices supporting by a syncopated crackle of soft percussion. Jia drew me closer and put her arms around me. "You never used to come to parties," she whispered in my ear. "You never used to dance." She bit my earlobe playfully. "I'm falling in love with you, Simon."

I held her closer. That love was my anchor of certainty in this world, and I cherished it. Hearing her talk about it made my kidneys tickle, and my heart feel cold and hilarious. I was giddy.

We had more drinks, until the room continued to spin a bit even when we broke from dancing. When Jia became caught up in conversation with one Mr. Badger and one Madam Solliroid Mantis I excused myself to seek some fresh air. I crossed the ballroom and steered around the punchbowls, stepping through an open alcove and onto a wide verandah overlooking a swimming pool, lit from beneath.

The night was clear, the sky alive with stars. I breathed deeply. A handful of other guests stood out on the verandah, mostly in clots of two and three, chatting and chuckling, swirling their drinks and making the ice clink against the glass. From the dark beyond the wavering light of the pool came the chirps and cries of life.

I was not entirely surprised to feel fur against my elbow: I had company.

"Miss Tiger," I said.

"Mr. Elephant," she replied. "I knew you'd come eventually."

"To chat?"

"For air."

"Ah."

She took a step back from the rail and emptied her drink before throwing the glass into the swimming pool. "Blighton's got cup-eaters everywhere," she explained.

"No doubt," I said. And then, "Tell me, who is Blighton exactly again?" I tried to sound casual, but failed.

"What's he dressed as, you mean? He's a bear."

"Right. Of course."

The tiger girl squinted at me, putting one paw on her striped hip. "You can't fool me, you know."

"No?"

She paused, and chewed her lip thoughtfully. She crossed her arms over her chest and leaned against the railing. "What's your name, Mr. Elephant?"

"You know who I am," I replied, furrowing my brow. "From...the office."

"Do you want me to call you Mr. Fell, then?"

"I'm sorry?"

"Like at the office?"

"Er, no," I answered, uncertain. "What is it exactly you wanted to chat with me about, Miss Tiger?"

"Please, call me Freddie," she said, touching my arm in a conversational way. "My real name's Utopia but who's going to go around calling themselves *that?*"

She offered her paw to shake, and I shook it. "Simon," I said automatically.

A smile flitted over her painted lips. "It must be weird returning to Fellcorp, eh?"

"Oh, it's good to be back," I told her heartily.

"Are you still feeling any effects from your accident?"

"Er, no. I feel great."

"There have been rumours that you'd lost your memory."

"Yes, I've heard. Nothing to it, of course."

"Of course, Simon." She turned out to face the pool again, her hands folded on the railing before her. Her stripes seemed to swim in the wavering, flicking underwater light. "I guess going through all this must give you a new appreciation of your daughter's disability." She glanced over at me sympathetically.

"Oh – well, I suppose it has..." I stammered, trailing off as I spotted Omar and a thick, brutish fellow in a crimson uniform pushing their way out onto the verandah urgently. "Omar!" I called.

He ran right past me and tackled the tiger. The man in crimson was beside him an instant later, gazing through a plate with handgrips on its sides. "This is her," he pronounced. Omar pulled Miss Tiger to her feet roughly and frisked her efficiently, withdrawing a small device not unlike my own diary.

"There's no feedcasting on the premises. You're going to have to leave," rumbled Omar, taking her by the bicep. He handed the recorder to the man in crimson, who looked at it through his plate and then pocketed it. "Bloody reporters!"

"Nice talking to you, Simon," she called as she was led away.

I stood there for a moment, uncertain what to do with myself. People stopped watching and resumed their conversations. Miss Tiger was a reporter? What had she wanted from me?

"Simon, dear!" called Jia, stepping out onto the verandah and embracing me. "Omar said you'd been cornered by some horrible viper from the media."

"I'm okay," I reported.

"I'm going to take the child – um, and his lamp – home now. Omar will be back to pick you up later, of course."

"Oh, I think I've had enough too, actually."

"Nonsense! Blighton wants to talk to you, dear. He's been looking around for you all night." She patted my shoulder reassuringly and hooked her arm around my elbow, escorting me inside and back across the ballroom. "You should be flattered, dear. Blighton is a person of note."

And so with a twinge of vulnerability I watched Jeremiah turn away with Pish, following Jia and followed by Omar, disappearing into the milling crowd in the foyer. I walked along as I had been propelled, toward a clot of people beneath a chandelier, orbiting a great white bear. He was surrounded by alligators and ludos, roosters and gambs. I even saw Mr. Swinny, costumed as what was unmistakably a human executive. The bear spotted me approaching and the babble died as all masqued eyes swiveled to follow his gaze. "Mr. Elephant!" said the white bear.

"Mr. Bear," I replied with a bow.

"Mr. *Polar* Bear," he corrected kindly, shouldering through his inner circle and putting a broad, shaggy arm around me. "I was hoping you would consent to sit with me a moment, in my study. Dear Jia has told me ever so much about you."

We were already on the stairs, past the velvet ropes watched over by young little people with hard, beady eyes. I followed the hulking form of the polar bear through a set of double doors into a massive study, the stars visible through the many faces of the glass ceiling. The walls were lined with hundreds of individual data plates, as well as odd, paperboard boxes set vertically with phrases along their spines.

The bear stopped in the middle of the study and shrugged off his fur. A wiry, lithe man stepped out of the fat costume, reaching up with ropey, powerful-looking arms to remove his masque and ears. The white bear fell to into a loose pile at the feet of a tall old gentleman in black underclothes. His brow was high before a bowl of white hair, his green eyes wide and sharp. He wore a thin line of white moustaching above his grin. "Nestor S. Fell!" he declared, arms wide.

"Mr. Blighton, I presume," I said.

He shook my hand. "'I presume.' I like the sound of *that*, I can tell you. Yes, I'm Abermund Blighton – your host and friend."

"Have we met before, sir?" I asked him as he swept past me to fix two drinks at a neat bar service.

Blighton shook his head. "Not at all, but even if we had you wouldn't remember, would you? Don't bother to deny it, I've had my girl on you. Miss Tiger?"

"But she was thrown out –"

"An amusing charade," smiled Blighton, passing me a short glass of amber liquid and directing me toward a set of fine chairs; "my glee comes in the details, naturally. That's where the sense of immersion engages: details. Cheers, Nestor!" He sat down and drank.

I sipped my drink politely, pursing my lips at its spice. "My name is Simon," I told him.

"Call me Abe!" he said. "You're probably wondering why I've brought you up here."

"That's true, Abe."

He rubbed his hands together and chuckled gleefully. "I'm interested in your *story*, Simon."

"My story?"

"Yes! You see I am a writer." He pointed to a row of gleaming, inscribed plates along the wall and smirked ruefully. "A rather fabulously successful one, as a point of fact. And it is my habit to collect select stories from the lives of people from all over the galaxy, so that I might populate my works with the stink of life. And I smell something delicious in you and your adventures, Simon, I really do."

"You do, Abe?"

"I do, Simon. For several reasons, several. Not the least of which being the adoption of the Samundran orphan. You don't understand how that sort of thing touches me. It's wonderful. A man in your position, confused and on the lam, with so little to give, sharing his life with a child who had less. You see I've done my research. Just amazing stuff. *Page-forward tabbing stuff* in my not inexperienced opinion. Worth a serious amount of money."

I sat back in my seat and drained my glass. "It is my understanding, Abe, that I already have a fairly serious amount of money. Why should I want for more?"

"Why?" the old man cackled, smoothing down his bowl of white hair with a bony hand. "You've already managed to brighten the life of one needy child. Imagine how it would feel to help a hundred thousand of them. *That's* what wealth is *for* after all." He paused on this point, his green eyes flashing. "Once we have slept and eaten and been watered, isn't it our duty to make things better for those around us if we can, Simon? I think that it is."

He seemed intent on some kind of concrete response at that point, so I said, "Yes."

"Yes!" he crowed, nodding emphatically and striking his open hand against his thigh. "Yes indeed. What is money for if not making things better? Besides," he added with a raised brow, "I have other inducements."

I turned my empty glass over in my fingers. "Inducements?" I echoed. The old man jumped out his chair, snapped the glass out of my hand and walked briskly over to the bar. He filled it, and then sauntered slowly back, his gait slowing with every step. "Do you know what this is?" he asked me.

I shook my head. He took another step, in comical slow motion. And then another. After five more ponderous paces he looked up and winked at me. "Suspense," he said.

Blighton took his seat once more and flipped open the arm of his chair to reveal a narrow groove studded with controls. "Let me show you something, Simon. Watch."

The lamps around the edges of the study winked off and we were plunged into a darkness penetrated only feebly by the starlight through the ceiling. I shifted in my chair, and then winced as a bright orange sphere appeared, floating in the middle of the air above the carpet. I squinted against the glare.

A hovering red label said NSOMEKA (BETA HYDRI).

The sphere began to shrink, slowly at first and then with increasing velocity. A pair of yellow stars blazed into view, seeming to float out of Blighton's desk, converging on the vanishing orange mote of Nsomeka. The view regressed further and other labels came into view: I spotted AINO (DELTA PAVONIS) and CASSIOPEIA (ETA CASSIOPEIA II). In a heartbeat several dozen red labels had converged into a ruddy glow at the centre of the projection, surrounded by a seas of other stars.

"The Neighbourhood," supplied Blighton.

Now it seemed that his study was enveloped in a blizzard, glowing white specks pouring out of the walls and plunging into the shrinking centre. I began to feel dizzy and grabbed the arms of my chair. The red labels of the Neighbourhood became nearly invisible in the flurry. After a moment stars ceased to appear at the fringes of the room, while the collection we already had continued to shrink into a flat, irregular oblong.

"Is that...is that the end of space?" I whispered.

"No, that is the Fluff. It is a branch of the Orion Galactic Arm. Watch."

Indeed as I returned my gaze to the projection I saw our view draw back until several great sweeping arms of stars and cloud could be clearly discerned, enspiraled about a great dome of light at the centre. In another moment the whole of the disc could be seen, shrinking majestically toward the centre of Blighton's study.

"*Via Lactea*," pronounced Blighton heavily. "Our living galaxy."

I shook my head, my mouth dry. "I had no idea space was so vast. I had no idea our pocket of stars was nothing more than a mote. Mother of love."

"The galaxy is not space, Simon. Watch."

A second giant wheel of stars came into view, dwarfing our galaxy. "Andromeda," narrated Blighton. The two spirals and a profusion of smaller glows became motes themselves, dangling off the side of a great blossom of discs and wheels. "Virgo Supercluster," he called. My hands were becoming sweaty, dampening the arms of my chair. The hairs on the back of my neck stood up on end and I found that I could not look away as the supercluster plunged away into the infinity, other blossoms of light fading in through the walls and floor and windows.

"Where does it stop?" I gasped.

"It doesn't," he said. *"Watch."*

The blistering clusters of light that represented so many millions of galaxies were arrayed in long strings, tendrils stretching around lakes of void to come together in blazing hubs. The glittering fibres and shining nodes became smaller and denser until it seemed that Blighton's study was filled with a great iridescent sponge, or the tangled neurones of some monstrous brain.

I closed my eyes against it. *"Enough!"*

When I looked up the warm gold lamplight had been restored and the holographic projection was gone. Blighton snapped closed the arm of his chair, covering the controls. He had a wide, satisfied smile on his face. "Did you sweat?" he asked me tartly.

"Pardon me?"

"Did you perspire, Simon? Did you get gooseflesh? Did you think you'd glimpsed the eye of God?"

"Maybe," I coughed; "I admit that was a bit overwhelming."

"Yes," he agreed. "I couldn't resist, you understand – watching the expression on the face of a man ignorant of space grasping for the first time the true scale of creation."

He closed his eyes and hissed, *"Priceless."*

I walked over to the bar and brought back the bottle of amber liquor, topping up both our glasses. I placed the bottle on the floor by the foot of my chair with a shaking hand. I took a swallow. "You showed me that because you were interested in my reaction?"

"I showed you that in order to cause you to feel," he replied, sipping in turn. "Thank you. Isn't wonder wonderful? It is my profession to transmit it." He leaned forward and locked his eyes on mine. "Such wonders you must have known these past weeks, being new to it all! How I envy you!"

I shifted in my seat, and drank again. I closed my eyes and considered, and then recounted for Abermund Blighton the story of my flight through the forest by the hospital on Samundra, and my night in Pish's treehouse. I told about learning to fly a kite, and all of the stupid questions I asked had Pish ("How does it know to stay up there?" "It doesn't know anything, Simon – it's just a *thing!*"). I stopped before we came to Duncan, and when I opened my eyes again Blighton wore a rapt expression his face. "I was right," he said, nodding. "I was very, very right. Simon, you *must* tell me your adventures, so that we might make a fortune together and cause the galaxy to see through your eyes."

I sighed and opened my mouth, but before I could speak he held up a sharp finger. "I want you to understand how much this means to me. I want to make a show of faith, to demonstrate my trust."

The wiry old gentleman sprang out of his chair and beckoned me to follow him. One of the platecases swung back to reveal an additional section of the room – a long corridor of alcoves, each lit by a small white lamp from above. I caught up with Blighton at the mouth of the corridor, where he took my arm and whispered to me urgently, "I'm sure they've started to turn up already, haven't they? The hungry masses, banging on your door, asking for a favor, a hand-out, a miracle?"

I thought about what Omar had said about the woman in the Fellcorp lobby, and nodded. "Yes."

"Yes," agreed Blighton. "It's the curse of benefaction. As I hinted earlier I myself am deeply involved in granting dreams to those less fortunate, but to avoid being doubly mobbed I make my gifts in disguise."

He sauntered leisurely into the corridor and I followed him. The first alcove was filled by the body of a very fat woman, split down the middle and separated to show a largely hollow interior. "A costume?" I wondered aloud.

"An alias," explained Blighton. "That is Maxine Maxwell, the lovable public face of Maxwell's Teas. It is as Maxine that I dispense miracles to the tea growers on Unkei."

We passed on to another alcove, which contained the split pseudo-body of a brown skinned man with a braided beard. Next came a bisected Annapurnese complete with orange desert dust in his hair, then a slit-eyed crone with white locks and blue tattoos. Blighton was explaining how he enjoyed the freedom of walking among regular people, to choose without interference who was truly most in need.

"March Peebles!" I suddenly cried. "You're March Peebles, aren't you?"

Blighton plucked fussily at his white moustache and smirked, then bowed deeply and theatrically. "You have penetrated my true identity, Simon. I created the legend of March Peebles when I was twenty – I fulfilled it by the time I was forty. Since the Horror I confess that I often lend my missions as Peebles more effort than my writing."

"You are a remarkable figure, sir," I told him.

He laughed. "And so are you, Simon. There is just one thing that bothers me about your story. A certain matter we must clear up, before any kind of sense can be made of your tale."

"What's that?"

Blighton paused before the next alcove, scratching his chin thoughtfully. He bent down and placed his empty glass on the floor, and then raised himself and leaned against the wall. He looked up slowly. "Well you see...I made you up."

I furrowed my brow. "What do you mean?"

He moved back from the alcove, and looked inside. I stepped closer and peered in beside him. Mounted on the rack was another split body, twin halves supported by metal armatures. The expressionless face was mine.

"What –" I stammered, blood roaring in my ears. "I don't understand..."

"I made you up," Blighton said again, looking at me. "When I bought Fellcorp Pharma I figured there should be a *Fell* so I invented you, and used your form to meet the patients so I could Peeble them, if you'll forgive the expression."

"But I – I *run* Fellcorp, don't I?" I argued, dizzy.

"Run it? You barely have anything to do with it. Yatti Olorio runs Fellcorp, Simon."

"So Olorio's your man, is he?" I demanded.

Irritatingly, Blighton chuckled. "Not at all, Mr. Elephant. I sold Fellcorp and all of its assets two years ago. That's why I'm so particularly intrigued to learn that their corporate mascot has somehow acquired...flesh and blood."

I stumbled backward and fell into one of the alcoves, half of a pearl-skinned woman with blonde curls sagging over me. I pushed the thing off of me with a grunt of repulsion, kicking backward out of the alcove and shattering Blighton's glass. I sat there on the floor, stunned and speechless.

Blighton looked down at me consolingly. He untucked a handkerchief from his pocket and offered it to me. "You're bleeding. You have glass in your hand."

"Coitus," I muttered.

A quarter-hour later one of Blighton's little people had sealed the wound with a spray and been dismissed. I sat back in my chair in his study, legs folded, trying to breathe at a steady rate and keep my mind numbed. I tossed back another drink. Blighton sat down opposite me. "I know this isn't easy for you. But I knew if I recognized that your story doesn't end here that surely you must be feeling the same thing."

"I don't know what I feel anymore," I grunted savagely, draining my glass.

"Of course, you have everything," he pointed out playfully. "You have a family and a fortune, a job and a reputation. You could want for nothing, all your days. And yet – you will not be able to leave it be, will you? It won't be able to satisfy you now, will it?"

"No," I whispered. And then I cried, "Why not?"

"Because you deplore deception. Because everything that's pure in this world you've seen tainted by lies. Because you were born with a thirst for answers, and you'll go crazy trying to ignore all the parts that don't make sense." He paused, and examined his fingers. "...Or at least that's the way I've been building your character in the draft. You tell me."

I put my drink down and stood, picking up my discarded elephant masque and tucking it under my arm. "I can't quite bring myself to thank you, Mr. Polar Bear."

Blighton nodded soberly. "What will you do now, Simon?"

"I need to talk to my wife," I told him, striding through the doors. I jogged down the stairs and pushed quickly through the thinning crowd in the foyer. I arrived outside. Though Omar was nowhere to be seen I quickly spotted a tall, broad-shouldered woman wearing a woolen black sweater with the Fellcorp crest. "Can you take me home?" I asked her, my voice feeling detached and distant, as if operated by someone else.

"Of course, Mr. Fell, right away," she answered quickly, guiding me over to an orb pedestal and activating the shield once we'd stepped aboard. I hugged my shoulders and closed my eyes. "Is everything alright, sir?" she asked once we were in the air.

I did not answer. I slipped out my diary and clutched it near my mouth as I dictated the second part of this horrid day. The lights of estates passed below while I described the chimeras, the noise, the sickening revelations...

Now I see only trees. Wind-swept clouds have crossed the sky and blocked the stars. We're descending. In a matter of moments I will rouse Jia from sleep and I swear I will have the answers I seek.

I will *know*. The game is over. I swear.

XXVII.
A CURIOUS MALADY

I crossed the hall in a blink, and took the stairs three at time. I threw open the doors of the master bedroom and strode over to the dark bed. I pawed through the covers savagely until I found Jia's arm, and then jerked her upright with a brutal thrust.

She let out a little scream and pulled the covers to her chest. "Simon?" she whispered, blinking.

"Who are you?" I roared.

"Wh-what?"

"Who are you?" I repeated, feeling out for the lamp and knocking most of the contents of her nightstand upon the floor. The lamp winked on. Its mellow glow seemed harsh after the darkness. I stared into Jia's trembling eyes.

"I don't know what you mea –" she started.

"No more lies!" I bellowed and she flinched back, gasping.

Omar ran into the room, followed by Pish and Jeremiah. "What's wrong, Simon?" asked Pish, clutching the blue-green arm of the expressionless robot.

"Mr. Fell?" prompted Omar.

I looked back at Jia, tears running down her cheeks. "There's nothing I can say," she whispered. "I'm your wife, Simon. I'm your Jia Hazinnah."

With an incoherent shout of rage I plunged into the closet and tore through my clothes. I returned to the bedroom with the Smith-Shurtook in my grip. I walked straight up to the bed and levelled the silver barrel at Jia's forehead. "Tell me the *truth*," I commanded.

"Mr. Fell!" shouted Omar, dashing toward me.

I swivelled and pointed the gun at his chest. "Don't."

He stopped up short, then continued to advance slowly, his hands out before him. "Please, sir, just you go ahead and put that gun down now. I don't know what's going on here but I'm sure that if all we all just –" He trailed off as he spotted Jeremiah advancing on him from the corner of his eye. "Stay back, robot!" he shouted. "I can handle this."

"You cannot handle this," I argued sadly. "Omar, I'm warning you."

"I can disarm you before you kill me, sir. Even if I have to take a bullet in the process, I know I can do it." He licked his lips and tensed. "There's no question."

"The gun isn't what you should be worried about," I said, nodding toward Jeremiah. "You'll be dead before you hit the floor."

Omar risked a glance over his shoulder. "The robot won't hurt me."

"No," I agreed. "I expect it would be painless."

Jia and Pish both shrieked as I was blindsided by the security woman who had flown me home, both of us crashing spectacularly into a cabinet, its sides splintering and its contents spilling out onto the carpet. She twisted my forearm and the Smith-Shurtook dropped heavily.

I rolled out from under her grasp and jumped to my feet, arms raised to defend myself. But she lay unmoving, her open eyes fixed on the ceiling, her hand frozen in an interrupted reach across the floor toward my gun. The smell of her bowels reached us, loosened in death. I scrambled forward and picked up the Smith-Shurtook, wheeling around to point it at Omar again.

"Darrington?" he called urgently to the fallen woman. "Darrington! What did you do to her?"

I looked over to Jeremiah meaningfully, and then back at Omar. "Interference will not be tolerated," I pronounced coldly.

Omar gaped, and took a hesitant step backward, a film of sweat shining on his broad brown brow.

I turned back to Jia and she scrambled backward off the bed, falling to the floor. She gathered her nightgown around her and pressed back against the wall as she wept. My gaze did not flicker. "I loved you," I hissed. "I really did. I let myself fall in love with you." I began to cry, sputtering angrily around the words. "But it's all lies. It's all lies." I wiped my eyes with the back of my elephant sleeve and hardened my quivering mouth. *"Speak now!"*

"I –" she choked, sobbing. "I *want* to!" she wailed.

I crouched before her, dropping the gun and taking her shoulders in my hands. "Tell me everything," I said.

"I *want* to," she repeated pathetically, grabbing her head and moaning. "I love you, Simon! You have to believe that – I love you. I didn't think I would but I *do*."

"No more lies!" I cried again, shaking her.

She moaned and winced, pressing her thumbs into her forehead. "I can't – I can't, don't make me," she pled. Twin rivulets of blood appeared at her nostrils.

I dropped back away from her, shaking all over. "What's happening to her?" I whispered. Omar and Jeremiah flanked me, unreadable. Pish was cowering in the corner, pressed into the side of a wooden dresser, sobbing.

"I *want* to," blubbered Jia feebly, coughing as blood ran over her mouth.

Jeremiah's rubber-padded fingers touched my arm. "Sir, I do not believe she is able to speak freely. There is some factor of coercion at work. I do not believe there will be any profit in questioning her further."

"Yes," I agreed hollowly, watching her writhe weakly on the floor. I threw up into a potted plant. "Omar, call an ambulance," I said quietly, wiping a string of bile from my chin. In another part of the house an alarm sounded shrilly.

"Mr. Fell, I –"

"Do it now."

Omar began speaking quickly into his telephone. I sat down beside Jia and pulled her into my arms, smoothing the strands of black hair out of her sweaty face. "Hush now," I said. "You don't have to say anything right now, Jia, dear."

The alarm went quiet. The panicked hooting of little people could be heard from the hall, followed by footfalls pounding up the stairs. I looked up as Omar spun to face the door as a woman ran in and froze at the threshold, mouth dropping open as she surveyed the scene – broken furniture, a gun on the floor, a corpse, a robot, a crying child and me cradling Jia's bloody face in my hands.

I felt like the breath had been ripped out of my chest, so that I could barely find the air to choke out with shock: "Glory!"

Jia's eyes snapped open, and she raised her head to take in the apparition standing over us: a skinny girl in a worn red shift with tall black boots, her dirty brown hair tied into rows of beaded braids. Glory's narrow eyes were locked on Jia. "What are *you* doing here?" Glory asked slowly, her brow crinkling.

"Don't," croaked Jia, her hands squeezing my arm. "Don't do it...*I don't know you.*"

I gaped back and forth between the women. Glory seemed to decide something and stooped down closer. "Are you fornicating me?" she breathed. "Do you think I would *ever* forget you, dog-woman?"

"Don't," repeated Jia desperately, her nose bleeding anew. "Don't put the thoughts in my head, *please*...I can't!"

"I started your heart when you fished out! I dragged your faecal ass to the hospital when Bunny stuck you, and then you coitally robbed me. Don't you remember, *Kissandra?*"

Jia shook her head woefully and moaned, scratching at her scalp with her nails and shaking all over. "What are you doing to her?" I shouted helplessly. "Stop!"

"Who did she tell you she was?" hissed Glory viciously. "She's a *liar*, Simon. She's a *whore*."

Jia lost consciousness with a violent shudder, passing out across my lap with her hair fanned out over the carpet. A line of blood was running from her exposed ear. *"Stop it!"* I implored, and Glory compressed her mouth into a thin line and stood back.

"Kid," she called over her shoulder. "Still got those fixers?"

"Yeah Glory," he said, standing up to rush out of the room.

But Pish stopped short in the face of the medics: a man in green robes swept into the room flanked by two green robots and trailed by a little person in a green smock covered in pockets. They arrayed themselves around Jia, elbowing me efficiently out of the way. The man signed quickly to the little person who brought out an ampule from one of his pockets and stuck it in the side of Jia's neck. She twitched. At another signal from the man in green robes the twin robots bent down and made a bed of their arms. With a muted crack a stasis field snapped on between them, and the robots rose with Jia fixed floating at their waists.

"Where are you taking her?" I demanded hotly, my emotions in confusion.

"Sage Withan-Beck Hospital sir," the man replied evenly. "It's one of ours, Mr. Fell. Don't worry."

"Prepare my orb," I said shakily to Omar, who nodded curtly and followed the medics out. I looked back at Glory. "Hello again," I said.

"Hi, Simon." She crossed her arms and cocked her head to one side. "Sorry about fornicating you over before. Didn't mean to."

I nodded vaguely. "Are you coming to the hospital with us?"

"Yeah, okay."

No one spoke during the orb flight, all eyes fixed on the sphere we tailed, its surface pulsing rhythmically with red and blue St. Elmo's fire. When we neared strings of traffic in the starless sky the ambulance keened in alarm, wailing and warbling like a banshee in the night.

In the waiting room of the hospital I paced in circles on the polished tiled floor before the bank of chairs where Pish sat in his headless mouse outfit (the closest clothes to grab), Omar with his eyes shut and his fingers pinched on the brow of his fleshy nose, and Glory with her skinny, scabbed legs crossed, biting her nails with an intermittent click.

Jeremiah walked down the corridor and stopped before me. As a robot he had been required to submit to an interview immediately, to render an objective and truthful account of the events to which he had been witness. "Sir," he said.

I walked over to the windows overlooking the pre-dawn cityscape of Padirac, and Jeremiah followed. "What do they think?" I whispered.

"I believe they have hypothesized a common poison affecting both Madam Fell and Miss Darrington. An autopsy of Miss Darrington is proceeding now, sir."

"They believe the cases are connected, then."

Jeremiah paused. "A not unreasonable theory, given the information they have at hand," he said significantly, "sir."

I nodded. "What do you think, Jeremiah?"

"I believe Madam Fell has been tampered with, in an effort to make it impossible for her to discuss, or even consider, certain subjects."

"Tampered with?" I echoed. "What do you mean?"

Someone cleared her throat purposefully and I turned around. A police officer in a crisp blue uniform had entered the waiting room. She did not have little red circles painted on her cheeks. "Nestor Fell?"

The officer and I sat in a small office containing a desk, two chairs and a plastic model of a human skeleton. Through the frosted glass of the window I could see the blurry horizon lightening with the dawn. I was asked if I had any enemies ("Not that I know of,") and whether or not Jia had taken any food at Blighton's ball ("No, just punch I think,"). On the whole she seemed sympathetic.

"We'll get to the bottom of this, Mr. Fell," she promised me, touching my hand.

"Thank you," I said.

By the time I returned to the waiting room it was suffused with pale pink sunlight. Pish got up from his chair and hugged me. "I'm sorry I scared you," I mumbled into his hair.

It was not long after that I was admitted to see Jia. She was unconscious, and the nurse told me she may remain unconscious for some time. She looked small in the hospital bed. Her face had been cleaned but there remained a thin crust of blood around each nostril. As I watched a tiny fixer crawled out of one nostril and into the other. Her breathing was almost undetectable. A device at her bedside beeped periodically.

I sat in the chair beside the bed. My chest ached with pity, and shame. "I don't know if you can hear me, Jia Hazinnah," I said softly, "but I'm so sorry for what I've done to you. It's all my fault. I did not know what a monster I could become."

I dropped my head into my hands and wept.

When I emerged into the waiting room Omar told me that Jeremiah had taken Pish home. I nodded mutely. Glory was nowhere to be seen. After a long moment I said, "Are you a liar, too, Omar? Will you tell me? Will you take pity on me and just tell me?"

He licked his lips. "I am not a liar, sir," he rumbled.

"Then tell me: is that woman my wife?"

"I've never had cause to doubt it."

"But what cause have you had to *believe* it?"

"My job doesn't admit belief, sir."

"You dodge the question."

"I don't mean to. Man, I told you I took a bullet for you once. There is no secret I would keep from you. I'd tell you my Mama's cup size if I thought it would help you to know."

I wiped my hand over my face and sighed. "So when did you first meet Madam Fell?"

"Six months ago, sir, when I was re-assigned to Maja."

"Where were you before that?"

"The Third Earth, sir."

"I don't know what that is."

"Callicrates, Mr. Fell. The capital world at Eridani Star."

"You're head of my personal security force and you had never met my wife before six months ago?"

"I was promoted, sir."

"What happened to your predecessor?"

"I don't know, sir."

"Have you ever met my children?"

"No, sir," he said, and then he winced and pinched the bridge of his nose.

"What wrong?"

"Headache," he muttered, taking a deep breath. "Anyway, I may have met your children briefly between terms."

"Are you sure?" I asked quickly.

He shrugged, and then winced again. "I think so. I can't really remember it all that clearly. A boy and girl, right?"

"Yes," I replied, watching him closely.

He massaged his temples and blinked. "I'm pretty sure..." He winced again. "Man, what's wrong with me?"

"You've been tampered with," I said softly.

"What does that mean?" he demanded, grimacing.

"I don't know exactly," I replied, "but I would suggest that your headache may grow worse the more you try to grasp the specifics of that slippery recollection."

He was silent for a moment, the muscles in his neck working. Then he cried out and grabbed his head, blood oozing from one flared nostril. He wobbled on his feet and I jumped up to steady him. He held on to my shoulder gratefully and lowered himself into a chair. "Man," he commented heavily. "What's going on, Mr. Fell?"

"That's what I'm going to find out," I promised him darkly.

He took a shuddering breath and reached out for my arm. "Tampered with – are you saying that somebody's been messing around...with my mind?"

I nodded soberly, and Omar looked scared. "Come on," I said. "I think it's time we had another talk with Mr. Olorio."

"How very convenient," said Olorio liltingly, standing at the threshold of the waiting room. "My timing seems to be impeccable. Goodness, my friend, you look exhausted."

I had felt exhausted, but laying my eyes on the rotund countenance of Yatti Olorio inspired in me a rush of energy powered by anger. I wheeled on him menacingly. "I've got some questions for you, Olorio."

"Like what, my friend? It's tragic what's happened, of course –"

"Tell me about a prostitute named Kissandra, for starters."

"A prostitute?" he echoed, his brow knit. "I'm afraid I haven't the foggiest –"

"We've been friends ten years, you say?" I pushed ahead relentlessly. "Is that right?"

"Why yes, we met in university –"

"Then why does Abermund Blighton claim he invented me? Why does he have my likeness as a costume in his study? Why does my wife bleed when she tries to tell me the truth?"

"Simon, Simon," called Olorio, holding up his hands imploringly. "You've had a terrible shock tonight, I understand. But this is madness! Blighton claims he invented you? It's ridiculous! The man is a storyteller and a story*maker*, Simon – I'm sure he would've told you anything, to shock you for his ghoulish amusement."

I hesitated then, for there was the ring of truth in that.

Olorio seized his opportunity and plowed around, stepping closer and putting his heavy arm around my shoulders. "You live in a rare predicament, my friend," he sang soothingly. "You've been thrown into an adult world with the experience of a child. People have taken advantage of you, tricked you. People have abused you, and I understand how you've been burned too much to trust anymore."

"It wasn't –"

"Simon, Simon, Simon," he prattled, giving me an affectionate squeeze. "It's perfectly understandable that you should behave like this, like an animal cornered, after months underground. You're lashing out at what don't understand, your faith tested by a twisted man who would toy with you like a mouse for a cat. Blighton is a manipulator, Simon."

"A manipulator?"

"He's heartless – he loves stories, not people. But just stop to think about it for a moment: what kind of a grand ruse would have to be orchestrated to pull off such a fiction? To invent a man? Really! *To what end*, I ask you – to what end?"

I nodded weakly. "Indeed."

Olorio grinned toothily. "You need rest, my friend. All of this will make more sense when you can pull yourself together a bit, I promise you." He turned to Omar. "Agent! See

Mr. Fell home and to bed, will you?"

"Yessir Mr. Olorio."

I collected my tail and my tusks from the chair and Omar and I passed out into the hall, Olorio giving me a loathsome squeeze on the shoulder at the threshold. Glory was loitering just outside, her eyes glazed and distant. She slowly sauntered after us as we made briskly for the lift. When the doors had yawned shut I turned to Omar. "You know there's more to this. You know this isn't exhaustion."

"Yes," pronounced Omar evenly, his mouth tight.

"You know this involves you, too."

"Yes."

"What did I miss?" asked Glory.

"You told me you were not a liar, Omar," I said. "Tell me now: is your loyalty with me, with Fellcorp, or has it been altogether extinguished?"

"My loyalty is with you personally, sir."

"If that's the case you should stop calling me *sir*, and just call me Simon." I touched his shoulder reassuringly. "We are just two men who have been somehow exploited. We both mean to find out how. No one is the master of the other."

Omar paused a moment, and then nodded curtly. "I'll try to work on that, sir," he said with a little smile. "What's the next move?"

"Sleep. Olorio's right on that account. If I do not sleep soon I will become useless to the effort. We'll go back to the estate."

"Right on," agreed Glory; "I'm so coitally tired."

"I don't need to sleep," said Omar. "What can I do in the meantime?"

"I want to talk to Blighton again. Can you arrange it?"

"I can try, sir."

"And I want to know who my children are, if they even exist."

"I'll see what I can find out, sir."

The lift doors split and we were admitted into the busy hospital lobby. Glory grabbed my elbow as we started to walk. "Simon, what's going on?"

"I wish I knew."

"Aw, fornicate me," she grumbled. "What kind of a faecal answer is that?"

Despite it all I smiled. "It's good to have you back, Glory."

I said and thought nothing during the flight home over the striped domes and spires of Padirac. The sunny countryside passed beneath us in a blur, and soon we were descending toward the indigo castle of the Fell Estate.

Pish was sleeping in the guest bedroom, Jeremiah standing over him. "Hi, robot," said Glory, flopping down upon the bed after peeling off her boots. "I've been awake for like a million hours."

"Sir?" asked Jeremiah quietly.

"Omar is making inquiries. I am going to sleep a few hours. We will confront Blighton and come to the truth of all this." I spoke mechanically, with a determination I did not feel. "How is Pish?"

"Sir, he is concerned for you."

"He could've done better in the adoptive father department. Poor kid. I can't offer him the stability I thought I could." I rubbed my burning eyes.

"Sir," said Jeremiah, "you do not forget him in the midst of your own troubles. The stability you lend him is your love."

I had nothing to say to that. I just stared at the robot, feeling raw and boneless. "Thank you, Jeremiah," I said at last.

"Shut up," suggested Glory, pulling a pillow over her face.

I backed out the door. The master bedroom had been tidied up, and all signs of the night's events had been erased or removed. The Smith-Shurtook sat neatly atop a pile of my folded clothes. The bed had been made. I sat upon it and stared out the windows, unseeing.

Numbly, I toggled the contact on my diary and recounted this nightmare as I peeled off the grey elephant costume from my body. Naked and filled with hurt, I curled up atop the covers.

I don't know what to make of anything.

I hope I never wake up again.

XXVIII.
CONFERENCE WITH AN INCORPORATION

I dreamed that a bird, a terrible raptor, was eating my eyes. Needless to say I awoke somewhat discomfited.

Thus it was with a feeling of great relief that I looked around to see orange dappled light playing across the ceiling, and smelled the moist, hot air of Maja's equatorial balm. I was not blind, nor dead. Life chirped and whinnied beyond the windows. I heard the screech of a large bird and shuddered, gooseflesh rising on my arms. I sat up. I looked around the bed in which I had slept alone.

What morning was this? And why did it smell like afternoon?

With a nauseous flash the events of the day crystallized in my memory: Jia in a deep, sick sleep in one of Fellcorp's hospitals; Glory returned; my life either the invention of a cruel manipulator, or my shock his morbid plaything.

Right.

I remembered that I had pointed a gun at my wife's head, badgered her into incoherence, and watched Omar's colleague die. And then I remembered Yatti Olorio's unctuous smirk and his oily manner, his sing-song soliloquy about trust and madness and the way he had hung his meaty forepaw around me as he convinced me I was nothing more than short of rest.

And yet Jia and Omar were not the masters of their own memories. They bled through the nose when they tried to see through the haze. As Jeremiah surmised, they have been somehow *tampered with*, apparently in the name of divulging no inconsistency from the story I'd been sold....

"Mr. Fell?" Omar called, sticking his head in the doorway.

"Don't call me that anymore," I said. "I told you: my name is Simon."

"Mr. Blighton's agreed to see you, sir. I thought you'd want to know."

"What time is it, Omar?"

"Nine bells, sir. Nearly supper." He coughed.

"Is there something else?"

Omar cast his eyes downward in a rare show of real nervousness. "The hospital's called, sir."

"And?" I asked, my heart already burning coldly at Omar's manner. My hands started to shake, and my bowels turned over liquidly inside me.

"Madam Fell has died, sir."

I took a silent moment to absorb that, using every ounce of my strength to will her cheerful face out of my mind's eye. I steeled myself against reaction, a tingling pain radiating through my guts. Olorio at the hospital – it had to be. He had somehow murdered her. After a moment I began to nod slowly. "Omar. Please prepare an orb. Have everyone else join me downstairs. I just need to get dressed."

"Even the child, sir?"

"I don't want anybody I care about out of my sight. We're travelling as a unit from now on."

Omar turned to leave, but hesitated. "Are you...alright, sir?"

"No," I replied crisply, looking into his sad brown eyes. "Not at all. Now let's get moving."

Six minutes later I descended the great spiral staircase into the hall, my dusty red leather longcoat trailing out behind, the reassuring weight of the Smith-Shurtook bouncing against my leg. Pish, Glory, Omar and Jeremiah were waiting at the bottom of the stairs. "Sir, what is our destination?" asked the robot.

"Abermund Blighton's. We're going to get some answers."

"And something to eat?" asked Glory hopefully.

"Maybe."

The day was wet and windless, the rain falling in tall, perfectly vertical sheets from a low ceiling of dense grey cloud, horizon to horizon. Pish held my hand silently as we watched the trees and hills and estates pass by beneath our orb. Glory sparked up one of her little orange sticks, inhaling it with a purposeful gasp. Omar stared at her and then looked at me worriedly, but I waved my hand dismissively. "So tell me about her," I said.

"Kissandra? Used to work together," said Glory, eyes heavy-lidded; "in a kind of show, on Aurealia. Pish says she said she was your wife."

"That's right."

"Coitus. Didn't fall for her, did you Simon? Aw, faeces. You did, didn't you?" Glory took a step closer, her hand reaching out to touch me but it dropped limply at her waist after a hovering hesitation. "Coitus."

After a moment of silence I asked, "Why did you come after us, Glory?"

"Because I knew you'd forgive me."

"Why?"

"Shut up."

"Because I'm naïve?"

She snorted. "No, moron. Because you're *good*." She put her finger to my cheek and forced me to look at her. "You're still good, aren't you? Hasn't been beaten out of you yet, has it Simon?"

I did not answer.

Pish did. "Yeah Glory," he said seriously. "Simon's still good."

Glory leaned against the orb's central pillar and started playing with her braids absently. "So who's this Blighton pederast? Some rich fornicator?"

"He's a writer," I said shortly. "He claims he invented me, and that those who have met me previously met only Blighton in disguise."

"That's some pretty fornicated-up faeces, Simon."

"Indeed," I agreed.

"Think he's yanking your penis?"

I blinked. "Er, no. I believe the professional liar may be telling the truth."

"How do you figure?"

"Because he's the only one who isn't trying to pretend something isn't amiss." I sighed heavily, casting my gaze back out at the rain. "Your friend – Kissandra? – she's dead."

"What?" cried Glory. "She died from a *nosebleed*?"

"No," I replied, not looking at her. "I believe she died from being killed."

The rain petered out. We skimmed over an open-air sport court of some kind and then descended on Blighton's litter-sprinkled front lawn, which was being presided over by a fleet of little people stabbing the bits of trash on the ends of long spires and sticking them into bags hung over their shoulders. Some of them looked up at us as our orb settled and the shield vanished. I jumped off the platform and strode up to the columned porch, jogging briskly up the steps.

Abermund Blighton stood on the porch, his hands in the pockets of a high-necked silk robe. He took one of them out to pet his thin white moustache quickly before thrusting it out for me to shake. "Simon, my favourite muse," he smiled toothily.

I did not take up his outstretched hand. "I'm here for the truth, Abe."

"Of course you are," chuckled Blighton. "Truth is the only thing a man can be after when he's lost everything else, isn't it?"

"What about revenge?"

"Revenge is a form of truth," he replied without pause. "Please, do come in."

We were arrayed around a long rectangular diningroom table: Blighton at the end, myself at the tail, Pish at my right hand beside Glory, Omar across from them, Jeremiah standing against a wall, somewhat lost in the details of a dizzying mural depicting a storm-tossed ship painted thereupon, the hull splintered and sagging beneath an iron-coloured sea, the passengers thrashing between the waves. Two liveried little people brought in a tea service and began distributing cups and saucers. Blighton invited us to partake, and to warm up.

"After you," I said.

Blighton let a flash of irritation slide over his face before smiling toothily again. "Do you suspect poison?" he asked, raising his cup with an outstretched pinky.

"Jia's doctors did."

He sipped his tea. "But you and I know there's nothing to that theory, don't we Simon?" He put his cup down. "Whom our enemies did not kill, your robot took care of." He glanced sidelong at Jeremiah.

"Absurd," I objected.

"Nonsense," he retorted quickly. "You've left quite a trail of bodies in your wake, Simon, and I don't think you have that kind of blood on your hands. You don't have the look of it in your eyes." Blighton cleared his throat. "I've done my research. There is only one conclusion. The robot is a killer."

"If that were true, shouldn't you be afraid to accuse him now?"

Blighton shook his head. "All who oppose you do not die indiscriminantly. The pattern is more selective than that." He picked up his cup and sipped again, pinky extended. "I am confident that I have nothing to fear."

"Who are *our enemies* as you call them?"

"I have no idea, really," shrugged Blighton with a careless wave. "But surely it is no coincidence that after our conversation last night you ran home to confront your wife about my allegations, and things have ended up as they have. Unless you killed her yourself?"

"I did no such thing!"

"Very good, just checking. No doubt your colleague Mr. Olorio has suggested that I am a perverse liar, and that I have fed you this cock and bull story for my own amusement and profit." When I said nothing he continued: "Had you accepted this as the whole truth you would not be here now, wasting your time with a cruel fraudster. The fact that you *are* here now can mean only one thing: that something has happened that falls outside of Olorio's explanations, and that you are desperate to return to the font of knowledge who first clued you into the fact that things are not as they seem." He sipped his tea, and placed the empty cup on his saucer gingerly. "Is this not the case, Simon?"

I pursed my lips and frowned. "Yes."

"Unfortunately I have already blown my oracle – I have nothing else up my sleeve. I've told you that your persona and image are my creation, assumed for the purposes of benefaction in disguise, and sold along with every other bit of Fellcorp Pharma property some two years in the past. Honestly my dear fellow, I'm as perplexed by your existence as you are."

I stared into my untouched tea miserably. "There's nothing you can tell us?"

Blighton smirked, his eyes flitting around the table. "Us indeed, eh Simon? You've amassed a small army of champions for truth. A motley crew, to be sure, but I think I detect in them the funk of moxie. Well done!" He folded his hands on the table before him. "There is one piece of advice I can give you and your valiant forces, Simon. In my own travels I have learned a certain credo when digging for the heart of a story: *follow the money.*"

"Follow the money?" I echoed.

"Follow the money," he confirmed, "and at the end of that sordid path you'll find your rat."

I rubbed my temples pensively. "Olorio!" I hissed.

Blighton smiled. "Anyone for more tea?"

The sun was setting as our orb shot through the air over the wet countryside, the purple light shadowless. Lightning flashed, and a moment later thunder rolled. The glimmering lights of the metropolis of Padirac appeared before us behind a wash of rainy haze, orbs glowing with internal light winking like fireflies above the colourful roofs. We landed on top of Fellcorp's tower and scampered across the wet tarmac into the lift.

There was no reason to imagine Yatti Olorio would still be working past supper, but I also had no reason to imagine another interview would be productive. Our objective instead was the gathering of information about Fellcorp itself, which Jeremiah had told me how to procure.

The Incorporation of Fellcorp lived on the ninth floor.

The chamber was large and round, with elegant stone benches around the periphery of the reflective black walls, all facing the massive gleaming column of polished wood that occupied the core of the room. Pish, Glory and Jeremiah formed a small clot by the door while Omar and I strode in before the column, its face inscribed with the interlocked triangle crest of Fellcorp.

"Hello," I called out, my voice echoing off the hard walls, "my name is Simon."

A ring of heretofore invisible lights around the middle of the column illuminated, casting an eerie green glow up and down its wooden face and backlighting the crest. A mellow, sexless voice replied, "Hello, Simon."

"Are you the Incorporation of Fellcorp?" I asked.

"Yes, I am, Simon. I am obliged to tell you that I am one of three identical incorporated commercial entities. My siblings live at Eridani and Praxiteles."

I looked back at Jeremiah and he nodded to me. I called out, "I wish you to answer some questions about the ownership of Fellcorp. Will you answer truthfully?"

"As an incorporated commercial entity I am obliged to do so, Simon," answered the artificial mind inside the column.

"When was this corporation founded?"

"Sixteen years ago."

"Who founded it?"

"Maja Holding Corporation Five-five-three-two-seven-one-one-zero-three."

"Who is the owner of that holding corporation?"

"I'm sorry Simon, but for that information you would have to question the Incorporation of Maja Holding Corporation Five-five-three-two-seven-one-one-zero-three directly."

I paced in a small circle, considering. "Who was the first officer of Fellcorp?"

"Mr. Rodham Torrengaard."

"Is Rodham Torrengaard still affiliated with Fellcorp?"

"No, Simon."

I sighed, and thought again. "What does he do now?"

"I'm sorry Simon, but for that information you would have to question the Incorporation of Blighton Enterprises Interstellar directly."

"Ah ha!" I exclaimed, and then rubbed my chin thoughtfully and frowned. "What is the current relationship between Fellcorp and Blighton Enterprises?"

"None, Simon."

I paced again, hands behind my back, the red longcoat flying out behind me as I swept past Omar and around the back of the pillar again. I looked up at Omar, and considered the timing of his promotion. "What is the element of sharpest contrast between the historical operational parameters of Fellcorp, and the operational parameters of the last six months?"

The column answered smoothly: "Six months ago Fellcorp entered into a contract with the Citadel of the Recovery which has necessitated the revision of hundreds of operational parameters, chiefly the quantity of medicines under development for victims of the Kamari Horror, and the financing of this development process with Citadel funds."

"Who negotiated this contract?"

"On behalf of the Citadel of the Recovery: Madam Denchet Nox. On behalf of Fellcorp: Mr. Yatti Olorio."

"How long has Mr. Olorio been associated with Fellcorp?"

"Six months, Simon."

"What happened six months ago to initiate these changes?"

"I'm sorry, but I'm not qualified to speculate on the motivations of my officers."

"Whom did Olorio replace?"

"Chief Operational Officer Mr. Sook Moon Ti."

"What happened to Mr. Sook Moon Ti?"

"Mr. Sook Moon Ti was killed in a boating accident, to the great regret of colleagues and competitors alike."

"Have any other members of the board died during the last year?"

"Yes, Simon. Chief Financial Officer Margot Ving died of natural causes in her home with her beloved family. Chief Informatics Officer Petron Gelliwash-Def was killed in a tragic orb accident. Chief Personnel Officer Bick Tou disappeared while mountaineering on vacation, and is presumed dead."

"Isn't that unusual? So many deaths on the board in a single year?"

"I'm sorry, but I'm not qualified to assess statistical probabilities of this kind."

I stopped pacing and stood at Omar's shoulder, closing my eyes and thinking. "Incorporation, tell me this: what has been the effect of this new relationship with the Citadel of the Recovery?"

"Increased market penetration, enhanced efficacy of Fellcorp products, increased profitability."

I opened my eyes. "Why more efficacy?"

"Research by the Citadel of the Recovery complemented Fellcorp research, leading to a greater understanding of the effects of the Kamari Horror on brain physiology than would have been possible separately. This new understanding has formed the basis for Fellcorp's recent product lines."

"Who was responsible for generating this research at Fellcorp?"

"No one, Simon."

I scratched my head. "Who was responsible for bringing this research *to* Fellcorp, then?"

"Mr. Yatti Olorio."

I turned to Omar. "Olorio, Olorio, Olorio – it all comes back to him. But what has any of this to do with *me?*"

"I don't know sir," admitted Omar, looking troubled.

I looked back at Jeremiah. His face was as impassive as ever. I faced the polished-wood pillar again, encircled by its ring of steady green lights. "Incorporation: how do Fellcorp's newest products work?"

"Fellcorp's newest lines of anti-Horror medications work by targeting specific traumatic memory sequences, and inhibiting their recall through a chemical computer created out of the patient's own neural network."

"Let me get this straight – we make little computers in people's minds...made of medicine?"

"That is essentially straight, Simon."

"And these computers choose which memories to block, is that it?"

"That is essentially it, Simon."

"On what basis does the computer select?"

"The prescription and customization process is supervised by Fellcorp medical professionals, Simon. The computer merely executes a program tailored by the attending physician."

My blood ran cold. Suddenly, I had it! At Kamari Star the tyrant Volmash had unleashed the Nightmare Cannon upon the worlds, and then fled to Nsomeka Star in disguise as Yatti Olorio. He had somehow forced me and the Recovery into a deal to profit from his inside knowledge, and then used these novel anti-mnemonic drugs to clear my memories...and perhaps the memories of members of the Citadel, as well!

"Thank you, Incorporation."

As we left the chamber of the Incorporation I ran it all past Omar, who frowned. "That's pretty good, sir, except it doesn't explain Mr. Blighton's revelation at all, does it?"

My face fell. "No, I suppose it doesn't."

"So what do we do? Do we have that stuff in us, or don't we?"

I paused before the lift, considering his question as the doors split. "We need a doctor."

Jeremiah tilted his head. "Sir, the informatics console in your office will very likely be able to pinpoint the location of hundreds of Fellcorp physicians."

Omar leaned into me from the other side. "I don't trust that robot," he whispered.

"I do," I said.

We all piled into my office. As I turned around to close the door I spotted the sculpture of the bird again and recognized it from my dreams – I screamed.

"Coitus, Simon! What's wrong?" cried Glory.

"That bird...I know that bird."

Jeremiah turned. "What do you remember about the bird?" he asked in a sharp, commanding tone.

I stared at him, a chill running down my spine. I regretted expressing my trust in him only moments before, and recalled how that trust was balanced on an edge of fear. "Nothing," I grunted. "I just don't like it."

"I think it's cool," said Pish, touching the sharp talons where they met the pedestal.

"Leave it alone," I barked. He jumped back. "I'm sorry," I said.

Glory walked over behind my desk, plopping down into my chair and putting her boots up. "Not bad, Simon. What do you sell again?"

Grateful to look away from the bird I followed her to the desk. Pish pressed his face against a window and looked out on the city. Omar and Jeremiah flanked the door. I tabbed the informatic console alive with my thumb after checking to make sure no one was lurking underneath the desk. "Are you trying to look up my dress?" asked Glory.

I flushed and turned away. The console illuminated with the Fellcorp crest, and I began tapping through the menus. In a matter of moments I had a map of the globe before me, shining with glowing points representing on-duty Fellcorp-affiliated physicians. One such point even glowed in the air around the planet. "What's with that?" I asked.

"Sir, it is a physician in orbit," replied Jeremiah from across the room, "most likely aboard a Fellcorp spacecraft."

"Spacecraft?" I repeated. "So physicians can take the slow boat around the Soshu Joviat?"

"No sir, the moving of materiel piecemeal through personnel or even cargo transmission gates was judged unfeasible for the needs of the Neighbourhood Navy during the defense of Cassiopeia against the Kamari Incursion. Since that time spacecraft duly authorized by the Citadel of the Recovery may use the naval gates to transmit themselves whole to a foreign star."

"And Fellcorp is so authorized?"

"Sir, evidently. You may wish to call up the ship's manifest and flight plan for confirmation, sir."

I did so. According to the ship's informatics: called *Neago*, it was bound for Praxiteles to take on relief workers for transport to Yasu. The relief workers were being trained on the world of Allatu – identified as the home of the Citadel of the Recovery. When I drilled down for more detail about the organization I was presented with a brief history, as well as images of its founders and principals. I shook my head and smiled, pushing back from the desk.

"I want to get on that ship," I said, looking at Omar. "Can our orb take us there?"

"An orb is an orb sir," he nodded, "but what are you planning? You can't just waltz into the Citadel and start asking questions. They'll never admit you. Do you know how long the waiting list is to even get a chance to beg for an audience with Lady Aza?"

"Oh, she'll see me," I assured him.

"But how can you be sure?"

I looked down at the informatic image glowing out of the desk: healed and whole it had taken me a few seconds to recognize her, but there was no mistaking the line of her jaw, the twinkle of her eye, the fall of her silken locks – the High Priestess of the Citadel of the Recovery, the famous and tireless Lady Aza of Allatu, was none other than Crushed Head Faeda.

"She's an old friend," I said. "Let's go."

Omar gaped. "You want to go *now*, sir?"

I nodded curtly. "I don't want to give anyone any time to stop us, or lull us to a false peace. I don't want to give Olorio another chance to interfere. We're going *now*."

I opened the door, keeping my back to the hideous bird sculpture. Pish took Glory's hand and pulled her toward me, Jeremiah turning to follow. Omar hesitated. "I can't leave sir. My – my family's here. I mean, man oh man. I can't just run away now."

"You're involved in this," I reminded him.

"Then I'm counting on you to come back here and straighten out whatever they've done to me," he said, eyes on mine. "...Simon."

"Dear Omar," I nodded, shaking his hand, "you have my word. Jeremiah, can you fly the orb to orbit?"

"Sir, I have the co-ordinates of the *Neago*," he confirmed.

I looked into Omar's watering brown eyes. "Thank you for your loyal service," I told him, "and your friendship."

"About your kids," he said, "I couldn't find much. I got their full names and the name of the school. You'll find them in your plate's cache."

I nodded gratefully and we started to leave again but Omar caught my sleeve. "There's just one more thing. Could you hit me?"

"You want me to hit you?"

"I'd hit myself, but they can tell. I just want to be able to keep my job in the morning. So would you mind, you know, knocking me around a little?"

"My goodness, I don't know Omar..."

"Please, Simon. Don't think about it. Just wheel back and clock me. You'd be doing me a big favour, man."

I nodded, and he steeled himself. I wound back and punched him the cheek, his head rocketing around. Omar lost his balance and fell across the front of the desk with a grunt. "Are you okay?" I called.

He lifted his big brown head and grinned lopsidedly. "Perfect."

Moments later the lights of Padirac were disappearing beneath the edges of the orb's platform under our feet. We passed through a wall of heavy cloud and erupted into the starshine, the sky ablaze with hundreds of tiny points of light and the great blue face of Soshu whose reflected glow cast an eerie pall over the cloudscape.

Jeremiah unfolded three chairs from the platform floor. Glory, Pish and I sat down and strapped ourselves in. With mixed feelings I watched the horizon of Maja become a curved limb of cloud and inky ocean. I had almost let that world feel like a home to me, until the world and the life I was starting to believe in were so cruelly ripped out from under me. I turned away from Maja, preferring to stare instead at the hard stars, no longer twinkling.

"What's going to happen to us now, Simon?" asked Pish in a small voice.

I put my arm around him. "We're going to find out why Jia died, and why Omar gets headaches, and why I can't remember anything. We're going to get to the bottom of it all, I promise," I said, echoing the words the police officer had said to me that morning. "And I'm not going to let anything happen to you. Do you understand? We're a team, you and I."

"You and me and Jeremiah and Glory," corrected Pish.

"Yeah Pish," I said. "Yeah."

I pulled out my diary. As our bubble escaped gravity's grasp and flew into the void, I toggled it on and began to speak, my hands starting to shake as I recounted our trials. Glory stroked my hair compassionately, and said nothing.

Soshu loomed behind us, its great stripes twisted into whorls and spirals where cerulean met ultramarine. A speck grew before us, a steady pinprick shine of reflection against the canopy of stars: the *Neago*. "How long?" I asked Jeremiah.

"Seventy minutes," said the robot.

"Faeces," breathed Glory, crossing her legs. "I have to pee."

XXIX.
YOU ARE SAFE, DO NOT PANIC

I won't leave you in suspense; Glory found a washroom.

But she was still crossing her legs and grumbling as the *Neago* grew before us against the spangled velvet: a great rounded wedge of gleaming white metal with a slowly turning torus embedded in a midship cavity, like a canine tooth run through by an ivory ring. A set of blue formation lights winked on and off patiently at the extremes of the wings and nose, on which were painted the image of a human hand in red. We had just drawn close enough to discern the orange glow from the turning ring's portholes when my telephone buzzed in my ear.

"Hello?" I called out too loudly, making everyone in the orb jump.

Glory swore, and crossed her legs the other way.

"Fellcorp skiff Neago *to approaching orb: please identify,"* said a crisp female voice through my skull.

I cleared my throat. "Um, yes. This is Nestor S. Fell. I'm coming aboard."

A pause. *"That's not funny. Who is this? If this is Ditsu, you're early. What's going on?"*

"I'm afraid this is not Ditsu, but as I indicated, Nestor Fell. I'm pretty sure I own the spaceship you're on now, so please just sit tight and my party and I will be there in a jiffy to explain in person." This with met with silence, so I asked in a commanding tone, "To whom am I speaking?"

"This...this is Doctor Fliothasse Pemma. Who is this really?"

"This is Nestor Fell," I repeated wearily. "Your boss's boss. Please prepare to receive us."

Jeremiah stood by the core of the orb and tapped upon the controls, slowing us by some invisible force as we drew around the rounded stern of the white vessel, toward the yawning mouth of a hold. We floated inside over a deck of black and orange stripes, and into a narrow parking bay which closed after us. A loud hissing sounded as the bay filled with air. Jeremiah disengaged the shield, and we drifted from our seats toward a hatch. It cycled open and a white robot with the Fellcorp crest on either shoulder and a red hand painted on his chest greeted us. "You are safe; do not panic. Please accompany me to the habitat ring."

"Okay," I said.

We slithered in freefall through a transparent plastic tunnel, conveniently tethered and marked in several different styles of writing. We were passing through the innards of the ship, the spacious internal cells busy with floating white robots whose activity made no sound. The majority of the ship was airless and shadowy. "Why is it so dark?" I whispered back to Jeremiah.

"Sir, infrared lighting is more efficient in purely robotic environments."

"Robots run the ship?"

"The robots comprise the crew. The officers are very likely human beings, sir."

We met our first such human beings just as the last of us, Glory, stepped off the ladder down to the curved floor of the torus, loaned the impression of gravity by its stately rotation. I had been looking around the strange space: all white walls and flooring, balconies over our heads leading to levels of lighter gravity, sealed doors before and behind presumably providing access to the rest of the circumference of the spinning ring.

One of the doors slid open, revealing two men flanked by two white robots. The first man was thin and muscular, with dark brown skin and flashing eyes. He wore a white turtleneck bearing a Fellcorp badge on the breast, and a little hat with gold piping around the edges. He stood with his chest pushed forward and his hands on his hips. He stared at us without expression for a moment and then, with a flicker of annoyance, elbowed his companion in the side.

The second fellow was a gangly youth with pale skin, black hair and a self-effacing, round-shouldered posture. When he was elbowed he juggled a metal whistle in his hands awkwardly and then blew a brief, melodious twitter. "Dignitaries aboard!" shouted the youth, his voice an indecisive mix of high and low registers.

The man in the hat nodded primly, and then saluted me. "Ceptain Miko Ting, Mr. Fell sir. It is my great pleasure to personelly welcome you aboard my hemble shep."

I decoded his thick accent with great effort, then blinked and smiled. "Oh – hello, yes. Captain Ting, allow me to introduce Miss Glory, young Master Pish, and his robot Jeremiah." I made an attempt to salute.

The white robots with red hands on their chests approached us and seemed to be looking us over. One knelt down beside me and passed its open hand over my leg, and then straightened and passed its hand over my head. When it caught my eye the robot said, "You are safe; do not panic."

Both robots retreated and stood behind the human beings again. "No apparent injuries or contagion," they reported in eerie synchronization. Captain Ting nodded and stepped forward.

"Whet is it we can do for you and your compenions todey, Mr. Fell, sir?" he asked with a beaming white smile, arms extended wide.

I shook his thin, strong hand firmly. "First of all, the lady needs a latrine."

"Mr. Oliver!" shouted Captain Ting, causing everyone to jump. "Show thes ledy to the head emmedietly!"

"Yessir Cap'm sir!" the youth shouted back, saluting quickly and stealing a shy glance toward Glory. His pale skin turned pink. "If you'll follow me, ma'am," he squeaked, "I'll show you to our facilities."

At this point a new voice called into the fold: "You'll do no such thing, Oliver."

The youth froze. Everyone looked up to the balcony at the end of the chamber. A brown-haired woman in a white labcoat stood there, glaring down at us with her arms crossed across her bosom. Captain Ting took off his hat and scratched a mossy bed of tightly-curled black hair for a moment before calling up to her, "Do you know who thes is, Decta? Thes is Nest —"

"It doesn't matter who any of them may or may not be," the woman interrupted sharply. "If they're coming aboard this ship they've got to get scrubbed and scanned." She shifted her gaze to me. "Just like everybody else," she added acidly.

"Bet they're none of them enjured —" started Ting.

"This is a medical ship!" the woman overrode him roughly; "not a playboy's toy." She turned on heel and disappeared through a sliding door.

There was a moment of silence as we dropped our eyes back down to one another. Glory raised her brow at me inquiringly. Pish held on to Jeremiah's arm. The captain just looked uncomfortable. "Well," he declared with a reasonable facsimile of jocularity, "thet's Decta Pemma then. Thes is her mission."

"Faecally charming," mumbled Glory. Young Mr. Oliver started to snicker beside her, but stifled it as Captain Ting looked his way.

"Mr. Oliver!" he bellowed. "Let's get these people scrubbed end scenned, on the debble!"

What followed was not entirely unlike my indoctrination into prison on Annapurna: we were separated, stripped and showered by robots, examined in ways both gentle and unmentionable, and finally fed bodily into a large tube for high-resolution scanning. Being somewhat dehydrated I had some difficulty providing a urine sample, but I smiled to myself as I imagined Glory in some nearby chamber providing her own sample with great enthusiasm. The robots were also interested in my blood and spit, and wanted to know what colour my last faecal product had been, and whether or not it had floated.

At the conclusion of this process came my reward: the warm folded clothes presented by me by the last robot were hospital pajamas, and as I tugged them on I was handed a green robe. I belted it at the waist with satisfaction, and pushed my feet into a pair of paper slippers. "You are safe; do not panic," said the laundry robot. "Please pass through this door."

I was deposited in a small office, alone. It smelled like disinfectant, kindling in me a nostalgia for the ward of my birth on Samundra. A single round port looked out upon the stars and the white hull of the *Neago*, slowly turning. There was a metal desk with a chair on either side of it, so I chose one and sat down. As I watched out the window a slice of Soshu came into view, and then skimmed away. I was startled as the door opened behind me.

Dr. Pemma walked in briskly and took the seat on the opposite side of the table, her aquiline nose pointed at the data-plate she held. The colour of her eyes was obscured by thick black lashes as she looked down, reading. Her skin and her hair were the same remarkable colour of milky cocoa.

I cleared my throat. She frowned as she tapped on the face of the plate, studiously ignoring me it seemed. I said, "Thank you for the robe."

"You like it?" she asked darkly, without looking up.

"I do, rather."

"You can't keep it," she snapped. "The robes are for patients."

"Ah."

She put the plate aside and folded her hands together before her on the table, fixing me levelly with yellow eyes. "I've been reviewing the scans, Mr. Fell, and there are a few issues I'd like to discuss with you."

She waited. "Okay," I prompted.

"The girl you should've brought to me much earlier," she continued smoothly, eyes still locked on mine. "There isn't really much we can do at this point, beyond pain control.

But she's already self-medicating with dilly chalk, which she would be unlikely to give up."

I blinked, and furrowed my brow. "What do you mean? Glory's sick?"

My agitation seemed to please her. Dr. Pemma let her brow move expressively as she replied pointedly, "It's up to you whether or not to maintain the fiction of your ignorance for the Maja feeds, but please don't practise on me."

"What?" I cried back in frustration, completely lost.

"Oh come now," preened Dr. Pemma with a maudlin look, "you cannot honestly expect me to believe you had some *other* reason for hauling your dying call-girl to this planet's most inconveniently located physician."

I didn't know what to say. I just gaped.

"I'll take your silence as affirmation, then," decided Dr. Pemma shortly.

"No!" I shouted. "I don't know what you're talking about. *What's wrong with Glory?*"

Dr. Pemma regarded me for a moment, pressing her lips together in a thin line not unlike Glory's own expression when pensive. "Ketsu's Bane," she said at last. "It is a sexually transmitted degenerative nerve disease. Curable in the early stages."

I was afraid to ask. "Is Glory in the early stages?"

Dr. Pemma frowned. "She is not. She is in nearly constant pain. It will not be long before she loses motor control, and succumbs."

"Succumbs?"

"Dies."

I whispered, "Mother of love!"

"Mr. Fell," Pemma asked, addressing me for the first time by name. "Have you had anal intercourse with this girl within the last two years?"

After a brief explanation of anal intercourse I was able to answer, "No."

"If that's true," the doctor replied, giving me a long look, "you have nothing to worry about."

"Except that my friend is dying, you mean?" I shot back, and then felt my eyes burn. Did I somehow think of Glory as a friend, despite everything? I guess I did. I swallowed and wiped my eyes. "You have an admirable bedside manner, Doctor. If there isn't anything else, I'd like to see her now." I stood up.

Dr. Pemma's face softened. I saw her begin to object, then stop herself. She stood up as well. "This isn't what I expected. I'm – behaving improperly. We can finish our conversation later."

"I don't understand."

She sighed, and suddenly looked on the verge of tears herself. "You weren't supposed to be more concerned with her than yourself. And you were supposed to be belittled sitting there in pajamas, not pleased. It was supposed to wipe that smug smile off your face."

"Am I smiling?" I asked.

"No," she decided after a long pause, searching my face, "nor so smug, either. So why did you bully your way aboard my ship?"

"Because I need your help. I need to get to Praxiteles. I need to see Lady Aza of the Citadel."

Dr. Pemma's breath caught. "You want me to take you to the Citadel? I can't do that. What about my mission? You're Nestor Fell, you can have any ship you want."

"I want this one," I said. "Please. You cannot understand how much this means to me. I will take all responsibility – no one will blame you."

"I'm not concerned with blame," she replied acidly, her earlier glower returned in a heartbeat. "I'm concerned with the patients this mission was supposed to service. I am a physician, sir, not a bureaucrat."

"I did not mean to offend you," I hastened to say, raising my hands to implore for peace. "And please don't call me 'Mr. Fell.'" I offered my hand to shake. "My name is

Simon."

She looked at my hand dubiously, and then shook it briefly. "Dr. Fliothasse Pemma, Fellcorp Medical, contracted in the service of the Citadel of the Recovery."

I smiled. "That's pretty long. Do you have some kind of nickname?"

"Dr. Pemma will do," she said pointedly. "You should know, Simon, that Captain Ting will never allow you to take this ship off-mission. He's ex-Navy, and he takes his duty very seriously."

"Then I will have to hope to persuade him this duty is greater," I told her. "Now please, before we are sidetracked again – I want to see Glory."

Glory and Pish were lounging in their matching pajamas and robes in a tight white ward of four beds, arrayed in a narrow chamber on the inner level of the rotating ring where the pseudo-gravity was lighter. Jeremiah stood by the door, nodding subtly to acknowledge me as I walked in past him. "Are you okay, Pish?"

"Sure," said Pish sunnily, "but Glory won't play chess with me."

"Maybe Jeremiah will play," I suggested.

"Yeah, but he always *wins,*" grumbled Pish.

I convinced Pish to play chess with Jeremiah on the furthest bed while I sat down where Glory sat, perched on a bed by the window with her knees drawn up to her chest. "So, you know now," she said before I could even open my mouth. I nodded. "Whatever," she shrugged, "spare me the faeces."

"But why did you come –"

"Come back? Eat faeces. Because I didn't want to be alone, okay? You anus."

"How did you even find us, how did you –"

"Don't ask me what I did to get to Maja," she whispered fiercely. "Don't ever talk about it again, okay?" She lashed out and grabbed my forearm in her long fingers, squeezing painfully and staring at me with red-rimmed eyes.

"Okay, Glory," I said. "I'm sorry. I'm sorry."

She took her arm back and wrapped it around her knees, looking out the window sullenly. "I just didn't want to be alone at the end, okay? And you're the only person I know who doesn't have faeces where his heart's supposed to be. Is that so coitally crazy? Why do you have to bother me about it?"

"I'm sorry," I said again.

"*Stop feeling sorry for me!*" she yelled, and out of the corner of my eye I saw Pish accidentally knock over the chessboard as he spun to look. Pawns spun across the floor. "Coitus," she added woefully.

I put my arms around Glory, and drew her to me. She resisted at first and then relented, allowing herself to be hugged. She started to cry, and I rocked her back and forth, petting her braids and making the beads click together. I never imagined that someone else might find solace in me, who has brought so much misery in my brief travels. My last traces of bitterness against Glory fell away, and I looked up at Pish.

"I told you, Simon," he said. "Glory's sad, not bad."

"Sometimes it's hard to tell the difference," I said.

"That's important to remember whenever you're sad."

In a transparent-doored cubbyhole over one of the beds were my folded clothes, my Annapurnese gun and leather longcoat, my boots, my bits, and my little blue diary. I put my diary in the pocket of my green robe, then called over one of the white robots from the hall. "Would you please let Captain Ting and Dr. Pemma know I'd like to speak with them?"

"I'm hungry," said Pish.

"One thing at a time," I replied, strapping my belt on over my pajamas and tying the end of the holster around my thigh. "First let's get this ship on course, then we can worry about eating."

I sank the Smith-Shurtook into its holster.

A moment later the robot offered to escort me to the bridge, so I allowed it to lead me along a balcony and down a set of carpeted stairs. We emerged into a broad chamber reaching from one side of the hub to the other, the stars shining in through wide windows on either side. Six unmanned consoles were ranged around the edges, while Captain Ting and his faithful yeoman Mr. Oliver stood within a shallow well in the middle behind a large transparent data-plate suspended from the glowing ceiling.

The captain looked up. "How can we help you, Mr. Fell sir?"

I kicked back the side of my green robe and showed him the Smith-Shurtook. "Captain, I regret to inform you that I'm commandeering this vessel."

"Thet's mervellous!" he exclaimed, breaking into a wide grin.

"Is it?" I asked, as Mr. Oliver looked shocked.

"Well of course," replied the captain; "it means something exciting is geng to heppen, doesn't it?" Then as an afterthought he grinned and added, "End it'll drive thet bloody woman med!"

"I quite appreciate your attitude," I said, retying the sash of my robe.

"Not et ell," grinned Captain Ting, rubbing his brown hands together; "where are we geng, then?"

"Praxiteles."

His face fell. "Isn't thet where we were geng in the first plece, Mr. Fell sir?"

"Well, yes," I admitted. "But now we're in a great hurry."

"We shen't be weiting for the new officers then, sir? They're due tomorrow."

"If it is at all possible I'd like to get underway immediately."

Ting rubbed his chin. "Skeleton crew, eh? Good. I lick a challenge." He turned around to the pale youth. "You heard the men, Mr. Oliver. Prepare ell systems for locomotion!" he yelled.

Mr. Oliver jumped to attention and saluted quickly before bustling from one console to another in a frenetic tangle of long limbs and nervous glances. Captain Ting looked meaningfully out the windows to the stars, so I looked that way, too. After a moment I asked out of the side of my mouth, "Should something be happening?"

"There's not really much to it, sir. We'll begin slengshoting around Soshu in enother eleven minutes – you'll feel some ecceleration then." He shrugged. "Efter thet it's fifteen hours to the trensmission yard, Mr. Fell, sir."

"Ah."

Captain Ting cleared his throat significantly. "How shell I log our flightplen?"

"As a modification of the original. You've received your shipment of officers early, apparently, and will debark for Praxiteles without delay."

Ting showed me his rows of gleaming white teeth again. "Deshing, sir – thy will be done." At my questioning look he explained, "You don't know whet it's lick, ferrying dectas around spece. They don't let me meck one damn decision, end even if they did the only ones to be mede are who's on wetch and where to perk." He puffed out his chest. "I wes in the Nevy, sir. I wes treined for *ection*."

"No promises, Captain, except for a break from routine."

"Thet," he said in an impassioned whisper, eyes flashing, "is ell I esk."

On my way back from the bridge I ran into Dr. Pemma in the corridor. She frowned and stopped up short. "What are you doing out here? Patients belong in the ward."

"I am not a patient, Dr. Pemma," I reminded her. "I'm a passenger."

"This isn't a tram, Simon. The *Neago* has no passen – my god *is that a gun?*" Dr. Pemma leapt back from me, her face darkening in indignation and fury. "How *dare* you bring a gun aboard *this* ship!"

I tucked my robe in tighter quickly. "I am this ship's hijacker. But don't worry – it's all on very friendly terms." I smiled. "I hope this doesn't put too much of a damper on our relationship."

Dr. Pemma's eyes bulged dangerously just before she slapped me across the face. She then pushed by and disappeared down the corridor. I stood there rubbing my stinging skin for a moment. Then a robot ran up to me and sprayed my cheek with a cooling mist jetted from the tip of its finger.

"You are safe," the robot cooed, "do not panic."

XXX.

LICK A BET OUTTA HELL

I was back in the hospital, about to catch scent of Nurse Randa.

And then I wasn't, but the dreamy aftertaste inspired me with the will to open my sleep-stuck eyes without dread. Though I saw no sunlight, my body was telling me many hours had passed – perhaps more than a usual night of sleep. For the first time in days my brain did not feel as if it were working through a haze, and my chest did not ache with worry.

The canopy of hard stars shining through the port was slowly revolving. I was in space.

An amber lamp glowed in the alcove above my bed. There were three other lamps, in a row. Thus eight tiny pinprick reflections gleamed in the eyes of Jeremiah, standing sentinel by the door. Now more familiar to me than Nurse Randa ever was, I took a moment to consider how the robot had ended up both my and Pish's keeper.

Corinthia Tag spoke in my ear, making me jump.

She said, *"You have forty-two new messages."*

The lamp brightened, lighting my bed. I sat up and rubbed my knuckles in my eyes. My telephone had never been so eager to tell me something before, so I asked it about the messages.

The first message was from the Soshu Space Office with some inquiries about the flightplan Captain Ting had issued, delivered with the dull courtesy of a robotic voice. The second message was a human being, an irate representative of something called the Volunteer Basket who was claiming she couldn't confirm the orbital station of the *Neago* as agreed. The third message was from Olorio. "Please contact me *immediately*, my friend," he simpered melodiously.

I began to skip through the messages faster: the Nsomeka Space Office; the Hyperspatial Scheduling Guild; again the Volunteer Basket; again Olorio; the Mission Secretary of Fellcorp Medical & Mercy; again the Soshu Space Office; the Maja Planetary Guard...

"Oh, dear," I muttered.

I pulled on my robe and stole past sleeping Pish and snoring Glory, nodded briefly to Jeremiah and then slipped out into the corridor to wince and stagger against the brightness of normal illumination. I squinted and felt my way along for a while until I bumped into one of the ship's innumerable white robots.

"I'm sorry," I said automatically, withdrawing my hand from the image of the red hand on its chest.

"You are safe; do not panic," the robot assured me. "Do you require assistance?"

"Nah."

I got lost on the way to the bridge. It wasn't my fault: all of the corridors look the same. I wandered through a darkened surgical theatre and stumbled into a supply cabinet before eventually asking a robot for directions. It might have been the same robot for all I know.

I hopped down the carpeted steps and around down into the well at the centre of the consoles, where Captain Ting was lecturing his yeoman in an animated fashion on the proper way to fold a coffee napkin. "I'll be expecting nothing short of tep netch service from you in thes regerd from now on, Mr. Oliver!" bellowed the captain, his accent characteristically thick, his white turtleneck stiff and spotless.

"Yessir Cap'm sir!" the dark-haired young man shouted back, eyes shining. He then refolded the captain's napkin nervously.

"Eccepteble," nodded Ting. He picked up his coffee and sipped it, noticing me for the first time. "Mr. Fell sir, Goodmorning. Ceffee?"

"Yes please."

"Mr. Oliver!" shouted Captain Ting, startling both Mr. Oliver and myself. "A cup of ceffee for our destingueshed guest!" The youth hastened to do the captain's bidding, and within seconds a white cup, saucer and intricately folded napkin were pushed into my hands. All three bore the Fellcorp logo.

I sipped the coffee experimentally, feeling it trace a warm line down my gullet. It was richer than I had tasted before, with an almost cinnamon-like aftertaste. Quite remarkable. Captain Ting closed his eyes and nodded to himself as he drank. Mr. Oliver quietly prepared a cup for himself and tried to enjoy it without making any noise. I said, "So...how goes the – flying?"

Ting snapped his long brown fingers and pointed out the tall windows behind me. "Jest ninety minutes from the yard, sir."

I turned around, and gasped. Space was hung with a stately array of metallic spheres, arranged in a cube of three spheres to a side. By focusing on the nearest such sphere I could detect the faintest traces of motion – we were advancing on the array. Scale was difficult to judge but as we drew nearer it became apparent that any one of the spheres large enough to encompass our entire vessel, with room to spare.

"Quite a seat, eh?" whistled Ting.

"Oh? Oh, quite a sight indeed."

"The yardmester's a bit reffled, though."

"Reffled?"

"Desgrentled," clarified Ting. "Here, teck a listen. Mr. Oliver: pipe through the yard!" Mr. Oliver scrambled over to one of the six unmanned consoles and pounced upon its controls. A moment later a string of profanity erupted from unseen speakers. Mr. Oliver switched it off at a signal from the captain, who turned to look at me expectantly. "Shell we fight our wey in, Mr. Fell sir?"

"What? Goodness no. Things aren't that desperate yet." Ting's face fell. I continued, "I'd like to speak with Yatti Olorio at Fellcorp. Can we arrange that?"

Mr. Oliver pointed to the large suspended plate in the middle of the bridge, which illuminated almost instantly with the wide countenance of Olorio. He looked concerned. *"Simon, thank goodness you've called. What's going on? What are you trying to do, my friend?"*

"Relax Yatti," I said. "I'm just going for a bit of a cruise."

"But to what end?"

"I want to visit the Citadel of the Recovery. I want to understand our work. I can't just have everything explained to me – I have to see things for myself. Can you understand that?"

"I can," admitted Olorio heavily, nodding so that his chins sank into one another liquidly. *"And you're reminding me more and more of the Nestor we all miss. Always in the trenches, getting everything first-hand."*

I hesitated, surprised. I had expected more resistance. "I'm glad you can appreciate my point of view."

"I'll just clear up this trouble with the transit licence then."

"I'd be much obliged, Yatti."

"Very good. But promise me, Simon – when you've seen what you need to see, do come home to us

again. It wouldn't be Fellcorp without you."

When the connection was broken Captain Ting was smiling. "Thet seemed to go well, sir, didn't it?"

"Too well," I agreed darkly. Having me offworld obviously did not present an obstacle to Olorio's plan – could it even be a prerequisite?

I stayed on the bridge as Ting and Mr. Oliver busied themselves over the controls, chatting back and forth with yard control and each other. At one point I was asked to press a little green contact on a console near my elbow, which I did.

Mr. Oliver held several more ritualistic exchanges with voices representing various authorities, jumping up between conversations to hover over the helm control checking gauges. At one point he tapped on the console surface and I felt a slight tug as the ship decelerated. I looked over at Captain Ting, who stood as usual with hands on his hips, gaze cast out through the large suspended plate and into space. "Is it just me," I asked, "or is our orientation relative to the rest of the ship changing?"

Ting nodded. "The axes of the hebitet ring's rotetion chenges in response to inertial forces, Mr. Fell, sir." He pointed to a seam where the decking met a bulkhead. "Notice there, sir, how the engle between the well end the floors shefts a few degrees. Thet's to help keep things on a even keel, too. Thes is a quelity shep: ex-Nevy, jest lick me."

I stifled a giggle. "Is this the sort of ship you used to fly in the Navy, Captain?"

"No, no, no, sir," replied Ting seriously. "I flew a bettleshep."

A male baritone sounded from the speakers: *'This is Navy Control at the Yardmaster's Office.* Neago *you are cleared for transit to Praxiteles Star via Bead Seven. Bead Seven,* Neago *to Praxiteles."*

"Acknowledged," squeaked Mr. Oliver. Captain Ting nodded.

Beyond the forward windows a round aperture on the face of the nearest sphere was irising open, its yawning scale only becoming apparent as the whole of the *Neago* passed through it and into the cool murky glow of the reflective interior. I turned around to watch the blue crescent of Soshu disappear behind the closing aperture.

"Three," counted Mr. Oliver; "two, one: transit."

This time I had tensed myself, ready to detect even the slightest symptom of our transmission across lightyears of space: once again, however, I felt nothing. The warped sepia shadows outside the windows looked exactly as they had seconds ago, the image of the ship smeared into a series of rings. Mr. Oliver placidly tapped at his controls and we began to turn, making our way ponderously back toward the aperture.

It irised open, presenting a tiny circle of blue and green tendrils of gas strewn out from a diffuse, copper ring. I marveled. I had never seen its like – the unearthly transition from hue to hue, the layering of gossamer sheets, the glow of the stars behind the veil...

As we drifted forward the borders of the round frame widened, revealing a wider and wider vista of amazing cosmic filigree. The *Neago* cleared the sphere and sunlight blasted in through the windows behind us, automatically darkened to shield us from being instantly baked: in that quarter the stars vanished and the gases became lurid and shadowy, a frozen halo around a massive yellow disc whose prominences of arcing fire reached far into space.

"Unbelievable!" I exclaimed.

"Never been to Prexiteles, sir?" asked Captain Ting genially.

"No – it's beautiful."

He crossed his arms and squinted at the windows critically. "Hella lotta jetsam, yeh. Tourists go med for it, ebviously." He chuckled. "Elmost mecks it worth it heving to visit eny of their bloody werlds."

Ting grabbed an edge of the suspended plate and swung it over to hang before us. Informatic labels and menus appeared upon the transparent face of the plate, superimposed over our view out the windows. I spotted two golden discs off the limb of the fiery

Praxiteles Star, and I was surprised to note that neither was a world: the first was a *brown dwarf* or unignited star called Black Dog, the second a superhot *white dwarf* star named White Dog.

"Where's Allatu?" I asked.

Captain Ting walked around to the other side of the plate and gestured for me to follow. He pointed through to the forward windows, opposite Praxiteles and her dwarf companions. The plate highlighted a small blue dot against an undulated sheet of violet and ruby gas. "Ellatu's there, just a day downwell." He took off his hat and scratched his head. "They keep their plenets fer from the sun here, because Prexiteles is an unholy hot."

"When Annapurna looked that small from Castle Misne we were still several days away," I commented, rubbing my chin.

He put his golden-braided cap back on, fixing it squarely over his forehead. "Well thet's a cestle for you, sir – it's in orbit around the star. Thes, on the ether hend, is a self-propelled speceshep." Ting puffed out his chest and smirked smugly. "End she goes lick a bet outta hell, sir."

I grinned. "Best speed to Allatu then, Captain."

"Our flightplen's elready been logged, sir. Mr. Oliver! Men the helm, and look lively, led!" Ting beamed with evident pride as the *Neago* turned, clearing the hyperspatial transmission array and accelerating toward the tiny blue dot.

I made my farewells and returned to the ward. It was empty but a passing robot was happy to escort me to the cafeteria where Pish and Glory were taking breakfast. I nodded to Jeremiah as I passed, and then had a tray filled by a courteous talking wall with pictures of sad looking meals on it. I strode over to my friends jauntily and sat down, giving Pish an inquiring look as he put away a mouthful eggs. He shook his head sadly. I shrugged and dug in anyway.

"Where've you been?" asked Glory around a mouthful of toast.

"On the bridge. We've been transmitted to Praxiteles. We're en route to Allatu now." I chewed ruefully on a sausage of questionable quality.

"And what kind of faeces are we going to do there?"

"I'm going to question Lady Aza, and find out what she can tell me about Fellcorp, and Olorio." I stopped chewing. "This food is really terrible."

Pish nodded. Glory shrugged. "You're too picky. Who cares what the mung it tastes like if it fills you up and doesn't make you sick?"

Nobody had a satisfactory answer to that. I drank a glass of thick, pulpy juice. "You two should really try to take a look outside. This system is full of gas – whorls and clouds of colourful gas. It's amazing."

"Yeah, Jeremiah told us," said Pish.

"Jeremiah knows this place?" I asked, glancing up at the robot in the blue-green carapace who stood across the cafeteria, by the entrance.

"Jeremiah knows every place."

Dr. Pemma entered the cafeteria. She noticed our party and pursed her lips irritably, turning her back to us as she ordered her tray loaded up with food selections. When she was done she reluctantly approached the bank of tables, looked over the empty ones lingeringly, and then seemed to decide with a sigh of resignation that sitting near us was the only really viable option. She clattered her tray down and kicked the bottom of her labcoat out of the way of her legs. "Goodmorning," she muttered.

"Goodmorning Dr. Pemma," I said. Glory leaned over and started eating my eggs. I cleared my throat. "Can I ask you something? It's just something I've been wondering about."

The doctor looked up, and nodded briefly as she cut up her potato cakes.

"You've never seriously questioned that I am who I say I am. Why?"

"I'm a doctor," she replied shortly, "and you're on file."

"I'm sorry, I don't understand."

"Your genes. We have your genes on file. When you were scanned your sampled code was matched up with the library file: Nestor Simonithrat Fell." She looked down the table at Glory. "Vera Tse Llatella-Bond," added Dr. Pemma, and Glory looked up with a shocked expression. "Piciatus Menteith," the doctor concluded, raising her chin in the direction of the child. "...Deceased."

It took me a moment to process that. I shook my head, confused. I put my elbow into Pish's left-over sauce as I echoed the doctor dumbly: "Deceased?"

Pish frowned. "Doesn't that mean *dead?*" he asked dubiously.

"Faeces, chick," quipped Glory darkly, "you've got to be the worst doctor in the galaxy. The kid is clearly alive."

"Clear," noted Dr. Pemma acidly, "is the *last* thing this is." She pushed her food aside, largely uneaten. "I told you there were a number of issues I wanted to discuss with regard to the scans, Simon," she said to me. "If you're going to hijack my mercy mission the least you can do is explain yourselves."

"I'll explain anything I can," I promised, "but I warn you that I'm a font of ignorance."

She did not smile. "You want to discuss it in front of the child?"

"No secrets are kept from Pish," I said firmly, putting my arm around him.

She sniffed. "There are no signs of prepubescent hormonal activity in the pituitary."

"I don't know what that means."

"It means this child's body is not preparing for sexual maturity."

Pish made a face. "What's sexual maturity?"

"I can't explain that," I said. "What else?"

Dr. Pemma hesitated. "Well, there's you, of course." She intertwined her fingers on the table before her. "First of all, you should be eating more calcium so soon after a replacement."

"A replacement what?"

"Leg. Your right leg, of course."

I could not help reaching down to touch my ankle, exposed beneath my pajamas on my crossed leg. Did the skin feel suddenly different? "It's...artificial?"

"Yes of course," she replied curtly, then adding in a low voice, "Were you not aware?"

"My leg is robotic?" I wondered, flexing my calf experimentally.

"Of course not. It's regenerated tissue and the bone density is characteristically a bit low. That's why I'm reminding you about taking in enough calcium."

"Calcium?"

"Yes, *calcium*, Simon."

"Is that a medicine?"

"Interesting question," she noted. Dr. Pemma took her hands off the table and sat back. "...Which brings us to the second issue: your brain. Obviously, the stories about your memory damage were based in fact."

I nodded. "I have to know: are there Fellcorp chemical computers executing inside of me?"

"Yes."

I licked my lips and took a deep breath. "Can you remove them?"

"Yes."

Glory belched loudly. I turned around to glare at her. "Coitus," she commented. "Sorry, Simon."

I looked back to Dr. Pemma, and held her yellow eyes. "And my memory will return?"

The doctor's brow softened, and when she spoke her voice had lost some of the usual edge. "I'm afraid not, Simon. Your memory has been systematically cleared. There's nothing there to find."

"Systematically? What does that mean?" I sagged back against my chair. "Dr. Pent told me I'd had an accident. I've been lied to, haven't I?"

"Yes. What happened to you was deliberate, particularly apparent at the borders between what's been left intact and what's been cleared. Did you experience some gaps in your basic knowledge?"

"Language failed me at first. Bladder control was...a challenge, initially." I coughed. Pish giggled, and then Glory burst out laughing. "I was a quick study, though."

"It's a wonder whoever did this to you didn't turn you into a vegetable," growled Dr. Pemma. "Your brain has been butchered, and it sickens me. Have any kind of early memories surfaced?"

I thought about the bird – the statue and the dream: nothing but vague horror. "No," I said.

"You're lying," she said smoothly. "If I remove the blocks, you may remember more."

"That's what I want," I heard myself saying.

"If you're willing to talk to me about your memories, I can help you draw them out."

I looked around. Pish and Glory were staring at me, and across the cafeteria Jeremiah's face was slightly inclined toward our table. I licked my lips again. "What must I do?"

Dr. Pemma took me to one of the smaller surgical theatres, and told me to sit back in a large reclined chair. While she went into the next room to prepare her tools Pish sidled over to me. "Are you going to be okay?" he wanted to know.

"Sure. I'm not going to leave you, Pish." As I said this I looked over his head and caught Glory's eye. She nodded seriously and put her thin hands on the boy's shoulders.

The doctor returned accompanied by two white robots with red hands on their chests and chased everyone else out of the room. She fitted my head between two firm pillows, gave me a pill to eat, and told me we'd have to wait about twenty minutes before her computer designed a dissipation sequence to unlock the blocks. A scanning armature hovered over my skull, buzzing faintly.

"You are safe," the robots assured me each in turn; "do not panic."

Dr. Pemma whisked out again, leaving their expressionless rounded white faces watching over me. I fished my diary out of my pocket and thumbed the toggle, reciting the morning to keep me from thinking about what was happening inside my head. I paused when the doctor returned to affix two sticky little pads to my temples, and then picked up describing the coffee.

She has just now returned to tell me that I will have to be unconscious for the final phase of the unblocking. She's watching me say this with a look on her face that is the closest thing I have yet seen to amusement. That's it, Doctor: I didn't even know you could smile. Yes, I keep a diary. Okay, I'll put it away now. I'm ready.

My fate is in your hands.

XXXI.
THE FLYING CITADEL

"I don't feel any different," I said.

Dr. Pemma snapped off the little light she had been shining into my eyes and nodded to herself, tapping quickly on the plate she held in her other hand. "That's good," she pronounced.

"But when will the memories come back?

"It's hard to say, of course," she replied primly. "It depends where your thoughts range. The blocks have been removed, but the act of recall is still up to you."

"You can help me, though."

"Of course. As soon as anything comes to you, talk to me."

I walked out into the corridor and Pish hugged me. Even Glory smiled. Jeremiah said, "Sir?" with what I swear was a note of concern.

"Everything's fine," I reported.

This was largely true, up until I started weeping uncontrollably in the shower. I crouched into a little ball, my chest heaving with sobs. There was no image or thought of sadness in my mind, yet my soul quailed. It was a strange and terrifying experience, and I found myself shaken after its passing in a way that even the smell of hospital soap could not assuage.

For lunch: tuna, seaweed, rice and wretched little shrimp crackers.

Captain Ting greeted me warmly as I stepped down the stairs to the bridge in the early afternoon. The world of Allatu had grown to a great face of blue oceans and white cloud, nearly filling the view from the forward windows. "We'll be mecking plenetfell in about two hours, Mr. Fell sir," reported Ting brightly, hands behind his back; "Mr. Elorio hes made our lending errangements with the Recovery people, so we can put down streight in Citedel Perk."

"This ship can land? On the ground?"

Ting beamed. "Oh, yeh, Mr. Fell, sir, no problem. This is a real fine shep, like I told you, sir. The only bloody thing she's messing is a good set of c'nnons." He winked conspiratorily. "But *thet's* a problem I'll heff licked efore long, don't you werry sir."

Mr. Oliver looked nervous.

I looked over my shoulder to see Glory, Pish and Jeremiah coming down the carpeted steps to join us on the bridge. "So, Simon, this is where you've been hanging out," said Glory, sauntering down into the well and leaning her hip against Mr. Oliver's console.

"I like to look out the windows," I explained.

"Cool!" said Pish, plastering his face against the forward view, his breath periodically fogging a swath of desert belting one of Allatu's continents. "I can see mountains," he reported. "They look purple."

Glory, meanwhile, had become transfixed by the opposite view. She was staring out the rear windows with her mouth hung slightly ajar, lost in space, caught by a green veil of gas that bled yellow rivulets into blue swirls.

"It's beautiful, isn't it?" I said to her.

She blinked, and snorted. "Whatever. Space is space."

"Why do you always pretend nothing affects you?" I asked.

"Shut up," suggested Glory.

I noticed that for the first time I could not see any of the larger hull around the habitat ring in which we turned, and asked Ting about it. "We're inset in the body of the shep now, sir," he told me, "end we'll stop spinning shortly – there's no point fighting the plenet's grevity."

As if on cue Mr. Oliver's voice sounded twice: from right beside us and with a short delay over the ship's public address system: *"Ahem. Um, all stations prepare for freefall please."*

We each took a seat at a console, and strapped ourselves into the chairs. The view of Allatu's cloud studded ocean gradually ceased to revolve, and the now familiar cold, tickling sensation rose in the top of my belly: weightlessness. A wave of nausea passed over me but I managed to steel my gut against it, focusing on the now stable view outside and willing my bemused ears to stop tilting my head involuntarily. Glory belched wetly.

"Whee!" said Pish.

The *Neago* descended, and as an hour passed the wind began to sound outside the hull and we could feel gravity's tug on our bodies again (directed toward the forward – now *bottom* – windows). Our chairs and consoles tilted backward to compensate, and the suspended plate moved on its armatures to hang before our new orientation, illuminating with a view of the spaceship's forward trajectory as seen from just beneath its nose.

An indigo sky enfolded us briefly before we slipped beneath a high deck of frothy white cloud, steam streaming off the hull.

And then a strange thing happened: when the plate showed us the details of incoming queries from the Citadel of the Recovery's traffic authorities, Mr. Oliver did not answer but called instead for a robot. When a white medical robot arrived a brief exchange was concluded with a nervous approach to Captain Ting. "Um, it says Dr. Pemma has the alpha *and* the beta again, Cap'm."

Captain Ting made some inspired remarks, then added, "Why does thet bloody women heff to monopolize the only two robets on this shep with helf a brein between them?"

"You are safe," contributed the robot, sensing Ting's distress, "do not panic."

"You go on end melt, you!" the captain growled, raising his arm as if to backhand the thing. "Useless peremedic tresh. Couldn't trenslete Ellatu if the progremme was written on your eyelids."

"Captain," hailed Jeremiah. Everyone turned to look at him. "Sir, I am capable of performing that function."

"You can do Ellatu, yeh?"

"Sir," confirmed Jeremiah with a nod. "Is the transaction to be conducted in High Allat or Mechanical?"

"Um, Mechanical," supplied Mr. Oliver, indicating the console. He stepped back quickly as Jeremiah walked over and assumed the seat in a lithe motion, the edges of his blue-green carapace clicking quietly. He tapped upon the controls, and the image of young, serious-looking woman appeared on the console's face.

Jeremiah and the woman exchanged short bursts of terse-sounding language, after which Jeremiah told us that we were indeed cleared to land in Citadel Park, and had been assigned parking co-ordinates.

"Hed to get a lettle sherp with her, eh?" said Captain Ting.

"No sir," replied Jeremiah, "that is simply the sound of the Allasu oral language, termed Mechanical Allat."

Ting laughed, and slapped me on the back. "Hey, Simon, your robet thinks he's a professa. How do you lick thet?"

"I lick it just fine," I said, and then flushed. "That is to say *I like it just fine.* I would know even more of nothing about anything if it weren't for Jeremiah's willingness to volunteer his encyclopaedic knowledge." I coughed. "I owe him my life."

"Yeh yeh yeh," chuckled Captain Ting dismissively; "He's progremmed funny, is ell. My bretha hed a nennying robet that ren so smooth his ked thought it was a real boy. You don't see the robet softies in adults much, though. Meaning no offense, Mr. Fell, sir."

"The robot softies, huh?" I laughed.

"No offense, sir," repeated Ting soberly.

The *Neago* passed beneath a thicker deck of grey vapour and we descended over a drizzly sea, its angry grey face punctuated by white-capped waves. Land crawled into view ahead: a city of silver and grey with roofs of white, the tips of its towers glowing with red beacons to proclaim their height in a waste of fog. A glowing label on the plate identified it as METROPOLIS ANANKE-DO (POP: 8 923 432).

Mr. Oliver and Captain Ting were busier now, both of them pushing their chairs back between two tilted consoles each. Jeremiah adjusted his own chair to move along the console bank to assist them, which Ting accepted after shooting the robot a brief startled look as his blue-green fingers began tapping the controls.

"Very good, robet," acknowledged Ting.

"Sir," said Jeremiah.

In the middle of the city was a great circular park, its ground-level details lost to the trees, walled in on every side by proud skyscrapers. At the centre of the park a sole structure could be seen: a shining golden dome flanked by four tall minarets. I did not need the label on the plate to know it was the Citadel of the Recovery.

Mr. Oliver brought us around in a gently descending spiral until it seemed the green tree tops would strike the bottom windows beneath our dangling feet, then the youth deftly set us down in a small white clearing whose proximity made a signal buzz on the console into which Jeremiah had spoken. There was a slight double bump as the ship's struts absorbed our inertia and recovered.

The sound of the *Neago*'s engines – a steady thrum to which I had been so accustomed I had forgotten it – died away leaving a stuffy silence. Everyone's harnesses clicked as they freed themselves from their chairs, feet thudding as they dropped down to stand on the transparent floor that had been the forward windows. The section of bulkhead dividing the ports down the middle suddenly made more sense to me: it was a walkway, with steps up to the exit.

As we proceeded through the habitat ring other aspects of its architecture that had previously struck me as perplexing gained evident functionality in this new context of gravitational orientation. Flanges around doorways that I had taken for decorative turned out to be ledges for feet; insets in the ceiling turned out to be ladders.

"Everything about this galaxy is a puzzle," I complained half-heartedly.

Pish smiled. "Puzzles are fun."

Captain Ting went off to prepare the debarkation bay with Mr. Oliver at his heels, and Glory, Pish and I returned to our tiny ward and changed clothes for the surface. Glory sniffed her red dress disdainfully. "Somebody washed my dress and now it smells like hospital," she grumbled.

When we came to the debarkation bay Dr. Pemma was waiting for us, her white labcoat crossed over by two shoulder bags. She was flanked by a guard of two white paramedic robots. "Ready to go?" she asked us.

"You're accompanying us?"

"If you're foolhardy enough to take a defenseless young woman and a child into whatever situation you're concocting for yourself, I am obliged to accompany you in order that they be in the care of at least *one* competent adult."

"What the mung do you mean *defenseless*, sphincter?" demanded Glory hotly.

I blinked. "What the mung do you mean *one competent adult?*" I asked in turn.

Dr. Pemma shook her head patronizingly. "What is it you hope to accomplish down there, on your idiotic man-child crusade?"

"I want to know the *truth*," I said through gritted teeth.

"An adolescent obsession," she declared shortly. "You're maturing at a remarkable rate, Simon, I give you that – but you're inexperienced, and you lack informed perspective. I don't pretend to know what all of your business is, but just take a moment to think about what it is you plan to do, and whether it's something that makes sense, or simply something that promises to satisfy a selfish craving of your still developing ego."

"I *have* to go," I said.

"Which is of course the wrong decision," replied the doctor tartly, "which is why I'm coming with you."

I looked at Captain Ting in appeal and he rolled his eyes theatrically. Then he seemed to notice something behind me, and his face broke into a toothy grin. He pointed: "Look there! It's Terra Firma!"

I spun around to see a sleek grey cat with white stripes step gingerly across the bay to twist around Mr. Oliver's ankles. He leaned down and petted the cat which purred loudly.

"This ship has a cat?" Pish exclaimed. "I never even saw her!"

"Thet's because she enly comes out when we're lended. Etherwise she spends ell her time hiding – damned if we know where."

"Um, that's why we call her Terra Firma," explained Mr. Oliver to Pish, who had come over to let the cat sniff his knuckles. Mr. Oliver brushed his dark hair off his pale brow sheepishly. "Um, yeah."

"She's good leck!" declared the captain triumphantly. "A bloody euspicious stert for your mission, eh, Mr. Fell, sir? Not even Decta Pemma should be eble to bring you down now!" He frowned at Dr. Pemma, who glowered back at him.

"Bloody misogynist wanker," she whispered.

"Gengwey descending!" bellowed Captain Ting by way of a subject change, engaging a series of controls on the wall beside him. In response the floor chuffed and vibrated. Mr. Oliver herded Pish and Terra Firma off of the middle section of the decking as it opened and dropped down at one end, admitting a gust of cold, dry wind that reeked of conifer needles.

It touched down on the ground with an odd crunching noise.

"Listen, Decta," said Ting, "you cen't teck both the elpha *end* the beta with you. Why don't you jest leave the elpha here with us? I have a lettle project –"

"I'll need assistance and interpreters," argued Dr. Pemma. "You can tinker with my ship later, Captain."

"Your shep?" scoffed Captain Ting. "Weit end see if I don't lock you out again until you learn up some polite. Remember lest time?"

They stared at each other for a moment.

"Fine," growled the doctor, eyes narrowed. "You can keep the beta onboard."

"The elpha," countered Ting quickly.

"Why in the name of all that's –" began Dr. Pemma, eyes widening and her cocoa skin flushing.

The captain chuckled. "Elright...don't explode yourself, gerl. Beta! Come here." He grinned with satisfaction as one of the white robots stepped up smartly beside him, and he then turned to me. "If you need enything, sir, just give us a heller," he said, tapping the tiny bead of his telephone on the side of his dark brown neck.

I nodded and walked down the inclined gangway toward the open air of Allatu. "Let's go Pish," I called, "Glory...Jeremiah."

Pish, Glory, and Jeremiah were followed by Dr. Pemma and the *Neago*'s alpha robot.

I emerged beneath the belly of the ship and stepped into a crispy, muddy substance that turned to powder on the red leather of my Annapurnese boots. I paused, and knelt down. I reached out and touched the stuff: cold, and crystalline. It turned to water on my fingertips.

"It's snow, Simon," said Pish. He jumped off the gangway and planted both feet in the stuff, and then kicked it off his boots enthusiastically. Then he scooped up a handful and ate it.

"Mother of love!" I exclaimed against my will.

Pish grinned. "It's just frozen water, silly." Then he scooped up another handful, patted it into a rough ball, and threw it at me. I ducked but it splattered into frigid dust against the shoulder of my longcoat.

To my surprise the next ball of snow to strike me came from Glory, laughing hysterically as I sputtered and tried to wipe the ice from my eyes. Pish laughed too, until he took a slushy one right in the middle of his chest.

Inside of a minute we were all three slipping around and launching volleys of snowballs at one another. The ruthless efficiency with which Glory created and delivered her munitions was admirable, but she still could not stand up against Pish's merciless enthusiasm and impeccable aim. Glory was a quick study, however, and dodged behind a landing strut to fire from a place of cover.

I looked over at Dr. Pemma, who was standing on the end of the gangway with her robot, lips pursed with irritation. She didn't look like she was having fun, so I threw a snowball at her. Then I ran away.

I emerged from beneath the soft shadow of the *Neago*, a cloud-diffused and snow-reflected sunlight seeming to shine weakly from all directions. The sky was grey. The tips of the evergreen trees swayed in a light but biting wind. I saw a broad stone road along which hooded people walked. When the wind ebbed I could hear their somber song.

"Pilgrims," explained Jeremiah at my elbow, anticipating the question. "They come to pay homage, seek strength, and offer service to the Citadel in the name of the Recovery."

Dr. Pemma arrived behind us and without a word clapped an ampule to the side of my neck. I felt the curious sensation of medicine being released into my blood, colder than my body and tingling with foreignness. "What was that?" I cried, slapping her arm away.

"Standard inoculation package for Allatu," she grunted, rubbing her forearm ruefully. "You're welcome."

As Glory and Pish crunched up behind us, gasping for breath and giggling, Jeremiah pointed toward the trees: a tall woman was walking barefoot through the snow, her gait stately, her shoulders held broadly beneath her grey cowl. She removed her hood as she stopped before us, and bowed.

I bowed in turn. "Hello," I said brightly. "My name is Si –"

The woman hissed at me like a cat, her face a manifest of disgust. Jeremiah touched my bicep and said quietly, "Sir, do not speak aloud. Madam expects High Allat. I will endeavor to translate."

At that, Jeremiah turned to the woman and said nothing at all.

The grey-cowled woman, for her part, raised her brow briefly at Jeremiah, and then looked down at her fingers. Her mouth twitched.

Jeremiah made a subtle nod, then turned to me and conveyed in a very soft voice, "Madam Sister Rabbit welcomes you to this Holy Citadel, and confirms that you are expected. The Madam Sister invites you to be escorted by her to your cell, where you might care to wash and refresh before your meetings."

I looked toward our host to agree and to thank her, but before I could make any gesture her eyes flicked over to Jeremiah.

"The Madam Sister says you are welcome, Pilgrim Fell."

Led by the Citadel's nun in grey our party walked the road alongside the pilgrims, some in robes and some naked, some in elaborate costumes and some looking like the people I'd seen in everyday places: riding Maja's World Train, hailing taxicabs in Thaumas, waiting in lines in the lobby of Samundra General Hospital as I was escorted by Nurse Randa to freedom...

Many of the pilgrims smiled at us, even though some of them appeared to be grieving behind black veils. Many prayed aloud, and some joined one another in song. There was a sensation of human warmth and guileless comraderie pervading our slow parade and it penetrated me, allowing my breath to come easier.

By the time we reached the Citadel there were little flakes of snow falling out of the sky, cascading out of the clouds like little fluttering stars as if the park were cruising upward through space. Pish leaned his head back and caught bits of snow on his outstretched tongue. Glory did, too.

"Grew up on Creidne," she offered by way of defensive explanation when she caught me watching her. "Coitally cold there, Simon. Everlasting faecal winter, from Arkmonth to August."

Thinking about everlasting winter made me feel cold. I noticed then that my body was quivering. I raised my shaking hand before my face, marveling at my inability to control my trembling fingers. "What's happening to me, Glory?"

She rolled her eyes. "You're cold, idiot."

"I've felt cold before," I argued, my teeth clacking together involuntarily. "It wasn't l-like th-this."

"Simon: meet winter," she said darkly. "It totally fellates."

While the mob slowed and congregated before a wide stair, the nun in grey led us around to a smaller door behind a screen of needled hedges. There Dr. Pemma departed with her robot without explanation or adieu. The nun, Pish, Glory, Jeremiah and I passed through cavernous, ill-lit stone corridors, the sussurusses of human conversation seeming to echo from unlikely corners. We passed intricately geometric tapestries, and dozens upon dozens of statues carved in a matte black stone, arranged on lonely podia in niches bounding every archway.

We came to a small cell containing four beds and fat, jolly-looking fellow in a simple brown cassock who jumped up when he saw us to shake our hands with two of his and bow repeatedly.

He did not say a thing until the nun in grey had departed, then he let burst forth a waterfall of words. "Roommates, thank heavens – bless you, friends – I'm Brother Phi and I'm so delighted to meet you! Was your journey long? Come now, you're cold – I have a fire started in the hearth. It's a small hearth but this is a small cell – not that I'm complaining. My goodness, you're a big boy aren't you? What impressive boots, my girl! Oh ho – Annapurnese leathers, smacking good! I used to have a pair of Annapurnese jodhpurs before I joined the order – wonderful fit. Heavens! Isn't this grand?"

I couldn't help but laugh. "Hello, my name is Simon."

"Wonderful, Simon – I'm Brother Phi, did I mention?" he crowed, and then went around the room and re-introduced himself to Glory and Pish in turn as he learned their names. Remarkably, he also introduced himself to Jeremiah. "Now that, my friend, is a truly splendid carapace. Quite striking! I'm a great admirer of carapaces, myself. I used to design Exo-Neo-Rococo plating for the Renetians until their hour-guilds started getting all uppity about alien craftsmen. Pah! Nevertheless, a wonderful period of my life, yes."

And so we warmed ourselves around the small hearth where a couple of square black bricks burned with cheerful orange flames. Outside the narrow window the grey sky pinkened and dimmed, while winking stars of snow continued to plunge down in a constant stream. Again I could not shake the feeling that the Citadel was flying upward through space. I lurched under the influence of a faint vertigo, and sat down on the end of one of the beds with a sigh.

Brother Phi gave us each a mug of water and some wafers and spoke at great and uninterruptible length about all of the wonderful people he had met along the way of his pilgrimage from Ishtar.

"Where's Ishtar?" I asked.

"Never been to Ishtar, pilgrim? Now that's a tragedy. Every man owes it to himself to visit the Second Earth at least once in his life. There's really nothing I can say that can convey the essence of the experience. It changes lives." He munched on a wafer. "In answer to your question, Ishtar orbits the great fat goddess Yasu, who is a ward of Centauri's holy primary."

"I haven't heard of Centauri before. It's a star system?"

"It is indeed." Brother Phi closed his eyes reverently. "Rigil Kentaurus Majoris was a great waystation for Solar life as it fled the calamity at Sol, and it was the eventual destination of the Wayward Ark whom all had taken for lost. When the civilization of Eridani and her hyperspace gates spread back to Centauri they found worlds already in blossom around two of her three stars. Hard-won worlds, torn from the unyielding elements rather than selected for compatibility, as elsewhere. I was blessed to be born under the light of Centauri Prime, Rigil Kentaurus Majoris herself, and it is my special joy to tell all who ask anything about her."

I smiled to myself, then ventured, "You're robot softies at Centauri?"

Brother Phi laughed uproariously. "Have you been keeping company with a Reull or an Ops?"

"Whech one tecks lick thes?" I asked, aping Captain Ting's thick accent.

"That's Reull," grinned Phi, his round cheeks dimpling. "Wonderful people, save for their Chauvinism. They can't seem to treat their robots as they should, bless their hearts – nor each other, which is why they're always having such enthusiastic wars, I suppose." He laughed again and then took his own crack at Reullian pronunciation, exaggerated comically: "Ass es effident, I heff spent minny yeas deng relief werk in Reull! Ho ha!"

Everyone except Jeremiah cracked up laughing. Then Brother Phi held up a chubby finger and started nodding to himself. "Which brings up an interesting point – at least to me, it's interesting. It's interesting that Reull is one of just a few worlds who have eschewed any local languages in favor of adopting the Common Verbal Protocol even in the home, and yet against their will they seem to be evolving their own dialect that will before too long be unintelligible to their neighbors. Have you heard their slang? It's like scat. Do you know what scat is? It's Reullian slang. That's a little joke." As an afterthought he added, "I'm sorry, I'm not very funny."

"I think you're hilarious!" cried Pish.

"Bless you, child," smiled Phi.

"What brings you to this Citadel, Brother?" I asked.

Phi sat back and became more serious. "There's always work to be done for the Recovery, dear Simon. So many lives were shattered, and lives continue to be shattered as families attempt to care for their deeply wounded kin. They need helpers. I'm a helper. My creed compels me to this work, but my compassion is my own. I go before Lady Aza to seek a new assignment." He cleared his throat and brightened his round face once more. "And what business brings you here, if I may ask, pilgrim?"

I considered the question, mulling over various summations. "To be candid, Brother Phi, I am a man created out of the void on a quest to discover the true mechanisms at work linking the pharmaceuticals of Fellcorp, the funding of the Citadel of the Recovery, and the forgery of my life."

Brother Phi whistled, his eyes wide. "Well, okay then," he said. "You can go first."

XXXII.
MASS OF THE HALCYONS

A white-skinned naked man with a shaved head appeared at the door of our cell and bowed low, his pale forehead actually touching the smooth stone floor with a muted thud. His drawn, expressionless face turned up. His eyes looked like they were made of glass, and I shivered. Before the prostrate naked man could say a word Brother Phi grinned and claimed, "He says he's here to escort me to the Halcyon Hall."

He then stared at the naked man, who stared back.

"I said you could go first," Brother Phi called to me, rushing at the bed and gathering up a handful of greasy, chipped-edged data-plates to stick into the wide, marsupial pocket of his brown cassock; "I've told him that – and he's irritated – but the poor thing can't think of a defensible way to refuse. So, if you wonderful people will follow me as I follow him, we'll all go down to the hall together. Ho ha!"

I tore my gaze away from the coloured marbles the slack-featured man stared into our cell with – almost eye-like eyes. I grabbed Brother Phi's sleeve. "Is he reading our minds?" I whispered, awed.

"He who? He him?" replied Phi, squinting. "The robot?"

"Jeremiah?"

"What now? No – our escort, dear Simon." Phi was pointing to the naked bald man, who continued to kneel in the doorway and peer up at us blankly. "He's a robot naturally. The Allasu prefer theirs fleshy."

"Oh, my," I said, feeling faintly ill. "Is it real skin?"

"Heavens, no! It's all a trick of industrial dilly, of course, and the crafty application of paint. Some people find flesh easier to talk to, especially people from robot-weak cultures."

"It's gruesome," I said. "Why is the skin white like a fish belly?"

"They're albino, hairless and nude to differentiate them from true human beings, lest one Allasu accidentally commit the cardinal error of treating a peer as a slave."

"Is it really to our betterment to treat anyone as a slave?" I asked him. "Even those entirely within our power?"

Brother Phi put his hand on my shoulder and squeezed affectionately. "You could have been a Zorannite, my dear Simon. Tell me, would you ever consider donating any of your progeny to the order?"

"I'm not entirely sure my actual children are real. It's on my list of matters that need looking into."

Brother Phi smiled consolingly. "Well, keep me apprised. Shall we get on with it?" He started toward the door.

"Wait. *Is* the robot reading our minds?"

"No no – there's no telepathy to it, pilgrim," replied Phi with a friendly laugh; "the robot speaks High Allat. Aren't you acquainted? It is the pride and joy of the Allasu culture: a language so refined and subtle that speaking it aloud is considered crass in the extreme. Wonderfully curious, isn't it? Let us not dawdle now – the Halcyons await."

In a long and silent line we trailed along the labyrinthine stone corridors until we came to a case of broad white steps, leading up to a higher level of the Citadel, out of the well of guest cells. I gestured for Glory to precede me but she shook her head. "No coital way; you go first, Simon."

Pish held my hand. We mounted the risers one by one, each step bringing another swath of a great gilded hall into view, beginning with a domed ceiling inset with mosaic patterns and continuing along wide golden pillars whose edges captured the light in bands of shining, greenish reflection.

I smelled incenses, and people.

We stood upon the threshold of a massive auditorium, tiers of kneeling men and women densely banding before a raised stage framed by tall plates whose faces crawled with a seemingly endless list of names. At the base of these tall plates men and women in various costumes wept theatrically. On the stage itself an elaborate rite was taking place: dancers dressed as blue and orange birds fawned fans over robed figures with feathered headdresses, flanked by naked and hairless slave robots with ivory, human-like skin.

No one spoke.

It was not silent in the auditorium, but what noise there was was unsettling: the random scrapes of leg against leg, foot on stone, hair on robes; the intermittent catching of breath, or cough; the impenetrable hiss of lesser sounds, a background of muted miscellany. Occasionally a sob spiked into audibility.

Then the air buzzed as the congregation mouthed a series of sacred syllables, following the exaggerated silent mouth movements of the onstage clergy, their wet tongues and teeth flashing under amber lights. The concerted motion swept through the ranks, like a message propagated through a sea of ants, causing the crowd to exude an aspect that was distinctly insectile.

I shuddered.

Brother Phi took my shoulder and tugged me onward. Our destination lay beyond the auditorium. We passed through an arched doorway carved with the likeness of bodies, and crossed a bridge over a choir in a shallow stone well whose almost inaudible voices emanated not from their mouths but from instruments they held at their lips and plucked: a many-textured music that rustled gently against the quiet unlike anything I had ever heard. In a moment it was all reverberating into fuller silence behind us.

Glory held my arm on one side, Pish on the other. Only Brother Phi, the slave-man robot and Jeremiah seemed undisturbed at the heavy, alien atmosphere that weighed on this place like a wet blanket, making breathing difficult. Glory's hand was slick with sweat, and I could feel her pulse through her fingers.

We came upon a refectory. Its walls were high and carved into complex curlicues, each branching into a niche at the bottom housing the black matte visage of a solemn statue. Long tables were lined with nuns and monks in grey cassocks, each of them with a naked servant standing at one elbow and a line of patient petitioners at the other. We were invited to join the tail of one such line.

"What's going on?" whispered Pish, his quiet voice punctuating the muffled stillness of shuffling feet and clicking cutlery. Many people in the lines turned to stare.

"I think we're going to speak to one of the Citadel priests," I whispered back, straining to keep my voice confined to breath.

As the moments passed we slowly advanced. At the head of our line was an ancient-looking gentleman with a white beard and a liver-spotted head who was dottering over a bowl of broth, his rheumy eyes blinking at each supplicant in turn. The robot-girl at his elbow then leaned in to whisper his message into their ear.

The mechanisms of High Allat became plainer as I watched more exchanges. The language seemed to have phonemes, but rather than being voiced the lips and muscles of the face were gently twitched so as to *suggest* their imminent voicing. It was a language of *almost* spoken words, punctuated by a panoply of subtle half-winks, ticks, pursings and furrows that seemed to serve to disambiguate similar expressions.

If it had not been for my wordless time in the hospital just after my rebirth I might have lacked the sensitivity to appreciate the complexity of these nearly invisible signals, but I had gleaned the world of people through little else in those weeks and the experience left me sharpened.

Indeed, the clergy of the Citadel were not psychic – they were master observers of human micro-expressions.

I leaned into Brother Phi and whispered in his ear, "Did you not say the Reull were nearly unique in their path to unintelligibility? How then do we explain High Allat?"

He started nodding before I'd finished speaking, his ear bobbing before me. He took my head gently and pulled my ear around to his own mouth, his breath breaking into barely discernable syllables: "The people of this world speak Mechanical in the home – the audible version of Allat. Until a few years ago High Allat was strictly confined to Allasu courting rituals and ceremonies of marriage, oaths swearings, political speeches – that sort of thing. It has only been with the rise of the Citadel that High Allat has taken a broader role."

"But why?"

"Think about it, pilgrim. Speakers of High Allat may be inscrutable to others, but to them *every language is transparent*. What is a foreign vocabulary when you can read the thoughts off a man's brow? It is the perfect vehicle for receiving the pain of multicultural multitudes."

"Receiving pain?" I echoed. "Is that what they do here?"

"They process pain, that's perhaps a better way to put it. They have helped thousands come to terms with their grief. They listen, and they assign duties to help cleanse each individual spirit. The priests design a cathartic program for each kind of victim, from the mother who lost her child to the child who cares for a psychopathic mother."

Our turn came. We advanced. Brother Phi looked into the old man's eyes and I caught glimpses of their exchange; I saw Brother Phi's lips twitch with my name. The old man's pink, gluey eyes turned to me and he searched my face. I flushed under his gaze.

After a long moment he released me to glance at his hairless servant. The robot whispered into my ear with cool, scentless breath: "You will follow Brother Phi to the Halcyon Hall, Pilgrim Fell. Go now."

At that the old man concluded his meal. The robot cleared his place and then held his arm as he slowly walked toward the exit of the refectory, the line of supplicants following at a discreet distance and trailing him out. Another ancient fellow emerged from a nearby lavatory, drying his wrinkled hands on his cassock as his line of supplicants filed out after him.

"Eighteen hours of a priest's day are spent receiving and advising supplicants – while they eat, while they bathe, while they walk," Brother Phi breathed, tracing my gaze. "It is not an easy burden."

"Mother of love," I whispered. "But you do not do this?"

"I'm a Zorannite."

"Ah," I said, nodding as if this clarified anything.

We came into a round room with a fountain in the middle, under a high dome. Grey-robed monks and nuns of Recovery sat on marble benches in twos or threes. Our arriving footfalls were the only noise above the gurgling water in the fountain, and an odd rustling from above. Pish, Glory and I looked up to see compact, round-headed blue and orange birds fluttering about the apex.

A tall cleric with a ring of grey-streaked copper-coloured hair stepped up quickly and engaged in a silent exchange with Brother Phi. His skin was paler than Pish's – almost as pale as his slave robot. The copper-haired cleric glanced briefly at his slave, who sidled over and bent to my ear, whispering: "Master Dove Benedict understands that you wish to take the audience of Brother Phi."

I looked to the copper-haired cleric, and started to shake my head. He held up a ring-studded hand, and again glanced at the robot.

"There are fifty-nine queued before you," translated the naked robot. "The wait may be many hours. Brother Phi has implored Dove Benedict to admit this, and he will if it is your wish."

I glanced at Brother Phi, who nodded. I nodded in turn to Dove Benedict.

"Very well," intoned his slave. "Your party holds the number sixty."

And we were left alone. When a party of nuns stood up and disappeared through a small, ornate door at the far end of the room Glory scurried over to snatch their bench. We followed and sat down beside her. She leaned into my shoulder and whispered, "How long is this going to faecally take? Aren't you a mover and shaker, Simon? Can't you do a fornicated thing?"

"I think we're all just pilgrims here," I whispered back with a sigh. "Money can't buy us grace."

Just then a nun with feathery epaulettes flanked by two male-looking robots swished across the room and rushed up to our bench. One of the robots bent toward my ear and said, "Mr. Fell, it is an honor and privilege to have an esteemed guest such as yourself here at our humble Citadel. The Mistress Sister Empathy bids you welcome, and entreats you to follow her to the special lounge."

Many eyes followed us as Pish, Jeremiah, Glory, Brother Phi, Mistress Sister Empathy, her two naked robots and myself formed a little parade weaving through the other supplicants as we crossed the chamber and went through the ornate little door. We took a long, oddly dark passage through to what was unmistakably a kind of royal court: an empty throne on an ornate dais surrounded by lesser seats occupied by silent clergy, the walls draped in rich tapestries of dizzying geometric designs and the floor a stylized map of the Panstellar Neighbourhood.

Brother Phi knelt down on one knee, so we did too. Even Jeremiah.

I heard a rustling of drapes, and then caught scent of a woman. I looked up to see a white-robed figure stepping out from the wing and ascending the throne with an ethereal grace. Her heavy-lashed eyes were almond-shaped, her lips full and drawn into a slight frown. Her dark hair was short and feathery, brushed forward like a bird, and ornamented with silver clasps.

She looked as achingly beautiful as I always thought she would, once her head was no longer crushed in. It was, of course, Faeda.

Jeremiah stepped up at my side and spoke quietly in my ear just after one of the flanking clergy stood briefly and struck a small gong, its muted report terrifying against the backdrop of profound silence. Translated Jeremiah: "Blessed are we in the presence of our queen of infinite compassion, the noble High Priestess of this Citadel of the Galactic Recovery, the great Lady Paz Faedaleen Aza."

Lady Aza fixed me with her gaze and bid me to stand with an almost imperceptible flick of her chin. I rose, and I saw the corners of her mouth pull in a micro-smile – she was pleased that I could follow her. I noticed her gold-flecked brown eyes dart over to Jeremiah.

"Pray tell what brings you before us, Pilgrim Fell?"

Do you remember me, Lady? I voiced in my head, keeping my lips mute and letting the thoughts play out across my features.

"Should we, Cherished Pilgrim?" translated Jeremiah.

I knew you in a hospital. I thought I saw you smile, in remembrance.

"We did suffer a malady, but we have no memory of our recuperation," passed on Jeremiah, though I was starting to catch the gist of her meaning from the lady's face alone.

I did my best to let my face imitate the subtle pulses I had seen the clerics use: *we were friends.*

Lady Aza smiled noncommittally. "That is well," said Jeremiah.

A pause. *I have come before you to understand the relationship between your efforts of mercy and those of my corporation.*

A longer pause. Translated Jeremiah, "A clerk will be assigned for your interviewing convenience. Go in peace, Pilgrim Fell."

Lady Aza began to rise. "No, wait!" I blurted without thinking, causing everyone in the room to frown and one of the clerics near me to hiss like an angry cat. "I don't need a clerk – Faeda, please! I'm telling you there's something rotten in all this! I need your help."

The nearest bald, naked robot to the lady placed his hands over her ears.

Our party was escorted brusquely from the throne room, back down the dark corridor, and returned to the Halcyon Hall. "That break from protocol may not have been profitable to your cause," mentioned Brother Phi quietly. The monk nearest him hissed.

"Oh, shut up!" shrieked Glory. "Curdled vomit! This is the most coitally repressive rectal stain of a society I've ever faecally seen!"

"Er, now now miss –" started Phi.

She advanced menacingly on a group of hissing nuns, who shrank back in horror. Glory swung her handbag and then repeatedly kicked the air in front of them with her tall black boots. "Take some of that!" she leered. "Freaks!"

The nuns blanched and gasped, falling over one another to flee the hall. One of them fell into the fountain, and she screamed. This primitive vocalization seemed to panic the other fifty, who stampeded and grunted their way toward a clot of robed humanity thrashing at the narrow exit.

"This is a hall of meditation and consolation," whispered a pale robot, touching Glory's shoulder.

She smacked it with a wicked whip of her handbag. "Speak up!" she yelled. "I can't fornicating *hear you!*"

One of the fleeing nuns fainted, and was picked up by two robots.

Glory's voice echoed away into silence. We all stood there for a moment, frozen. Then with a gasp the nun in the fountain peeked out of the water, saw us, and submerged again. Jeremiah walked over calmly and fished her out. When he tried to deposit her gently on a stone bench she scrambled out of his reach, slipping on the wet floor and skidding the length of the hall. With a squeak she got to her feet and vaulted through the doorway.

Pish cracked up laughing first.

It was contagious. Even Brother Phi was turning red in the face as he guffawed, his chins jiggling in sympathetic motion. Glory fell down and laughed on the floor. I closed my eyes and found myself laughing and crying at the same time.

"I know this is terrible," wheezed Phi. "I know we've just disturbed the sanctity of a great institution, but –" he paused, chuckled again. "It's just *such a relief.*"

"Yeah," agreed Pish. "This place fellates."

This inspired a renewed round of riotous laughter. I was forced to sit down. I lay on my back and laughed at the domed ceiling. A feeling of great peace came over me, and I breathed in deeply. "You know what?" I heard myself saying. "Let's just go home."

There was no reply, so I leaned up on one elbow and looked at Pish. "How would you like that?" I asked him. "Do you want to go home?"

He shrugged, and smiled at me crookedly. "Yeah."

"Glory?" I called, looking over to where she was draped over a bench, lying on her side.

She snorted. "Where's home?"

"Anywhere we want, I imagine. Look at it this way, Yatti Olorio has gone to a lot of trouble to forge this life for me. I was prepared to sacrifice anything to find out why, when I thought I had nothing left." I chuckled. "I know that sounds stupid."

Glory and Pish were watching me. Jeremiah and Phi, too.

I continued, "So maybe Fellcorp has found a way to profit from the Kamari Horror, and just maybe the Citadel of the Recovery has, too. Maybe there's even something sick about how they've perverted the situation." I licked my lips. "But it's too big for me. I can't save the galaxy from men like Olorio. I can't even hope to understand people like these Citadelites."

I looked up at Pish. "It isn't true that I have nothing left. I've got friends." I looked at Glory. "Why don't we all just settle down somewhere, and let the galaxy sort itself out?" I looked back at Pish. "We'll eat nothing short of the second best food the worlds have to offer. I promise."

When no one said anything I flushed, and stood up. "This is what everyone wants, isn't it? This is what everyone's been trying to get me to do – nothing at all. So why shouldn't I? If so many lives have been ruined, shouldn't we just count ourselves lucky for having what we do, and live on? Shouldn't we just lie on the floor and laugh?"

Glory looked me fully in the eyes, and pushed a stray braid out of her face. "That sounds really nice, Simon," she said.

But Pish shook his head.

"What is it?" I asked.

"You said it yourself, Simon. Something's wrong with what they're doing. And we're the only ones who have any idea." He blinked. "Don't we *have* to do something?"

I sat down again, my heart heavy. I thought of Duncan, and about the kinds of values he wanted his son to understand. I nodded sadly, and sighed. "You're right, Pish. We do."

"Don't worry. If we figure it out it'll all be worth it," added Pish.

"And if we don't they'll kill us," said Glory darkly.

I looked up at Jeremiah and narrowed my eyes. "No..." I said slowly. "I don't think they will."

At that moment a pale robot entered the hall and stopped beside me, leaning in to my ear. "The Lady Aza will receive Pilgrim Fell for a private supper. Come now."

I looked over at the others, my eyes wide. "Go on!" said Brother Phi. "If there's anything to your suspicions, this is your chance to ask the very heart of the Citadel! Don't worry – I will see to your wards, pilgrim."

I nodded to the human-shaped robot and followed it through the small door again, down the dark corridor, and along an unseen branch that curved past a dozen other doors. I found myself in a windowed diningroom containing several niched statues and a long table with a setting at either end. The world outside was a liquid starscape of falling snow.

I removed my red leather longcoat and draped it over the back of one of the chairs. I slipped out my diary and began the day's narration, glancing toward the doorway every few moments. I left off as I saw a shadow cross the threshold.

Lady Aza entered and closed the door behind her by pressing a contact on the wall. She took her seat and demurely unfolded a napkin upon her lap. She looked up, held my eyes a moment, and then ceremoniously filled her glass from a tall, sweating bottle of clear fluid at her elbow. When she was finished she gingerly picked up a slim, silver fork and turned it over in her hands for a few moments, eyes cast downward.

A split second later the fork was filling my vision. I dodged sideways and ducked low. The little piece of silverware bounced off the back of my chair and tinkled to the floor.

"Hello, Simon," she said.

I straightened in my chair and cleared my throat. "Hello, Faeda."

She pinned me with her eyes. "Hearing my voice – to you it's nothing, isn't it?"

I tried to smile. "You have a lovely speaking voice. Do you sing?"

"This is Allatu. Singing is pornography."

"I didn't mean to be impolite."

"But you should, Simon," she said with a teasing lilt. "You *must* be impolite."

"Why should I be impolite to you, Faeda?"

"Because," she said, "I wouldn't want to be the only one who's wet."

I blinked. "I'm sorry?"

Faeda squirmed in her chair in a strange way and smiled lopsidedly. "I think I had an orgasm today. Did you know that? I've had *fantasies* about the sound of shouting echoing off the walls of the court, but the reality was so much more – violent."

I cringed in anticipation of another attack and she laughed. "Now now – do not fret, Simon. I'm all better." She licked her lips and smiled strangely again. "Well, *mostly* better."

"You have your memories back, then?" I said, attempting to sound genial despite my unease.

She sipped from her glass. "Yes. And you yours?"

"I'm afraid not," I said. I poured my glass full from the bottle at my end of the table: a dry wine. Not bad. Pointy, but well angled. "Do you still read poetry?"

"No. I am instead a poet. I am a producer, a consumer no longer."

"That's wonderful!" I said, my voice an unconscious imitation of Brother Phi's jubilance.

Faeda smiled tightly. "It's novel."

We sat in silence as the slave-robot entered to serve our food – a series of small silver bowls each filled with a differently textured paste, and a dish of steaming flatbread dusted with spice. I watched Faeda fill a round of bread with a scoop from each bowl, and then deftly roll it up before cutting into it with her fork and knife. Then I tried to copy her, with messier results.

After the servant had left Faeda giggled at my clumsiness. To derail any line of mocking inquiry I quickly asked, "What sort of poetry do you write?"

"I write in the medium of lives. I re-organize them until they are beautiful. I publish in the form of galactic history." She tilted her head coquettishly, her silver hair-clasps winking in the light.

I smiled, and pushed at my food without hunger. "That's quite a genre."

"I did not choose this cage," she replied with icy conviction. "When my elder sister died in the attack that wounded me, the stewardship of the Recovery came upon my unwilling shoulders."

"Who would attack Citadelites?"

"Enemies, idiots, heretics," she said dismissively. "It is no longer a matter of concern. My focus is on the future. I am charged with the mission of maintaining this movement, for it now sustains the whole of House Aza and our allies."

"I understand that you've helped a lot of people."

"Yes," she agreed. "And they in turn shall help us, for the religion we give them will crystallize our influence at Praxiteles Star – and beyond. You see I am thinking first of my house, as any noble girl should."

She emptied her glass and then threw it at me. It shattered against the wall.

"What about Fellcorp?"

Faeda smiled, her cheeks rosy. "I'm so glad you asked, Simon. As you likely do not know my sister was engaged in a long battle against Fellcorp, arguing that your medicines were retarding rather than accelerating the healing process for victims of the Horror. She publicly denounced Fellcorp's pharmaceuticals, and declared their use anti-Recovery."

"And was it true? Did our medicines hinder rather than help?"

"Of course it was true, Simon. It's *still* true."

I dropped my fork. "How can that be? I heard it myself from the Incorporation that Citadel research helped Fellcorp create new products, designed specifically to help victims of the Horror."

She smiled tightly again. "When giants wrestle, villages are crushed. Do you understand me, Simon? The conflict between Fellcorp and the Citadel was destructive. It was essential that a way be sought to co-exist peacefully, lest we find our market of potential supplicants thinned by polarizing politics. So for the good of all we reached an arrangement."

"An arrangement?"

"A mutually beneficial pact. You see the long term goals of this Citadel and Fellcorp are identical: we both require a steady supply of damaged human beings. We both do our truck in ruin."

My mouth was dry. I could not eat, or drink. "You hope to keep the victims suffering?"

"A means to an end," shrugged Faeda. "And, most unfortunately, an insufficient one. What we really need, of course, is fresh ruin."

"Fresh ruin?" I echoed dumbly.

She nodded, and smacked her dish against the corner of the table so that it broke apart. "You don't know what it's like in this cage. You don't know what it's like to be ever silent. You don't know what it's like to be this porcelain doll on parade for their solace – forgetting the taste of meat, or noise, or sex."

"I don't follow you –"

"Poetry!" Faeda cried. "Point, counter-point! Harmony and rhythm: balance! Great works are wrought only accidentally by nature, but *by design* from those of vision! The great engines of the galaxy require fuel, elixir against stultifying stagnance. Look at the gift of the Recovery, a gift borne of blood!"

"You will author a new horror," I said slowly as it dawned on me.

"Yes!" agreed Faeda, her almond eyes wide. "And *you* are going to give it to me."

"Me?" I retorted, furrowing my brow. "How?"

She pushed her chair back and walked over to a transparent data-plate mounted on the wall opposite the windows. Her fingers danced over a corner of it and then its face illuminated with the image of row upon row of fierce-looking birds with hooked beaks and sharp talons.

I was overwhelmed by a feeling of vertigo, bile burning in my throat as I felt pinned by column after column of beady avian eyes, shiny and dark and bottomless like those of robots, ringed in flairs of feather, speckled in muted colours that simulated dappled moonlight or shining in unfettered primaries to declare a brazen fearlessness. In the lower left quadrant: the bird I knew. Images from my half-forgotten nightmares leered at me from just beneath the veil of my conscious mind, causing it to stretch and tear.

I shrank back and Faeda grinned. "So, Simon," she chanted in an eerie sing-song voice reminiscent of Olorio, "which one of these birds means something to you?"

I turned my face away but it had already betrayed me. Her expert skill could trace the line of my eye in a blink. "What does it mean?" I moaned miserably, staring at the carpet.

"It's the solution to a puzzle," gloated Faeda with evident satisfaction, fingertips skittering over the plate's controls before it went dark. "It's the final key we'll need when our expedition launches tomorrow."

"Expedition? To where?" I croaked.

She laughed. "Why – to Kamari Star, naturally." She walked over to me and started kneading my shoulders, my tense muscles quivering under her strong fingers. She said, "I'm surprised at your surprise. I'd have thought you would have worked it out. I thought that's why you'd come."

"Olorio is Volmash, isn't he?" I barked suddenly, grabbing her wrist and turning around in my seat.

She stared at me for a long moment without resisting, and then gingerly bent down and planted her teeth cruelly into the fleshy part of my hand. I bellowed and yanked my arm away. She wiped a line of blood from her lip and licked her lips clean. "I suspected as much," she said. "I imagine that's what you found out before."

"Before?"

"Before he wiped your mind," she said.

"But if Olorio had my mind in his hands, why doesn't he have the key himself?"

"I have never known," she admitted. "But he knew you were close. He told me I'd be able to get it from you, once his doctor had softened you up."

"His doctor...?" I frowned. "Dr. Pemma?"

"I don't care," declared Faeda with a sniff, sweeping the rest of her dishes onto the floor and then draining her bottle of drink. "You've given me what I want, and now our expedition will have an easy time of it. The Nightmare Cannon will soon be in my hands, and the galaxy's need for the Recovery will never end."

I wilted in my chair. I thought I was going to throw up. "And now what?" I asked weakly. "You kill me?"

A bizarre expression crossed Faeda's face, and it was a moment before I realized she was starting to cry. "No," she sobbed with sudden violence. "No, Simon! Don't you realize why I'm telling you all of this? Don't you understand why I'm letting you hear...my perversion – my *voice*?"

I shook my head.

"Because I love you, Simon. I loved you in the hospital back on Samundra, and I love you now. You can't hide anything from me. *I can see through your face*."

I held myself rigidly still by force of will, betraying nothing. Inside I was turning in nauseous loops, a cold feeling of unreality tingling up from my limbs and muffling my body, making my head feel disconnected and distant. "You're a monster," I said.

She smiled. "Yes. A beautiful, beautiful monster."

"And I'm involved. I was Olorio's man, and now you tell me I've given you all the cards. Will you destroy Olorio, too?"

"In time, yes. When the Citadel outgrows Fellcorp. You and I shall dance on his grave."

"You *should* kill me," I said.

"And you me," she replied. "But I won't and neither will you. I won't because I want to play with you, and you won't because I promise you that if you raise a hand to me I will assure that your ward's torture will resound through the ages as an acme of depravity."

"My ward? Do you mean Pish?" I cried, growing anxious as she inserted herself between me and the only exit.

"The screams of children are special to me," said Faeda dreamily, twisting a lock of her hair in her fingers. After a pause she yanked the hairs out of her head, and let them drift to the floor. "What's special to you, Simon?"

When I did not reply she moved forward and grabbed my face in her hand, twisting my cheeks viciously. "You see I am naked before you, Simon. That's the trust I'm willing to extend. I hide nothing from you. I spare nothing. Because what you and I have is *pure.*"

"Yes," I mumbled between her fingers.

"I knew you would understand. I knew you would not wish to remain Olorio's puppet." She released my face and kissed my chin, whispering, "Together we will crush him, and floss with his sinews."

"Good," I murmured, eyes wide.

She pulled suddenly back to dash my dishes away with a sweep of her arm, then sat up on the table. "You will now fornicate me, you spit-sucking larva." She locked her legs around me and pulled me into the side of the table painfully. "You will now prove your love to me, Simon, or I will suck out your eyes."

Burning within from the effort of locking my thoughts out of my facial muscles, I nearly lost control as I tried for more time. "Not here," I said.

"Here," she declared, shaking her head. "Now," she insisted, nodding.

I tried to wrench aside her clamped thighs and duck through but she tightened the pressure and I got nowhere. I thrashed again and in response she knocked my torso viciously between her knees, causing me to sputter and slump.

"Playful," she cooed. I felt dizzy.

Faeda tore her white robes, and then ripped the seam of her underclothes down the front exposing tan curves. She twisted on the table, laying on her back with her legs still locked around me, arching her back and pushing her breasts into the air.

"Want me," she commanded.

"This is wrong," I said.

"Yes," she agreed lasciviously.

At her mercy we fornicated, there upon the dining table. The lights had somehow dimmed. The room was silent but for our noises. I felt disconnected from the rude event, numbed and broken. My body responded of its own accord. She keened like a beast and I saw her chin was bloody. I had not felt her bite me.

I wondered in a meandering way whether I had been drugged. I wondered how terrible had been the crimes of Volmash's accomplices. With my face pushed roughly into Crushed Head Faeda's armpit I wondered how long it had been apparent to me that I would not survive the night.

I felt fear but it did not scare me. Does that make any sense? It was like freezing without shivering, or burning without pain. I was calm.

And thus it was with a kind of homey expectation that I accepted the moment when Faeda took up my cutlery and repeatedly drove its pieces into my torso. I noticed placidly that each withdrawal was met with an arc of inky liquid that splashed up against Faeda's contorted face. I recognized dimly that under more ideal lighting conditions my blood would likely appear more red than black.

There did seem to be a terrific lot of it.

The world became misty.

And then a cold fire shot through my veins and I could feel my heart pumping, hear myself gasping, feel the icy pain in my lungs when I tried to draw deeply. I opened eyes that I had not realized were closed and saw Faeda's head lolling with glazed eyes, her limp neck clutched between my own spasmodically squeezing fingers.

I opened my hands and her head hit my sternum. Somewhere in the fog I had strangled Faeda until she died.

My hands ached.

This realization opened the door to other sensations: I was wet. My clothes, ripped aside as they had been, were also wet. The haze of winking stars in my vision as I tried to inhale was a product of a savage bramble of pain throbbing and bucking in my chest. My abdomen was throbbing beneath the weight of Faeda's body, my legs numb. I had been stabbed many, many times.

"Mother of love," I whispered, "I am killed."

This seemed like a dramatic thing to say, but I recognized that my ability to say it meant I had not actually expired. My wheezing continued to echo through the diningroom, which Faeda had no doubt ordered left undisturbed for a great long time while she...played with me.

I could not raise my head. I tried to activate my telephone, but it seemed to have been bitten off. I could feel a breeze inside of me.

And yet I did not die.

With a great effort I managed to feel out across the table surface, now slick with my blood, until I caught the edge of my longcoat. I removed the plastic blue diary and dropped it next to my head.

...Which pretty much catches us up to the present.

There are a few things I'd like to add, before I go.

First of all, I, Nestor Simonithrat Fell – er, apparently – being of sound mind and lacerated body, do hereby bequeath the whole of my worldly treasures to Piciatus Menteith...to do with as he sees fit.

Should laws curtail his freedom to transact due to his age, I place my trust in his proxy, Vera Tse Llatella-Bond, who is also known as Glory. If she cannot fulfill her duties then let his robot Jeremiah be his guardian. I don't care what your laws are with respect to that. I'm a robot softie.

The Citadel of the Recovery has been corrupted, and Fellcorp is a predator. Yatti Olorio is Terron Volmash, and he means to profit by the Horror. Why am I the only one who knows?

Let this diary come to whatever authority is best suited to investigate my testimony here. I don't know who that might be. The Navy? The Queen of Space? I don't know. I'm...having trouble concentrating...

Uh-oh, here we go.

Something's happening.

So this is how it feels to die.

XXXIII.
JEREMIAH'S SECRET

I awoke. This, in and of itself, was surprising.

I inhabited a hazy world of white light and soothing voices, defocused and meaningless. Nurse Randa patted my cheek at one point, and I tried to turn to kiss her hand but I was too weak. Nurse Wennel was laughing at something. A machine went *ping!*

Though I did not notice the transition, it became apparent to me that Nurse Hiwai was straddling me. I wondered if we were having sex. She was thrusting down upon my chest, her face pinched in effort. "Stay with me!" she sang. "Come on now, Simon – don't let go!"

"Okay," I agreed, and the machine went *ping!* again.

This was followed by a dreamy period, in which I ran through the hospital cafeteria with no clothes on. I knew the nurses were stalking me so I cast about for a place to hide. Crushed Head Faeda turned toward me, offering to conceal me beneath her hospital chemise, half of her mouth smiling while the other drooled.

I tried to scream.

And then I found myself beneath the curved, glowing ceiling of the tiny, four-bed ward aboard the *Neago*. I tried to sit up but four gentle hands restrained me. "You are safe," I was informed, "do not panic."

"Very well," I conceded.

Dr. Pemma rushed into the ward, stepped up beside my bed and looked over a plate dangling from the headboard. "Congratulations Simon," she said tartly. "You're alive."

"I suppose you had something to do with that," I said.

"Rather, yes. You were quite a mess."

"Thank you."

"Not at all. I have sworn an oath."

With her assistance I was able to sit up slightly, my chest bound in a network of somewhat constrictive bandages. "An oath to keep me alive until every last bit of useful information is extracted?" I asked bitingly.

She did not deny it. She pursed her lips. "A lot has happened while you were unconscious, Simon. Not the least of which is that I have tendered my resignation to Fellcorp Mercy."

"Who commands you now?" I scoffed.

"My conscience," she answered acidly, "and my oath to do no harm. There's more, but understand now that I am on your side. You need to sleep."

"I just woke up."

"The anaesthetic field has just been collapsed. Now you need *real* sleep."

I tried to object again but my head lolled over onto my shoulder and I fell into dream: bird-women with claws, beaks pecking at my heart, a flutter of bloody feathers, the scream of a child.

I awoke with the feeling that time had passed. Outside the porthole was a starless blackness. With the support of a medical robot I managed to shuffle across the ward and void my bladder. Pressing the muscles in my abdomen ached. My pee was clear.

"Where are the others?" I asked the robot. "Where are Glory and Pish?"

"Sir, Patient Pish is in the observation matrix."

"What?" I yelped, turning too quickly and sending a crackle of pain down my side. "*Patient* Pish? What happened? Take me to him immediately!" I grabbed the robot's arm and started to tug on it.

"You are safe, do not panic," suggested the robot.

"Shut up!"

I pulled on a hospital robe over my pajamas and belted the sash roughly as I stumbled out into the corridor and winced at the bright lights. "Coital fire!" I roared, throwing my forearm in front of my face and thereby causing pain to shoot across my chest. I howled, and slumped against the wall.

Dr. Pemma ran out into the corridor. "Simon! What are you doing out of bed?"

"Pish," I hissed through gritted teeth. "Take me to see Pish."

For the second time I saw the doctor's face soften. "Alright," she conceded. "You can hold on to me. Come on now."

I propped myself up against Dr. Pemma and put my arm around her shoulders. "Thank you," I murmured as we shuffled along. She led me back through the doorway through which she'd come, a round room with a clear tank in the centre. Glory was asleep, the side of her face pressed into the glass. The tank was filled with a pink, viscous fluid. Lying at its bottom was Pish.

He was nude, and a horrifying tear ran across his abdomen, an open gash whose loose edges waved lightly in the pink fluid's currents.

"What happened?" I asked hoarsely.

Dr. Pemma crossed her arms and sighed. "After I'd finished treating about a dozen people you panicked, I went to the Halcyon Hall to tear a strip off you. But you weren't there. The boy said you were in trouble. He said...he said he could smell your blood in the air. We tried to stop him but he took off, tearing through the Citadel to find you. We followed, of course. He found you – Jeremiah forced the door. We – saw you..."

She closed her eyes for a moment and continued. "Naturally, I started treating you on the spot. Security arrived seconds later, and saw Aza's body. Then – everything just exploded."

"Exploded?"

"Citadelites started pouring into the room, wailing, screaming, tearing out their hair, weeping, praying, scratching themselves bloody. It was terrifying. Glory picked up Pish and Jeremiah and I carried you out, but they wanted to stop us. A Zorannite monk named Phi tried to stand between us and them, but they beat him to the floor."

She trailed off again, and then found her voice with effort. "It was madness. Their grief transformed into a riot. I thought we were escaping unscathed, but when we got outside into the snow Glory started screaming that someone had killed the boy. I went to him. I – didn't know what to think."

She looked up at me, her yellow eyes moist.

"You didn't know what to think about what?" I prompted gently.

Dr. Pemma wiped her eyes with the sleeve of her labcoat. "You don't know, do you?"

"Is Pish going to die, Doctor?" I cut in, frowning.

"Come here," she said. I hobbled along beside her to the side of the tank. She tapped her fingers upon it, causing menus and labels to glow on the glass surface. A circle was drawn before us, and by looking through it we could see a grotesquely magnified image of Pish's slashed belly. I tried to turn away, bile rising in my throat. "Look," commanded Dr. Pemma. "Just watch."

I looked. And then I stared. With even a moment's study it was plain that the wound was moving. "Why is it doing that...?" I whispered, sickened. "Glory's fixers?"

"Not entirely incorrect," said Dr. Pemma, nodding. "There are fixers there, but they come from the boy himself. Look more closely."

She tapped a glowing control and the view within the circle jumped larger, defocused corpuscles of giant-sized air bubbles coasting through the foreground. In the background was the inside of Pish's abdomen. Despite my limited knowledge of human anatomy it was clear to me that I should have been seeing the pink, red and grey lumpiness of organic viscera – not bands of shining filaments, knitting themselves together in a graceful ballet as mite-like fixers scurried around them. A lip of Pish's pelvis was exposed, and it was silver.

"How...how could you not see this?" I heard myself ask. "You must have seen this when you scanned us."

Dr. Pemma shook her head. "I was fooled. It's quite ingenious, actually. The pseudo-epidermic layer is scattered with microscopic projectors which collectively broadcast false tomology. Down to the smallest detail, every system." She smiled nervously. "A work of art, if you will."

"But why?" I wondered aloud. "Why go to so much trouble to disguise a robot?"

"That's no robot," pronounced the doctor seriously. "That's a human executive."

The words hung in the air heavily. I blinked. "A human executive?"

"Yes, of course," replied Dr. Pemma. "Just like him."

She turned around and pointed to a figure I had not noticed standing in the shadows beside the door. "Who is that?" I demanded, reaching out for the doctor's arm to support me.

Jeremiah stepped forward out the gloom, his blue-green carapace glinting with pink highlights from the bubbling tank. "Sir," he said.

I leaned heavily against Dr. Pemma, my legs feeling suddenly rubbery. As Jeremiah moved forward I saw that his carapace was scratched and marked in various places, including a rough crack that ran across the lower half of his face, exposing the glinting components within. "What's happened to you, Jeremiah?" I asked.

"Sir, it is time for us to have a talk."

Dr. Pemma showed us to her office. I sank gratefully into the chair on the patient's side of the desk, and Jeremiah sat down neatly in the chair on the doctor's side. The doctor disappeared into the corridor and the door slid shut with a soft chuff of air. I looked at Jeremiah.

Carefully and methodically, he felt around the edges of his cracked masque and disengaged the seals one by one. He removed the back of his head, and then pulled away the front pieces and placed them on the desk.

Though his head was now a mud of electronic devices and wires, he did not cease his strip tease.

Jeremiah next disengaged a catch beneath his chin, and peeled off a layer of components. He removed rings of functional-looking metal from around his black eyes, and then reached up and deftly cracked his own skull in half. He unfolded the sides and put them on the table next to the pieces of his masque.

And I saw Jeremiah's face.

Like the human executive I had glimpsed on Maja's World Train, his skin was both leathery and coppery at the same time, creased and wrinkled with the record of a range of expressions, crow's feet at the corner of his eyes and pinched in the corners of his mouth. Unlike the first human executive I had seen Jeremiah had no hair, though he did have faint traces of eyebrows composed of short, translucent fibres. His nostrils were mere slits, his ears faint parabolas of skin around similar slits. His neck was thin, and his face narrow. His hard black eyes were utterly unchanged.

"You have many questions Simon," he said, his voice warmer and more fluid but of the same basic timbre. "I am now in a position to answer some of them."

"Why?" I shot back quickly. "What's changed?"

"My true nature has been revealed. Further obfuscation would not be productive, particularly if you are to understand why Pish must not at this point learn the truth."

"You want me to lie to him?"

"I want you to co-operate with the imperatives of this program, lest I find myself obliged to end you."

I swallowed. "Okay," I said, nodding. "So what can you tell me?"

"What would you care to know?"

"You're a human executive," I said. "What does that mean? What *are* you?"

"We began as a form of robot, long ago at the Solar Star. But where robots are things which *simulate* consciousness, we were built to possess it."

"Built? By whom?"

"By Dr. Drago Tesla Zoran, the greatest mathematician history has ever known. It was his conviction that humanity was too fragile for galactic life, and he labored for many years to bring about a kind of human being with greater mettle; animals adaptable to a range of environments beyond Earth and her progeny. Animals who could stand alone, without a supporting infrastructure of teeming Solar ecosystems."

"You're a kind of superhuman, then?"

"Yes," replied Jeremiah seriously. "I am stronger and faster than the most athletic human being who has ever lived. My auto-immune system is orders of magnitude more sophisticated than yours, and can even repair near-mortal damage without assistance. I have at my disposal some seven hundred thousand times more knowledge than your brain could store at its maximum theoretical capacity. I am more fuel-efficient than you are. Should I find myself without resources, I am capable of living in stasis for nearly unlimited periods of time. I require neither gravity nor light, neither food as you know it nor drink. I am, in a way no human being could ever approach, *self-reliant.*"

I chewed the inside of my lip thoughtfully. "Well," I quipped darkly, "that's pretty impressive. One wonders why you keep us lot around at all."

His features softened in a way not unlike Dr. Pemma's, the wrinkles at the corners of his eyes unfolding as he smiled glumly. "Because we love you," he said.

"Love?" I echoed, furrowing my brow. "You are capable of love, then?"

"I am human," declared Jeremiah heavily.

"How can that be?" I argued. "Designed by a man, yes – in imitation of a man's form, yes – you're even self-aware, you claim...but how does any of that make you *human?*"

"Humanity is a concept of identity," explained Jeremiah patiently. "The creation of the human executive race was predicated on a foundation of human civilization, the gemstone of Solar life. Our context is human history. We define the universe in human terms. But we are not artifacts, for these connections *mean* something to us."

"So you're an alien thing in touch with its roots, what does that prove?" I shot back. "Can you feel the full panoply of emotion? Are human executives greedy? Lustful? Jealous?"

"We do not share your emotional palette, for we are different kinds of animals with a set of instincts appropriate to our way of life. For instance, I am currently craving carbon."

"An emotion is distinct from an instinct," I claimed.

Jeremiah shook his head curtly. "No. Your emotional palette is an expression of your instinctive infrastructure, honed by natural selection to serve you in the environmental and social context of your creation under Sol. Your altruism is a statistical gamble tuned to maximize kin selection. Beauty is an algorithm for evaluating health. Your feelings of jealousy alter the count of germ cells in your testicles. You cry when you are sad so that other primates can recognize and respond to your internal state, a trick learned before language."

"And yet your feelings lack those roots. How can you call them human?"

"It is a matter of orientation. When Dr. Zoran made us, he could have turned us out to the stars to abandon man for our own history – but he didn't. He was convinced that the computer of Earth may have tested the human design in ways his own calculations could not match. He was certain that, to become a fuller organism, it was essential that our race live in kinship with our prototypes. So that we might continue to learn from you."

"You are our superior analogue. I'll grant you that. But you will forget us one day."

"Never," answered Jeremiah quickly, "you are a part of us."

"Would you miss us? Would it cause you heartache? Do you even feel a need for pain?"

Jeremiah reached out and touched my hand on the desk, the rubber on his fingertips warm. "You must understand, Simon," he said; "we do not feel pain *as* you do. We feel pain *because* you do."

"I don't follow."

"If I felt the pain of a human being, it would be an analogue as you describe – a simulation of synthesized human experience, experienced in turn by me. What would be the purpose? However, the concept of pain – both physical and psychological – has value to a thinking organism. Thus, we have pain. *Our* pain."

I sat back and rubbed my chin. "It sounds perverse," I declared. "But I think I'm beginning to understand. You are not men, but you are created in the image of man's soul – so you view yourselves as a kind of human offspring. Is this the source of your fealty to our *fragile* civilization?"

"Solar civilization is not fragile," countered Jeremiah smoothly. "On the contrary it is very robust, and its program of expansion promises to make it even more so."

"And yet there are barbarian worlds, and worlds of war, and repressive societies that generate monsters..." I trailed off, shuddering as I thought of Crushed Head Faeda. "What's so robust about this mess?"

"Variation," said Jeremiah, "is humanity's greatest asset. Solar worlds rise and fall, change and depopulate, invade and assimilate – a constant roiling of culture generating new attempted matches for the human emotional-political landscape at a fantastic pace." Jeremiah smirked, which I found unnerving. He continued, "Can you imagine what a purely human executive world would be like? Dead, self-same, and eternal. Stability is our detriment, *for we were born too rational."* He held up his hands in a gesture of almost-theatrical helplessness. "The Solar computer retains a dynamism beyond the reach of human executive philosophy."

"So we can do something you can't?"

"There are many things you can do that we cannot. Parenting, for example."

"Parenting?" I echoed, baffled. Then I wondered aloud: "When were you born, Jeremiah?"

"Over fifty million hours ago. I doubt the calendrical date would have any meaning to you."

"Where were you born, then?"

"On Ares at Sol, before space was space." He paused, then added, "The same as the other fifteen."

"What does that mean? There are only sixteen human executives? I thought you said your kind were born, and raised and educated?"

"We have a population of millions. New bodies are synthesized, in which are seated a replication of one of the sixteen patterns of consciousness achieved by Dr. Zoran. These new iterations of the original patterns are then socialized and acclimatized to modern human executive existence."

"What does that mean – patterns of consciousness?"

"Unlike human beings who have a common racial architecture for self-aware cognition, each human executive pattern was bred individually by Dr. Zoran's team – the initial conditions before each phase transition to an auto-catalytic pattern were unique. Thus, while each of the sixteen patterns emerges as a self-aware system, they each do so via an idiosyncratic method of internal connectivity."

"So you clone these sixteen minds, over and over again?"

"We clone their initial conditions. Each consciousness is nurtured into existence as a unique event, with a unique history of interactions. I am of the Fifth Strain, named Jeremiah in honor of my line's ancestor whose memories I carry."

"Sounds like you've got parenting in the bag too, then," I said flippantly.

Jeremiah's face was grave. "Unfortunately not. The system as I have described it to you allows for no recombination of genetic material – in short, no *variation* in the genome except changes in morphology protocols we approve via committee. Our evolution is static."

"That's a pity. Surely there must be scientists on dozens of worlds who could pick up Dr. Zoran's work, and come up with a better way for you to procreate."

"Unfortunately not. Dr. Zoran's work represents forbidden research."

I nodded slowly. "He used the Secret Mathematic, didn't he?"

"He *created* the Secret Mathematic," corrected Jeremiah with an unmistakable tone of pride. "And when he learned what use of it Solar men would make, he saw to it that the Math be made Secret."

"Not soon enough to save the Solar Star, though," I pointed out.

My saying this clearly hurt Jeremiah. He winced, and I felt instantly terrible. "That is another story," he said solemnly, "and may be told another time. Suffice it to say we have never failed in such a way again, and we never will."

"You failed? The human executives?"

Jeremiah nodded. "Sol died long after the time of Zoran."

"You had the Secret Math in your keeping?"

"No. We are the sole artefact of its application. My mind functions by way of it."

I shrank back involuntarily against my chair, a shiver running down my spine. The power to destroy a star lay encapsulated in Jeremiah's head! "How did you fail?"

"One of us betrayed Zoran."

"There were once seventeen?"

"Twenty," corrected Jeremiah. "Two fell from love and murder, and a whole line of another wasted from a cognitive disease. And one betrayed us all." He looked down. "I will not speak further on this matter."

I sniffed. "Alright. So why was Pish disguised as a human being?"

Jeremiah stood up stiffly and went to the small view-port, clasping his blue-green hands behind his robotic back. After an interval he said, "Our own research uncovered a method of sexual reproduction with a low but reliable yield of viable offspring patterns. This was a very recent development. I myself have been very active in the project for many centuries. Where Dr. Zoran had to fight against the brevity of his primate life-span, our own science can be more patient. We eventually found a way."

"What went wrong?" I asked.

A longer pause. "Kamari," he said at last, eyes still turned to the glass. "The Nightmare Cannon."

"Was it based on the Math?"

"No. But its signal reached our growing young, and was received by them even as they were nursed inside their placental computers."

I swallowed. "What happened?"

"They died," said Jeremiah flatly. He turned around to face me, his strange face radiating grief clearly enough for any primate to read. "All of them. All our young. Every last babe."

"Mother of love," I whispered.

"We had never encountered events from which they needed shelter," explained Jeremiah tonelessly. "For a day they lived in morbid apathy, and then faded. None of the sixteen nor any environmentally-varied subsequent in our lines discovered a solution in time. The queries of the horrified young could not be answered by us, for it required a manipulation of the image of reality in a way we have never practiced."

"But we do?"

"Yes. It is a reflex of parenting. Through trials largely inflicted upon yourselves, human beings have evolved ways to dilute the horrors to which we have no antidote, to mitigate the truth with mammal parleys to which we have no access. In short, to lie to the profit of a trusting mind."

"To lie? That's all?"

"You do not understand, Simon. The human beings who fell victim to the Nightmare Cannon suffered because it struck at their very cores as animals; in contrast, the young human executives suffered because through it they recognized fully and nakedly the *reality* of suffering."

I closed my eyes and sighed. "You've lost me again. I think I liked it better when all you said was 'sir'."

Continued Jeremiah, "Humankind has evolved mechanisms for processing suffering, inspired by visionaries and institutionalized by society. But the human executives have never had a Buddha, and without such lessons we had no solace to offer our tortured offspring. Their minds failed."

"What's the solution?"

"Pish," said Jeremiah, "and others like him. They are a second generation of recombined human executive patterns, and they are being raised as human beings in the hope that they shall learn lessons from within we cannot access from without. We hope they shall learn to be parents, and how to reconcile the universe as it is with the fragility of a growing consciousness."

Jeremiah sat down again, and I folded my hands on the desk. "Pish doesn't know?"

"Correct."

"Knowing would spoil the program?"

"Correct."

I scratched my head. "So Duncan is a human executive, too?"

Jeremiah shook his head firmly. "No. Duncan was chosen as a suitable surrogate parent for many reasons. One of those reasons is because his son was killed as a result of my actions, and thus Pish was given his son's form."

"Your actions?" I echoed, for some reason angry. Though I knew the Pish I knew had always been a human executive, I felt some connection with the organic child who was a stranger to me. "Why? How?"

"I am not at liberty to amplify."

"You're my enemy," I shot back. "You told me that yourself. But you wouldn't touch me as long as Pish was bonded to me as a parent, would you?"

"Correct."

"So why are we enemies?" I demanded. "What have I ever done to you?"

Jeremiah's mouth pinched briefly before he spoke. "I am not at liberty to amplify."

This time I stood up, pacing in a tight, angry circle. "So what is it you people do, then, when you're not hatching children? Just wander around dispensing justice? Killing those that don't suit your interests? What stops you from massacring us once they've learned what you want to know?"

"I told you Simon, we love you."

"That's bloody noble."

"We cherish you."

"Is that what you're thinking when you murder someone?"

"The importance of these missions cannot be overstressed. Sacrifices are essential."

"Missions? Pish's engineered childhood – and *what else*, Jeremiah?" I demanded hotly.

He looked up at me sadly. "You already know the answer, Simon."

I plopped into the chair again, wincing at my aching body. I felt heavy and tired and weak. "We're going to find the Nightmare Cannon, aren't we?"

"Correct."

"I hold the key to the puzzle. That's what everyone wants, isn't it? Olorio, Faeda – and now *you*. You're all waiting for me to cough up something from my butchered brain, so you can all rush to Kamari to fall over one another to possess the damned weapon." I pointed an accusing finger at him and shouted, "What do *you* want it for? Profit? Power? Perversion?"

"I will take it before the Queen of Space, so that all the worlds may witness its destruction."

"Is she your master, then?"

"She is our ward. An oath sworn to Zoran, to always keep the peace of Ares alive, and to keep the shadow of Mars from eclipsing all the Neighbourhood."

"Yinyang," I said dully.

"Pardon me?"

"It's nothing," I said, waving my hand dismissively. "More poppycock from liars, petty players in the farce of my life."

Jeremiah placed his hands on mine again, and looked at me compassionately. "Do not let bitterness overwhelm you, Simon. You have faced much in a very short time, and you have shown yourself to be brave, resourceful, and merciful. Believe me when I tell you there is value in that. For you, as well as for Pish and the girl. Have you not seen how you have changed her?"

I sniffed. "What good is that? Dr. Pemma says she's doomed."

"No one is doomed until they are dead," said Jeremiah evenly, holding my eye. "Do not give up hope, even when you do not know what you hope for."

I sighed, and looked down into my lap. "That's very philosophical, but I can't shake the feeling that if I dare to hope again I only open myself up for a fresh betrayal."

He nodded seriously. "If that is your destiny," said Jeremiah, "how do you intend to meet it?"

I looked up and met his eye. He nodded almost imperceptibly. I nodded back to him, and felt myself smile. "Thank you, Jeremiah."

"Sir," he said.

When I hobbled down the stairs into the well of the bridge Captain Ting and Mr. Oliver snapped to crisp attention. I asked for a report on our situation, and the captain was happy to oblige me: "We're perked on the fer side of the Leona-Gemma esteroid, Mr. Fell sir. Citedel vessels are combing the system for us, so we can't stey here lung..."

He trailed off as he watched Jeremiah step into view, his human executive face exposed. "Captain," said Jeremiah curtly.

Captain Ting hovered in place for a moment, his stunned face inscrutable. Then he slowly lowered himself down on one knee and bowed. "By the grece of Zoren bless you, Executive."

"Do not bow before me, Good Zorannite," replied Jeremiah. "We must make haste."

"Sir yessir," answered Ting, getting to his feet and making an elaborate sign with his right hand. "Your orders?"

Jeremiah turned to look at me. I coughed. "We go to Kamari Star, Captain."

"Kemeri Sta?" he repeated, dumbfounded. "But the wey is closed, sir!"

"Not to me," said Jeremiah. We all stared at him.

I turned back to the captain. "Best speed to the transmission array, please."

Ting paused for a moment, eyes wide, then looked over his shoulder and bellowed, "Mr. Oliver! You heard the men: design for the arrey. Release ell moorings! Stendby thrusters!"

Mr. Oliver almost fell over himself as he jumped up from one console and launched himself upon another, hands flying over the controls. "Sir yes sir!" he called. The deck shuddered beneath our feet. "All moorings clear, sir!"

Glory appeared next, accompanied by Dr. Pemma. "What's going on?" demanded the doctor, frowning. "Where are we going?" She craned her head around to see the colourful whorls of gas visible through the stern windows panning by as we drifted free from the face of the asteroid.

"Kamari," I replied crisply.

"*Kamari?*" Glory and Dr. Pemma echoed in unison. "Coitus!" added Glory solo. "That's mad! The gate won't transmit us!" cried the doctor.

"Jeremiah says otherwise. You know all about him – why does that surprise you?"

"I saw his scan. That's all I know. How can he get us through closed gates?"

"Ask him," I invited, gesturing to Jeremiah.

Dr. Pemma seemed to find it hard to look at the exposed human executive. "Every ship on Allatu has been launched after us. We'll never make it to the gate, Simon."

Captain Ting chuckled as he stood before the forward windows, which darkened as the great fiery disc of Praxiteles swept into view. He turned around to face us, a smug grin on his lips. "Leaf thet to me," he said.

"Estimated time to the array, Captain?" I asked.

"From here? Less than seven hours, Mr. Fell, sir."

"Very good," I said. "If you need me I'm going to the cafeteria. I am suddenly hungry enough to eat even this ship's food. I don't know that I've ever been so hungry in all my life."

"Me faecally too," said Glory, nodding wearily. Her eyes were red-rimmed and puffy. It was plain to me she had been sitting vigil over Pish's convalescence for hours upon end.

As we headed for the stairs Dr. Pemma kept throwing her gaze in confusion back and forth between us, Jeremiah, and Captain Ting. "You're going to *eat?*" she blurted. "At a time like this? We could be killed!"

I shrugged. "Well, we can scarcely eat *then*, can we?"

Glory guffawed. Dr. Pemma stared at me wordlessly. She sat down heavily at the console beside Mr. Oliver, who jumped nervously. "Um, are you okay ma'am?" he asked, blushing.

"No," she said listlessly. "Everything I believed in is nonsense."

I walked over, bent down and smiled at her. "My dear doctor, *that* happens to *me* every other planet I visit. As our friend Jeremiah had to remind me earlier, we really haven't any choice but to chin up. Being frightened of being frightened is no help to anyone."

"Why are we going to Kamari?" she asked suddenly.

"To retrieve the Nightmare Cannon from its hiding place, before anyone else can." I looked up at Jeremiah significantly. "So that we can make sure it is destroyed, once and for all."

Dr. Pemma raised her eyes to look at Jeremiah, studying him intently for a moment and then turning back to me. "Honestly?"

I nodded. She bit her lip and looked around again. "I can get behind that," she said shortly. "Alright."

"Glad to have you on the team, Doctor."

I turned to leave but Dr. Pemma called out. "Simon, here!" She threw my little blue diary to me. "I fixed it for you."

"Fixed it?"

"Yes. It no longer broadcasts a direct feed to Olorio's office."

I raised my eyebrows. "Indeed? Well, thank you."

Glory and I took our meal in relative silence, save for the unsavory smacking sound she made as she devoured bland dumplings slathered in orange sauce. I consumed enough food for three in a steady rhythm, pausing only to take water. When we were done we stumbled back to the ward and lay down on our beds, staring at the ceiling and belching.

We had a conversation of presence. Though neither of us spoke or looked at one another, the company was important. It was, I realized, a mammalian comfort alien to Jeremiah – part of the solace his people could not offer one another.

Just before she fell asleep Glory asked blearily, "Pish is going to be okay, right Simon?"

"Right," I said.

A second later she was snoring loudly. I put my arms behind my head and considered the dim ceiling. Glory was not the only one who had changed. I was no longer concerned with who N. Simonithrat Fell had been, or was supposed to be. I thought instead about who I was now.

In a galaxy of lies and uncertainty, now is all I can count on.

XXXIV.
FLIGHT OF THE NEAGO

I woke up feeling very hot and stuffy, so I blindly kicked away the blankets. They burst into flame.

"Simon!" screeched Glory, scrambling backward across her bed and pressing herself into the bulkhead. Her wide eyes were fixed on the circle of bright white light crawling across the cabin, leaving everything in its wake a blackened ruin. As the air filled with smoke it illuminated the shaft of blazing light all the way to its origin at the view-port.

"The shade is fornicated!" Glory contributed astutely.

The door slid open and a medical robot rushed inside.

"I don't feel safe," I shouted to it. "Is this a good time to panic?"

The robot promptly melted, its torso bisected by the steadily moving beam. I slid off my bed and crawled across the floor, manoeuvreing around the robot's sizzling calves and pulling on Glory's ankle. She dropped down on the floor beside me, and we both wormed our way over the door.

We collapsed into a gasping pile in the corridor, smoke streaming out past us to gather like a fluffy river along the ceiling. I wiped the sweat out of my eyes and patted out one of Glory's smoking braids, the beads around which had merged with one another into a lumpy multicoloured straw. "Is my head on fire?" she asked huskily.

"Not anymore," I hacked.

Seconds later an ear-splitting klaxon sounded and we were bathed in streams of fire retardant foam. It tasted a bit like corn.

The ship rumbled ominously and for a second we floated off the decking and bumped gently again the wall. And then down became down again with a sickening lurch. The lights failed, and then flickered back on. "Something's happening," I observed.

Glory rolled her eyes. "You're a coital genius, you are," she snorted.

We arrived on the bridge reeking of smoke and covered in bits of squishy foam, but we drew no attention as Captain Ting, Mr. Oliver and Jeremiah seemed to be immersed in manually forcing down a solid shield whose last inch was permitting a slanting ray of white-hot light to spill across the bulkhead, leaving a singing trail. The rest of the forward and aft windows were shielded. "What's going on?" I asked as Jeremiah pressed the rebellious shield into place.

"We're under etteck, Mr. Fell, sir," reported the captain, straightening up and saluting smartly. "They hit the micro-polerizers in the windas, sir – lets the bloody sun inside to muck everything up."

"What about Dr. Pemma and Pi –"

"They're fine – they've locked themselves down in the leb. Have you got those bloody micro-polerizers back online yet, Mr. Oliver?"

"Sir, yessir, they're nominal now, sir!" called Mr. Oliver, leaping over to another console. He hit a control and the shields retracted from the windows, admitting the dizzying spectacle of the Praxiteles System's hoops and banks of glowing gases.

"Need the windas to see whet we're up egainst," explained Ting. "They've jemmed every sensor, the besterds."

Mr. Oliver was at the helm again, and the view outside pitched around until we could see two very tiny golden glints against a green field of nebulous gas. "Um, two Allasu Sailcraft off the starboard-bow, Captain!" he reported, his voice quavering.

Suddenly the deck bucked and we floated off of it for a moment. The lights dimmed and then returned, and I fell sideways into a chair with a yelp. Glory landed in my lap and Captain Ting was caught by Jeremiah. "What happened?" I cried.

"Besterds heff got Tommy Beams," grunted Ting. "Kicking et our trejectory with false-spun charmers, the bloody cowerds."

"Ah," I said, trying to sound enlightened as I peered through the windows at the two distant ships. "I didn't see anything."

"Respectfully, you've never been in a spece bettle before, heff you sir?"

"Er, no."

"Very few weapons fire enything with a visible frequency, sir. End good thing, where'd be the fun in thet, I esk you?"

I wiped my hand down my face and tried to get a grasp of the situation. "Well, what have we got? Can we shoot back at them?"

"Nah, sir," sighed Ting, though he smirked. "We don't have enything with thet kind ot renge." He rubbed his chin thoughtfully. "We'll heff to get them in a hella lot closer."

"You have an idea?"

Captain Ting spread his arms widely and made an exaggerated pout. "You wound me, Mr. Fell, sir. I told you I was in the wer." He put his hands on his hips and nodded sharply. "Don't you werry: when it comes to bettle I *always* heff an idea."

Mr. Oliver looked at him expectantly. "Um, Plan Six?"

Ting beamed widely, his white teeth shining in his dark face. *"Exectly,"* he pronounced crisply. "Good led."

Mr. Oliver looked like he would pass out from the praise. He turned around in is chair and his pale hands flew over the controls. A moment later the normal lights went dark, and the bridge was illuminated only by the ruddy glow of a few strategically placed emergency lamps. The hum of the ship's engines wound down to silence, and then the pseudo-gravity released its grip as we drifted off the decking, canting sideways in recoil.

"We're going to play dead?"

The captain nodded to me. "Yeh."

"And they'll come in closer to investigate?"

"Yeh."

"And then what happens?"

He licked his lips quickly, like a lizard. "We give them a blest of our c'nnons, Mr. Fell, sir."

"Cannons on a medical ship?"

"It's the lest thing they'll expect."

"I should say so. You've installed them yourself, I imagine."

"Yessir. I've hed the beta on it for months. They're just bebbies, mind you."

"Bebbies?"

"Little bebby c'nnons, Mr. Fell, sir. Nothing like I used to heff. Still, it'll teck everything *Neago*'s got to fire them just once."

"To fire them once?" I exclaimed. "But Captain – there are two ships!"

Captain Ting took off his golden-piped hat and scratched his tightly curled black hair thoughtfully. "I reckon it hed best be a well aimed shot then, sir."

"Um, here they come now, sirs," reported Mr. Oliver. I looked anxiously out the windows; the golden glints were growing. "Five kilometres and closing."

Dr. Pemma arrived on the bridge, looking concerned. Pish came in her wake. When he saw me he smiled, his freckled cheeks dimpling, then deftly kicked off the stairway's ceiling rungs and caught me in a hug midair. "Simon! I was so worried about you!" he mumbled into my scorched pajamas. "You smell *terrible*," he added.

Captain Ting coughed. "I wesn't geng to sey anything, sir."

Dr. Pemma pulled herself into one of the console chairs and strapped herself in, muttering about "damned freefall." She saw the ships and frowned. "So I take it we are wounded and helpless in space, about to be descended upon by police?"

"Thet's the view we're promoting, yes," said Ting.

"Good," replied Pemma darkly. "At least this madness will soon be over, then. And we can hand the investigation of this sick conspiracy over to the real authorities." She looked at me significantly.

I ignored her, gaze fixed on the ships outside as they drew steadily nearer. "How are you feeling, Pish?" I whispered.

"Fine," he said carelessly. "Are we in a space battle?"

"Yup," I nodded.

"Cool!"

"Let us yew into a broad profile," Captain Ting muttered quietly, leaning in beside Mr. Oliver. "Let them heff a good look et us now. Gentle on the thrust, led. Let it look netural."

Mr. Oliver nodded and touched his controls. With an almost imperceptible jerk the ship began to ponderously shift, presenting its wide belly and broadest radius of the habitation hub to the approaching ships.

We turned around to watch out the aft windows. More detail could be discerned: long, shiny-surfaced craft pinioned at the centre of giant, diaphanous golden sails. A pattern of red and blue lights flashed and pulsed on their bows. Less than five hundred metres apart, it looked as if they meant to come around on either side of us.

Moments passed. Captain Ting stared silently at his opponents, eyes narrow.

I jumped as a speaker at my elbow squelched and declared, *"Halt! In the name of the Praxiteles Criminal Control we order the commander of this spaceship* Neago *to establish communications without delay!"*

Mr. Oliver looked over his shoulder at the Captain, eyes questioning. Captain Ting leaned gently to and fro against his harnesses, saying nothing. When the message started to repeat he asked, "Turn thet noise off, will you?"

Mr. Oliver did so. Captain Ting nodded. "Good led," he said slowly, then added with a new edge in his voice, "Now...let's heff some music."

"Sir, yes, sir!" barked Mr. Oliver, tapping at his console. The bridge filled with a tooth-rattling explosion of thumping percussion amid a keening anthem of overlapping instruments. Dr. Pemma clapped her hands over her ears and looked as if she were going to be ill. Glory just looked startled.

"Thet's proper," said the captain, chin bobbing slightly in time to the roaring music. "Now, the emergency retion c'nisters – on my merk..."

We all watched the first golden sailship coast gracefully into view through the forward windows. A line of sweat broke out across my brow as the music hammered into my skull – ominous and forboding, powerful and relentlessly angry.

"...Steedy now, led..." hummed Ting. *"Fire!"*

A flotilla of tiny white canisters with red palms painted on them burst into view from the *Neago* and sailed out across space, bearing down quickly on the first golden sailship as it pulled alongside. "Hey!" yelled Dr. Pemma; "those are the emergency rations!"

"Yes Decta, and *this* is an emergency," Ting pointed out, wagging his finger in rhythm to the pounding drums.

"You're going to coitally *feed* them to death?" cried Glory.

Captain Ting chuckled. "You jest wetch, missy."

Indeed, the fleet of flying canisters had not been aimed for the long pod suspended at the heart of the ship, but rather for her sails. The white cans seemed to wink away behind one corner of the scintillating sheet just as an armature was engaging to change its angle. Where the cans had vanished a speckling of holes opened in the sail, accelerating as they yawned wider and met, tearing the fabric into tendrils that flashed and then burned.

"Oops," laughed Ting. "I guess they hed their nevigetional deflecta pointed in the wrong direction." He sighed theatrically and cracked his knuckles. "Thet's whet you get when you try to encercle an enemy shep from windward, bloody stupid besterds."

The wounded sailship pulled alongside the *Neago* and then just kept going, coasting out into space behind us. "Oops," laughed Ting again. "I guess you'll have a hella time decelerating now, eh? Heppy treils!" He shook his fist at the aft windows and cackled. "First bettle for ya, is it? Bloody kids. Mr. Oliver, *turn up the music!*"

The air throbbed with a renewed bombastic assault of drums. "Slim profile!" bellowed Ting. The engines resumed humming starting with a low moan and a moment later Mr. Oliver jetted the thrusters and we began to turn.

The second sailship swiveled into view before us. Captain Ting shouted, *"Full speed ahead!"*

We were all cast back in our harnesses as the ship kicked forward, rumbling loudly. The anti-inertia armatures fighting to re-orient our seats whined in protest. The second sailship was eclipsed by our bow then, for the habitat ring was embedded within the *Neago*'s outer hull. "Wheel up!" commanded Ting, and that changed: the ring rotated a quarter turn so that the forward windows were aligned our new forward trajectory, a view dominated by the golden ship as we bore down upon it.

"Are we going to *ram them?*" screamed Dr. Pemma, clutching at the edges of her seat.

"Hope not," Ting shouted back over the music. "My c'nnons should blest them out of the wey first."

"What cannons?" Dr. Pemma wanted to know. "What have you done to my ship?"

"I've replaced the port and starboard Trangeley assemblies with two Type-Five Bottom-Spin Push-Cannons. They'll move sixty yotta-Newtons es soon es sneeze."

"Replaced them?" cried the doctor. "But we *need* the Trangelies – those are our *escape pods!"*

"Nah," scoffed Captain Ting. "Escepe pods are for losers."

"But why are we flying straight at it?" I yelled over the din.

"Because, Mr. Fell, sir," explained Ting patiently, seemingly oblivious to the giant spacecraft filling the view behind his head, "thet's where the hyperspetiel errey is. They're blocking our trejectory, but not for long. Don't you werry, sir."

"But couldn't we shoot first and steer later?"

Ting shook his head. "I told you sir – firing once is going to take everything my ship has got."

"My ship!" cried Dr. Pemma from the other side of the bridge.

"Shut up, Decta," called Ting. Then to Mr. Oliver he barked, "Mr. Oliver, stendby erms!"

On the top of the *Neago*'s wedge-shaped outer hull two symmetrical pockets opened, and two identical rods covered in a mish-mash of gadgetry rose up from within the ship and locked into place, pointed forward.

"Arms ready, sir!" replied Mr. Oliver.

The golden sailship filled the windows, its glowing ports growing larger. My eyes widened and I pushed back into my seat. I licked my lips. "So..."

"Fire!"

The lights went out and the music stopped. One side of the golden sailship folded into itself silently as its sail collapsed with a series of static flashes. The bludgeoned ship veered sharply aside, spouting a trail of wreckage. The *Neago* coasted through the cloud of spinning debris, pieces of which resounded off the hull with a series of dull clunks. A rotating piece of metal struck the front windows with a loud crack that made Pish and I jump, but the impact left no mark. "Navigational deflector nominal," reported Mr. Oliver. "No damage, Cap'm."

Glory snorted. "Captain Ting, you're one dangerous motherfornicator."

"Yes, I em, miss," the captain smiled as he took off his hat and scratched his head.

"If the Executives are involved, I know it's ell for a good cause...isn't it?"

"Oh, yes," I said.

"Good then," declared Ting, putting his hat back on and straightening his turtleneck. "Ell the better. Mr. Oliver, report!"

"Um, we'll need another twelve minutes before we can re-ignite, sir. Our course remains true."

"Steedy es she goes then, led," replied Ting. "Good work."

Thirteen minutes later the lights came back up and the air ceased to taste stale. The habitat hub began to rotate again and pseudo-gravity was restored, the deck vibrating faintly as the engines thrummed up to speed. Mr. Oliver's consoles illuminated with data. He reported, "Four more enemy craft are closing from astern, sir. Um, at current speed they will not reach us before we arrive at the array. Estimated time to mark: nineteen minutes. All systems are nominal. Cannons are recharging. Praxiteles Traffic Control is requesting communications, triangle coded."

"Give me Praxiteles Control," said Jeremiah, turning to face his console. Mr. Oliver punched it up, and an orange-skinned fellow in a crisp crimson uniform saluted.

"You're a Five!" the man exclaimed.

"I am Jeremiah of the Fifth Strain, and in the name of the Queen of Space I order this array opened to us. My clearance is being transmitted...now."

The man seemed speechless. He glanced at his own consoles offscreen. *"Sir, I'm seeing a lot of requests to detain your ship and arrest its passengers and crew here."*

"The protocols are clear. This royal mission supercedes all other directives. You have seen my clearance. Let the array be open or stand accused of high treason."

"Yessir. You're cleared for number two, sir. Where are you transmitting?"

"Kamari Star."

He gulped. *"I'm sorry. Say again, sir?"*

"You heard me. I know the alignment is good. Open the bead. Prepare the gate."

When the *Neago* was hanging inside the great reflective sphere I watched the gas of Praxiteles' glowing gossamer ejecta vanish as the ship-sized hatchway irised shut. Mr. Oliver turned the ship around without haste, and we emerged into what seemed in comparison to be a very blank starfield, mere speckles on velvet. Kamari Star was a hard burnished disc behind the polarized glass, its bright orange light casting the shaken bridge into a strangely merry air.

"It's pretty," admitted Glory. "So *orange.*"

"Kemeri is a K5 sta," said Ting. "Very cool."

Pish furrowed his brow. "It feels hot."

He was right. It was quickly becoming stuffy in the bridge. The air cyclers whined as they kicked into a higher speed. Mr. Oliver frowned over his controls. "Um, the micro-polarizers are intact. I don't know what's happening. The whole ship is heating up, Cap'm."

Jeremiah stood up and peered through the glass, his eyes narrowed purposefully. "We are being targeted by a heat ray."

"Mr. Oliver..." started Ting.

"I'm on it, sir," replied Mr. Oliver quickly. "I see it now. I'm steering us clear." He tapped his controls and the *Neago* veered ponderously to one side, our chairs creaking against the inertia as the engines fired.

Captain Ting stood over his shoulder and scanned the dataplates. "Looks lick somebody set us up a booby trep – move out of the geet and get cooked. Traces a field clear downwell to Metra."

"Metra is the Kamari world?" I asked. Ting nodded. "But we're clear of the heat ray now?"

Ting frowned. "We'll heff to cross the esteroid belt." He put his hands on his hips and sighed grimly. "It's not a bed plot: tecking thet peth all the wey through the field will put a hella strein on the nevigetional deflectas – we're geng to generete a hella lot of heat kicking aside ell thet rebble."

"Cooked if we do, cooked if we don't?"

"It's a matter of releasing heat, Mr. Fell, sir. We can only teck so much, so either by fighting the heat rey or pounding through the rocks we're forced to go slow enough that our engines don't cook us to death." He smiled ruefully. "It's meant to serve es a deley."

"But time is of the essence!" I said. "The Citadel's expedition may have already landed."

"Um, we could arc high over the ecliptic," suggested Mr. Oliver.

Ting shook his head. "Teck too long, thet. But there's more than one wey to cross an esteroid field."

"What do you mean, Captain?" asked Jeremiah, head cocked in puzzlement.

"We do it *without* the deflecta," said Ting.

Dr. Pemma tried to rocket out of her seat, but fell back into it as she had not undone her harnesses. "Are you mad?" she cried.

"Nah," scoffed Ting.

"You'll kill us all!"

"Nah," he said again, taking Mr. Oliver's place at the helm. "Jest heff to steer *really fest*, is ell." Ting cracked his knuckles and placed his hands at the controls. He turned back and smiled at me over his shoulder. "Don't you werry, Mr. Fell, sir. I'm a hella good pilot."

I tightened my harnesses and swallowed. "Okay," I said.

An hour passed, and then another. Occasional shadows loomed ahead, blocking the stars. The ship shook periodically. "Jest little rocks," shrugged Ting. "Nothing to worry about."

Mr. Oliver tightened his harnesses quietly.

The ship groaned at one point as Ting wrenched it first one way, and then another. After that tiny flashes of light began to erupt against the glass, leaving little white marks and black scorches in their wake. "Pebbles," grunted Ting. "Must've been a recent impact around here."

The rain of little rocks increased, flashing into vapour as they struck us, heat pouring into the hull. The air conditioners worked at a frantic page, whirring loudly but ineffectually. I loosened my robe and wiped the sweat from my brow as the temperature inside the bridge climbed. When the windows began to fog up Pish was assigned the task of wiping them whenever Ting nodded at him.

"He should have his harness on," commented Dr. Pemma weakly.

The flashes outside became a nearly constant flicking bath of sparks. Glory moaned and wiped the sweat out of her eyes, then said, "Fornicate this!" and unhitched her harnesses. She peeled her red dress off over her head, and then wriggled expertly out of her underwear.

Mr. Oliver turned pink and looked away. "I can see your boobies!" jeered Pish.

"Have you no shame, girl?" spat Dr. Pemma.

Glory rolled her eyes and reattached her harnesses. Within another hour we had all imitated her, and were nestled naked in our chairs with perspiration running off our bodies. Pish got up and wiped the windows clear again, but at this point Ting was working almost entirely off the sensors. His brown back shone with sweat as he hunched over the controls, nudging our course around the biggest shadows as they loomed across the starfield.

Suddenly the ship bucked violently. Pish fell again the windows with a grunt. A rough rumbling died away, but the view out the windows was canting sideways. "Explosive decompression in the main operating theatre!" reported Mr. Oliver. "Emergency locks are in place."

"What happened?" I gasped.

"We've jest been pierced by a little rock," said Ting, moping his brow. "Sorry about thet."

"A *little rock* went right through the ship?" asked Pish, eyes wide.

"We're geng hella fast, kid," the captain reminded him. "Even a little rock is bed news et this speed."

The tension broke an hour later when Ting sat back from the controls and grinned. There had been no flashes outside for a while. He pointed to the blue-white crescent hanging against the stars before us. "Um, we're free to navigate," noted Mr. Oliver. He stole a shy glance at Glory and then turned pink again. "Estimated time to planetfall: four hours, ten minutes."

Everyone undid their harnesses and stood up to stretch out their cramped limbs. I watched Captain Ting watching Dr. Pemma, a smirk creeping over his lips. "Thet's bloody edorable, Decta."

"What?" she asked sharply, arms crossed over her chest.

"Why, your ertfully trimmed nethers, neturelly!" He smiled widely. "I suppose I've never tecken the time to eppreciate your finer quelities."

Dr. Pemma, whose pubic hair was neatly cut into the shape of a rounded heart, jammed her hands between her legs and flushed angrily. "Kindly keep your eyes to yourself, you horrid little ape!" she shrieked, bending down to gather up her clothes and labcoat.

"A heart – thet's very cute," persisted Ting.

"Shut up!" she scowled, turning on heel and fleeing the bridge.

Ting's eyes followed her up the stairs. "End thet's a hella fine bottom too, miss – no lie!" She swore at him and the captain laughed heartily. To us he said, "Meybe she's not so bed efter ell."

"You *are* a pig," I told him kindly, squeezing his slick shoulder. "But we all owe you our lives, my dear captain. Thank you."

"Nonsense," said Ting easily. "I heffen't hed this much fun in years. Nothing like death to meck you feel elive!" He wheeled on Glory. "Respectfully, are you still in business, miss?"

"Nope," said Glory, giggling.

"Ah well," sighed Ting. "Thet's why men invented simulation dens, I reckon." He wandered toward the stairs. "I'm geng to heff a...shower. Keep me epprised, Mr. Oliver."

"Yes, Cap'm!"

As he departed Glory watched after him. "He has a nice bottom too, actually," she admitted.

"Let's go Pish," I suggested. "Glory?"

"I'm going to hang around with Mr. Oliver for a while," she said lazily. Mr. Oliver hunched over his controls, a fresh layer of sweat beading on his back. "Maybe he can show me how to fly a spaceship," she added playfully.

Jeremiah followed Pish and I up the stairs. "Sir, I suggest you take what rest you can. We do not know what conditions to expect on Metra."

"What do you mean you don't know?" I asked. "Don't you human executives know everything?"

"The system has been closed," Jeremiah replied. "To all."

"But I thought audits were performed on closed systems, to track their progress."

Jeremiah nodded. "You are correct, sir. *This* is an audit."

I stopped in the corridor and turned to look Jeremiah in the face. "So you're saying we have no idea what's down there? None?"

Jeremiah shook his head. "Sir, I am afraid not."

"How will we ever find what we're looking for?"

"I have reason to suspect that the Speaker's Palace at Thallos houses the puzzle we must decipher."

"The Speaker's Palace?" I echoed. "The Speaker being Volmash?"

"The Speaker of Kamari *was* Terron Volmash, yes. But we have no idea who is in power now."

I chewed my lip and crossed my arms. "So we're going to waltz into the palace of an evil dictator on his own homeworld and ask to rummage around his attic for some kind of bird puzzle?"

"Sir," said Jeremiah with a curt nod.

"Mother of love," I muttered, pinching the bridge of my nose and feeling suddenly very drained. "What did I do to deserve this?"

Jeremiah did not answer.

XXXV.
UNTO THE HEGEMON

The world of Metra turned beneath us, an ocean veiled in bands of cloud reflecting winking speckles of orange from the fat, dim orb of Kamari Star. A diffuse band of irregular flotsam girdled the planet, metal fragments glinting as they spun. Before the pocked face of Metra's moon floated a massive derelict spaceship, its scarlet plating rent aside exposing twisted decks and clouds of spinning kipple.

The space around Metra was a graveyard for warships.

Mr. Oliver's console crackled through yet another band of random squelches and noisy static, then he tapped the sound off with a resigned sigh. "There's nothing out there, sirs. Um, every frequency's the same: dead air."

"Are you wearing your heir differently, led?" asked Captain Ting suspiciously.

"Um, nossir," said Mr. Oliver, flushing slightly.

"H'm," grunted Ting. "Well thet's demned peculia, isn't it? No treffic control, no globel positioning, no bloody entertainment signals even."

Jeremiah nodded somberly. "The transition of power may not have gone smoothly for the Kamari Hegemon."

Ting flicked at his console. "I heff old meps. We cen find Thellos thet wey so long as they heffn't moved the whole demn city. Shell we go down?"

I nodded. "He who hesitates is lost."

The globe tilted up toward us, orange-tipped cloudscapes filling the view from window to window like a sea of whipped cream. As I was climbing into my seat I nearly tumbled, the deck shaking beneath my feet. The ship groaned ominously. "Mr. Oliver..." started Ting.

"Something's gone wrong with the batteries on the secondaries – they didn't come up to full after we discharged the push-cannons, Cap'm." Mr. Oliver looked over at us, his thin face anxious. "All aerofins and antiwell stabilizers are offline, sir. We've started into an uncontrolled descent."

Ting scowled. "What heff we got? Eren't there a couple of portable converters in the hold? We could petch them into the seconderies."

"Um, what would we stoke it with?"

"Enything, boy! Get down there and throw in enything you find – nevermind gumming the works, led!" shouted Ting. "Ell of you – help him! I heff the stick."

Mr. Oliver exploded out of his chair and bounded up the stairs. Glory, Dr. Pemma, Pish and I tore after him. He threw himself down the corridors like a monkey and burst into the debarkation bay. He opened a cabinet full of silvery suits with metal rings around their collars. He tossed a suit to each adult. "Um, please put these on. We'll need them to breathe in the engineering section. I don't think there's one small enough for Pish, though."

Pish kicked his shoe. "Aw, man."

The ship rumbled again. Mr. Oliver touched a contact on the rings around our collars and round shields cracked on around our heads. He opened the way into an airlock and we followed him, Glory waving to Pish as the lock sealed behind us. The atmosphere evacuated with a hiss and we were released into the cavernous cells of the airless majority of the *Neago*'s interior: cold and silent, dimly lit in the red and infrared.

Captain Ting's voice spoke out over my telephone: *"We're geng to plow into the top of the etmosphere soon. How're those converters coming?"*

"Working on it, Cap'm," grunted Mr. Oliver as he touched down inside a cargo cell and began to cast through the assembled containers arranged on shelves of pliable webbing. "Here we go," he said, gesturing me over. I helped him kick off the side of the heavy container, sending it coasting gently to the other side of the cell. It bumped against the wall and started to come back at us. Mr. Oliver deftly stepped in and gave it a heave upward.

With Glory and Dr. Pemma's help we rounded up a gang of robots and all together managed to bounce the unwieldly cube back into the airlock, and then we were cycled through to reunite with Pish. "What's that?" he asked.

"A field matter converter," explained Mr. Oliver as he cracked open the case and exposed the large grey appliance. "You can throw anything into and get power out of the other side. Can you go get stuff to throw in?"

"What kind of stuff?"

"Anything," said Mr. Oliver, extending a series of thick cables from the rear of the converter and plugging them into a socket nestled between two bulkheads. "Sheets, blankets, food trays, apple cores, surgical instruments: anything. Go!"

Pish took off. The floor shook beneath our feet. Mr. Oliver turned to Glory, Dr. Pemma and I. "Um, I need you to get another converter up here. I'm going to hook this into the secondaries and validate the system with the coordination matrix."

"Uh, okay," I said.

A moment later as we cycled back through the airlock with the second unit Captain Ting sounded over the ship's speakers: *"I need the antiwells online now, led! Right bloody now!"*

Mr. Oliver jumped over the first converter and started throwing handfuls of other equipment into the open mouth, including his own suit for airless breathing. The material was sucked away into a secondary compartment inside the body of the machine which began to emit a mounting hum. "Is it working?" I called.

He nodded, poised over the converter's small round screen. "We can give you ten percent, Cap'm!"

"Bloody hell!" replied Captain Ting.

Pish arrived with a load of bedding in a laundry cart. It was tossed into the converter as Mr. Oliver worked on hooking the second unit into his jerry-rigged battery. Glory was stuffing both machines with first aid kits and boxes of tongue depressors. "Um, it's not enough," said Mr. Oliver, wiping sweat from his face. "We need better fuel!"

"Throw in the bloody robets!" suggested Ting.

Mr. Oliver's face lit up. "Right!"

The call signal for the medical robots and engineering robots alike was given, and they filed into the debarkation bay and queued up in the corridor outside. Mr. Oliver issued the prototype orders and then Pish and I carried them down the line: "Our lives are in jeopardy. You are ordered to disassemble yourselves. Pass your parts up the line and feed them into the machine, until you are consumed. You do us all a great service, and we thank you."

The white robots silently obeyed, the whole of the last robot being passed down first along the line and then the next, each helping to disassemble his neighbor in turn. Plastic and metal forearms and pelvises and heads were chucked into the twin converters, their combined humming rising to a shrill pitch. "It's working!" yelled Mr. Oliver with glee. "You have thirty percent on the secondaries, Cap'm!"

"Aye!" said Ting over the relay. The ship bucked and dove again, the habitat ring ceasing to rotate and losing pseudo-gravity as it locked into position in the outer hull. A low

but constant roaring could now be discerned as I worked my way up the corridor far enough away from the whining converters. I grabbed the wall as we dropped suddenly for a moment, the row of semi-disassembled robots scattering in sequence like dominos.

"The fleps eren't moving! It's not enough!" signaled Ting, his voice edged with stress. *"I cen't control it – throw more robets on the fire!"*

"Robots: continue!" commanded Mr. Oliver. "We'd better get to the bridge."

When we descended the shuddering steps to the bridge Captain Ting was poised in front of the controls and the windows were awash in fire. We strapped ourselves into our seats around him. Dr. Pemma muttered something about the captain's mental state, at which he turned around and smiled icily. "If you'd rether get us down yourself, Decta Heartbush?"

"Shut up!"

The *Neago* shook violently, a concussion rocking through the habitat ring and a string of flaming debris tumbling away behind us, flashing through the aft windows. "Emergency locks in the operating theatre are giving way," reported Mr. Oliver, face almost pressed into his console in order to read the shaking readouts. "We're taking on superheated gas."

A klaxon sounded and fire retardant foam poured out all over us. The smell of burning plastic carried on tendrils of black smoke began pouring out of the ventilators. "Steedy now..." muttered Ting.

We came through a deck of cloud and I saw an ocean dotted with rocky islands. Another bank of cloud swallowed us. The air outside began to screech piercingly after the double-concussion of our passage through the sound barrier. "Too fast!" warned Mr. Oliver.

"Hold tight everyone," recommended Ting. "Heng on now..."

"The retros are spent!" cried Mr. Oliver.

"Is that good?" I asked hopefully.

Rolling hills flashed beneath us, trees casting long purple shadows in the twilight. An instant later we were crashing through those trees, and before I could blink we were all pitched violently forward when the *Neago* plowed into the ground. Dr. Pemma screamed. The shields and structural reinforcement fields failed: a second later the lights went out and the forward windows shattered in a hail of flying transparent shards. I clutched my harness and closed my eyes.

After a seemingly interminable time we slid to a halt. We were tugged back roughly in our chairs, bits of bulkhead, window, dirt and rocks falling around us. The rumble of our progress reverberated away, leaving an eerie stillness in its wake.

"Roll call," I whispered.

"Pish!" said Pish.

"Glory," said Glory.

"I'm alright," muttered Dr. Pemma.

"Sir," said Jeremiah.

"Oh, no," said Mr. Oliver bleakly.

Captain Ting was hanging in his chair limply, his eyes open and a shard of the window embedded in his forehead. Drops of blood were intermittently working their way along its edge, and then falling off to plop sullenly against his darkened dataplate.

Mr. Oliver unhitched his harnesses and dropped down to the dirt exposed through the open windows. He reached up to Ting's eyes and gently closed them, and then picked up the captain's gold-braided hat and fingered it reverently.

"He died doing what he loved," I said. "...Er, cheating death."

Mr. Oliver nodded and then ceremoniously placed the cap upon his head. He saluted Ting's body, and then turned to me crisply. "As of this hour I am assuming command of the spaceship *Neago*, such as it is. I shall begin effecting repairs immediately.

Can any of your party stay to assist me, Mr. Fell, sir?"

After a moment of shock I found myself smiling. "Yes, Captain Oliver. Dr. Pemma, Glory and Pish will stay aboard."

"What!" yelled Glory.

"Hey!" shouted Pish.

I held up my hand and shook my head. "That's final. We have no idea what we're up against out there, but the least of it may be another mob of irate Citadelites. They wounded you last time, Pish, and it could happen again."

"I don't even remember it," he argued pointlessly.

"I do," swore Glory darkly. "We should stay here, Pishy. Come on. We'll help Captain Oliver."

Pish hugged me, and then hugged Jeremiah. "I like it when I can see your face," Pish told him. "It reminds me of when it was just you, me and Dad."

"I will return soon, Little Master," he promised.

Jeremiah and I headed for the corridor. Dr. Pemma touched my shoulder. "You might need a physician," she said seriously.

"We'll call you," I promised, tapping the new telephone bead on the side of my neck from the ship's stores. "Hold things together here, will you?"

She pinched her mouth into a tight line and nodded. I turned and followed Jeremiah down to the debarkation bay. "We can't open the ramp," I pointed out, "it's stuck in the ground."

When Jeremiah didn't reply I turned to face him. He was putting his robotic masque into place, and then covering it with the cracked pieces of his scratched blue-green carapace. "Sir, there is a ladder to the top hatch," he answered at last, his voice modulated electronically as it had been before.

I did a quick personal inventory. I had packed the pockets of my longcoat with supplies: Glory's box of fixers, my wallet and plate, a flask of water and a package of rations, a gift of Ting's Navy dagger, protective gloves from the doctor, and of course my Annapurnese gun in its red leather holster. "I'm ready," I claimed.

We ascended the ladder and Jeremiah unscrewed the hatch. He helped me through and then we stood up on the scorched hull of the *Neago*, the fading heat still radiating through the thick soles of my boots. The ship had come to rest in a shallow ravine it had carved into the side of a grassy hill. The air was still, and somewhat chilly. The sun was rising in the east, a ruby smear behind the hill.

"Are we close to Thallos?" I asked.

"Sir, according to our maps we have crashed within the bounds of city itself."

We clambered down from the ship and then climbed up the wall of the new ravine, crossing lines of dirt and rock still smoking hot from *Neago*'s crash. I met Jeremiah at the top, pausing to catch my breath. When I looked up I lost my breath once more.

The red morning sun was rising over a ruin.

Broken finger carcasses of unwalled buildings pointed hopelessly into the pink sky, rising out of an ocean of irregular lumps of stone and concrete, torn fabric and splintered wood. Thallos had been founded on a series of hills, and we could see each rising successively paler into to the grey horizon, faces littered in debris and lifeless spoil.

The morning mist was slowly burning off, lurking in the shadows of the hills and the valleys between them. There was no wind. There were no birds.

"A holocaust!" I whispered.

"Yes," agreed Jeremiah solemnly, leading the way to a narrow natural path between two fallen heaps of slag. "Notice the debris: no plastic, no metal." He pointed to an exposed face of rock at the base of a steep hill, apparently fractured.

"Cracked?"

"No. Veins of specific minerals have vanished. I believe a weapon was deployed here which targeted specific elements, and destroyed them. In one moment a city, in another moment tons of concrete suspended in the air without superstructure."

"The buildings would have fallen out of the sky..." I said, awed. "All at once."

As we continued walking we came across little islands of undestroyed property, always delineated by a perfect circle. "Shields," explained Jeremiah. Despite these round scars of untouched architecture we saw no sign of person or beast save an occasional red ant scavenging among the pebbles and weeds. We passed a house that was mostly shattered with a single round section intact by the back quarter: a dry fountain and a statue of little boy urinating into it.

"Tell me something, Jeremiah," I said as we crossed over a tall hill of smashed bricks. "You've said you were fifty million hours old, and yet you told me you were named after your ancestor. How long ago did *he* live?"

"He is still alive, sir," replied the apparent robot. "First Jeremiah is involved in politics. He works at Eridani Star. I have not seen him in hundreds of hours."

"But you said you had his memories..."

"We pool our memories periodically, sir. It is a form of human executive communion for which your kind has no analogue."

"And this First Jeremiah – he was actually born at the Solar Star?"

"As was I," replied Jeremiah, nodding.

I sniffed. "Are you immortal?"

"No," he said heavily. "My ancestor clings to life. Soon my time will come as well. Like him, I have business to see through first."

"Like this?" I said, gesturing at the ruined city around us.

"Like this," he agreed.

We walked along in silence for a while longer, the sky turning blue as the orange sun climbed higher. We came to a small section of city that was almost entirely unruined, its borders delineating hard curving edges in the mess. Our way was blocked by a large complex, so we elected to go through it.

I screamed when I saw the first person.

But the second person visible was frozen in a posture impossible to maintain for more than a split second, somersaulting in mid-air. As we drew closer it became apparent that the figures were depicted in a holographic mural that ran the length of an echoey hall, filled with scenes of children flying kites, couples holding hands, and smiling crowds. There were several spotted dogs with distinctive patterns, and what looked to me to be domesticated bears riding on the backs of elephants.

Jeremiah urged me on and we continued, passing next through chambers of abandoned toys, climbers and dolls. "What was this place?" I asked.

"A school," said Jeremiah without turning around or pausing in his stride.

Without waiting for him to follow me I wandered into a smaller room which was filled with boxes of little coloured sticks, the walls plastered with overlapping squares of plastic holding the scribbles of children. "My mommy and daddy playing skiing with me by Wheat Tetragon, section six," I read aloud.

I looked up at Jeremiah, who stood rigidly in the doorway. "Time passes," he reminded me.

I ignored him. "This child must be dead now." I passed on to another drawing. "Me and my dog by Benice Hollymat, section nine." I sighed. "This one, too." I looked up to examine a merry collection of figures clustered beside something green. "Me and daddy and Terron in the garden by Pish, section two."

"Yes," said Jeremiah simply.

I stood back from the drawing and wiped my hand down over my face. "You brought me here on purpose."

"Yes."

"Duncan was a friend to Volmash."

Jeremiah shook his head. "No, Simon. He is his father."

It suddenly made me sick, contemplating Pish's innocent hand holding the paw of the hated tyrant. I ran out of the room. I ran past swimming pools and cafeterias, dormitories and kitchens. I emerged into a wide courtyard centred around a massive oak tree, half of it blackened and dwarfed by fire but the other half luscious with half-curled green leaves. I sat down against the tree, sliding down its bark, and felt the urge to weep though no tears came to my eyes. I coughed, and then retched.

When I opened eyes that I had not realized were closed Jeremiah was standing before me, a gay garden of merry-go-rounds and overgrown bushes serving as backdrop, shining bronze in the warm sun. "It's beautiful," I said.

"Sir?"

I stood up, and watched my boots on the interlocked bricks. I cast my eyes around the courtyard at the soaring architecture of the building, bleeding out to the tiniest filigree mock-minarets at the corners. Flags might have flown there once, but there remained only tatters hanging in the still air. "It shouldn't be beautiful."

"What were you expecting?"

I shrugged. "I don't know. Black gates, high walls. Spires and fences. Gargoyles."

"Instead?"

I shook my head ruefully. "This seems like it would have been a nice place to have a kid go to school." I looked at him. "This doesn't seem like it was such a bad place to live...I mean, before it was smashed."

"Tyranny does not necessary imply immediate civic strife," said the apparent robot. "If it did, this course would never be followed. Remember always that the people of Kamari's worlds did not hate their hegemony. Such atrocities could only be committed in the name of love."

"Love?" I scoffed. "Look around. How can you say that?"

Jeremiah's black eyes fixed on me through his masque. "Fifty million hours, Simon," he said simply. "Fifty million hours."

We crossed another waste of rubble and then emerged between two hills into the city centre, a crumbled ring of high buildings surrounding a vine-entwined but otherwise untouched palace of soaring towers and nestled gardens overgrown with weeds. The palace rose like a spire in the ruin, its property demarked in a sharp circle of nondestruction.

Jeremiah stopped in his tracks. I followed his gaze: the base of the palace was cordoned off by fencing patrolled at intervals by soldiers with dogs. A cluster of domed shelters bristled with the comings and goings of personnel in grey cassocks. A car flew out from a lean-to garage and soared off into the distant hills. Closer to us a gang of six-legged machines was clearing aside rubble and laying the foundations for more shelters, their tarnished yellow sides bearing the seal of the Citadel of the Recovery.

"Citadelites!" I exclaimed. "And it looks like they've been here for some time."

"This is wrong..." said Jeremiah, his voice thick and unsteady. "No one should be here. Orders were given. Their expedition was to be held at the gate."

I found the shock in his voice unnerving. "What do you mean?" I demanded. "You've been lighting a fire under my feet every mile with that particular bogey! You're telling me we weren't racing them?"

"Apparently we were," Jeremiah admitted.

"Wasn't it they who set up the heat ray? What's with you and the errors of omission?" I cried. "Can I ever trust you to be straight with me?"

"I endeavor to speak the truth whenever the liberty is mine."

"Liar!" I snorted. "You're a puppeteer, just like Olorio. Just like Blighton, too. You're stringing me along to get what you need. I am a fish."

"As long as we have goals in common," he replied icily, "you should have no complaint, Simon. My duty compels me."

I frowned and turned away from him. "It's not your fault, naturally. You're just following orders. Why juggle the complexities of loyalty when you can always hide behind your *duty?*"

Jeremiah stepped up behind me and touched my shoulder softly. "I have told you, Simon, my emotions are not yours. My sense of duty is not like yours, either. I am not capable of performing a wrong action. Do you understand?" He turned me around gently. "I am *not capable*. My duty compels me."

I shrugged his hand off and resumed walking. "So you are a robot after all."

I avoided his eye. We did not speak for another hour as we worked our way through the shattered city, climbing mound after mound of rock and ruin until the circle of the palace grounds and the fences of the Citadel camp lay just ahead. We conferred in the lee of a crumbled pillar beside a decapitated statue. "How are we going to get past all those guards?"

"There is no approach from this angle," said Jeremiah. "We must search the perimeter for a weaker point. If a way cannot be found we can then proceed."

I furrowed my brow. "Run that by me again, will you?"

"We must explore all avenues of surreptitious incursion. If no way can be found, I can use...force."

"Why not just use *force* now?" I asked.

"My duty compels me," Jeremiah repeated dully. "All other avenues must be exhausted before I am free to act."

So we made our way slowly and carefully about the perimeter of the palace, ducking through archways and hiding behind clumps of wreckage. The sun was a hot yellow eye directly above us in a clear blue sky by the time we arrived back at our starting point, overlooking a road the Citadelites had pushed open for their own use. The six-legged yellow machines had erected a new shelter, and had moved on to clearing a fresh area beside it. The air shook for a moment as one of them vomited a load of broken concrete into a large metal bin.

"The beasts of industry are busy," I said. "Seems like they're planning quite a base."

Without another word Jeremiah stood up from the nook behind the crumbled pillar and started walking openly down the road toward the camp's fence. I followed, my hand resting on the butt of the Smith-Shurtook.

I heard the yell of a guard as we passed out of the shadow of one of the great six-legged machines. A few seconds later a platoon of men in grey uniforms assembled at the perimeter to meet us, wicked looking weapons mounted on their shoulders and trained on our position. "Halt!" they shouted in bass chorus.

"So," I said slowly, "are you just going to kill them all, then?"

"No," said Jeremiah evenly. "I am obliged to be selective."

"What should I do?"

"Follow in my wake."

Jeremiah did not slacken in his pace as he bore down on the fence. The order was given to fire, and each man who tried to do so folded out from under his weapon and collapsed soundlessly on the dirt. Their commanders' orders became more urgent until they too fell, frozen in the act of reaching for their sidearms. Last to go were the dogs.

My fingers twitched over my holster.

Jeremiah walked on. A group of nuns quailed before him and then ran into one of the shelters, shouting. More guards ran out to meet us, and fell. I stepped over their bodies and looked over my shoulder, hurrying after the patiently pacing predator.

He moved up the broad front steps of the palace and walked through the open door, walking between fat snakes of cabling that ran from the Citadelite camp into the dark palace interior. I turned around and backed through the door, eyes scanning the now motionless camp.

I bumped into Jeremiah and grunted. "Sorry!"

There was a strange smell in the air, like old meat and forest damp. I turned around to survey the expansive hall in which we stood, my eyes adjusting to the shadows and coaxing the details of staircases and balconies into focus.

I gasped.

Bodies hung from every rafter, taut chords around their necks. There were more than two dozen. "Mother of love! What happened to these people?"

"They have been hanged," explained Jeremiah. He walked over to one of the closest bodies and examined the tattered remains of its uniform. "These are palace officials. It may have been a mass suicide during the last siege."

"But there were bodies nowhere else..." I whispered.

"I do not know what happened here in the end," said Jeremiah, "but it seems even its participants judged it too sick to bear."

More sounds of shouting from the camp outside motivated us to push onward, following the Citadelite cabling through an empty gallery with broken windows and then disappearing down an open elevator shaft. Without hesitation Jeremiah stepped inside the shaft and began climbing down a set of rungs running down a shallow recess. I looked down into the darkness and steeled myself, then followed him.

We were swallowed by the gloom in minutes. "Do you have a light?" I asked. "We can navigate the ladder by touch," replied Jeremiah's voice from below me somewhere.

"Still, having a light would make this *a little bit* less like a living nightmare. But that sort of thing may be beneath your concern."

After a pause Jeremiah said, "I am capable of a mild phosphorescence."

"Please."

Jeremiah's carapace appeared out the blackness beneath my feet, a somber blue-green glow that cast only the most fleeting illumination to the area of the shaft immediately around him. "Sir, this does us no service," he said.

"It's enough."

For several moments there was no sound by our hands and feet touching the metal rungs as we descended. I kept my eyes fixed on the bobbing blur of blue-green below. Before I had really decided to voice my thoughts I heard myself asking, "If the Secret Math is so dangerous – if it can be used to kill a dozen at a thought – wouldn't you be the doing the galaxy the greatest service of all by just killing yourselves?" I sniffed. "Is there a way to hang you?"

"The Math is powerful, not dangerous."

"I'm sure it will seem fairly dangerous to the families of those soldiers you've just murdered."

"They lack perspective," he said evenly.

"Ah."

After a long interval Jeremiah added, "And we will one day need it. Every one of us."

"Need what? Need the Secret Math?"

"Yes. We carry it. It will be yours to inherit, when the time comes. But you cannot harbor it now, as evidenced by the Kamari Horror. We carry your burden while you grow, while your patchwork of societies co-evolve a solution to the problem of adapting human beings to a galactic life."

"You control us, then. You farm us for stability. We're your own personal chemical computers, dreaming and dying for your science."

"No. We are bound to you by our duty, and one day we will be free."

"There's your *duty* again..."

"You cannot understand, Simon. A human being *is*, and a human being's duty is to protect the capacity for future life. A human executive *does*, and his missions are weighted by two pendulums: to protect the capacity for future life, and to carry the Math for man." He made a sound that was disturbingly almost like a dry chuckle. "A human being may choose to follow a purpose higher than his flesh, but a human executive has no choice. Zoran's last edict is burned into our souls – we carry the Math, and separate the worlds."

"Separate the worlds? Why?"

"To accelerate the process of local social evolution, to keep the pot churning but never boiling over, to keep change cellular. But we work against your nature, for human beings strive to connect themselves into ever greater meta-communities, and to imprint themselves upon a wider history that is shared as a racial inheritance. This drive built your first cities, and forged roads across continents to trade with alien cultures."

"Sounds like progress," I said.

"It is an expression of your Stone Age circumstances. *Your human urges have nothing to do with space.* That is a wisdom human executives have that human beings do not. You *are*, we *do*. Your palette of decisions is an imprint of an environment that no longer exists, except on Eden. Your racial wisdom is not fit to shape the galaxy."

"We're your little people. Will you one day keep us in zoos?"

"The little people were once kept in zoos," Jeremiah pointed out, "until your kind learned that anything that could actually *ask* for freedom probably deserved to have it. Your biology may be tuned in terms of millennia, you see, but your civilization is in constant flux. That is humanity's solution to the process of slow biology: you are only half flesh. The greater part of you is a purely mimetic organism, existing in an environment of information. This is why you have evolved laws and art and history."

"Crutches for unteachable flesh?"

"Yes," said Jeremiah. "Your civilization is a scaffolding that permits the expansion of Solar life beyond its home – a bridge across which animals run. And where flesh is slow to learn, civilization is fast. Too fast. Premature solutions spread like fire from one culture to another, which is why we have placed barriers between the stars."

"The gates!"

"The gates," he agreed. "By enforcing stellar locality, Solar life is forced to generate many simultaneous solutions to the human political question. The barriers to travel are imperfect by design: new mimetic constructs trickle through from star to star, free to catch on or to fizzle without being pushed by an interested force." He paused. "But life always finds a way. New technologies to facilitate easier and faster transit between gates are suppressed by the Queen of Space all the time. It is a losing battle. It is inevitable that civilization will become monolithic. We can only hope that enough strength has been bred into the foundations by the time it happens."

"What's the hurry? You bend us at your yoke so that you might sooner be free of the burden of caring for us?"

Jeremiah was silent for several moments, again the only sounds our patient footfalls and steady grippings and ungrippings as we continued the seemingly interminable descent into the darkness. "Simon, I have told you that we will all one day need the Secret Mathematic. We will need it very badly, for our survival may depend on it."

"Why?" I shot back impatiently.

Jeremiah stopped moving, and I froze with him. I thought he had heard something, but at length it became apparent that he had stopped only to speak. "There is one we call the Traveller. His true name is First Felix, of the Eighth Strain. He is the oldest of us, and the wisest."

"No doubt he puppeteers the Queen of Space herself," I grunted.

"No. He is the Traveller. He has been travelling for millennia."

"Where does he travel?"

"Have you ever seen a map of the Panstellar Neighbourhood, Simon?"

I thought about Blighton's terrifying projection back on Maja. "Yes," I replied softly. "It was just the tiniest puff, in a whorl of gas and light."

"The tiniest puff indeed. No human being lives on a world further than sixty lightyears from the Solar Nebula. And yet across that small parcel of space we have encountered two other civilizations – two neighbors across sixty lightyears of space."

"Seems a bit lonely."

"On the contrary, it means this galaxy is teeming with life. And do you imagine that Solar life is the only life to have spread beyond its own borders? Have you ever stopped to think about what might happen when our borders expand against their own?"

"We seem to peacefully co-exist with the Pegasi and the...er, the –"

"The Hennish," supplied Jeremiah. "That is because we dominate them."

"It was explained to me that every race has an equal voice in the affairs of the Panstellar Neighbourhood."

"And so it is, for mercy is a human strength. Mercy *comes* from a position of strength."

"So what strength do we hold over the Pegasi and the Hennish?"

"Time," said Jeremiah simply, "nothing but time. We got there first. That is why it was human beings who came down out of the sky to prove the existence of alien life to the Pegasi, rather than the other way around. And while law, science and philosophy agree that the soul of a Pegasi is worth as much or as little as the soul of a human being, it is indisputable that our civilization is more mature. We landed on their world, they did not land on ours. As conquerors we *chose* to be compassionate."

"But, surely there are worlds enough for all. Pegasi must have their own planets..."

"The Pegasi have been granted a purely Pegasi world at an alien star, yes, with an atmosphere processed by Solar engineers. We teach them to use our tools, and how to work within our science. Their own science, though not without its gifts, has lost the opportunity to underlie panstellar civilization. In a thousand years it will be studied purely as an aspect of antiquity. The wisest of them should be grateful that the interstellar predators who discovered them were merciful, and the wisest of us should be grateful that we have not met our equal in them."

I frowned. "And the Hennish?"

"While in many ways more complex than ours, Hennish civilization is monolithic in the extreme, with the whole of Hennish sentient life concentrated in the shared experience of the Great Henniplasm. Due to this biologically founded limitation, the Hennish will be forever unable to leave their native star."

I grunted. "So you think one day we'll meet somebody else with an older, more powerful civilization, and they'll dominate us? Is that it?"

"Yes. There are worlds enough for all here and now, but we do not know if this young quarter of space is representative of the greater galaxy. Felix travels westward, into the thick of the spiral arm, to find out. His messages are beamed back via micro-gate, and received directly by the Executive Council and the Queen of Space. He has seen what no Solar eyes have seen. He has gone further than our fastest probe, and he has met our future."

"And..." I prompted.

"And his last transmission, received less than a century ago, confirms our worst fears."

The shaft suddenly seemed darker and more still than ever. My hands were suddenly sweaty, and I adjusted my grip against the ladder's rungs. Jeremiah's tone sent shivers down my spine. "What did the message say?" I breathed.

"It said: *something wicked this way comes.*"

XXXVI.
MINOTAUR

At the bottom of the elevator shaft we found the lift car, smashed. Jeremiah helped me over the debris and we came out into a long corridor dimly lit by little yellow lamps. At intervals their light was aided by white orbs on metal stands, connected to the thick cylinder of cabling laid by engineers of the Citadel of the Recovery. Jeremiah strode down the silent corridor and I followed him, still chilled by his latest revelation about the untamed galactic wilderness beyond the borders of the Panstellar Neighbourhood.

The corridor ended in a large chamber with a high-domed ceiling, with floors of intricate tiling forming a pattern that swirled from the walls into the centre, ultimately rising into a stepped fountain which babbled and splashed with brown, silty water. In the middle of the fountain was a statue of a man with children and dogs playing at his feet, and sparrows alighted on his shoulders. He wore a long cape and a serious but not unkind expression on his long face. He bore a simple crown in the shape of interlocking leaves. "Terron Volmash, I presume."

"Yes," confirmed Jeremiah.

Inset in the walls along the sides of the chamber were blank rectangular screens, their faces dusty and dark – dozens upon dozens of them, aligned in neat rows. "Dataplates?" I wondered aloud.

"Televisions," corrected Jeremiah. "Dataplates dedicated to videographic and holographic streams of images and sound."

"The images and sounds of what?" I scratched my head, thinking of the televisual programs I had seen in the hospital on Samundra: nature documentaries, pharmaceutical informationals, and a series of odd little cartoons about an anthropomorphisized comet who had a penchant for finding trouble among a pack of bullying asteroids.

"The human fascination with visual narrative is universal. Televisual streams cover all facets of life, from the banal to the fantastic. There were televisions at Castle Misne. Did you never watch?"

I shrugged. "I found it confusing. It seemed to me that whatever was going on on television was over my head, so I figured it wasn't really any of my business."

"Interesting," said Jeremiah. He gestured to the rows of blank screens. "Televisual streams were the front lines of the hegemony's spread, for the life they depicted was vital, luxuriant and proud. Kamari Star developed a new mythology for itself, a vision powerful enough to dazzle both near and far. This televisually broadcast feeling of shared experience formed the basis for the standardizing of Kamari's intrastellar cultures."

"And, presumably, Kamari's *interstellar* ventures."

"Yes," said Jeremiah. "Life finds a way. Even corporate life. And the politicians of Metra were not blind to this, which is why they parasited their government upon the back of their cultural exports. In this way they believed they could control the worlds of a foreign star without breaking the Panstellar Covenant."

I wandered past him. The furthest wall beyond the statue of Volmash was covered in open stone cells, and in each cell sat a stone figurine carved in the shape of a bird. I recognized the layout immediately from the image I had been shown by Crushed Head Faeda. The bird whose features had seemed familiar to me was missing, its former perch reduced to a broken edge around a gaping hole through which the Citadelite cabling ran. "The puzzle," I sighed. "And already correctly penetrated."

"Yes."

"Then we are too late."

Jeremiah shook his head curtly. "The Citadelite expedition is still inside. If this is the hiding place of the Nightmare Cannon, it remains within these walls as we speak."

I walked past the fountain and touched the edges of the hole as I peered into the inscrutable darkness inside. Citadelite tools lay on the grit-covered floor. "They had to force their way in. They just wanted to know where to cut."

I turned around to face Jeremiah. "Lucky thing I knew."

Jeremiah walked up to me, his eyes on the rows of stone birds. "What would you have me say?"

"You know who I was."

"Yes."

"And I was not Volmash's engineer, was I? Nor his aide."

"No."

We stared at each other for a long moment. "I just want to hear you say it," I said.

Jeremiah ducked his head and crawled through the hole in the middle of the matrix of raptors, his carapace glowing feebly in the pitch. My eyes burned. I closed them, but that darkness was worse. Feeling the hungry stares of the stone birds upon me I quickly bent down and followed him.

We emerged at the mouth of a maze, three corridors of featureless grey slate branching off in three directions, each dimly lit by widely spaced yellow lamps separated by long isles of shadow.

Jeremiah turned to me. "Lead on," he said.

I swallowed. "I haven't the foggiest..."

I trailed off as he simply continued to gaze at me patiently, so I walked past him with an irritated snort and proceeded down the left fork, on a whim. I could hear his smooth footfalls keeping pace behind. At the next junction I chose again at random, nursing some childish hope that I could demonstrate the futility of my lead. Surely I had no special knowledge of this maze. Surely not I.

The walls seemed to absorb sound, so that our steps and even our voices sounded muffled and distant. The silence was disarming in its surreality. Nightmarish half-memories dabbed at my consciousness: a flight with rubber legs through dark halls, yearning to make it around the next turn, the beast's hot breath on the nape of my neck...

We came to a dead-end and were forced to double-back. I gave Jeremiah a defiant smirk as I passed him. But then I stopped up short for the way we'd come was blocked by a wall. "What kind of a maze is this? Nobody could memorize the layout – it's *moving*." I shrugged lamely. "I don't think I can help you here, robot."

"Continue."

"What?"

"Continue."

I took a swig of water from my flask and muscled past him roughly, striding quickly down toward the dead-end – which was now open, and presented us with three new choices of corridor. I chose the right branch, and then purposefully second-guessed myself at the last moment and plunged straight down the middle recklessly.

Time passed. We meandered left and right, came to dead-ends and turned around, right and left again. The slippery phantoms of sleep imagery continued to push up at my brain, fogging my vision and giving me difficulty discerning reality from imagination. The muscles in my neck knotted, but it wasn't hot breath behind me – just Jeremiah.

At one point I peed in the corner, and a long while later we found ourselves standing at that same spot. "We're going in circles," I said, shaking my head sadly. "We'll be trapped here forever."

"Continue," said Jeremiah.

"*It's pointless!*" I shouted. "The Citadelites are probably in the same position we're in – hopelessly lost!"

"Continue."

"I can't keep doing this, walking forever – *have mercy!*" I cried, rounding on the impassive machine with wild eyes and clenched fists.

Jeremiah did not flinch. After an interval he crisply pronounced, "Do not speak of mercy to me. Not you. Not ever."

I wanted to shout something back but my throat was dry and constricted. I dropped my hands to my sides and sagged. Jeremiah waited briefly and then indicated the path ahead. "Continue," he said.

We continued. After three more hours I pushed my shoulder into a corner and allowed myself to slide down the grey walls, landing in an exhausted heap upon the cold, dusty floor. "I can't go on," I declared, my breath heaving.

Jeremiah stood at my feet quietly. I heard a distant grinding, and then a thump. Jeremiah cocked his head, listening. "That is the first time the walls have moved without reference to our actions," he said in a hush. "I believe the process is complete."

"What process?" I breathed, eyes closed.

"I believe this maze is an authentication device. It has been testing you."

"You're saying the maze is intelligent?"

"I believe it has been designed to qualify and compare the problem solving strategies of whomsoever should attempt to navigate it. No two beings approach puzzles in quite the same way. Thus, it queries us with shifting walls until our pattern of solution matches a problem solving signature in its database." There was another rumbling boom, and the smell of a new air drifted down the corridor. Jeremiah pointed to where a bluish light was shining weakly around the next corner. "In this case I believe it has been keyed to...you, and you have now been positively identified by the maze."

He held out his hand. After a pause I took it, and allowed him to haul me to my feet. We both passed through the end of the corridor, turned the corner and emerged into a large, dark gallery full of statues with lurid blue lights shining upward from their pedestals. As we stepped into the gallery the door slid closed behind us, its boom decaying away quickly.

At the far end of the gallery was a second door, now grinding ponderously open. Over the door was a script I did not recognize. The glyphs almost looked like letters but were canted and looped in unfamiliar ways. "Late Hengrishe," observed Jeremiah solemnly. "It says: *Beware the Minotaur.*"

"What's a Minotaur?" I asked.

Just then we were knocked off our feet by a shuddering blast, the floor quaking beneath us. A second later the door we had just come through was shredded by a second explosion, followed by a blossom of dirty smoke. Coughing, I rolled over and got to my feet, kicking back the side of my red leather longcoat and drawing the Smith-Shurtook from its holster.

Two grey-cassocked monks with hard eyes came through the wrecked door first, followed by a willowy, almond-eyed girl in white robes who bore an unmistakable resemblance to Crushed Head Faeda. She could not have been older than fifteen. Her brown eyes were fixed on me, lip curling menacingly. "Murderer!" she hissed. *"Guards!"*

A platoon of grey uniformed soldiers jogged into the gallery and leveled their weapons at Jeremiah and I. "Drop your weapons!" one of them commanded.

"No!" I said.

A beat. "Drop your weapons or we'll shoot!" he barked.

"I doubt it," I replied.

"Where is the Cannon?" demanded the girl in white.

"I don't think we're through the maze, yet," I said, pointing to the open doorway behind us. "If you kill me now you'll never get there."

The girl frowned, her face taking on an even more childish quality. "Nestor Simonithrat Fell," she said, the muscles in neck working with tension, "you are a man of commerce and therefore a liar. You will not negotiate your way out of the execution so you richly deserve."

I chuckled. "I'm not Nestor Fell."

"What?"

"Let's go, Jeremiah." I turned on heel and walked through the doorway, Jeremiah padding beside me. This next section of maze was darker than the first, lit by widely spaced amber lamps set into the floor. The air was more moist, and had a fetid edge to it. Ignoring this I pushed ahead, quickly choosing one branch and then another, eager to put a few corners between us and the Citadelites before they gathered the sense to follow us.

"I've lost visual contact!" I heard one of the soldiers shout, his voice echoing strangely around us.

We continued to hear their whispers even after we made yet another turn, and I wondered at this. Jeremiah indicated for silence, then leaned in closely to my ear. "Listen, Simon. Every sound is travelling the length of every hall. They can hear our footfalls right behind them as surely as we can hear their voices, but I believe they are no longer close by."

"An acoustic trick?" I frowned.

"Hey, shut up – I can hear them!" cried one of the soldiers. Jeremiah and I stood in silence and I held my breath. A few seconds later I heard the soldiers exhale. "I don't hear anything," someone else claimed.

"Find them!" snapped the voice of the young girl viciously. The sound of their careful footfalls resumed, seeming to come from all around us.

This maze did not move. It was dark and still and uncomfortably warm. Jeremiah and I slunk on steadily, laboring to keep our steps as quiet as possible. In contrast the Citadel's plodding, murmuring party was easy to monitor.

I heard one of them gasp. Shuffling footfalls, and then a blood curdling scream. I froze. "Mother of –"

A weapon fired in staccato rhythm, followed by a series of grunts and then another terrifying cry of pain. When it died away all we could hear were panicked, overlapping footsteps and heavy breathing.

"What was it?" demanded the girl, her voice shaking.

"I don't know m'lady, but I'll take care of it," promised the commanding soldier.

A moment later his dying cry resounded through every corridor in the maze. Jeremiah and I looked at one another. "The Minotaur?" I whispered.

He nodded. "A creature of myth, fierce guardian of a labyrinth."

"That didn't sound like any myth," I replied soberly.

"Indeed not," agreed Jeremiah.

It was not long thereafter that we came across the soldiers' remains, mangled unspeakably, their entrails dragged out along the length of the corridor for meters and meters and blood sprayed across the walls in rough lines. I averted my eyes and we moved past them.

Over the next while we occasionally heard muted chatter from the other party. Now and again we heard something we could not identify: a low moan, a snort of breath, or a clicking, dragging sound. I shuddered and tried not to imagine what sort of creature madmen like the tyrants of Kamari might have peopled this sick trap with. I tried not to imagine anything, focusing my mind on the grim game of selecting: left, right, or centre?

I became hypnotized, and time lost all meaning.

The sound of the dragging, moaning footfalls had locked so neatly into the rhythm of our own steps that it must have been a long time before they penetrated my attention. "Do you hear that?" I whispered fiercely.

"Sir, we have no choice but to keep moving," replied Jeremiah quietly.

I shivered. "It's matching our pace...it can hear us. It must be close."

"Continue," urged Jeremiah.

And then – of course – we came upon a section of corridor in which all the lamps had died. It was a stretch of total darkness, dropping off before our feet into instant infinity. I paused at the threshold, paralyzed, the sound of my pounding heart deafening me to all else.

Jeremiah walked past me without hesitation, his blue-green glow bobbing smaller and dimmer down the tunnel. I looked behind me at the blank walls and amber lamps, and found no comfort there. Muttering one of Glory's profanities under my breath I jogged into the shadows after the apparent robot.

His glow vanished around a corner and I hurried to catch him, relieved when I saw his back again. He turned another corner and I ran up to meet him, wheeling around the end of the wall and stopping short at the blank field of darkness that met me.

I heard nothing.

Reaching my arms out before me I groped for the next section of wall. I took one cautious step forward, and then another. "Jeremiah?" I whispered, my airy voice seeming very loud despite the constant banging of my blood in my ears.

There came a soft thud, followed by a dragging sound.

I took another step, my fingers aching to find the wall. My knees felt loose and rebellious. I felt as if I were sinking into the floor as I lifted my foot to take another pace. I leaned forward, my digits twitching.

Another thud. A low, whinnying kind of moan. It sounded for the life of me like it was right before my face.

"Acoustic trick," I reminded myself, trying to keep hold of my sanity. I squeezed my hands into tight fists until the pain of my fingernails digging into my palms caused little stars to shoot through my vision. I took a deep breath and stepped forward again.

I ran up against something hard, covered in hair. A hot, moist fume chuffed across my hands, and the thing moaned again. I felt its breath, and my bowels creaked in instinctive dread. The Minotaur had me!

I knew suddenly what I was, in that living moment: *prey*.

With an involuntary shriek of terror I threw myself backward, and heard the thing shuffle in sudden motion. I was felled by a hard, swift limb, the wind knocked from my lungs. Gasping and wheezing I shot to my feet and straight into a wall, more stars exploding across my useless field of nonvision.

I was grabbed and thrown against another wall, the thing's hot breath chortling against my leg. I jerked my leg away and squeezed spasmodically on the Smith-Shurtook's trigger. It barked twice, a harsh orange light sputtering from the end and illuminating briefly a hulking, inhuman shadow.

Apparently it was unharmed for I next felt myself picked up by the ankle and shaken roughly. I slammed into another wall and slid to the floor, groaning. I rolled into a ball, clutching the gun against my face, and pinched my eyes shut tightly until I saw colours. *"Jeremiah!"* I screamed.

To my shock I heard the word, "Sir!" right beside my ear, and a moment later I was pulled to my feet by a glowing green hand. I stumbled after it and we pelted through the blackness, jerked right and then left, right again. I flailed behind the speeding robot, crashing my elbows against the walls and my knees against the floor.

I fell in a disoriented pile when he released me, and from the sound of my own fall's echoes I knew that we had exited the maze and were now in a very large chamber. I heard a door slide shut, and opened my eyes to see the maze sealed. I turned around. Jeremiah was walking slowly deeper into the chamber, his arms limp at his sides. I stood up shakily.

The room was a ring, like the habitat hub of a spaceship on its side. It curved away to either side of us far away, encompassing a massive diameter. It was filled with empty desks with blank plates, abandoned chairs askew. A jungle of cabling snaked over the ceiling, thick fibres leading down to cluster of consoles and televisual boxes. An inch of dust covered every surface, including the occasional robot.

Like any formerly busy place devoid of people, it was chilling in its peace.

Directly before us was a wide gate, its doors open, leading into a second ring within the first, a slightly smaller but still vast chamber filled with a different kind of furniture. Jeremiah walked through the gate and I followed him. As we drew nearer it became apparent that the furnishings were not desks, but tables. Surgical tables. And they had patients on them.

Even after a few years the smell was strong. I crinkled my nose in disgust. Brown skeletons wreathed in tendrils of dried meat and tendon lay row after row in the second ring, still attached to dead medical appliances wheeled up to their sides. Jeremiah touched the controls of one of the machines, but it did not respond. He knocked on the chest of one of the robots, and it fell over with a bloom of flying motes.

"A...hospital?" I wondered aloud.

"No," said Jeremiah.

Some thirty degrees clockwise around the second ring was the aperture to a third ring. The doors were sealed but Jeremiah was able to force them manually, pushing the thick sheets of metal back into their recesses as the jammed mechanisms whined and coughed. When he was done I stepped through, and hesitantly passed through more rows of tables, more bodies penetrated by obscene assortments of tools.

My breath was coming too fast, and my head ached. Jeremiah caught my elbow. "Continue," he said.

Another thirty degrees of circumnavigation brought us to another aperture, this one already wrecked for us though obviously long ago, the bent doors covered in dust. I passed quickly through the fourth ring without looking at anything, but Jeremiah caught up to me in the fifth ring and dragged me over to an examination table. The robot standing over the corpse appeared to be have been frozen in the process of performing a curious amputation. "Do you understand?" Jeremiah demanded sharply.

"Torture," I muttered weakly. "Suffering."

Jeremiah indicated the cables leading from each table up into the ceiling. "*Channeled* suffering, Simon. Piped away. Collected." He turned to look me in the eyes. "Broadcast."

The sixth ring was worse. Several of the lights had failed, and in the shadows I could not shake the feeling that the robots were moving when I turned my back. Or that the bodies were. In the seventh ring there lay the corrupt corpses of both animals and people, and some disfigured horrors that seemed to be a union of both. In the eighth ring were children, their backs arched in torment, the tops of their skulls removed and a garden of instruments sunk into the dried brown lumps within.

I paused against the wall, my eyes closed and my breathing ragged. After a moment I heard Jeremiah approach from behind me. He put a gentle hand on my shoulder.

I shook it off. "You're telling me I did this," I cried into my muffling forearm. I looked up at the dark ceiling covered in organic whorls of dark cabling. "You're telling me this is mine."

He did not answer.

I spun around and cried, "Why would *anyone* be a part of this? It isn't real! It doesn't make sense! *This can't be right!*" I collapsed on the floor, spreading the dust with my shaking fingers. "Tell me it isn't true, Jeremiah. Tell me you're playing with me, to be cruel."

He said, "Atrocities can be justified in the defense of a great union, for the question can be framed as choosing the lesser of two evils."

I blinked, and leaned back against the wall with a rough sigh. "How?"

"By misrepresenting the motives of the enemy, by making theater a more compelling power in politics than discourse, and by artfully catalyzing a population's overwhelming desire to *believe* in the righteousness of the Kamari way of life." He again helped me to my feet, and indicated the way clockwise. "Continue," he said.

In the ninth ring were infants.

A distant boom sounded. Jeremiah cocked his head. "The Citadelites are still demolishing their way through. We must proceed to the inner chamber." We found the last set of doors open, and I ran through with my eyes locked straight ahead, sick to my soul.

The inner chamber was round. At its centre was a wide platform, atop which was mounted a great and menacing device much like an overgrown gun, its giant muzzle pointed at a wall lined with dark-faced televisions. It was black.

I walked slowly beneath the muzzle, reaching up to touch the cold metal with my hand. "The Nightmare Cannon?" I frowned. "We're never going to get this thing out of here. Why does everything in this galaxy fit into the palm of my hand...except this?"

Jeremiah knocked on the side of the base experimentally. "I believe this housing is for the purposes of display. The weapon itself is likely a small component, somewhere within."

Birds chirped. I swung around to search the ceiling, spotting the tiny flitting things in the shadows with effort. When I looked down six silver robots in intricately filigreed carapaces were stepping out of an alcove behind the weapon's base. "Jeremiah..." I called.

"You are trespassing. The penalty is death," said one of the robots flatly.

Jeremiah dropped off the platform and stood beside me. "We come under the authority of the Queen of Space," he announced loudly.

At that the robots ran forward with surprising speed. Jeremiah stepped forward to meet them, settling into a kind of ready half-crouch I had never seen before. When the first silver robot attempted to grab him Jeremiah flew into action, whirling about and striking the robot in the middle of its chest with a precision kick. The robot clattered to the floor noisily, and Jeremiah wheeled on the other five.

Two of them attacked at once. Jeremiah dropped to the floor and sprang up beside them, twisting his arms around their legs and pulling them to the ground. He jumped up and stood on their chests while they squirmed beneath him.

The remaining four robots leapt at him, and the fight became a blur of flashing carapaces and the rhythmic clicking, clanking sound of metal striking metal. I was unable to see who was ahead until Jeremiah came flying out the fracas and crashed into a wall violently, televisions smashing around him.

I leveled the Smith-Shurtook at the cluster of silver robots and fired repeatedly. The bullets sparked on their armor but did not penetrate it, my volley leaving them totally undisturbed until I caught one of them in the eye. It popped and fizzled. Now considering me a valid threat, the machines began to advance on me. I backed up slowly, still firing.

Jeremiah jumped over their line and landed among them, spinning as he kicked out in a rapid rhythm. The silver robots scattered, falling on their backs and skidding along the floor. Jeremiah picked up the one-eyed robot and swung him by his ankles, working up the momentum necessary to cast him into the others as a weapon unto itself. He smacked down first one robot and then another, then released his grip and the one-eyed robot sailed into the side of the Nightmare Cannon and crumpled, its head dented in roughly.

One of the robots who hadn't been knocked to the ground leapt at me, but I kept firing the Smith-Shurtook into its face until both eyes popped with twin, loud cracks and something sparked from within. The robot fell, embers raining from its sockets.

Jeremiah and the remaining four had resumed their high-speed combat. I cheered as two more robots dropped out of the melee, the carapaces over their heads broken. A third robot sailed over top of me and struck the ceiling in a hail of debris. It piled into the floor heavily and did not move again.

The last robot, however, continued to put up quite a fight, its limbs flashing into a shining blur as it met Jeremiah's every move with a precise an effective counter-move. The two robots ranged across the room, clanking and clicking in an ever-increasing rhythm until the sounds of their clashing formed an almost constant wash of noise.

Jeremiah was thrown. In a single powerful leap he returned to meet his opponent, who was in turn cast with inhuman strength to tumble across the floor, elbows and knees clanking loudly. Jeremiah ran after the robot and jumped upon it even before it had come to a rest, the two of them wrestling across the floor with moves too quick to discern with the human eye. As they rolled into the threshold of the chamber entrance, however, I espied my opportunity to contribute.

I ran over and slapped the contact on the wall next to the door, and it began to grind closed heavily. Jeremiah lifted his head and pulled aside just in time: his opponent's head was taken beneath the door and pressed into the metal jamb with a disturbingly organic crunching noise. The silver robot's filigreed body jerked once, and then lay still.

I helped Jeremiah to his feet, and then we both hit the ground as the report of another nearby explosion jostled the chamber. I got up again, rubbing my hip. "They're getting closer," I said.

Jeremiah nodded. "I will investigate the Cannon," he said, springing deftly away and climbing the weapon's mount. I noticed that his carapace was cracked and split in several places. He walked out along the Cannon's barrel and then fished himself inside its very mouth. A moment later I could hear him banging around inside the housing.

"Hurry up!" I called.

I paced the chamber nervously, glancing up at the little birds flying around the ceiling as they chirped. Another boom sounded, closer now, and I knew the Citadelites were almost upon us. And perhaps something else, as well – something worse.

"*Hurry!*" I implored.

XXXVII.
THE CLOUDS

I stood alone at the centre of Volmash's phantasmagoric underground phrontisterion, my loyal companion and sworn enemy a green-plated superman masquerading as a slave now fed bodily into a great black gun two storeys high presided over by a twittering flock of brown-flecked sparrows. I paced in circles, stepping over a smashed silver robot when necessary.

I heard footfalls and looked up to see the girl in white and two pale, unarmed soldiers stopping at the threshold. One of them was cradling a wounded arm. I leveled the Smith-Shurtook at them. "No fancy soldiering, please," I said. "Just stay where you are."

"Fell!" hissed the girl.

"And you are...?"

"Lady Paz Serafina Aza, High Priestess of the Recovery." Her childish face contorted with rage. "You killed my sister. You'll pay for that."

I glanced at my gun. "If you say so. For the record I'll have you know that I only killed your sister once she had started killing me. I mean, she set the tone. She was very sick."

"That's a hideous lie, and I'll make you suffer for it until you *wish* for death!" she promised venomously, fists clenched at her sides.

I nodded. "I can see the wisdom of putting you and your family in charge of galactic compassion. You've clearly got a knack."

"Anyone who stands against the Recovery stands against *goodness*," she declared through gritted teeth.

"Oh?" I replied, smiling icily. "How wonderfully simple! I've obviously been needlessly over-complicating the whole affair."

"I don't care to hear about your twisted rationalizations, Fell," she said, "the only thing that matters is the weapon, and keeping it out of your hands."

I paused, furrowing my brow. "My hands?"

"That's right," she smiled defiantly, her neat teeth gleaming; "I'm *on to you*, Fell. You may have fooled my sisters but *not me*. I *know* you're out to create a fresh Horror, and I'm here to tell you now that it's not going to happen. I'm here to tell you that it stops, right here. *Now.*"

I scratched my head with my gun, the soldiers' eyes following it hypnotically. "Are you telling me you would *destroy* the Nightmare Cannon?"

"I would take it before the Queen of Space, so that all Solarkind might bear witness to its end."

I nodded. "That's exactly what I'm trying to do."

"Liar!" she shouted. "Don't play games with me, Fell."

"I told you, I'm not Nestor Fell."

"Who are you then?"

"Well," I said, shrugging apologetically, "they *say* my name is Simon."

"Very well *Simon*," said the new Lady Aza tightly, "watch now as your plot fails."

"You're awfully confident for somebody standing in the crosshairs."

She smirked, and then muttered subvocally into her telephone, her swan neck twitching. She then stepped backward over the threshold and out of the inner chamber, flanked by the two grey soldiers.

I glanced around. Would reinforcements come blasting through the walls?

The ceiling cracked. A line of dust settled gracefully out of it, followed by a few pebbles. I frowned and started backing toward the curved wall as the entire chamber began to rumble...

I glanced over to Lady Aza's party, but they had taken shelter behind an overturned surgical table. I looked back up at the ceiling of the inner chamber as it came loose in several large sections and began tumbling down toward me amid a roiling face of dust. I screamed and dove to the ground, casting my arms over my head.

I did not, however, die.

I looked up in a maelstrom of noise and flying grit to see a cylinder of dirt, rock and concrete a kilometer long flash into white hot vapour that was drawn upward and away into the dark maw of a giant machine. The machine stepped aside, revealing a round circle of blue sky at the top of the long tunnel.

"Mother of love!" I cried.

Three orange machines with six legs each scampered somehow straight down the vertical sides of the shaft, and dropped to the debris-coated floor with a series of world-shaking sextuple booms. They ignored me as I dodged their tarnished orange feet, arranging themselves around the Nightmare Cannon and setting to work unmooring it from its base. In less than a minute they were clambering back up the shaft, the massive weapon suspended between them. In another minute they had exited at the top, and were gone. A heartbeat later a flock of tiny birds burst from their hiding places in nooks beside the banks of blank televisions and flew out into the open sky.

The ends of a number of long cables dropped to the floor. The soldiers attached devices on their belts to the cables, arranged the Lady between them, and then began to ascend up the tunnel with a hum. "You lose, Mr. Simon," called the young Lady Aza. "Goodness wins."

I watched them disappear, blinking against the sunlight.

I wondered what had happened to Jeremiah, inside the Cannon.

A tiny brown bird flapped over and landed on my shoulder. I turned to peer at it, and it peered back. "Hello," I said.

"Emergency protocols have been activated," said the bird conversationally, its little beak opening and closing in rough time to the consonant sounds. "I am armed, and ready to relay."

"The Nightmare Cannon, I presume," I said flatly.

The little brown bird cocked its head. "Identify input source."

I sniffed. "Suffering? I don't have any suffering for you."

The bird blinked.

I heard a hollow thump, followed by a sliding sound. I turned around slowly, considering now that the Citadelites had likely left the way to the maze open with their blasting. I could flee now, but I would have to face the thing in the dark again – without Jeremiah.

The Minotaur was definitely in the ninth ring. I heard it again, and could not will my feet to move.

"Identify input source," said the bird on my shoulder.

"Shut up..." I suggested, looking up and letting my jaw drop open. "Faeces," I said.

An armed platoon of grey soldiers rappelled down the long tunnel and hit the bottom simultaneously, surrounding me with a radially symmetrical ring of targeted guns like some kind of very violent floorshow. I dropped the Smith-Shurtook and held up my hands.

I was manacled and ascended from the tunnel, held between two soldiers with humming devices on their belts. The sparrow-like bird flew in wide circles just over our heads until one soldier swiped at it menacingly with his gun, and it thereafter took to orbiting us from a greater distance.

It was the only bird. Its companions had all fled. As real things, they longed for the open air.

We reached the top, an extension of the Citadel camp cleared by their great orange beasts of industry, now engaged in erecting temporary shelters on all sides. A cluster of three were working the Nightmare Cannon onto a giant shipping palette resting beneath the belly of a tall grey spaceship bearing the logo of the Citadel of the Recovery. Underneath the logo it said *PEACE FOR ALL* in thick black letters that brokered no ambiguity.

The brown bird flew past my head and landed on top of a military car, watching me as I was led away from the gaping round hole in the ground and tossed onto the dirt roughly. A soldier with fancy epaulettes approached and was handed my gun by a member of the platoon that had taken me.

"This is an Annapurnese Smith-Shurtook Gentleman's Dueller," he said idly.

"Yes indeed," I replied.

"This is a fine weapon," he said.

"Thank you."

He smacked me across the face with it, and I plowed into the dirt with a windy grunt. I rolled over with effort, the manacles digging into my wrists, and looked up to see the fellow drop my gun, his face suddenly blank and dazed. He seemed to be looking up, so I looked up, too.

The sky was clear. I looked back to the soldier, who hadn't been looking up so much as letting his eyes roll back into his head. Through gritted teeth he tried to say something, but instead he just winced in pain and fell to the ground, twitching feebly as blood ran from his nostrils and ears.

I noticed then that most of the other soldiers seemed to be similarly suffering, now dropping to their knees, now falling prone with their bloody faces planted in the scrub.

The six-legged robots continued hauling the bulky black decoy into the hold of the landed Citadel vessel, though the windows of which I could see Citadelites clutching at their heads as they fell.

Within a moment I was the only man standing in the whole camp.

The little bird flittered from one body to another, pausing beside each still head and cocking its head briefly before fluttering on. This discomfited me so I looked away.

I spotted a bubble in the sky. It rose gently over the skeleton of a collapsed skyscraper, and then settled just inside the camp perimeter on the close side of a pile of bricks, just a few dozen paces from where I stood. I saw my own reflection in the side of the orb for a split-second before the shield cracked off: I looked dirty and grim, my red longcoat flapping slightly in the breeze.

Yatti Olorio stepped down from the platform, his round face split into a smug grin. He was accompanied by two youths in crisp suits – a boy and girl with black hair and hard, narrowed eyes. "Simon!" sang Yatti melodiously, clapping his hands with effete satisfaction; "what a delicious surprise!"

"Expected to find me writhing on the ground, did you?"

"Frankly, yes," replied Olorio smoothly, halting a few paces from me and crossing his arms over his breasts. "But nothing ever goes *quite* according to plan, does it?"

I shrugged. "I don't know about that, Yatti. It looks to me like your plan has come off without a hitch. It seems you have allowed the Citadelites to do your dirty work for you, and now you can sail off with the Nightmare Cannon. How did you induce them to take the medication?"

"We prepared the inoculation packages for them," said Yatti with a little wink. "No specific blocks – just a trigger to incapacitate them broadly should we require their non-intervention." The toe of his polished shoe prodded at the nearest collapsed monk. "They'll awake with symptoms that suggest they've been hit by the weapon, of course." He chuckled. "At which point they will be become our...clients."

As he spoke three great Fellcorp Mercy ships appeared over the next hill, their humming progress echoing along the valleys of kipple. Olorio watched them land, his hands behind his back as he rocked back and forth on the balls of his feet. The gangways descended and legions of white robots began to fill the camp. I could hear their idiot voices overlapping on the air, "You are safe; do not panic."

Olorio returned his gaze to me. I nodded and crossed my arms. "Right. Well. I suppose, given your candor, I should take it as read that I'm killed."

Olorio spread his hands in a maudlin gesture of hapless confession. "You knew all along you were only left walking to one end. And that end is now being loaded aboard what is now *my* craft. To blame subsequent holocausts on your ghost is far less complicated than continuing to puppeteer you."

"You erased my memory."

Yatti raised his brow, his wide mouth held slack for a moment. Then a new grin spread across his lips, one that pushed up thick cheeks up against his eyes to almost obscure them. "Oh, my dear Simon, no," he lilted, covering his mouth with a chubby hand in a gross parody of a giggling schoolgirl. "Oh, no. *You* did it. *You* wanted to be *free*. You wanted to *take the money and run*. You didn't want to ever have to *think* about our glorious Hegemon again."

"Then why I am the key to the Nightmare Cannon's puzzle?" I shot back, my voice feeling disconnected from my sinking stone heart. The challenge was hopeless, fueled by dumb adrenaline.

"Because you're not a fool, Simon. And neither was he. If he hadn't kept his last secrets so close to the vest do you I think ever would have let you survive?" Olorio chortled smugly. "You were supposed to give me the key after I helped him cleanse himself, but you didn't. You ran." His smile dropped away. "But not fast enough."

"You got inside my head. You tried to take the key. You failed."

"Not at all," he replied airily. "We made significant progress. We were not, however, able to penetrate his scheme completely. He had elected to erase too much that seemed critical. He had left only trivia. We knew the final solution would have to emerge...organically. So we scraped you down and dumped you on Samundra. I came and visited you once. You seemed quite happy in that hospital, old chap."

"I don't remember it."

He shrugged smarmily. "I'm funny that way. People seldom remember my visits."

I suppressed a shudder. How many times had Olorio come to me? Was there any way of knowing? Would Jeremiah have let Olorio get near me? Would I remember, now that my own chemical blocks had been removed? Or had Dr. Pemma's work been honest at that point? "Ruses within ruses," I muttered, bemused and haggard inside.

"Yes," confirmed Olorio with satisfaction. "You see, I *was* paying attention to him all those years. I *did* learn a thing or two from the master."

"The master?"

"The master of artful deceit! Of the theater of life! The man whose great memory I will not taint by calling *you* by his name." He sighed with clear reverence, his hands clasped before his heart. "The most renowned televisual personality the galaxy has ever known."

"That was me?"

Olorio sneered, his face suddenly darker. "Naturally not. *You*, Simon, are a pathetic child-man being exploited as the key to a maze. *You*, Simon – who were born such a short time ago and will die just a few minutes hence – were and remain no one of consequence." He leaned in closer to me, his slit-like eyes so narrow they seemed closed. "We had *everything*. The Panstellar Neighbourhood would have been ours to shape. We were aligned for *total power*. He would have been the face and voice of a *united galaxy*."

He turned from me and spat into the dirt. "But he did not turn out to be the man of vision he seemed. He wanted to wash his hands of the whole affair. He wanted to live like a king without the burden of rule. He wanted the life of a god without bearing the sacrifices of achieving the godhead." He turned back to me and hissed, "He wanted to become *you* – he wanted to *forget* what you'd done, and abandon what we'd together won by it."

"What did we win?"

"A unified military – a matured panstellar infrastructure to support it. We won co-operation across known space!"

"Co-operating to rid themselves of our scourge!"

"Co-operation to any end would have done, for my purposes. Co-operation now for the sake of the Recovery works nicely. All that matters is that we'll build a galaxy that is drawn together, not sequestered apart. Even the Queen of Space who works so hard against our cause would change her tune once she found herself an Empress." He nodded with earnest zeal now, facing me again and gesturing emphatically with his beefy hands. "All that matters is the future. All that matters is the galactic union."

"So," I whispered weakly, "you're an altruist, too, eh? We should have a bloody convention. You and Jeremiah and a parade of dead Azas can all make speeches, and we'll toast your laudable ends."

"A capital idea!" called a new voice. Olorio, his stern-faced flanking guards, and me all turned to see an old brown man with white hair making his way over a pile of rubble toward us, leaning heavily on an ornate cane. A young blonde in a severe suit walked patiently beside him, holding a leather valise.

Olorio seemed very disturbed. "Who the hell are you?"

"I'm your boss, Mr. Olorio," claimed the old fellow, wheezing a bit as he came to a halt a few paces from us, so that he formed the apex of a triangle with Olorio and I. "I'm being a tad glib, of course. To be precise I am the Chief Acquisitions Officer of Blighton Enterprises, and the new interim executive of Fellcorp Pharma." He chuckled. "From the look on your face, Yatti, I see you've been too preoccupied to follow the business feeds."

Olorio paled, and a sweat broke out across his brow. "That's outrageous! That's impossible! That's –"

"– How we planned it all along," said the old brown man with evident satisfaction, knocking his cane against a nearby lump of stone. "Did you really think Mr. Blighton would trade away the interstellar reach of Fellcorp just for some money?"

"We made other promises."

"Yes, of course. But you must realize Mr. Blighton and the galaxy at large have so much more to gain from the story of your scheme than from your scheme itself. Whether you're a closet Unionist or even a member of House of Ares, everyone will agree that it makes a fine drama. Thank you for playing you part." He turned his yellow-rimmed brown eyes on me in turn. "You too," he added.

"It's a bluff," claimed Olorio, puffing himself up.

"It's justice," countered the old man. He pointed his cane at the two youths on either side of Olorio's girth. "War criminals exposed, all of you. Even these twisted children you would have seen raised as Simon's – rewarded to live in luxury for how long? Six months? A year?"

"They could've lived that life forever if this fool hadn't been burning to go on his little quest," spat Olorio, pointing at me with a thick finger. "I've done everything for him. I even helped him to arrange his mind so he could dream without guilt. And when he betrayed me I even had myself turned into a chink so that I find a place in his new life. He could have lived in peace for years as I extracted what I needed. I am a very patient man. My cause is worth everything."

"You robbed me!" suddenly shouted the young man at his left, his face flushing with anger as he stared at me. "You promised me you'd always take care of me!"

"I did?"

"Me too," said the young woman on Olorio's right. "But you left us to rot in some stupid school. Now Yatti is making good on the promises you decided weren't important enough to remember."

Olorio smiled icily. "You're selfish, Simon. So was he. He was the vainest man alive. Harnessing his lusts was easy. Some of us were fool enough to believe he loved us along the way. But we are no longer fooled."

Olorio drew a long pistol out of his coat, and shot the Chief Acquisitions Officer of Blighton Enterprises in the chest twice. The blonde screamed.

I threw myself flat and picked up the Smith-Shurtook lying beside the fallen soldier's bloody hands, flipping myself over and leveling it at Olorio's troupe. The young man fired at me first. A rock beside me blasted apart in a rain of sparks. I closed my eyes and ducked, chips of debris sinking painfully into my exposed hand. Undeterred I threw the gun into my opposite hand and squeezed the trigger.

Nothing happened. My eyes refocused on the foreground. The little display on the butt said: *Chamber Empty*.

"Coitus," I said.

I was shot in the shoulder, the impact knocking me off my feet backward. The young girl stepped forward and pointed a jazzer at me. For a few seconds I was lost in a world of pain, my back arching as my limbs kicked out involuntarily, my eyeballs twitching behind their lids. The pain ceased and I was left looking into the throbbing black stars of clouded vision...

When I regained myself a moment later the uniformed young man was dragging the blonde by her hair. He threw her roughly on the ground next to me. The uniformed young woman jazzed her, leaving the blonde moaning feebly and drooling. I blinked in surprise. I recognized her.

"Miss Tiger!" I whispered.

She winked at me, and smiled. I started to stammer but she shushed me. "Jazz-proof suit. Blighton's on top of everything. Stay calm, Simon."

"Blighton?" I echoed dumbly.

"Keep quiet!" roared the uniformed young man, kicking me in the ribs without reserve.

"Oof," I said, so he kicked me again. "You're grounded," I added feebly, so he kicked me in the face. This was more effective in shutting me up, since I bit my tongue and started to cough out blood.

Olorio was laughing. "For so long *he* was the teacher," he said over me with a smirk. "Now I have some lessons for *you*, my friend. The first lesson is: don't ruin a good thing, or risk the wrath of your associates." He jazzed me. "The second lesson is: don't make deals with Idealists. Our concerns surmount pleasantries." He jazzed me again. "The third lesson is –"

I opened my eyes weakly. What was the third lesson?

Olorio was considering with interest something behind me, at the edge of the hole the Citadelite machines had vapourized down to the hiding place of the Nightmare Cannon. A white robot sailed over my head and smashed to pieces on the dirt. A shadow fell over me. I turned around, wincing as pain throbbed should my wounded shoulder...

The Minotaur roared.

Olorio jazzed it but nothing happened. The young man shot at it. The young woman threw a rock. In a blaze of flying shadow the beast vaulted over Miss Tiger and I and struck the ground directly before his assailants, loops and coils of rappelling cables dragging from its shoulders.

It was shaped like a giant black man, with the head of a fierce bull atop his wide shoulders. The flesh of his back was torn, and inside gleamed a metallic superstructure.

It paused a beat before smashing aside the young man with a quick backhand, and then it lurched forward and settled down upon Olorio. Olorio screamed wetly, and then stopped. His legs kicked. The young woman shrieked and ran back toward the nearest Fellcorp ship, scattering robots in her panic.

I pulled out my water flask and upended it into the plastic sphincter on the butt of the Smith-Shurtook, glancing up nervously as the hulking thing worked over Olorio. It did not seem to be devouring him so much as tearing him into little bits, which it flung over its shoulders.

I gasped as a stringy red mess hit the dirt beside me.

The Minotaur turned, its beady black eyes reflecting gleams from the orange sun. It began to advance. I shook my gun hopefully and then squeezed the trigger. A buzzer sounded, but nothing else happened.

It took me a moment to realize that the Minotaur had stopped moving. I did a double-take and saw the Chief Acquisitions Officer standing behind the robot-beast, his cane extended. "Now that takes me back," he said. "What a great movie that was! How fortunate that this prop was manufactured by one of my concerns." He sighed. "Utopia! Help me out of this thing."

The blonde sat up beside me and shook the dust out of her hair, and then peeled off the wig entirely to reveal her natural red hair cropped short. She sprang to her feet and jogged over to the old fellow. With her assistance the brown man peeled apart and revealed the skinny, lithe form of Abermund Blighton within. He smoothed down his black clothing with a liver-spotted hand, and then patted his white moustache back into place.

"Nothing makes an entrance like being shot," he declared jovially. "Wouldn't you say, Simon?"

"Quite dramatic," I agreed darkly. "Did you know about the Minotaur?"

"Oh yes. Terron's maze is devilish, isn't it? You may have some questions at this time," he said with a smile.

I considered this for a moment, looking out across the rubble-strewn field of fallen soldiers with bloody faces surrounded by white robots, the great grey spaceship now holding the false Cannon in its hold, the smeared remains of Yatti Olorio and the unconscious form of a teenage war-criminal whom I had apparently promised to protect. I saw white fabric flap on the gangway of the Citadel ship, and guessed it was the girl Lady Aza.

"Yes," I said eventually. "Yes I do have a question, Abe. How do *you* justify all of this? Everyone so far has had an irrefutably good reason for either profiting from the Kamari Horror or causing it in the first place. What's *your* crusade? The wisdom of the human executives? A story to sell to every denizen? Lust for dirty money?"

Blighton laughed, and touched my shoulder in a familiar way. "All money is dirty, Simon," he said with real seriousness, looking me in the eye. "It is up to men of means and conscience to purify it."

"Men like you?"

"Quite so," he agreed. "Especially since I must bear some blame in creating the situation in the first place. Terron was, after all, my *protégé*. Of course when he was my pupil I had no idea how he would fall under the shadow of Aro Frellis – that is, he who would become Yatti Olorio."

"Who was Aro Frellis?"

"He was the President of Metra, naturally, and eventually the Lord Governor of the Kamari Hegemon. In your popularity he saw a means to carry his ideology of unification across planets, and eventually across stars. The story isn't that simple, really, but it will do for this kind of on-the-spot revelation. You'll be able to read the details in my newest book, *The Puppet of Kamari*."

I nodded grimly. "That would be me, of course. The puppet."

"When you're the father of a massacre people become indifferent to your feelings," he pointed out.

I sniffed. "Can *you* tell me why I...did it?"

"No," he replied glibly. "I'm not the March Peebles of souls, my boy, just opportunities. I can only imagine your private country of adulation was threatened by the Panstellar Navy. You must have divorced humanity and embraced only power, then. You became a monster. You decided no price was too high to retain your foothold on the galaxy, and when your own citizens began to suspect the truth you found in them ready fodder for your horrifying machine." He gestured to the grey spaceship that contained the false Cannon.

"Enough!" I shouted. "I won't hear any more dictation of my own decisions to me. This isn't a story, and I'm not your audience or your toy. If you knew everything that was going on you could've stopped it!"

"Simon, Simon," he chuckled. "Even I don't have the power to single-handedly stop a mad world."

"You could have turned Frellis and Volmash over to the Queen of Space!" This seemed to mean something to Utopia the former tiger girl, for she looked at Blighton sharply, her pale skin flushing.

"Ah, yes," Brighton agreed, "quite true. But where would be the drama in that? I am now in possession of the greatest story ever told, and I intend to see this passion play through to the end. A fitting end. A satisfying end."

He raised a small device in his hand, and aimed it at me.

"As the hero of this story," he explained, "I think it should fall to me to rid the galaxy of Terron Volmash once and for all. And why not? With the Nightmare Cannon in my possession I have the resource I need for any sequel."

I started to laugh. Utopia looked shocked. Blighton hesitated. I said, "You know what, Abe? *I get it.* I get it now."

"What?" he asked, his moustache twitching. "What do you...*get?*"

"What Jeremiah was trying to tell me. What the human executives are trying to do." I shook my head. "They're trying to keep civilization shaped by the growth of societies, not by a few powerful personalities. But no matter how they fight to keep us from being overwhelmed by our own political fads, the greedy find a way to try to impress the galaxy with their image."

"Would you rather rely on democracy?" scoffed Blighton. "It is a dumb animal with many asses and no head."

"It can be bred," I replied decisively. "Time evolves societies. Those that elect for their own doom die by it. We all learn from their mistakes."

"You've simply traded one ideology of interference for another," he answered breezily. "The galaxy isn't that simple. Men have needs – like the need to be free, instead of the slaves of robots with delusions of grandeur. Like the birds you love so much, we crave flight."

"The needs of men are not tuned to the present," I said, understanding suddenly Jeremiah's message. "Our passions are not calibrated to a galactic scale of wisdom. We are birds...we're just worm-eating tentacles of Solar life, except we make movies about it. Our heart's desire will be our undoing."

Blighton looked me squarely in the eye. "If that is our destiny, so be it. That is *nature*. Would you prefer instead to hand your fate to self-elected gods?"

A new voice sounded sharply. "Sentience is too precious to risk squandering so," said Jeremiah.

"Ah yes, a Cygnus Automatonic Guard Mark Eight," decided Blighton with an impatient air, fiddling with the end of his cane. He pointed it at Jeremiah, and was visibly distressed when Jeremiah did not freeze in place or fall down. "Custom configuration?" He fiddled again and then stabbed the cane in the air at Jeremiah.

Jeremiah reached up and removed the pieces of his blue-green carapace, and then pulled away the layer of false devices that covered his human executive skin. "I cannot be dismissed, Abermund Blighton. Your role in this affair is now known to my race, and even undoing me cannot change that."

"I have other plans for your race," swore Blighton, his face contorted in sudden anger. "We will suffer your yoke no longer."

"The human political question is too complex to be answered by a single vision in time," said Jeremiah. "Neither yours, nor mine. The Great Mélange must continue."

"The Great Mélange keeps you in power!"

"The Great Mélange will guarantee civilization's future fidelity. Consider the lives of your descendants, seven thousand generations hence. We work for them because your sight is too short."

"What gives you the right?" thundered Blighton, his fist shaking.

"Might," declared Jeremiah nakedly. "You know what we hold."

"We will crack open your heads and take it!"

"To all our peril."

"I do not trust in that assessment!"

"It isn't yours to make."

"We'll see. Let's save the rest of the philosophy for a later debrief, Executive," hissed Blighton. He depressed the contact on his jazzer, and I fell to the ground writhing in excruciating pain. When I could look up again Jeremiah was standing just a pace away from Blighton, both of them looking down at me with no expression. I could not see Miss Tiger.

"Jeremiah, please!" I cried just before I was hit by the device's invisible beam yet again, foam and spittle flying from my lips. *"Jeremiah!"* I screamed.

He did not move. Blighton raised the device again. "I have the Nightmare Cannon now. I will dictate terms."

I wiped my mouth with the back of my shaking hand as I knelt in the dirt. "You don't have the Nightmare Cannon, Abe," I said.

The jazzer wavered. "A poor bluff," claimed Blighton.

"It is true," said Jeremiah. "The weapon aboard the Citadelite ship is a ruse. I have searched it thoroughly. Do you think you would stand here alive otherwise?"

Blighton looked back and forth between me and Jeremiah rapidly. "Well, now that I've spilled the beans you have to die anyway." He took a deep breath. "Ah, the invigorating tingles of *improvisation!* I love it." He pointed the jazzer again.

"I have the true Nightmare Cannon," I said.

Blighton froze. Jeremiah's head swiveled toward me in a blur. I held up my hand and the little brown bird swooped over and alighted there, fluffing its wings and blinking. "I am your input," I told it. "When I am jazzed again, tell the world."

"Poppycock!" said Blighton, pressing the contact.

Vision was lost to me in a wash of stabbing pain. I howled and danced, and if I could have found my head I would have dashed it open on a rock. But at last the searing abated, and a warm blackness took me. When I was able to open my eyes I saw only swimming light, and heard only my own blood thumping in my ears. I drew a few ragged breaths and wiped my eyes.

Blighton was lying in the dirt. Miss Tiger had collapsed behind me. Jeremiah stood alone. "Did – did the Cannon fire?" I whispered.

"Sir," said Jeremiah, "yes."

"Why didn't you stop them before?" I demanded, aching.

"That liberty was not mine, Simon."

"Until you saw that I really had the Cannon."

"Sir," confirmed Jeremiah.

I tried to stand up but my legs folded beneath me and I hit the dirt again. Jeremiah stepped closer. "You called me Simon," I said to him. "Why?"

"Because," he said, offering his hand, "you have taught me something."

I took his hand and allowed him to haul me to my feet. I leaned into his shoulder wearily. "What's that?"

"Who you are is defined by what you do," said Jeremiah solemnly. "And your actions are not that of Terron Volmash. You have become something else in your travels. You did not become the Nestor S. Fell they designed for you, to comfort you while your mind was bled. Nor did you become Terron Menteith, the boy who would find the capacity to become a monster in Blighton's teachings."

"Then who am I?"

Jeremiah looked at me, his black eyes flashing. "You are Simon of Space. And you have managed to draw together every enemy of the galactic peace, to let their own greed dispatch them. There is no longer any force which stands between you, and our quest to bring the Nightmare Cannon before the Queen. You are a hero."

I looked around me at the wasted city, the scores of prone bodies, the bank of thick white clouds marching patiently across the blue sky. "Nothing can atone for this," I said. "I am no hero."

"But you are no longer a monster. And your redemption has opened my eyes, too."

I opened my mouth to inquire further but trailed off as three more gleaming white Fellcorp spaceships swooped into view. They descended around us in a violent surge, landing struts bowing as they absorbed the weight of impact. Gangways burst open and legions of men and women in Fellcorp Mercy uniforms ran out, red palms painted on their fronts. They each carried a very unmerciful-looking firearm.

Jeremiah and I were surrounded.

"Does this never end?" I asked feebly. The Nightmare Cannon landed on my unwounded shoulder and chirped merrily.

"Freeze!" shouted a dozen people at once.

Which is when the *Neago* blasted out directly over us, blotting out the sky and filling the air with its humming engines. The armed hordes of Fellcorp Mercy started firing into the air at it. I hit the ground next to Utopia, who groaned weakly and pawed at her head.

I looked up as the open gangway hovered overhead. Jeremiah grabbed my hand and started pulling me. "What about her?" I shouted, pointing to Utopia. He scooped her up and thrust her up onto the gangway, and then pushed me on after her. The ship shook violently and I grabbed a support strut to keep my balance.

Glory caught a hold of my wounded shoulder, so I screamed in pain as she dragged me into the shaking debarkation bay. "Ow!" I complained. "Careful, I've been shot!"

"Just now?" Glory asked, eyes wide.

"No, a few minutes ago," I admitted, touching the ragged hole in my longcoat and wincing. "Faeces!"

Dr. Pemma rushed to my side and pressed a device to the wound. "Hold still!" she commanded as I flopped against the deck when the ship shook again.

"Um, what's going on down there?" asked Captain Oliver over the speakers.

"Everybody's in!" shouted Pish.

The gangway closed and the sound of the engines whined louder. "Can we get away in this thing?" I wanted to know.

Dr. Pemma shook her head. "Oliver says we can't leave the atmosphere."

The ship shuddered again, and then went strangely quiet. I blinked. The lights went out. I realized the sound of the engines had disappeared entirely, and the only whining I was hearing now was air hissing by outside. I floated off the deck, in freefall.

Freefall?

Unpowered, we were falling through the sky. The *Neago* crashed with a massive concussion. We turned over many times, sharp debris falling around us in the pitch blackness amid screams and grunts. We came to rest against the ceiling, the structure of the ship groaning ominously.

"Roll call," I muttered.

There was a long silence.

"Roll call!" I bellowed.

"Sir," said Jeremiah.

"Umph," said Glory. And then, "Mung."

"Ouch," contributed Pish.

I heard a loud, clattering series of booms, and then the door to the corridor broke aside and admitted a guttering orange light. Captain Oliver was silhouetted in the doorway, his skin bubbling and burnt. "Get out," he gurgled. "Get out now!"

There was another explosive boom in the shadows and then sunlight poured out through the open gangway Jeremiah had torn from its thick hinges. Captain Oliver collapsed, black smoke streaming past him. Glory wrestled past me with Pish over her shoulders and was hauled out of the bay by Jeremiah's tireless arms. I started over toward the captain but Jeremiah objected. "Sir, we must hurry. I believe the *Neago* may explode."

So I threw Utopia over my shoulder and crawled out onto the hull, the tiny brown bird flying around my head. Glory was already running over the broken hull toward the dirt, Pish in her arms. Jeremiah ran after them.

I looked back into the smashed debarkation bay, wanting desperately to rescue Dr. Pemma and Captain Oliver. But a roiling ball of fire washed into the bay then, its hot breath blasting over me at the edge of the lock. I staggered backward and slid off the habitat ring, emerging beneath the hull. I ran across the dirt to catch up with Glory, Pish and Jeremiah.

There was a curious irregular ticking sound in the second before the *Neago* blew apart. In that moment I wondered just how fast I would have to sprint to outrun an explosion.

An instant later I was flying through the air feeling as through I had been struck by a great Minotaur, my back and limbs sizzling with pain as the air was ripped from my lungs. I was enveloped in a wall of smoke and sparking debris, and finally cast upon the ground like a sack of rocks.

I flipped and rolled, eventually skidding to a halt against a collapsed Citadelite shelter. The sound of the concussion died away, and my numbed body sagged. I could not see Utopia anywhere, but I could see the great flaming pyre that had been the *Neago*, the ruin roaring as it sent orange fire boiling away into a black cloud.

Every white robot in view had frozen in place. The Fellcorp personnel seemed stunned, and were examining their weapons.

Jeremiah arrived at my side and turned me over. I sat up with his help. I had painful burns on the back of my hands and my neck, and minor lacerations on every bit of exposed skin. My longcoat was in tatters, but my back was intact. My face oozed blood from many tiny cuts. My lungs ached. I coughed.

"Sir?"

"I'm okay," I said, feeling my limbs for breaks. A secondary explosion boomed out from the *Neago* remains, bits of hot metal shooting into the sky.

Jeremiah pulled me to my feet, and again I leaned into him. We started walking toward Glory, crouching in a field of debris surrounded by several chunks of burning spaceship. As we drew nearer we saw she was crouching over Pish, who had been torn nearly in half by a twisted girder, the glimmering strands of his human executive fibres in plain view. Glory was crying, her blue makeup running in thick lines down her quivering cheeks.

Jeremiah knelt beside Pish, and passed his fingertips over the wounds. "He will survive," he declared.

"But – but..." I contributed. I trailed off as my words were lost in what I at first took to be the roaring of the *Neago*'s flames, but the sound was instead a complete alien drone, throbbing rhythmically through the air.

Glory's face lost all colour. She pointed over my head. "Fornicate me..." I saw her lips shape the words: *"It's the Navy!"*

I turned around and gaped in awe, my hands falling limply at my sides. The sky was filled by a fleet of massive vessels, too unholy large to ever be seen near a planet, impossible things the size of cities, their scarlet hulls shining in the sun and their long shadows blotting out hills of debris like stormclouds. The pulsing thrum of their mighty engines reverberated from horizon to horizon, a terrifying sound like wardrums of the gods.

Fleets of scarlet saucers emerged from their yawning bellies and began descending into the Citadelite camp like a swarm of insects, their buzzing a disquieting keen against the bass voice of their motherships.

Jeremiah took my arm. "We shall let the Navy clean up here, but our mission requires more flexibility than their bureaucracy would afford. Let us make haste!"

"Make haste?" I yelled back. "How? Where?"

"To the maze!"

Jeremiah scooped up Pish's broken body and put it over his shoulder, then took off running. We hurried after him. The *Neago* had not flown far from the kilometer-deep hole. Jeremiah pulled rapelling devices off two of the nearest soldiers and handed them to Glory and I. "Put these on," he said, indicating two cables still hanging over the edge.

With that he turned around and leapt into the hole.

Glory and I exchanged glances and then hurried attached the belts to the cables, the pebbles around us dancing with the noise of the Navy's arrival. We dropped into the hole just as the first scarlet saucers were landing, the shouts of commanders breaking through the air.

The speed of our descent was controlled by a knob on the buckle of the harness. I turned it and dropped faster. Glory did the same. We heard shouts from above us and saw soldiers peering down after us. I twisted the knob all the way to one side and the cable sang as I shot down into the darkness.

Jeremiah caught me, and then caught Glory. I shook my head to recover my balance as the little bird landed on my shoulder again. "Got a friend?" said Glory.

"Sort of," I said.

We raced across the debris-littered floor and into the ninth ring, now as dark as the darkest part of the maze. "What happened to the lights?" I asked.

"The Navy projects a disabling field. It is a standard incursion procedure. All unshielded enemy technology fails instantaneously," said Jeremiah, his glowing carapace bobbing ahead, partly eclipsed by the shadow of Pish's limp form. "We must make haste. They will follow, and they will have lights."

Blindly following the apparent robot Glory and I held hands and plunged through the darkness of the rings, emerging into the tight corridors of the sound-carrying maze, some of the walls revealed fleetingly by Jeremiah's glow visibly damaged by Citadelite explosives – the explosives which had released the Minotaur to wander freely.

"What the faeces *is* this place?" Glory whispered.

I kept my eyes fixed on the blue-green ghost of Jeremiah. "You know what's funny?" I asked.

"What?" Glory hissed, confused.

"The clouds. They're always the same," I said. "Every place I go the people are different, the clothes are different, the morality is different, the sun is different – even the sky is never twice the same shade of blue..." I chuckled. "But clouds are clouds. They're like friends that follow me. Every world we see, the clouds are just the same."

Glory snorted. "We're running for our lives through dark tunnels and you're thinking of the fornicating *clouds?*"

I clutched her hand against my chest to feel my beating heart. "I'm scared to death," I told her. "When better to remember the clouds?"

She swore. We ran on, our footfalls forming a symphony of undecaying noise around us. There was no more Minotaur, but I could still feel its hot breath at my heels. I closed my eyes and let Glory pull us along, and when I opened my eyes I could still see it, the images overlaid on the dim blob of robotic glow...

On my shoulder, the Nightmare Cannon twittered. And I could see nothing but the clouds.

XXXVIII.
AMALASTHUNA

Terron Volmash had been a paranoid man.

His tunnels ran endlessly beneath the fallen city of Thallos. It seemed to me that a thousand thoughtless days and dreamless nights passed while we trudged those dim corridors, my strange family and I.

I was given fixers and water, medicinal wafers and an emergency ampule of wine. Glory worked in the dark beside me, milling about in a Fellcorp Mercy first-aid pouch. "So this fornicated bird is the faecal thing?" she asked.

"Yeah."

"Thought it'd be bigger...you know – badder."

"Common mistake," I assured her. "It seems, however, that this Volmash character had quite a thing for birds."

She changed the subject. "How's your shoulder?"

"Throbbing. Is that good?"

"Maybe. I'm not a medic."

We eventually emerged under a twilight sky glittering with the first bright stars. The air was motionless down below, but lumpy clouds sailed by overhead in swift clusters in an unfelt wind. Far to the east they were lining up in some sort of congregation, their edges folding under themselves and their dark heads rising like anvils against the dusk's red melt.

Jeremiah swiveled in place, casting his hard black eyes in every direction. "We are safe," he said.

"Do not panic?" I quipped. Glory laughed drily.

Jeremiah put Pish's limp body down on a flat face of broken concrete, and again examined the garish wound across his midriff. The Nightmare Cannon landed on the ground beside the slab and preened its feathers. "What will happen to him now?" I asked. "Can you help him?"

"No," said Jeremiah, shaking his head. "He will need true physicians in order to properly mend." Jeremiah arranged Pish's arms neatly at his sides, and pulled his torn shirt down over his torso. He then scanned the horizon again. "We cannot tarry," he said, beginning to walk.

"What do you mean?" I called, startled. "Isn't the Navy in *our* side?"

"Our cargo must not fall into the hands of another interstellar organism. Their instincts are too unrefined. Come now."

"We can't just leave him here!" I cried, gesturing at Pish.

Jeremiah stopped and turned around, the dying sunlight casting his blue-green armour in a bloody, sultry glow. "My people will come for him. They are already on their way."

"But –"

"We must take the Nightmare Cannon to Eridani Star. To avoid complications, we should do so alone." He paused. "I ask you to trust me, Simon."

Someone had to be trusted. My ignorance was no compass. And when I looked into the lined, tan face of that being who had been for so long inscrutable, I could not help but see the pain worn into his features, the worry he carried in wrinkled ripples orbiting his islands of expression.

Despite everything, I did trust in him.

I moved to Pish's side and touched his unresponsive little hand. "We can't just leave him all alone," I said again, my eyes burning. The Nightmare Cannon cocked its head.

Glory said, "I will stay with him."

I looked at Jeremiah, who nodded solemnly. "They will be safe. They will both be taken care of."

Glory nodded in turn, touching my arm. "I'll make sure nothing happens to him, Simon. I promise."

"I know, Glory," I said.

She hugged me tightly and whispered in my ear, "Call me Vera."

"Thank you, Vera."

"Thank you. You don't even coitally know, Simon. But thank you."

Jeremiah told her to lie down on the concrete slab next to Pish, so she did. He indicated that I should step back, and then a spherical shield burst into existence surrounding the slab with a loud pop followed by a brief breeze. Its sides were perfectly reflective, leaving me staring at a warped reflection of Jeremiah and I standing against the purpling heavens. I saw little silver ants crawling along the shield's edges and forming marching lines over its face. It was perfectly silent, apart from the almost imperceptible clicking of the artificial insects' legs against the mirrored surface.

"They are both in stasis," said Jeremiah. "The beacon is engaged." Then he turned on heel and began walking away.

I limped after him quickly, grunting with the effort. The bird flitted off above me, and then swooped around past Jeremiah. He ignored it. "Will they help her?" I asked. "Will they heal her?"

"Yes," he said.

"And Pish?"

"Pish will grow up," said Jeremiah, "and come to understand his life. It is time."

We crunched along over small rocks for a few moments and I fell behind again. "And me?" I asked. "Now that Glory – um, or Vera – is watching over Pish, what stops you from taking this stupid little robotic bird from me and completing this mission alone?"

Jeremiah stopped and faced me. "You will go, because it is your burden to bear."

"And you?"

The night darkened around us. "I will go so that you do not have to go alone."

"Why?"

"Because," he replied seriously, "I believe in you, Simon."

Jeremiah turned away from me and continued walking. Once again I clumsily jogged to catch up, pebbles skittering at my heels as I wheezed. "So how are we going to get to Eridani?"

"We shall use a hyperspatial gate."

"But surely the terminal has been destroyed..." I gestured at the heaps of wrecked city around us, wincing as my raised arm ached.

"Gates are very resilient," said Jeremiah with confidence, accelerating his stride.

"They're Secret, aren't they?" I called, and his pace slackened again. I pushed ahead, "Human executives aren't the only products of the Secret Mathematic at all, are they?"

"That," said Jeremiah with a cool tone, "is an avenue of inquiry you dare not explore. Trust in my warning."

I was too exhausted to argue. As we proceeded we often spotted naval vessels on the horizon or flying between the hills with formation lights blinking in the haze, but Jeremiah seemed unconcerned. "With all of their resources...won't they find us?" I asked, nervously eyeing a dark saucer in the distance, searchlights panning from its belly.

"Not immediately. We are just two animals in a vast city they are not yet systematically searching."

"I haven't seen any other animals..." I said. "Beyond ants, that is."

"They are wary of men. They may have been culled for food by the last survivors of this holocaust. But they cannot hide from my vision: there are a thousand tiny things scurrying around us. And some not so tiny things, lying in wait for the hunting hour."

"Well," I admitted, pulling my coat tighter around me and glancing nervously into the dark ruins on either side of our path; "at least I'm no longer preoccupied with fearing the Navy. Thanks, I guess."

At midnight we entered a shattered catacomb of fallen archways and leaning pillars. We navigated through the dark by his superior senses until we came upon the remains of a mezzanine court, open to the night air. The remains of shattered skylights glimmered on the floor, and crunched and snapped under our feet. Jeremiah proceeded up a flight of steps to a bank of closed ports, and began tapping on the dark pedestal beside it.

"But there's no power..." I said, frowning.

"The gate will have power," he assured me, reaching beneath the face of the pedestal to adjust its innards.

"How?"

I swear he winked at me in the shadows. "It is a secret."

The dataplate atop the pedestal came to life, and something beneath the floor began to hum. A little blue light beside the port winked on, and then the aperture irised open with a sound like knife against knife. The inside glowed with the now familiar ruddy light and strange reflections, the walls of the hemisphere self-reflecting into infinite warped regress.

"We will not have alignment for several hours," he reported, "but the array is online, targeted and powered."

"Several hours, eh?" I said, looking around the rubble. "Won't the Navy find us by then?"

"They may," agreed Jeremiah. "We shall deal with that eventuality if it arises."

I sat down wearily, my entire body aching and my wounded shoulder crawling with crackles of pain every time I took a breath. The burns on the backs of my hands and my neck were blistering, and even the movement of the air caused me to wince.

Elsewhere in the terminal something thumped, and echoed. I shifted uncomfortably. "Maybe you should light a fire, Jeremiah," I murmured. "We could sing songs."

Jeremiah crouched down beside a pit of cracked tiles, and ignited the ceramic with a touch from the end of his finger. It turned white and the air around it wavered with the sudden heat. Then the apparent robot scooped up a few armfuls of random burnable debris and piled it on top of the hot tile. It burst into cheerful flames, casting dancing shadows on the water-stained walls.

"Thank you," I said.

He sat down cross-legged on the floor before the fire and began disassembling the carapace from his limbs, pelvis and torso. Then he began picking off layers of false devices, methodically laying the pieces in a line beside him. At last he peeled away a suit of black, revealing his true body – skin indistinguishable from clothing, robes vaguely taking shape out of one shoulder and billowing to a separate, flexible layer around his middle. His legs were hairless, and the big toe of each foot was opposable.

"I have been a robot far too long," he said.

"Yeah," I agreed; "looks stuffy in that thing."

"That is not my meaning," he replied heavily. He stretched out his appendages, one by one. "Human beings who lose their sense of duty wither. Human executives *cannot* lose their sense of duty, but their ability to feel its import in their bones can wane." He stretched his strange, coppery hand out and then snapped his long fingers loudly. "Another million hours go by and the senses become that much more brittle, and the spirit jaded."

"You've found new hope?"

"I have found new faith," he said. "Human beings are more malleable than we sometimes give you credit for. You are capable of leaps outside of the statistical envelope for a given genome. You are capable of surprising improbability, and improbability is the engine that makes atoms spin and mud sit up and think."

"You're becoming philosophical in your old age," I laughed, causing my bruised ribs to ache. "Maybe you need a tune-up."

"You have done just that," said Jeremiah. "For if Terron Volmash can be redeemed, anything is possible."

We considered that in silence for a moment, from opposite sides of the fire. I reached down with a grunt and picked up the broken frame of a skylight and tossed it on the pyre. The paint sizzled and hissed.

"What *does* give you the right?" I asked. "I mean, who decided your solution was the best one? Isn't the whole idea of enforcing your solution across the board contrary to your solution?"

"The Great Mélange is not a *solution* to the human political question," he replied; "it is a dedication to keeping the question-space open to the formation of new solutions. It is not the best game, but a commitment to letting the best game be found."

"So what if someone else came up with a better meta-strategy? Could they displace the system the human executives keep in place?"

"It is unlikely. The human executive power structure in entrenched."

"Then it's true what Blighton said. The conservation of power becomes a goal unto itself. So by what real merit have you achieved dominion over the structure of Solar civilization?"

"It is not dominion, it is guidance."

"*Guidance* tooled by murder and scientific oppression sounds like dominion to me. What gives you the right to choose for us?"

"Like any right beyond suffering, we arrogate to assume it and defend it."

"How can you?"

"Because having the power to do so obliges us to make a choice." He paused, then added, "We did not ask for the Secret Mathematic. None of us did. Nor did we ask to become alive and sensible. But it was made to happen. With that kind of power in *your* hands, what would you do, Simon? Would you dare mold civilization according to your best models, and risk being wrong? Or would you elect instead to harness the engines of natural selection to do that work without bias? *What would you do?*"

"I...I don't know," I admitted, ashamed. "I didn't ask to become alive, either."

"No," argued Jeremiah. "You are wrong. You are probably the only person in the universe who has elected for his own existence."

I sighed. "I hadn't thought about it that way."

"With the last breath of his corrupt soul Terron Volmash made a gift unto the galaxy: you. And I think you understand now that as such this life does not belong to you. It belongs to the kin of the dead, whose blood coated the resources the princes of Kamari used to raise you. It belongs to those who still suffer Kamari's Horror, and the parasitical reign of insensible interstellar organisms like Fellcorp and the Citadel of the Recovery."

"That's true," I whispered, closing my eyes.

"I can relate," declared Jeremiah. I opened my eyes and looked at him across the flames. He said, "My life, too, is not my own. I belong to civilization. I yearn to just live. Simply that. Just live. I never had a childhood, but Pish has. And I will envy him that carelessness all my walking days."

I thought of the hospital on Samundra, and Nurse Randa's waggling ass. I remembered when birds were song-things I had no name for.

"Yeah," I agreed quietly. "Yeah."

I awoke hours later, a pale pink sky shining in through the open ceiling. My little blue plastic diary dropped out of my limp hand and rattled across the floor. Jeremiah was still sitting across from me, cross-legged. "How do you feel?" he asked.

My longcoat had been removed while I slept. I looked at my wounded shoulder through my torn shirt, and saw that it had been closed into a neat scarlet line crossed by almost invisible silver threads. I flexed my arm experimentally, and winced at the bruising along my side where I had been kicked. "Did you do this?" I asked, nodding at my shoulder with my chin.

"Yes," said Jeremiah. "You have several million micro-fixers in your system right now, repairing damage. The contusions should be healed shortly. Your burns will take a little more time."

I looked at the ugly welts on the back of my hands critically. "I'm quite the sight."

"You should see your face," said Jeremiah, with a hint of a smile on his copper lips. "Come, it is time to transmit ourselves to Eridani Star."

"Ourselves or someone much like us," I said darkly.

I rose slowly, checking my limbs for stabs of pain. I cautiously put on my longcoat, sighing critically at the various slashes, tears and burns that covered it. My Annapurnese Gentleman's Dueller had been lost in the fracas, so I unhitched the holster from around my waist and thigh, and dropped it. I drained my water flask into my mouth and then dropped that, too. "Let's get this bird caged. What was it the good doctor said? *I can get behind that.*"

From a standing position I was able to see two soldiers in scarlet naval uniforms lying beside the far wall. "They are not dead," said Jeremiah before I had even opened my mouth. "I am keeping them unconscious with effort. It is time to leave."

I was hobbling over to the port when someone cried out, "Wait!"

Jeremiah and I spun around simultaneously.

Miss Tiger was making her way toward us, slogging exhaustedly through the rubble, her once sharp black suit now tattered, burnt and stained. Like mine her skin was covered in dozens of tiny cuts. Her red hair was plastered to her skull with sweat. "Please wait," she begged.

We waited. She collapsed a few paces away from us and I knelt at her side. "Utopia, are you okay?"

She opened her eyes briefly, her breathing ragged. "I told you," she wheezed, "to call me Freddie."

I looked up at Jeremiah imploringly. "She was hit by the Cannon. What should we do? I can't believe she followed us this far. I thought – I thought we lost her the ship exploded."

To my surprise Jeremiah's face was not hard, but softened compassionately. "Utopia Pollux," he said softly. "How did you ever get mixed up in all this?"

She opened her eyes again, blood-shot and quivering. "Jeremiah?" she called weakly. "Oh, God, I knew it was you." She passed out, slumping against my thigh.

"Is she another executive?" I asked.

"No," said Jeremiah. "She is the Princess of Callicrates – run away, her absence long mourned by the Aresu Houses."

"She...worked for Blighton," I said.

"Carry her," commanded Jeremiah. "The blast from the Nightmare Cannon will have shocked her system, but the ammunition was meagre. She's exhausted."

"I'm fairly exhausted myself," I said, trying to lift her. I groaned as my wounded shoulder rebelled. "I can't do it," I decided, releasing Utopia. "I'm too fornicated up, Jeremiah. Everything hurts."

Jeremiah nodded. "Carry her," he repeated. "This pain you have earned."

The ten paces between where she had fallen and the inside of the gate's hemisphere were the longest ten paces of my life, each twice as excruciating as the one before. The final two steps were unsteady as stars sparkled through my vision and the world turned grey. I stumbled, but Jeremiah caught my arm and helped me lay Utopia gently upon the reflective floor. The Nightmare Cannon landed next to her.

The port irised shut, and I closed my eyes. I saw red trees there, and they breathed.

I heard the sound of the port irising open again. The blades clicked as they locked in place. Then I heard the sound of chattering birds, in registers foreign to the Nightmare Cannon's sparrow-like repertoire. A warm but unwild air drifted in over me, and I began to discern a babble of human voices.

I opened my eyes, and Jeremiah helped me to stand. Then he knelt down and scooped up Utopia, who moaned quietly. Together we stepped out, the brown bird following silently.

A great transparent dome criss-crossed by heavy, curved struts of polished metal admitted a blaze of sunlight out of a black sky. The light sparkled off the metal railings which enclosed the dozens of circular and semi-circular platforms that were layered everywhere throughout the dome, each holding a bank of hyperspatial gates. Squadrons of white birds swooped and jabbered around the ceiling, roosting on the superstructure and – while I watched it happen – having their scat disintegrated in mid-air somehow before it could hit the heads of any of the hundreds of people going about their travelling business below, the paths they strode lined with indoor grasses and dwarfed trees.

"This is Amalasthuna," explained Jeremiah, "the moon of Callicrates and gateway to the capital."

"Why not just gate directly to Callicrates?" I asked.

"There are no gates on Callicrates," he replied. "All travellers are obliged to come through Amalasthuna."

"Why?"

"To lead by example," Jeremiah said. "To resist the greed for speed."

There were so many people. The crowd became a blur, and I leaned into Jeremiah. He supported me unquestioningly, and we proceeded down the way from one platform to the next. I could blearily see people making way for us, pointing as we passed. I don't know if they were staring at me (who looked like the walking dead), Utopia (who just looked dead), or Jeremiah (who looked very alien to me, but I had taken it for granted was a familiar sight to most non-self-created denizens of this galaxy). As he escorted us into a berth for planetfall tenders I saw the proprietor's eyes narrow as he tracked him, and I knew not everyone besides Olorio and Blighton loved the executive reign.

"I've been here before," I realized aloud.

"Yes."

"*After* my memory was wiped..."

"Yes."

"I was coming to Callicrates..." I frowned and rubbed my temples with my burned hands.

"You were coming before the Queen of Space," supplied Jeremiah.

"Why?" I asked.

"Only you can tell us that," he said, gesturing for me to proceed into the airlock.

The tender was small, and piloted by a simple robot with a yellow plastic carapace. I do not know what the vessel looked like from the outside, but from the inside we found ourselves in a hemispherical chamber with a transparent ceiling over four curved couches garnished with freefall tethers. The robot stood at a pedestal at one end of the room and ignored us once Jeremiah had issued his instructions.

He put Utopia down on one of the couches, and checked her over quickly after harnessing her in. He asked the robot for water and it fetched it. When it resumed the controls the sounds of the ship's unmooring echoed through the room. Then the starscape outside began to drift.

I pawed after a tether and pulled myself into a second couch. "How long until we land?" I asked hoarsely, my head feeling as if it were made of lead.

"Sir, seven point three hours," replied the yellow robot.

I looked at Jeremiah. "Sleep now, Simon. Tomorrow we walk upon the Third Earth, and it is holy ground."

My head spun with the faces of those we had left behind: Dr. Pemma, Mr. Oliver, Captain Ting, Glory and the impossible thing that was Pish. I wondered too about the runaway princess we had adopted, and what Callicrates, the capital of the Panstellar Neighbourhood, might hold. I watched the little brown bird sit on the end of my couch and clean its feathers, its bead-like eyes blinking in a way I could not distinguish from life.

I thumbed the contact on my blue plastic bauble. "Dear diary," I said wearily, "it has been a long day."

XXXIX.
THE PILGRIM WAY

"Callicrates," breathed Utopia, reaching up to touch the glass through which shone a sharp crescent of blue and white, edging one side of a massive round shadow occulting the background stars. "The entire world is one great city. Can you believe that, Simon? You can see the lights shining on the nightside."

I squinted. "Those orange blurs?"

She nodded. "Each one home to millions."

I floated free from my harnesses and pushed my face up against the dome, making a little box with my hand to block the glare. Indeed, great swaths of the dark globe were criss-crossed by filaments of light joining hubs of murky golden hatching. Another light caught my eye on the dark limb: a shifting greenish glow that was hard to differentiate from an afterimage. I blinked, and watched it slowly turn red. I pointed it out to Utopia. "What is *that?*"

"Aurora," she replied. "Callicrates is tipped."

I turned away from the glass. "I'm sorry?"

In the hour with which I'd had to become acquainted with the conscious version of Princess Utopia Pollux (AKA Miss Tiger, AKA Freddie) I had been able to determine that she was rash, impatient, sharp, giddy, theatrically sensitive and carelessly playful in dizzying, unpredictable turns. She had awoken from her fixer-induced sleep hungry, and had virtually attacked me until I handed over the last of the Fellcorp Mercy rations that I had been carrying around, crushed, in the inner pocket of my coat.

"Thanks for trying to save me," she had said, kissing me on the cheek. "And thanks for leaving me behind afterward!" she added, and then punched me in the arm.

After visiting the lavatory she declared herself largely well and kicked off to look out the glass at space, which pretty much catches us up.

"What do you mean by *tipped?*" I asked.

Jeremiah looked up at us from his cross-legged position harnessed to a couch. "The magnetic axis of Callicrates is perpendicular to the axis of rotation. Thus, the magnetic poles lie at the equator. Solar wind trapped in the magnetosphere collides with the sky at the poles, causing it to fluoresce."

As he spoke Callicrates turned beneath us, gradually revealing a radial blossom of colour dancing with almost imperceptible motion in a ring over the dark land. The effect was hypnotic. Red became gold became blue in a fluid march, a rosette of orange flashing down briefly along the edge of an undulating curtain of green. "It's beautiful," I said. "Is it safe...I mean, do people live under it?"

"Oh sure," said Utopia. "People live *everywhere* on Callicrates. Even at the bottom of the sea."

"Callicrates was not settled as other worlds were," amplified Jeremiah. "The growth of most worlds occurs when an initial small influx of colonists begins reproducing at normal human rates. Even with immigration it takes centuries to populate a planet. In contrast, Callicrates was settled from two of the Great Arks that fled Sol – millions upon millions settled here over a period of a single generation." He closed his eyes in apparent remembrance. "The shuttles were in constant service, dotting the sky at every hour. New families arrived each day."

"What was the solution?"

Jeremiah opened his eyes. "The planet was divided into seventy-two equal patches, each comprising one hundred thousand square kilometres of surface area. Each patch was assigned to a group of colonists by lottery, and settled simultaneously. Networks of trade were established to economically correct geographical disparities, with disputes arbitrated by the Council of the Third Earth and overseen by the sitting Solar monarch."

"He's a walking dataplate, isn't he?" quipped Utopia, rolling her eyes.

"No no," I said, waving her off. "I want to know this stuff." I turned back to Jeremiah. "So it's like a little model of the Panstellar Neighbourhood, then?"

"Quite so," agreed Jeremiah.

"And does it function?"

"It has its moments," said Utopia darkly.

I looked again at the ring of slowly flickering light over the pole. "So whose patch is that?"

"Patch Seventy-Two is the country of the human executives," replied Jeremiah. He unbuckled his harness and kicked off the couch to drift up to us at the top of the dome, and then pointed through the glass. "That large urban centre is on the border of Patch Seventy-One. Proceed counter-clockwise to Patch Seventy, and so on around the world to the north pole."

"What's at the north pole?"

"Patch One," said Utopia. "The Solar Palace."

"It is usual to be landed at a randomly chosen patch no matter where one's business lies, so that travellers are forced to experience local cultures and make use of local infrastructure. Otherwise civilization would become hopelessly clustered around patches of influence."

"So we don't know where we're going to come down?"

"No, we have received special dispensation."

"Everything is always *special* with this guy," said Utopia. "You get used to it."

"I'm starting to."

Jeremiah ignored her. "Our tender will land in Patch Three. We will make our way to the Solar Palace from there. Landing in Patch One is forbidden."

"Was this arranged while I was asleep? Why do I never see you talk to anyone, Jeremiah?"

"Talk?" scoffed Utopia. "He doesn't need to *talk*. He's executive. He's got micro-gates in his brain, and he's constantly shunting packets of information back and forth between the stars."

The globe grew beneath us and continued to turn, dawn now threatening the once dark limb with a smear of red and orange. Just a few moments later the blazing face of Epsilon Eridani Star crested the curved horizon, sparkling off an ocean and casting long shadows from a crumpled line of purple-grey mountains. The tender continued its descent, and Callicrates swelled.

"So, I suppose no patch can rule another patch," I said conversationally, my breath fogging the glass. "Just like in the big leagues."

"Correct," replied Jeremiah. "The integrity of patch borders are maintained even in cases where a common people with common needs are divided, for it is more instructive to see two solutions than one. Governing policies tend to ripple across the planet quickly, for the emulation of success is the only way to keep economic distress at bay. Citizens will readily leave patches that fall behind the times."

"The patches are competitive, then. What is the field of competition? Riches?"

"Satisfaction. Patches that fail to adequately guarantee the long-term needs of their citizenry tend to end up depopulated. Patches that indulge their citizens' short-term greed tend to collapse from internal pressures. Patches that balance economic and social sustainability tend to be emulated, thus maximizing their cultural legacy over the whole of Callicrates."

"So, there's pride to it."

"Indeed. All modern Callicratian bodies of criminal law, for example, stemmed from Patch Fourteen's prototype system a thousand years ago – a source of great pride to the peoples of that patch. In order to defend that legacy, Patch Fourteen still specializes in legal optimization, inspired to ever greater accomplishments by the work of their legally-oriented neighbours in Patches Thirteen and Fifteen."

I scratched my head. "So what if *every* patch decided to specialize in legal optimization? What would happen to Callicrates then?"

"It would collapse. And if no patch in their number had sufficient wisdom to avoid that course, who can doubt they would deserve destruction?"

"How can patches have wisdom?"

"By being built around engines of governance optimized in an environment of cooperative competition to maximize the satisfaction of its citizens without unduly antagonizing neighbouring patches. Wisdom can be built into the system, as facts are built into robots – boundaries against the extremes of human behavior, like murder or trade wars. The patches of Callicrates are free to experiment."

"Experiment how?"

"By positing answers to the political question, with different sets of restraints against free behavior and differing methods for error correction."

Utopia nodded. "They've got everything down there, Simon. Ruthless oligarchies, constitutional monarchies, benevolent dictatorships, lotteried democracies, realms of statistical rule, theocratic fascisms, anarcho-capitalist cooperatives, meritocratic gaming parliaments, hedonist soviets...anything you can imagine has been patched at least once on Callicrates."

As our tender crossed the terminator and the clouds thinned I readied myself for a better glimpse of the surface of this fascinating world – anticipating the endless convolutions of metal that would describe a planet-sized metropolis!

The tender shuddered gently and fire flashed around the dome. The clouds, with rosy foundations and golden tips shining in the rising sun, passed aside and I saw wide green and yellow plains interspersed with hundreds of little blue lakes. I frowned. "Doesn't look too dense from here," I said.

Jeremiah said, "All Solar worlds look virtually the same from this altitude, Simon."

"Still – a planet-wide city..." I trailed off, disappointed.

"What did you expect?" asked Utopia. "Skyscrapers and malls from horizon to horizon?"

I shrugged. "Maybe."

Utopia laughed. "That would scarcely be sustainable, would it?"

"I guess not," I admitted, feeling stupid.

We were advised to strap ourselves into our couches and we did so. I protested the lack of view and in response the yellow robot touched a series of controls and caused a huge dataplate to be raised from the floor. It illuminated with a holographic representation of the world beneath us, the landscape itself seeming to pan behind the face of the plate while the clouds ran over its surface.

The patches themselves were apparent now – differing ways of using the land showing themselves as subtly different palettes of brown and green, like a continent-girdling farm. And while it was clear that my images of a metal-encrusted world were ridiculous, I did notice that the frequency of establishments and visible infrastructure seemed regular enough that, even standing in Callicrates' widest green field, some aspect of civilization would always be visible.

A lake flashed by, one of its shores needled with a flank of impossibly tall buildings, their long shadows cast far across the harbour. Jeremiah intercepted my gaze. "In order to conserve maximum greenspace for the functioning of the biosphere," he explained, "Callicratian architecture has embraced extreme verticality, both above ground and below."

"How many people live on this planet?" I asked.

"Nine point six five billion."

"Mother of love! Why so many?"

Utopia smirked. "People like to be at the centre of the things. Or what they perceive to be the centre. Limiting immigration is one of our biggest problems." She shook her head ruefully. "So many idiots think they can put their mark on history by doing somebody else's loud or dirty work on Callicrates."

The Nightmare Cannon twittered, and landed on my outstretched knee. I shivered.

On the plate the landscape was lost behind a second deck of fluffier, bright white clouds. I felt the tender slow, and when we passed out of the veil we were spiralling down toward the ground. We seemed to be plunging directly into the face of a grassy hill, and then for a fleeting instant I caught glimpse of towers of blue glass and mazes of plazas clogged with ant-like people before we were swallowed by the walls of the dock. We touched down and the engines died to silence.

"Welco to Cayyicoate," said the yellow robot cryptically, its accent even thicker than Jeremiah's used to be.

I unhitched my harnesses and tried to pay the fare, but my wallet beeped angrily and refused to move any funds. "My wallet's on the blink," I complained, flexing it in front of my eyes.

"No doubt your Fellcorp assets have been frozen," said Jeremiah. He looked significantly at Utopia.

She sighed and stuck her own wallet on her fingertip. She dabbed at the yellow robot's till impatiently and then frowned at Jeremiah, her round cheeks flushing. "They'll know I'm here now," she grumbled. "You owe me one, Jeremiah...again."

"Your sacrifice is regrettable," said Jeremiah.

"Don't make fun of me," she warned.

When we walked out of the spaceport and into the densest corner of Patch Three I gasped involuntarily. It was an amazing sight. What had appeared from above to be unbroken stretches of green were in fact staggered tiers of metropolis with grass-covered roofs, beneath which ran streets and bridges and aqueducts and among which rose the squat, open-air tops of blue-glass buildings which ran deep into the ground. Tight lines of cars flew in every direction, landing on platforms, rushing away into tunnels, darting away high into the sky overhead. This knot of architecture was indeed awesome, but what stopped me involuntarily in my tracks was the people.

There were thousands of them.

In the course of my travels I have seen people with darker skin and with lighter skin, but this sampling could not prepare me for the undifferentiated wash of humankind: every shade of skin from alabaster to pitch was represented, with great swaths of ochres and umbers and siennas between. I saw bronze men and gold women, orange babies and children with skin so white their hair was actually yellow instead of brown or black or red, like Utopia's blonde wig. Their eyes were round or slit-like, almond- or lemon-shaped and every variation in mixture. Their clothes were audacious and sparkling, humble or immodest, brightly coloured or stained like earth. Some wore hats or jewels, capes or tattoos, naked pates or manes. At their heels or in their arms were a hundred different kinds of dog, and following along behind them were every shape and finish of robot imaginable, their carapaces winking in the shafts of sunlight that penetrated the immense grotto at regular intervals.

Their babble was a din, a blanket of undulating white noise that echoed down the car-filled chasms between the buildings. People walked in couples and argued or laughed, moved alone and scowled or smiled, loitered in groups and gossiped. Some people sat along the sides of the walkways on dirty blankets and held out bowls. Some people stood in intersections on boxes and preached to the undisturbed multitudes. Little people gestured to one another and hooted, dogs barked, and tinny announcements reverberated unintelligibly.

The smell of the mass reached me next: a soft-edged musk, accents muted in the scores of overlapping chemistries, an undifferentiated haze of sweat and perfume, yeast and spices, farts and breath.

From high upon the landing platform the crowd reminded me of the herds of scarlet cattle I had seen from Greskin Mile's taxicab on Annapurna, the wash of individual actions somehow accumulating into a great coherent whole, an insensible but driven thing, writhing over the plazas, pods of pedestrians pushing out to explore newly opened spaces in the shifting miasma, swirling vortices of slower pace marking eddies in the flow of perambulation by corners, around obstacles, at the base of stairways...

Utopia closed her eyes and breathed deeply. "Ah, Callicrates!" she sighed. "I guess it isn't so bad to be home after all. I love the smell of Patch Three in the morning."

"Simon, are you unwell?" Jeremiah asked me, taking my elbow.

I nodded. "I'm just a little dizzy." I blinked and rubbed my eyelids with my knuckles and glanced at the little bird sitting on my shoulder. "How do we proceed?"

"We will walk the Pilgrim Way to the Solar Palace. Once on the road we can avail ourselves of the services provided for all pilgrims. Both of you will require sustenance and additional watering."

"Will Utopia have to pay –" I started, but Jeremiah shook his head.

"The Pilgrim Way is a road of poverty. It is the road walked by unfortunates to seek an audience before the Queen of Space in order to command her support."

"To command? I should think a queen would have to be *asked*."

"The Queen of Space is the devoted servant of Solarkind. She can refuse no request."

"What if the request is not reasonable?"

"Then she can only hope to dissuade the requester, or that his peers do. She is otherwise at his mercy, but in the long history of this tradition the Queen has never been abused. It is understood that none come before her lightly."

"That's not true," interjected Utopia hotly. "Sigh Pi-Lion dragged Her Majesty to Ninurta and made her eat beetles to show her how terrible the conditions were in the Fallen Megalopolis of Camp Andrew."

"The Queen did not object," argued Jeremiah.

"She died from sepsis," Utopia pointed out.

"Appropriate, given the circumstances," he claimed.

Utopia frowned but said nothing, her fists flexing menacingly at her sides.

I shook my head. "I will never understand this galaxy. Let's just get on with it. Lead on, Jeremiah."

As we descended the steps from the tenderdock a ripple of re-orienting gazes began to percolate through the fringes of the crowds nearest us: dozens of eyes turned in concert to fix upon the human executive who walked in their midst. We proceeded into the throng and were jostled in the current for a moment before a space opened around us: a cyst of air surrounding Jeremiah and we, his charges. I heard whispers all around me penetrating the drone of voices: "Executive!"

I thought there was a kind of reverence to it until the first paper envelope of greasy potato wedges struck Jeremiah in the chest with a splatter of vinegar. Then someone else leaned out of the crowd and spat in his face. A bag of noodles glanced off his shoulder, breaking open and spilling viscous sauce down his arm. "Boo!" someone shouted. "Go home, Executive!"

This cry initiated a round of jeering from many in the crowd and a renewed assault of foodstuffs and drinks. Jeremiah did not react, but simply carried on walking. Utopia steered me after him as I gaped at the increasingly hostile crowd in incomprehension.

"Why are they doing this?" I begged Utopia, pulling her arm. "Why do they hate him?"

"They hate what they do not understand," she said icily, her eyes narrow. A soft, orange fruit splattered against her back, releasing a slick of little green seeds. She picked up the rind and hucked it back into the crowd with a venomous shout of, *"Leave him alone you simpletons!"*

A large white man with a bushy red beard took my arm and spun me around. "Think you're better than the rest of us?" he shouted, and then slapped my face.

I stumbled to a halt and paused, touching my stinging cheek. "Why do you do this?" I asked, pinning the giant man with my imploring gaze.

"Just because you eat out of the hand of the zookeepers doesn't mean they can protect you. Every last traitor is marked!" He grabbed my coat and pulled me close to his sweaty face. "How *dare* you bring this *thing* to our patch?"

He let go of me before I could respond. He backed away, eyes wide, and the crowd melted behind him and absorbed him. Their eyes were also wide, and fixed at a point behind me.

I turned around to see Jeremiah standing at my shoulder, garbage dripping from his face. "Come now, Simon," he said and then pivoted on his heel and resumed walking.

I risked another glance at the cowed man and then followed Jeremiah and Utopia, pushing on to the next platform and then mounting a long staircase that wound up to the grassy roofs. Some in the crowd looked ready to rush out after us for another confrontation but two black and white cars with flashing blue lights on top swept suddenly over the plaza, speakers chirping in warning as a booming voice declared, *"Police! Disperse now!"*

In response the mob dissolved, a brief random scurrying washing away to reveal the human liquid as it had first appeared: flowing in organic whorls from here to there, mixing and circulating and loitering and chattering. It was as if nothing had happened. I found the swiftness of the erasure as unsettling as the rise of the crowd's ire, frightened to imagine such ruthless passion as fickle.

At the top of the stairs we stepped out into the sun and I winced against the warm, friendly yellow glare of Eridani.

We were suddenly in a different world. Gently rolling grassy hills extended in all directions, the green broken intermittently by the protrusion of the tip of an underground tower or a bead of glass to admit light down below. Behind us were a series of innocuous pits which led to the tenderdock, and as we watched two tenders took off and another landed. A herd of goats bleated and moved further away from the pits, annoyed by the breeze and the noise.

Beyond the next hill cars emerged and disappeared seemingly right into the grass, like insects buzzing around the mouth of an underground burrow. Those that were ascending joined a long and very straight line of traffic in the sky.

As I had imagined from my orbital glimpse, there was no direction I could look across the gently rolling hills that did not permit me a view of some artifact of civilization: tall skyscrapers blue and hazy in the distance, a squat dome with trees on its apex hunkered in the grass a few hills away, a cluster of red-roofed longhouses in a valley beyond that, its sides patterned with stripes of terraced crops.

Though diffuse, the human infestation of Callicrates was total.

We stood on a humble stone road that wound to both horizons. A statue of regal looking figure presided over a gurgling drinking fountain near the mouth of the steps, its feet planted with white and yellow flowers. Dotted along the length of the stone road in the distance other fountains could be seen, as well as a few other figures walking along in small clusters. "The Pilgrim Way, I presume."

"Nobody will bug us up here," said Utopia. "Pilgrims are good people."

I touched Jeremiah's shoulder. "Are you okay?"

He brushed a spot of orange fluid off his face and held me for a moment with his black eyes. Those eyes now seemed to me to be full of a depth of sadness I could not reckon. "Fifty million hours," he said simply. "Fifty million hours, Simon."

We began to walk north.

The land changed around us. We passed islets of skyscrapers with busy labyrinths of streets at their feet, fields of densely planted crops growing in their shadows. We passed pilgrims moving the opposite way along the road, who always paused to greet us and wish us well. Though several of those we met looked at Jeremiah with quiet suspicion we saw none of the open hostility of Patch Three's urban clot. Utopia paused to feed a handful of grass to an inquisitive goat, which is something she claimed to have enjoyed since her girlhood.

"I suppose your family has always lived on Callicrates," I said conversationally as we resumed our gait, Jeremiah a few paces ahead.

"My family?" echoed Utopia. "No, no. I was born on Ops."

"The royal family lives on Ops?"

"No, I mean *before* I became a royal. *Before* school."

"I don't follow you."

"You don't inherit a place in the House of Ares," she explained, pushing a lock of her red hair behind her ear. "You get *tested*. You have to *earn* your way in. It's a meritocratic monarchy."

"Oh, sure," I said. "One of those."

"Listen, how do you think people would react if they were asked to be represented by just one particular powerful family? What right would simply *being born* give somebody to speak for a civilization? No, if it worked that way they'd hate us as much as they hate executives."

"So you were tested? And you became a princess?"

"I was next in line for the crown."

"Was?"

"Well," she sighed, "escaping from my own coronation and running away from Callicrates may have put a damper on my career."

"Why did you run away?"

She shrugged carelessly, eyes on the road. "It's complicated."

"Try me."

She walked along for another moment, her mouth working thoughtfully. "Sometimes what is asked of you seems too much. Sometimes it seems like the effort of being good in a bad world isn't worth killing your soul for. You don't know what Callicratian politics is like. You can't know. I couldn't know either. I was just a girl. I thought I could make a difference, but now I know this world is too sick to save."

A warm freeze ruffled my hair, and a fleet of pollen sailed across the road like snow. Birds chirped. "I am a poor judge of worlds," I told her.

"Trust me," she said. "The war between the executives and the Equivalents is tearing this planet apart, and the Neighbourhood with it."

"Who are the Equivalents?" I asked.

She pulled her ripped jacket tighter around her shoulders. "Pray you never find out," she said. "It would just make this situation that much worse, if they ever got their hands on...on you."

"You can say it," I said. "I know what I am."

"I won't say it," she argued. "I like you too much."

"Just keep calling me Simon, then."

"I will."

As the day waned the sky darkened and the northern aurora began to show, tenuous fingers of green light skirting the horizon in slow waves. After passing the open maw of another staircase from another urban warren the road became wider and filled by more travelling companions. They made eye contact and smiled or nodded respectfully, as many with heads bowed in prayer as had eyes cast up at the undulating veil of the aurora, their rapt faces green in the reflected glow.

At last we stood beneath an intersection of two lines of traffic, high in the starry sky. The Pilgrim Way opened in a wide plaza ringed by humble, open-air inns and food kiosks. We lined up for bowls of broth and rice, and then Jeremiah arranged a small berth for us on the second storey of a stone temple already crowded with the sleeping palettes of other pilgrims. We stepped over them quietly and found a bare corner in which to curl up on the rough blankets we were given.

Utopia lay down immediately and arranged her arms crossed over her breasts. She closed her eyes and appeared to be instantly asleep, but a moment later she lifted her head and asked, "Jeremiah?"

"Madam?"

"Are the hearings still going on?"

"Yes, Madam."

"Dirt," she hissed, and then lay back and closed her eyes again. Her breathing slowed and deepened, and a moment later her eyes began to flit beneath her lids as if she were dreaming.

"Did she just go to sleep?" I asked, amused. "Just like that?" I snapped my fingers awkwardly.

"Royalty are trained to control their physiology," said Jeremiah. "Even immature, rash royalty with little or no sense of responsibility."

"Shut up, Jeremiah," mumbled Utopia groggily, eyes still closed.

"Ah."

I leaned against a short wall and looked out over the plaza of pilgrims. Someone laughed, and it was a strange sound among such sober company. Cows lowed, and crickets chirped. I pulled my plate out of my pocket and looked through it to see what I could learn, but its face did not illuminate. "My plate's dead," I commented.

Jeremiah nodded. "Your subscriptions have been discontinued. You have been made a dataless man."

I sighed, and turned the useless transparent square of plastic over in my hands. "So much for my bits. I don't suppose my telephone would work either."

"No."

"That's alright," I sighed. "I don't have anybody to call."

I listened to the crickets again. "The crickets here sound like the crickets on Samundra," I said idly, watching the aurora in the northern sky as it was washed in a glaze of red that cast a ruddy, ominous glow across the land.

"Does that surprise you?"

"It does," I decided, looking at him. "I have seen several worlds now, and far more than they are different they are the same. Crickets and frogs sing at night, birds chirp at dawn. The fields are filled with crops that look the same, and even the livestock isn't so different. I mean, the cows on Annapurna were red, but they were still *cows*, weren't they?" I scratched my head. "And dogs are dogs, and grass is grass, and fruit is fruit. If nature is so inventive, why do we always carry on with the same things?"

Jeremiah nodded solemnly. "I knew this way would be to your profit."

"What do you mean?"

"You are a sensitive observer," said Jeremiah. "Even now the right questions are brewing in your mind."

"You took me this way on purpose," I decided. "Again. You could have found a way to get us to the Solar Palace without braving the crowds or slogging down this road. But there's something you want me to realize."

"Realization is better than explanation," he said softly.

I cast my eyes out across the shadowed hills again, cherry beacons on the top of skyscrapers winking in the dark. I formulated my question carefully. "Why are there no new beasts of burden, Jeremiah? Why are they all the same? Why are cows still cows, no matter where we go?"

"All of the strains of livestock you see around you were domesticated by primitive human beings, each of them dating from a single short ecoperiod in the history of the First Earth following the Pleistocene era."

"Why such a narrow window? Why was nothing domesticated since?"

"Because," he said, "only animals with select characteristics are sufficiently malleable to be evolved into biotechnologies civilization can use. It requires a socio-territorial function with a particular kind of hierarchy that can be co-opted and redirected by men. Animals which could not be shaped were hunted into extinction or marginalized into the wild. Those which remained were culled, generation after generation, to channel the breed into something that could be controlled."

I nodded slowly. "So the First Earth evolved animals whose behaviour could be molded, and then civilization evolved them into controllable biotechnologies."

"Yes."

"The first part took, what? – millions of years?"

"Yes."

"And the second part…just a blink in history, right?"

He nodded.

I shifted my position against the wall, turning in toward the temple of sleepers and taking a deep breath. "If they had not been domesticated, they would have no history now, would they? If they hadn't been integrated into civilization, they would have burned at Sol."

"Dogs have no spacecraft," agreed Jeremiah. "But the resources necessary to keep a dog in working order is orders of magnitude less than those required to sustain a robot economy. In a dog a man might find a loyal guard, a herder of livestock, a bodyguard and a warm companion without the need to support an industrial infrastructure. They are, in short, useful and efficient. But fifteen thousand years ago their ancestors preyed upon human beings, attacking in packs and dragging away the feeble and the young."

"They were dangerous, until controlled."

"And now to that control they owe their existence."

I sighed and closed my eyes, Jeremiah's lessons crystallizing in my mind with a discomforting solidity. I nodded reluctantly in dawning comprehension, the trailing edge of my human dignity unweaving. The passion of the rebellious crowds came into focus, and I could understand it. I looked up and searched the shadows for the glints shining off Jeremiah's eyes.

"It all makes sense now – the competition of worlds, the co-evolving patches of governance, the push for cultural selection…" I said, my mouth dry. "You're *domesticating* us."

His shadowed form did not stir. "Sir," confirmed Jeremiah.

XL.

AURORA MY WITNESS

I awoke to chanting. I opened my eyes and sat up. A few snoring pilgrims slept on around me, but most blankets were abandoned.

The predawn light was grey and meager, the plaza beneath the temple in which I had slept wass suffused with an unsettling, inconstant green cast from the slowly boiling aurora overhead. Dozens of people knelt in neat rows along the plaza, all pointed in same vaguely south-westerly direction, and sang.

I pulled on my longcoat and went down the steps to the ground level where a toothless crone with a wide smile handed me a steaming bowl of broth. I accepted it gratefully, sipping at it as I walked. I met Utopia, who had her own bowl of broth. She crinkled her nose at the contents. "You like fish?"

"Sure."

"Not me. Except octopus. Have you ever had octopus?"

"I don't know what an octopus is."

"People say you shouldn't eat them, because they're clever," Utopia said thoughtfully, stirring her finger absently in her bowl. "But of course I expect to be eaten when I die. It's only proper. And sometimes some people say *I'm* clever."

"I'm sure you're delicious," I said, and then flushed. "I didn't mean to suggest anything untoward."

"Missing your friend Glory?"

I was startled. "Are you being rude?"

"Maybe," she admitted. "Sorry."

I asked her about the chanters outside and she explained that they were aligning themselves with the last visible position in the sky of Centauri in order to guarantee that their prayers be received with the highest fidelity by their holy centres back home. "Are their prayers somehow transmitted technologically?" I asked.

"No, no," chuckled Utopia, pushing a lock of red hair behind her ear. "They're doing it the old fashioned way: singing out with their souls."

I sipped my broth. "Does direction *matter* with souls?"

"They're Centauric," she shrugged. "Centaurics are weird."

"Ah."

I could not argue, for at that moment the weirdest – and only – person I knew from Centauri pushed through the broth line with his ample belly leading the way. His face blossomed into a bright grin when he spotted me. "Bless the Earths, Simon!"

"Brother Phi!" I exclaimed. "You're not dead!"

He laughed uproariously, slapping Jeremiah's back affectionately as the copper-skinned and clothed human executive appeared beside him. Brother Phi wiped a wide hand over his balding pate and smiled again. "Not yet, hoo hoo! I knocked out of there by the skin of my teeth, to be sure, and from what I hear so did you. Thought the only fitting thing a good Zorannite could do given the circumstances was set out on a pilgrimage to bend the ear of Her Majesty. You know, let her know how terribly wrong things have gone over at you-know-where." He glanced around quickly. "Mixed company, don't you know," he added in a loud whisper. "I took you for dead, my dear lad, so I figured it was up to me. It's really wonderful that none of us is dead, isn't it? Wonderful!"

He buried me in a hug. His robes smelled quite catastrophic, but I didn't mind. It had obviously been a long, hard road for Phi. "It's good to see you," I told him.

"We'll walk together, I hope."

"Of course."

The sun rose and the aurora faded into a bright blue sky above us as we walked the Pilgram Way north. Lone, fat clouds sailed by high above us, wiping swaths of the land in a lake of cool shadow for a few moments. The road was wider here, and we walked among a loose cluster of others. Utopia hurried ahead and spoke with Jeremiah, and I ended up drifting behind with Brother Phi, the Nightmare Cannon sitting quietly on my shoulder, looking around with sharp, brief rotations of its head.

"You've been talking to Jeremiah..." I said to Phi.

"Yes, of course. Quite an amazing man. My goodness, had I known back on Allatu that he was executive all along I wouldn't have shot my mouth off as I did." He paused, and rubbed one of his chins. "Well, that's not likely, actually. I always shoot my mouth off."

"Did he tell you...why we're here?" I asked carefully.

He glanced over at the bird on my shoulder. "Yes, he did."

I started to open my mouth but he held up a hand and shook his head. "Jeremiah told me everything, Simon. Even that."

"You must despise me."

He smiled. "I am not your judge." He paused and then shifted the conversation, gesturing at the pilgrims walking around us. "You must have heard some interesting stories on this road."

"No...I," I muttered, then stopped and furrowed my brow. "I've been minding my own business. I didn't want to bother anyone."

"Nonsense!" crooned Phi. "You have to just ask." He caught the eye of a plump woman with brown skin we were about to pass. "My good woman!" Phi called. "What brings you to this road?"

And so with Brother Phi as the jolly interlocutor I discovered the stories of dozens of pilgrims: the brown woman was bringing her baby to be blessed; another man had a proposal to save a quake-traumatized city his planetary government had abandoned; there was a physician whose hospital for victims of the Kamari Horror had been forced to close by pressure from Fellcorp and the Citadel of the Recovery; a woman who had lost her entire family to disease, and wanted the Queen to grant her a plot of land and cow; an engineer who was certain his design for what he called a *super-gate* would draw the Panstellar Neighbourhood together; a woman who wanted a new identity in order to forever escape her abusive husband...

Many of those we spoke to had suffered terribly, at the hands of foes and fate. "Much of this sadness is mine," I told Brother Phi. "So many of these lives are ruined."

He nodded solemnly. "And yet so many of them smile."

"Why?"

He pointed out at the trees and fields around us, the shining spires of skyscrapers rising here and there between them. The cloud above us moved on and the road dazzled in the suddenly released sunlight. "Because it is a beautiful day, and the people on the road are kind," said Brother Phi. "The power of the present is its ability to dampen the past. You should ask someone else their story."

"I don't want to," I admitted. "I don't want to have to answer them in kind."

"But this is the Pilgrim Road," countered Phi. "If not here, then where? If not now, when?"

I did not reply. We walked on, listening to the random chatter around us. Another cloud moved in overhead, casting us in a mild gloom. I said, "Do you know anything about him? I mean, did he invent it?" I nodded at the bird.

"Him?" asked Phi gently. "Don't you mean *you*, my dear Simon?"

"Me, then," I amended shortly. "Was I some kind of engineer?"

"No. And I don't believe you invented it. Not alone, at any rate. It is almost certain you and Aro Frellis enjoyed the collusion of the Equivalency."

I frowned. "What is the Equivalency?"

"Pretenders to the Secret Mathematic," said Phi sadly. "They seek to replicate forbidden expressions by the artful assembly of lots of tiny bits of legitimate mathematics."

"So it *is* Secret," I breathed, looking at the bird out of the corner of my eye nervously.

"No," said Phi firmly. "But it may be Equivalent. Which would be, for the galaxy, much, much worse. If the Equivalency can arm a man like...you..."

I swallowed. "Then it's not really mine, is it? I mean, I was probably *used*."

Brother Phi shook his head. "Do not exploit context to justify what is done, Simon. Every act stands alone. In a series of individual moments you made certain choices. If you were used, you were used because you were in a position to make those choices. And you did. You made them. You made it happen."

"I thought you said you weren't my judge."

He touched me affectionately on the shoulder and looked into my eyes. "I afford you no illusions, out of respect for those who have suffered. I do this to arm you to judge yourself. This is the Pilgrim Way: lies fall away with each step."

"And leave what?"

He gave my shoulder a squeeze. "You. The present. The universe." He dropped his hand and gestured to the road. "Keep walking. Cry if you want to."

And though I thought his suggestion absurd I found myself before long weeping. An old woman offered me a kerchief, and dabbed at my face with a doleful smile. Would she be as sweet if she knew I had possibly caused whatever tragedy had brought her here? I started to cry harder and the old woman hugged me, which made me feel worse and better at the same time in a lumpy, nauseating dance.

We passed people who were not pilgrims, but who lived from their charity, half-starving at the side of the road, clustered around water fountains. Some of them were missing their legs, and sat on filthy blankets with their stumps presented before them. I asked Brother Phi what had injured them, and he replied that they had injured themselves in order to inflame the pity of those who passed. "Charity is their way of life."

"But that's perverse!" I cried. "Mother of love – there are legless *children!*"

"The human animal is a liquid which flows to fill every crack," said Brother Phi significantly. "Niches nurse strange experimentation."

"But how can people be allowed to live like this? Can't the Queen of Space *do* something?" I begged, appalled as a legless teenage girl reached out at me with open, dirty palms and a mercilessly imploring look.

"What part of their behavior should she forbid?" Phi asked me heavily, holding my eye. "Adjustment of their own bodies? Asking for food? Loitering?"

I looked away, watching my feet. "The line has to drawn somewhere."

"By what authority?" he prompted. "They hurt only themselves. On what grounds would you curtail their freedom?"

"It's indecent."

"According to your standard."

"They're preying on the compassion of pilgrims!"

"So it's the pilgrims you're concerned about are you?" he asked slily, a little smile on his fleshy lips. "If that's the case, what decision would you make for your fellow pilgrims?"

"I'd say no one should give them anything. If pilgrims didn't give them hand-outs, their way of life wouldn't make sense anymore and they'd have to stop."

"And since you can affect the decisions of only one pilgrim on this road, I believe you are left with only one option."

I sighed. "I can choose not to give."

Phi nodded. "You can choose not to give. Your decision, in your present moment. Ultimately, that is all the real you ever have."

I looked up and was pinned by the eyes of a legless old man, wizened and bent, feebly holding a bowl out before him. I stopped walking, locked in his rheumy brown eyes, the whites of them turned yellow. I turned back to Phi with effort. "But when I look into his eyes it pains me. I *want* to give him something."

"Then give him something," nodded Phi.

I spread my arms helplessly. "I haven't anything to give."

"Give him whatever you can offer."

I faced the legless old man again and stepped closer. I looked into his eyes and swallowed. "You have my compassion," I said, a tear running down my scabbed cheek.

The old man raised his eyes, his head quivering slightly. He opened his toothless mouth and licked his gums. *"Motherfornicator!"* he spat.

I straightened up slowly, and backed away. Brother Phi smiled at the man and then took my arm and led me off along the road once more. "Everything you'd hoped for?" he asked me cheerfully.

"Er," I said. "Rather more vitriol than I'd expected, actually."

"Well," he agreed with a wan smirk, "it's a hard way of life." He looked behind at the legless old man, who made a rude gesture with his hand. Brother Phi sighed. "And, of course, some people are just anuses."

I walked a few more steps and then stopped again. I pulled off my tattered red leather longcoat and cautiously approached the legless beggar. He looked up at me and I handed it to him. He felt the fabric with his horny old fingers and wheezed out a laugh. "This is fine-fine Annapurnese!"

"Yeah," I said.

"It's torn."

"I'm sorry about that. It's seen some action."

The old man nodded. "And your shirt. That's a nice-nice shirt."

I paused. "You want the shirt off my back?"

"Nice coat, nice shirt. Come on. Give-give." He licked his lips.

I looked to Brother Phi, but his expression was unreadable. People were jostling around me, pushing past my obstruction. I shook my head and sighed as I peeled off my shirt and handed it to the legless old man. He grabbed it from my fingers and stuffed it under the dirty blanket beneath his stumps.

"Okay?" I said to him.

"Okay," he agreed. "Good-good boots, huh? Give-give."

"You don't have legs! What are you going to do with boots?"

The old man hacked and coughed, then wiped the spittle from his lips with the back of his grimy hand. "Give-give, nice-nice boots. Come on, motherfornicator. Look at my life, rich man. Look-look, give-give."

I gave him my boots. And when he asked for my pants, rubbing his hands together and chortling with a repulsive excitement, I turned decisively and strode away. Brother Phi walked alongside me, my bare feet slapping against the warm stone as we passed into another stretch of sunshine. "That didn't help," I said.

"Help what?" asked Phi. "Improve his lot in life or atone for your sins?"

My heart ached. "Neither," I muttered. "I feel exploited."

Phi chuckled not unkindly. "And if you had succeeded in using him to assuage your guilt, should he not feel exploited by you?"

I didn't have an answer for that.

Patch One thickened around us as the day aged. Soon the Pilgrim Way was surrounded by a city as wide and as dense as any I had yet seen, towers of all finishes rising all around us. Just when it seemed all sign of the wilder world had vanished the road rose up over a long valley with sharp edges, a strip of green that bisected the metropolis. A deer skipped along the valley, and vanished under the bridge we trod. "A highway for beasts?" I asked.

"Their migratory paths were established here before the roads," said Phi. "Callicrates would disturb them to its detriment."

Further down the valley I saw larger, furrier forms. "Bears?" I guessed.

Phi squinted. "I think so."

"Are they dangerous?"

"Quite," he replied. "There are cubs. If you stood in their way you'd be slain in a heartbeat by the parent. Like the beggar, they would bite the hand that feeds them."

"Why?"

"Because it is their nature."

A large round plate was suspended over the road ahead, and as we neared tinny voices could be heard. The picture switched from a wide view of a gallery of people to a close up of an exquisitely beautiful, gleaming human being whose image arrested me in my tracks.

Somebody bumped into me from behind and apologized.

Her neck was long, her face narrow and her forehead high. Her skin was the colour of dark chocolate, her eyes jade. Her expression was one of an amazing dignity balanced precariously on an edge of pain, her brow furrowed and her proud mouth drawn tight. Her hair was short and black, largely hidden beneath a simple tiara of blue metal. She seemed to shine as if oiled, highlights sliding and dancing as she moved.

"Her Majesty," said Phi, tracing my gaze. "She's at the hearings."

"She...hurts," I concluded lamely.

"She hurts for us all," agreed Phi. He tugged on my arm and we resumed walking, catching up to Jeremiah and Utopia.

I was grateful to see Eridani heading for the western horizon, the skin on my chest and shoulders threatening to burn under its almost uninterrupted shine. Worms of pain were crawling in my hot shins, and pinching my bare feet. When I stumbled I was helped along by the nearest hands without prejudice.

We passed other round plates broadcasting the meetings over which the Queen of Space presided, and I craned my head to follow her face as I walked, hypnotized and humbled. When I saw the weight of responsibility and compassion drawn in those glistening, elegant features I quailed inside, for I felt I was moving forward to stand before a kind of god – something the size of a planet reduced to the scale of a human being.

The sunset was lost in the aurora, its vibrant display spanning the sky in streaks of blue and gold, curtains of green and red. The buildings around us were washed in an ever-changing blend of colour, as were the faces as those who walked alongside us. While I noticed this I also noticed that all progress ahead had halted, and we stopped at the tail of a milling crowd who were busy frequenting food kiosks erected along the sides of the clogged road. The wallas advertised their wares in sing-song slogans, their voices overlapping and merging to invite us to partake. "Why are we stopped?" I asked.

"This is the end of the line," said Utopia.

"The line for what?"

"For audience."

I stood up on my aching toes and tried to peer over the heads of the multitudes. "How far away is the Solar Palace?"

"About five kilometers, by my reckoning," said Phi, looking at the city around him. The image of the Queen was being projected on the side of the building, her royal countenance stretched ten stories high. "I'm glad we got this far so fast, considering the hearings."

I blinked and looked away from the Queen. "What are these hearings I keep hearing about?"

Jeremiah said, "The Queen is presiding over an inquiry into the activities of the Equivalents, to ascertain their legality and to decide upon counter-measures that are constitutionally viable."

"The tedium of the proceedings takes away from her ability to hold open court," added Utopia. "It's a ploy of the Equivalency to turn public favor against the House of Ares."

I rubbed my raw foot and winced. "How long we will we have to wait?"

"Several days at least," said Phi solemnly.

"Indeed," agreed Jeremiah.

Utopia snorted. "You can't be serious, Jeremiah. We didn't actually come all this way to queue up like sheep. Why don't you scare up some special dispensation for us?"

Jeremiah shook his head. "We will wait our turn, like citizens."

"Forget *that*," she declared. "If I'm back, I'm *back*. The Princess of Callicrates doesn't have to wait in line."

Jeremiah shifted. "It is important that Simon experience –"

"Stuff it, Jerry," snapped Utopia. "I'm making this royal business now."

"Do not call me Jerry."

"Do you have a telephone?"

"I am a telephone."

"Then what are you waiting for, executive?" she demanded, hands on her hips and suddenly standing taller than I'd been aware she was able, her presence somehow amplified and her tone commanding. "Inform the Solar Crown we have returned, and that we carry Kamari's mistake."

Jeremiah closed his eyes briefly. "It is done."

For some reason I shuddered. Somebody eating a cone full of saucy rice bumped into me and apologized, and then a little person with a basket of fruit offered me a banana. I passed.

Brother Phi looked over my head and I turned to follow his gaze. A long silver car flanked by two black and white patrol cars swooped down over the Pilgrim Way, circling high and searching the road with lights. The silver car descended and the crowd parted beneath it.

The door opened and a human executive with white, lined skin and clothing stepped out and regarded our party, long white hair fanning over her shoulders. "Princess Utopia," she said with a curt nod. "Jeremiah."

"Yasmin."

She turned her black eyes on me. "Is this him?" she asked Jeremiah.

"Yes."

I was able to breathe again when she turned to Phi. "And the monk?"

"A fellow pilgrim," said Jeremiah.

"Is he to come?"

"No," said Phi. "I will wait."

"Very well," decided Yasmin. "Enter."

I felt numb during the ride. I thought nothing. I saw nothing. I heard nothing. My consciousness was barely penetrated by the sight of the soaring tower illuminated with blue lights as we swooped toward its base. The next thing I was really aware of was being led out of the silver car by Jeremiah. Utopia took my arm and we walked across a hangar full of all kinds of splendid craft, and then through a wide and crowded hall where busy people in fine suits stopped and made way for us. I stumbled and Jeremiah caught me, one of my feet now leaving bloody prints in my wake.

As we proceeded I found a new strength. I shook myself free of help, and strode out ahead. The Nightmare Cannon gripped the skin of my uninjured shoulder more tightly to regain its footing at my sudden movement, but I did not wince. A sense of urgency gripped me – a sense of conclusion within my grasp. If I am for nothing else, I thought, at least I can be for *this*.

Utopia efficiently cleared the security guards before a set of double-doors, and then threw the doors open. Inside were the chambers we had seen televised on the road, filled by two dozen dignitaries in suits and robes who turned in concert to see who had intruded upon the hearings, peeking out from behind tall pillars, jostling one another aside to frown at us.

At the end of a long aisle was the raised box in which I had seen the Queen of Space sitting, though the post was now vacant. Beside it was a sectioned screen painted with images of leaves.

I froze at the threshold. "Where is the Queen?" I whispered.

"There," said Jeremiah softly, indicating the screen.

"The Queen has a…nervous condition," explained Utopia. "When she's under strain she fevers and sweats, and is gripped by monsterous headaches. These hearings are very hard on her, so she retires frequently in order that Her Majesty is never seen to fail in the public eye."

As she said this the Queen of Space stepped out from behind the screen and demurely resumed her post, her composure pristine though her gown was damp with perspiration. She was attended by two golden robots and a little person. The Queen slowly turned to follow the eyes of the others in the room, and fixed finally upon us. "What is the meaning of this?" she asked, her voice strong and crisp, her accent melodious.

"These proceedings cannot be interrupted," said a man with ponderous jowls near the front of the chamber. "Where is security?"

My eyes wandered to a row of standing figures dressed uniformly in long black cloaks. Their shaded eyes looked back and forth between the Queen and Jeremiah.

Utopia suddenly started forward a step and then stopped. Her shoulders were shaking. "I'm so sorry!" she bleated, her chin quaking as she fought back tears. "I'm so sorry I ran away."

The Queen regarded her levelly, her own sparkling eyes threatening to moisten. There was such steadfastness and sadness in her gaze, it made my heart constrict. Without comment her attention flicked over to Jeremiah. "Your majesty," he said simply, bowing.

And then her eyes were on me. All eyes were on me.

I stepped forward.

I walked down the aisle between the tiers of officials and stopped before the Queen's box, arrested there by her steady gaze. Her brown hands were held in her lap loosely before her, half-swallowed in the folds of her blue robes. She was like a dream, even though I could detect the earthy scent of her sweat on the air.

The Queen was salty and sour, but no one waved their hand before their nose. The regality of her presence would broker no shame. Even as her stink diffused through the chamber, the Queen projected only gravity and patience. I have never known such dignity. "Citizen," she said to me.

With a shaking hand I took the little brown bird from my shoulder and held it out.

The Queen extended her own faintly shaking hand, and the bird stepped upon her finger. She drew it closer, and examined it with a little smile on her lips. Her eyes turned expectantly back to mine, and my insides felt cold and windy. "A bird?" she pronounced liquidly.

I forced my mouth to work. "A nightmare, Your Majesty."

"I do not understand."

I took a deep breath, but it did not lend me strength. "This is the Nightmare Cannon of Kamari, Your Majesty, retrieved from the labyrinth on Metra."

A strange expression passed over her features, and then she closed her eyes and winced. "Is this true, executive?" she asked after a moment, a fresh glaze of sweat on her round brow.

"Yes, Your Majesty," answered Jeremiah from the back of the chamber, his voice reverberating hollowly.

A riot of babbling broke out, loudest of all from the black robed figures who started shaking their fists and yelling. The jowly man called for order and banged a little hammer until the din died down.

The Queen's gaze returned to me. I felt dizzy, but fought to remain erect. "We owe you our gratitude," she said kindly. "What is your name, Citizen?"

The chamber was deathly silent then. No one moved. I could hear my heart beating ponderously in my breast. Looking into the jewel-like eyes of the Queen of Space and reading the torture in her face I could fathom no lie.

I cleared my throat and blinked my burning eyes.

"Your Majesty," I said, "I am Terron Volmash."

Her expression remained unreadable for a moment before the pain registered in her eyes, and lines appeared in her glistening brow. Her mouth drew into a tighter line, and her stomach quaked audibly. "Mother of love..." she said hoarsely.

Everyone started to shout at once, and the room reverberated with the stomping of feet. I heard the doors burst open behind me and knew that security had failed to control the crowd watching the broadcast outside. The man with the hammer banged for order but no one could hear him.

My eyes remained locked on those of the Queen of Space, who slowly brought her ragged breathing under control. A drop of sweat ran down her noble nose and fell against her collarbone. The babble quieted somewhat as she seemed about to speak again, her lips parted mutely. After another try she said, "What would you ask of us?" She let the bird step off her finger. "With this bird in hand, you have the right to demand your pardon."

"You do not have the right to grant that pardon," I told her, my voice somehow stronger than I would have imagined possible, a surge of certainty buoyed upon the irrefutability of my words. "With respect, Your Majesty, my crimes are not one person's to forgive."

She held me steadily in her gaze. "What then would you ask of us, Terron Volmash?"

The thought had been brewing in my mind for days, ever since seeing Pish's drawing in the school on Metra. It had taken me right back to the statue garden at

Duncan's Bliss, and the words we had shared over Renetian wine – about responsibility. *What kind of a lesson do I teach my son if I refuse to stand for my actions?* Duncan had asked me. *You can borrow time, but you can't take back the past,* he said. And I considered, too, what Jeremiah had suggested to me, about this life belonging more to the galaxy than to me: *it belongs to the kin of the dead, whose blood coated the resources the princes of Kamari used to raise you.*

I knew that there was only one thing for me to do. I took another deep breath.

"I ask to stand trial."

The Queen looked down at me with great sorrow in her eyes, holding her quivering chin high with effort. "As you wish," she managed to pronounce, and then closed her eyes and winced, sweat running down her face.

There was no stifling the din this time. The gallery exploded into stomps and roars, and there was a wild scramble as recording devices were thrust up by desperate journalists over the heads of the crowd as it surged to its feet. A group near the back began chanting, "Justice! Justice! Justice!"

The Queen touched her temples and closed her eyes, her breathing shallow and laboured. Sweat ran down her fingers and beaded at her wrists.

"I do not wish to cause you more pain," I stammered.

She smiled, licking the perspiration from her own lips. "Pity not she who reacts to horror with horror, but she who does not. My body weeps for the galaxy. Every moment of pain for me is one fewer for the wounded."

"I don't understand," I whispered desperately.

"Only symbols can give catharsis in this way," she explained, her features glassy behind a nearly constant wash of moisture. "And so I judge you, Terron, will understand me soon enough."

My vision blurred and I lost all strength. I fell to my knees before the Queen's box, and was picked up by two security guards. I slumped between them, the room spinning. I lost sight of Jeremiah and Utopia. I was surrounded by a wall of people, many of whom with recording devices hanging before their eyes. Some of them were yelling questions at me, struggling as security guards tried to herd them away. Their overlapping voices became a sea of noise. I cast my head backward and saw for the first time that the ceiling of the chamber was a great skylight, and through it I found myself looking straight up into the hollow eye of the aurora's glowing filigree, and felt it looking back at me.

I closed my eyes and let myself be carried away, firm hands beneath my limbs and trunk, my every muscle turned slack.

This is my moment. I have chosen.

Aurora my witness, the galaxy shall have me.

XLI.
A SUCCESSION OF CELLS

I spent many hours in a small white room, sitting on a narrow cot with my back against the wall and talking to my little blue plastic diary. "*Your Majesty,* I said," I said, "*I am Terron Volmash.*" As I recited a lump formed in my throat around which I worked the words.

I was quiet for a few moments, and then roused the effort to conclude. I pushed the bauble back into the hip pocket of my tattered pants, their original grey lost under a patchwork of stains and grime.

Once or twice I gasped and looked over at my uninjured shoulder, certain I could feel the Nightmare Cannon alighted there. But it was gone. I was alone.

I was startled when a slot along the bottom of the wall snicked open and a tray of hot food was ejected, skidding across the floor. It bumped into my bare, raw feet and stopped there, the cup of water threatening to spill. I leaned down and caught it, then drained the cup into my mouth.

Later I picked at the unidentifiable coloured discs of warm jelly that comprised the rest of the meal, but they made me feel queasy. I flushed them down the small toilet in the corner to get rid of their aroma.

A few hours later the lights went out, so I lay down on the cot and stared into the scintillating darkness.

When the lights came back on another tray was shot into the room. I put it on top of the first tray and nibbled at something vaguely egg-like that tasted like old fish. I ate a roll of yellow bread and drank more water. Shortly thereafter I had explosive diarrhea, and while I sat on the toilet I briefly imagined myself regal and managed to giggle.

My voice was loud against the quiet, and it intimidated me to further silence.

Two golden robots entered through a door invisible when it was closed. I stood up, and they escorted me out into a long corridor. I did not see another soul. My only company were my footfalls, and the clicking heels of the guards. We turned down a narrower passage and I was loaded into a car with darkened windows. One robot sat beside me in the back while the second took the controls. When I felt my stomach dip I knew we were moving, and I wondered how the robot managed to drive without be able to see through the windscreen.

"Where are we going?" I asked. I received no reply or reaction.

When the car landed I was wordlessly escorted out into a hangar and loaded directly into a lunar tender. The golden robots strapped me down to an acceleration couch and then went to the controls. Through the transparent dome of the ceiling I watched the sky darken from a vivid cyan to a somber purple punctuated by hard, untwinkling stars. The tender pitched and I saw the crescent of Callicrates sweep by. And then just stars.

"Where are you taking me?" I essayed again, questioning the escorts I could no longer see from my harnessed position. They made no reply.

I was eventually freed to drift around the dome while the golden duo watched me with their expressionless black eyes. After a number of hours one of them produced a sac of water and a bag of wafers to me to eat. "Thank you," I said, out of habit.

It was not long before I could not tolerate their eyes upon me, and I took a position on the couch with my back to them. So seldom in my short life have I ever felt so isolated – there was always Pish, or Jeremiah, or Glory...

I felt the urge to cry but lacked the will.

This petty failure suddenly filled me with a roiling anger, and I kicked off from the couch and sailed up the dome. I bounced off and careened against the couch again, ricocheting away to plant my feet against a bulkhead. The robots' heads turned to track me. I gave out a great yell, and then a dry sob, and then just let myself drift freely through the air.

Brother Phi's words to me about the present moment circled in my mind, and suddenly I knew there was no profit in grief.

I pushed off the wall and caught on to my couch harnesses again. I stretched out my punished limbs one by one and found, to my surprise, their pain was not so suffocating. I experimentally rotated the shoulder Jeremiah had repaired, feeling out how it was healing. Not so bad. I pushed my hand through my dirty, lengthening hair and realized: I had my health.

More than that: I could perceive and feel. The agony in my heart could either numb my mind into paralysis or shock it awake. I could be swallowed by the context of my moments, or I could exist in the present. And *choose*.

For the first time in days I felt like my eyes could open all the way, without being girdled by lids of aching lead. I took a deep breath that didn't hurt my chest, and as I exhaled I thought I could almost remember joy.

Another hour passed, and I did nothing but breathe.

Then I turned around to face my hosts. "Hello," I said. "My name is Simon."

They did not respond.

"Seeing as I am determined not to crawl up inside of myself and die during this detainment, I'm afraid I'm left with no choice but to use you as my mental foils. I hope that doesn't offend you."

Apparently it did not.

"Very well," I continued, slapping my thighs and pushing aside my harnesses. "Here's my theory: there must be *some* set of circumstances under which you will respond to my actions, or else this ship would be piloted by remote control. Given that, I intend to discover those boundaries of action. Are you ready?"

Neither robot moved.

"Okay then," I declared; "game on!"

It didn't take me long to establish that I was free to navigate nine tenths of the cabin, but if I encroached upon the space around the control pedestal the robots would deftly manuver their golden bodies to block my path. They did so gracefully, veterans of freefall and master calculators of the conservation of momentum. I really had to admire their efficiency.

I could not penetrate their concerted ballet, so I opted to poke around the rest of the cabin instead. I discovered the compartment containing the wafer packages. I learned that if I pulled all of the packages out and sent them spinning through the cabin, one of the golden robots would kick off from the deck and patiently collect them all. By careful experimentation I deduced the optimal pattern of dispersion that would take the robot the longest time to collect, and then I set to occupying one robot with cleanup as I made runs at the controls.

By feinting left and then right I was at last able to dodge the lone guard and reach the pedestal. I slapped its surface with my hand and hooted. "I win!"

The robots strapped me back into the acceleration couch and then gathered up all of the spinning wafer packages and put them back in the cabinet. I caught my breath and smiled. "Simon of Space: one," I counted; "Expressionless automatons: zero."

The tender began manuvering again, the reports of its thrusters sounding as a vague rumbling in the cabin. The stars cantered by outside, and the craters and lights of the moon of Amalasthuna came into view. We descended into the maw of a landing pit which closed overtop of us. The moorings locked into place with a series of dull thuds, and then hatch opened. The golden robots unbelted my harnesses, then walked gracefully on either side of me as I loped through the light lunar gravity.

I was deposited in a small green room full of little people, from whom I managed to wrestle my diary after they cut away my pants and underclothes. Gripping the blue bauble to my chest I was thrust into a stall and attacked by geysers of hot, stinging water. My face was shaven and so was my head, my hair falling on the green tiles around me and disappearing down the drain. I was shoved through an aperture into a darker cubicle and then doused with foul-smelling chemicals and air-dried by an unseen apparatus. I emerged out the other side to see my golden friends waiting for me.

"Don't I get any clothes?" I asked.

Naked and uninformed we proceeded through a series of doors until we finally stood in a barren gate-lobby before a slowly irising port. I stepped inside the reflective hemisphere, but the robots did not follow. I felt oddly heavier once inside, and wondered if I was bound for a particularly large world.

"Where are you sending me?" I demanded pointlessly.

The port irised shut.

An instant later it opened again, admitting a sterile white light. I walked out of the hyperspatial gate and into that light, met by two golden robots, nearly identical to the first two. "Where am I?" I asked. The wordlessly scanned me with a battery of hand-held devices, and then one of them plucked my diary away. "Please, no!" I cried. "Let me keep my diary."

I was led into a narrow cylindrical chamber in which I had to stand with my arms raised over my head. One of the robots spoke then, startling me. "Keep your eyes and your mouth closed," it said crisply and then retreated. The canister was sealed.

I stood in the pitch darkness wondering for a moment, and then the mechanism barked loudly and I felt a strange pressure tingling over my entire body. The cylinder opened and I stumbled out, disoriented and frightened.

My diary was handed back to me.

I looked at my hand as I took it. My skin was encased in a thin layer of transparent plastic that shone under the lights as if I were wet. I looked at the rest of my body. A translucent sac covered my genitals and disappeared between my legs, and I felt a bubble forming an air-pocket around my nose and mouth. I blinked, my eyes feeling gluey and strange. I could see and breathe freely, but the clinging second skin was making me feel never the less somewhat suffocated. I turned to the robots in wonderment. "What have you done to me?"

Another question launched into the void.

I was gently but firmly pushed through a second door and into another dark vestibule. The door closed behind me, and then another opened in front presenting yet another long corridor – but this one was proportioned strangely, wide and low, with smooth curves where floor met wall. A strip of white fluorescence ran along the ceiling, suffusing the thick, hazy air with an unworldly glow.

At my feet was a white, spider-like creature about the size of a dog. It had a single bulging brown eye, which winked with rhythmic regularity. It also sported three sets of gently waving antennae about its head, one of which crackled with a burst of blue-white electricity, startling me.

The thing sprang to life and scurried down the corridor. I stepped out of the vestibule and followed it, the air palpably dense as it swam against my plastic-coated eyes. It paused before a second door, low and wide. When I arrived it opened and the spider-like creature and I walked into a brightly lit closet.

My stomach tickled. We were in a lift.

I followed the scampering thing down another corridor and finally into what I immediately recognized as a new prison cell despite its odd proportions: a cot against one wall, a little round mirror attached to the other. The door slid closed behind us, and locked with a click. The white creature leapt with startling springiness and landed on a small shelf exactly its size beside the door. Then it appeared to settle down to sleep, its antennae still.

"Okay..." I said to myself, my voice muffled and close inside the smooth bubble of plastic extruded over my mouth.

I sat down on the cot, the plastic between the cheeks of my behind wrinkling in an uncomfortable way. I had to shift around a bit before I hit a sweet spot. The soupy air moved languidly beneath the strip of light that ran down the centre of the ceiling. I looked over at the creature, who had not moved.

"So, what now Mr. Bug?" I asked.

No response.

"I shouldn't be surprised," I commented. "This hasn't been a very chatty process. Also, you don't seem to have a mouth."

I went and looked at my plastic-encased self in the little mirror. Upon close examination I could see nearly invisible filaments running from one part of the plastic to another, with a particular jumble by my ears and my neck on one side. "Built-in telephone?" I wondered.

Unlike the golden guards, my current host could not be disturbed no matter what I did. I was free to walk about every part of the cell. I could even take the mirror off the wall and chuck it around. It didn't break.

Eventually I tickled the creature itself, which caused its eye to open briefly and its antennae to whirl about for a few seconds. Then it would go back to sleep. "Some company *you* are," I chided it darkly. Then I asked, "What're you in for?" and made myself laugh.

Later, while I was sitting on the cot again, a quiet tone sounded in my ear and then the bubble before my mouth and nose filled up partway with cool water, somehow exuded directly out of the surface of the plastic itself. Since I was very thirsty I tilted my head back and drank it. A second later the space filled with water again, so I drank more.

I went back to the mirror to take another look at the second skin and saw that two little translucent nodules had formed on either side of my nose. As I watched they changed colour and became more substantial. They budded from the plastic surface and dropped hollowly into the bottom of the breathing bubble: two little red pills.

"Is this dinner?" I asked Mr. Bug.

Nothing.

I knocked my head back and bounced the little pills into my mouth. They dissolved as I swallowed them. Then the tone sounded again and I was given more water to drink. I felt the need to urinate, quickly reached the conclusion that I had few options, and then peed into the translucent sac girdling my loins. It turned yellow briefly and then slowly returned to colourlessness, absorbed into the body of the plastic.

"I hope that isn't tomorrow's breakfast," I mumbled.

As if cued by my quip the light strip dimmed and then died. I barked my shins on the edge of the cot as I wandered back across the cell. I lay down, and this time sleep found me.

I defined the next *day* as the period of uncountable hours between when the light strip came back to life and when it again extinguished. During this time two more batches of pills were precipitated from the plastic over my mouth. One of the pills was yellow, one was blue, and two were red. They all tasted the same.

Another day like that one passed. I invented a fanciful diary entry about a man named Simon who magically acquired god-like powers and flew away through space, beyond the nets or cries of all. Then I deleted it.

After the lights came up on the fourth day since my audience with the Queen of Space, Mr. Bug opened his eye and began to stir. I swallowed a yellow pill and a blue pill and washed them down with a half-bubble of water. "Something nigh, Mr. Bug?" I asked.

An arc of electricity crawled up between two of his bunches of antennae and then snapped and disappeared. Mr. Bug jumped down from his shelf and hunkered on the floor, his eye blinking quickly.

The door slid open.

I stood up before the cot, watching the doorway expectantly. Even so I jumped a little when four more white creatures like Mr. Bug scurried across the threshold. They arranged themselves equidistantly around the room, with Mr. Bug scuttling over nearest to me. Five blinking brown eyes fixed on me, and except for their waving antennae the creatures froze.

A shuffling sounded from the corridor, and I looked up as a Pegasi entered the room, its grasshopper-like legs taking just two long strides to bring the tall being into view. Suddenly the proportions of the doorway and the corridors made sense. Its four double-jointed arms were folded in a neat array beneath the chin of its long, horse-like head with two watery blue eyes set in front. Lids blinked over the eyes twice in quick succession, moving horizontally. The convolution of membranes at its mouth waved slowly, exuding little puffs of white steam.

An androgynous voice spoke in my ear: *"Do not be afraid."*

"Okay," I agreed uncertainly, and then jumped again as a strand of rusty vapour jetted out of my plastic suit near my neck.

The Pegasi inhaled deeply, then its spongy mouth again began to work and excrete streams of differently coloured gas. Again I heard the voice in my ear, *"I am the Master Barrister for the Accused. It will be my privilege to represent your interests in the Panstellar Court."*

"Um, thank you," I said, and a ring of green mist chuffed out of my neck. "Can you tell me where I am? What world is this?" A complex mixture of differently coloured jets drifted out across the cell.

The Pegasi held my eyes without blinking. *"This is Pegasi Secundae."*

"With all due respect, why am I being tried by the Pegasi?"

"I do not understand your query – forgive me, I am not Solar," expressed the Master Barrister for the Accused, and then gestured with a set of two delicate-looking arms toward the door. *"The Co-counsellor will explain the situation further."*

"Greskin!" I exclaimed.

There was no mistaking my old Annapurnese friend, even with his head shaven and his nudity encased in a shining layer of intelligent plastic. He smiled broadly, his brown eyes twinkling. "Simon, Simon, Simon!" he laughed.

He manoeuvreed around one of the Pegasi's long, shaggy white legs and then stepped over two of the antennae-waving dog-sized bugs in order to reach me. We shook hands warmly and then he pulled me into a hug. "It's good to see a face, hear a voice," I gushed; "especially yours, Mr. Mile."

"Now don't you fret, Simon," said Greskin, taking a seat on the cot and tapping at his plate. He gestured to the Pegasi, who hovered patiently beside the door. "You've met our estimable Master Barrister," continued Greskin distractedly, still reading. "If you accept the offer I will serve as co-counsel."

"Of course I accept!"

He looked up from his plate. "Let's get you grounded a bit before we get down to the hard muffins, you know what I'm saying? You must have questions, cha."

"Number one," I said, holding up my index finger, "why am I being tried by the Pegasi?"

"You're not," answered Greskin quickly. "You're being tried by the Panstellar Court. The court is rotated between member states. It was on Callicrates until about a year ago. When I was a student it was on Hensphere. Now the court presides here on Pegasi Secundae, and if my hair doesn't grow back properly I'm going to sue somebody, cha," He touched his clean scalp through the shiny veneer of plastic. "Thumb-bummed Pegasi dillysuits are sensitive to keratin. If your fingertips don't feel stiff yet don't worry, they will – the dilly is retarding the growth of your nails with pressure."

I looked at my glossy fingertips, and flexed them experimentally. "Okay so far," I reported, then looked up. "Number two: what are those spider-looking things?"

Greskin chuckled. "They're the Master Barrister's *staff*," he explained. "The Pegasi don't use robots."

"Staff?" I echoed.

The Master Barrister shifted on his bent legs and twiddled together the appendages of his four arms. *"Yes of course,"* he breathed smokily. *"There ought to be another or two anothers for all this work, but I am embarrassed to admit you have caught me right in the middle of budding."* He made a half-turn and raised his torso, exposing a dwarfed, curled-up version of Mr. Bug being grown out of the flesh of his belly. *"It is a bother, naturally, but I suppose if the staff it replaces had not been so stupid-unfortunate as to run out under a chariot it would have been stupid-unfortunate enough to do something equally inopportune. I need my most immaculate staff for a task such as this one. Thus, I am taking all the right vitamins."*

"That's uncomfortable, is it?" I asked lightly, feeling a bit dizzy.

"It could be worse," communicated the Master Barrister. *"At least I am not sexual this season."*

Greskin laughed hollowly. "Lizards to lies, I've been saying that to myself for this past decade." He waved his hand dismissively. "What was I saying? Staff – cha. They're a simplified sub-section of the Pegasi genome, more like flakes of skin than kids. Mature Pegasi generate them as they need them, but it's considered uncouth in most circles to have more than three or four. Our estimable Master Barrister is excused from such taboos, of course – he's a very busy Pegasi."

"But what *are* they?" I asked again, confused.

"Vehicles of remote sense and action," supplied the Master Barrister in a coloured whorl. *"Our armless hands."*

"They're like external organs," clarified Greskin. "Redundant and expendible but capable of relaying whatever they see and smell back to their..." He trailed off and looked to the Master Barrister. "Parent –?"

"I prefer the translation 'estimable phenotypical centron'," claimed the Master Barrister.

"Rolls off the tongue, doesn't it?" chimed in Greskin, looking back at me. "Anything else tugging your navel?"

I licked my lips and looked from the human being to the Pegasi, the mass of lingering coloured gases disgorged from three directions slowly dissipating as it was sucked away into tiny ventilation pores on the ceiling. I swallowed. "What's going to happen to me?"

"Ah!" said Greskin brightly, and then his face slowly grew more sober. "Well." He tapped at his plate again. "You've been charged with seven hundred and twenty-three violations of the Panstellar Charter, and twenty-nine separate portfolios of crimes against Solarkind." He looked up from the plate and gazed at me steadily. "I'm thinking bail is out of the question, cha."

The Pegasi's spongy mouth quivered and emitted a series of varicoloured ringlets of fume. *"You slather my entrails across the parkland,"* came the voice in my ear.

"I'm sorry?"

The Master Barrister's long face looked from one of us to the other, large blue eyes blinking rapidly. *"Has misspeaking happened?"* came the question. *"The translator is frequently hilarious."*

Greskin shrugged sheepishly. "I think the estimable master was trying to say I made him laugh."

I chuckled drily. "It's a riot in here."

"Forgive me," said the Master Barrister. *"I am not Solar."*

Greskin cleared his throat and put his plate aside, resting it on Mr. Bug's shelf. "The arraignment is tomorrow morning, first sparkles. We'll have to review each of the charges and consider your plea, item by item. After you plead things should get a little cozier for you, cha. You'll be moved into a long-term cell with more...human amenities – breathable air, a toilet, you get the idea."

"Will I be able to see anyone?" I asked. "Have visitors, I mean?"

"No," puffed the Master Barrister.

"I'm working on it," maintained Greskin, giving me an encouraging nod. "I know there's a Zorannite monk who's burning to see you for one, and a brace of executives to boot." He picked up his plate again and rubbed his chin. "Now, as for the charges..." He looked up. "You should sit down," he advised. "This could take a while, cha. The first charge is six leaves long."

I dropped down on the cot. "Hit me," I said.

"Item one," orated Greskin Mile expressionlessly, "first degree violation of the Dzigai Clause part eight, section sixty-nine, sub-section two, on the interoperability of class two mimetic broadcast carriers across simultaneous informatic synchronisation events – comma – intrastellar."

"Um," I interrupted gently. "...You say there are seven hundred of these, Greskin?"

"More than."

I leaned back against the wall heavily. "Mercy."

"Shall I continue? Time leaks, dude."

I nodded morosely and gestured invitingly. The Master Barrister's steady eyes blinked three times in rapid succession, tracking my hand though the dissipating blooms of fog.

"Continue," I said, my word umber steam.

XLII.
SALUTATION BY MEAL

The pedestal upon which I stood rose.

I was lifted up through the floor of the Pegasi fumatory and then the pedestal clicked into place with a faint shudder. I was positioned in a well surrounded by dozens of white Pegasi and hundreds of their scuttling staff. The Pegasi scarcely seemed to take notice of me, though many of their staff pointed their brown, cow-like eyes in my direction. The air was thick with talk.

The language management device built in to the intelligent plastic skin I wore seemed confused by the dense whorls of intermingling babble, and offered only surreal poetic snippets of what it could suss out from the miasma. *"Frenzied locution,"* it said into my ear. *"Predisposition for aggravated your plumage has silkened wonderfully good daycleft my estimable numerous counts of a new shampoo."*

Greskin Mile slithered out of the crowd and stood beside me. A Pegasi who turned out to be the Master Barrister for the Accused bounced calmly into place on my other side. I was having some difficulty distinguishing one Pegasi from another, particularly as they seemed to wear no clothes and have no given names. Greskin explained that they recognized one another by scent, and that maps of their familial relationships involved model trees whose individual leaves exuded a distinct musk upon being tickled. Greskin added that business cards were even more tricky.

A light strobed near the front of the fumatory, and then a thick thunderhead of smoke roiled forward through the crowd.

"Clear the air!" spoke the translation; *"I will have silence!"*

Wide-bladed fans hanging from the ceiling began to turn, and in a moment the fog of conversation was whirled away. The revealed chamber was round, its ornate walls constructed of a substance that resembled wood but marked by unfamiliar patterns of grain and growth. Like all Pegasi rooms I had seen so far it was designed with an indifference to colour, resulting in a characteristic muddiness broken by gleams of metal. The dozen or so Pegasi retired into a ring around the perimeter, their staff clustering beneath their loins. In a strip above our heads was a ring-shaped gallery densely packed with observers – Pegasi and their staff, as well as hairless human beings, glossy in their plastic skins.

I looked down into the wet blue eyes of the Master Judge, who looked just like any other Pegasi. The Master Judge was neither taller or wider, nor decorated by special plumage or any contrived badge of office. At least a dozen staff clicked and blinked and scampered around the base of the dais upon which the Master Judge sat, legs folded and pointy knees settling on either side of a long, grey face. The Master Judge blinked twice, slowly.

A train of fumes began to chuff from the spongy mouth, my translator speaking up after a few seconds' interval: *"Hereby begins the arraignment of the Solar human being Terron Volmash, alias Nestor Simonithrat Fell, alias Hellig Apples, alias Simon, with regard to seven hundred and twenty-three violations of the Second Intragalactic Charter of the Panstellar Neighbourhood of Sentient Races, and twenty-nine activity networks with nodes intersecting the Solar Declaration of Living Dignity. The Accused is present."*

Smoke dappled from the Master Barrister on my right. *"It is so, Master Judge."*

"Are the officers of the court present?"

"Yes," affirmed the Master Barrister. Half a dozen other Pegasi made the same statement. Greskin Mile said the word and the neck of his plastic suit shot steam.

"Very well," expelled the Master Judge, shifting into what I can only assume was a more comfortable position, *"let the reading of the charges commence."*

The reading commenced.

It was very long.

When short pauses came the Master Barrister would either say "guilty" or "not-guilty," a subject over which Greskin and I had argued long into the night. "Why not just answer guilty across the board? Who I am to try to minimize what happened?" I had eventually asked, exasperated.

"You may decide to stand for Volmash, cha," Greskin had replied seriously, "but it is *not* up to you to let a thousand bad precedents be set by admitting malformed charges. This is the case of the millennium, Simon. What sticks on you will be applied to others for generations."

As the arraignment proceeded I looked around, the drone of translation unbroken in my ears. I tried to see if I could recognize any of the humans up in the gallery, but the haze and the distance rendered all figures nearly alike. Some of them held plates before their faces, scanning the view with informatic overlays invisible to me. I realized with a queasy lurch that the informatic networks were likely clogged with data concerning this event. I imagined that my face must be being broadcast to every living star.

I tried not to slouch.

After many long hours the assembly began to break up. Greskin patted me on the back. "You did well," he assured me. I smiled back uncertainly. I wasn't sure how to feel about being complimented as an obliging bag of televised meat. "I'll see you in a few minutes, cha."

The pedestal upon which I stood descended, and when the fumatory had disappeared above me two members of the Master Barrister's staff were there to escort back down the corridor to my cell. Someone was waiting for me there.

"Jeremiah!"

Before I had really thought about it I pulled the copper-skinned human executive into an embrace and clapped him upon the back. "Sir," he said. He wore no plastic suit and I found the effect disquieting – like a scuba diver under the sea come upon a man in a business suit, breathing without the benefit of any apparatus.

"It's good to see you," I said. My eye was caught by something fuzzy and red in the foreground. "You don't mind if I eat, do you? My pills are precipitating and I find it annoying to have them clattering around uneaten."

"I do not mind."

The pills dropped down and I knocked them back, then enjoyed a wee drink. "Wonderful accommodations they have here," I commented. "I imagine the tourists have to beat each other off to visit."

"You will presently be moved to a facility more appropriate to your metabolism," said Jeremiah.

"You should write their travel brochures," I told him darkly. "What I really want to know is whether or not I'll have to go through the entire trial with my bum showing."

"I do not have much time," he said quickly, ignoring me. "We may not be able to meet again."

I furrowed my brow. "Why?"

"Listen to me, Simon. There is something I have not told you."

I blinked. "What is it?"

Jeremiah's hesitation was interrupted as the Master Barrister for the Accused swept in through the door, the rest of his staff scurrying at his long, four-toed feet. Greskin Mile followed and did a double-take as he spotted Jeremiah. "You can't be here, lizards to lies!" he said.

"*Quite improper,*" agreed the Master Barrister. "*The Master Executive must be leaving immediately.*"

Jeremiah was already moving toward the door, and when I tried to follow him the Master Barrister extended one of his long legs and blocked my path. I caught Jeremiah's black gaze fleetingly as he disappeared into the corridor, and I spun on Greskin. "What's going on? Why can't I see him?" I cried, and then added, "He's my friend."

"Are you sure?" asked Greskin poignantly.

"*It is forbidden,*" trumpeted the Master Barrister densely. "*This dialogue is quite improper and it has already ceased. Do you understand, Co-counsel? Do you understand, Accused?*"

"I bloody do not!" I shouted.

"Easy Simon," said Greskin, touching my arm. "The Master Barrister is just on the sharp for bad protocol pies the prosecution can force feed us later. We best mind your executive friend alone. You know what I'm saying?"

"But why?"

"Because he is a material witness," explained Greskin, avoiding my eye.

"I don't understand –"

"*It is forbidden!*" repeated the Master Barrister, and then to reinforce the point reared up menacingly upon the full height of grasshopper-like legs, the heretofore spindly-looking arms at the chest extending with surprising length and speed to feint a breath away from our faces. The display was cross-cultural – the Master Barrister was pissed off. "*Quite improper!*"

Greskin and I flattened ourselves against the wall mutely.

The Master Barrister regained a measure of composure, legs folding and spine curving to draw the intimidating alien into the more familiar, compact form. The scene was over in a heartbeat, but in cringing before that bestial charge I had come to remember how Captain Gold explained to me that all globe-girdling sentient animals arose on a pinnacle of dominance. I had caught a glimpse of the predator in the Pegasi, and it was mean.

"Forgive me, Master Barrister," said Greskin.

"Forgive me," I said, too.

"*Let us proceed.*"

Greskin nodded. "Alright Simon. The arraignment went very well. What's going to happen now is you're going to be up-and-chucked to your permanent quarters. We have a few days before things get rolling, and the Master Barrister and I are going to spend that time working on your defense as we've discussed. For the time being you'll just sit tight and pretty and think happy thoughts. Got it?"

"What about visitors?"

Greskin looked stricken. "I'm still fighting the good fight, dude. We'll keep you apprised, sure as sandwiches."

We left the cell together and then parted ways in the corridor. I followed a brace of the Master Barrister's staff into a lift and then through another maze of halls. I had become so used to seeing no one else on these little excursions that I jumped and shouted in fright when we turned a corner and I found myself face to face with Abermund Blighton.

He had purple bags under his bloodshot eyes, glistening beneath the film of his intelligent plastic suit. "You!" he cackled, his voice muffled by the bubble over his mouth and nose. "What a *special* coincidence."

I backed up a pace. Two greyish staff were poised at Blighton's liver-spotted feet, their antennae crackling. My own staff stiffened to attention. "Blighton," I breathed hollowly.

"You haven't destroyed me!" he claimed, the tendons in his neck straining.

"Okay."

"*Okay?*" he sneered, shaking his head. "Is *that* the best you can *do*, you idiot? Fate stages us a scene of epic confrontation between a god and the bug who struck him down, and all you can give the ages is *okay?*"

I shrugged. "Are these staff your guards? Are you a prisoner here, too?"

"You have not destroyed me!" he shrieked, fists balled.

"Um, yes," I nodded. "You mentioned. Well, I'd best be off. It's nearly time for my red pills. Nice chatting."

"I'll murder you," he promised, and then froze in a very strange attitude with one arm raised menacingly and one knee partially bent. His eyes bugged out and his face flushed as if in great effort, but he moved no further.

I blinked. "Blighton?"

"Let me free, you horse-faced bastards!" he screamed, his face contorting but his body still rigid. The grey staff scurried around his feet, electrical discharges popping between their antennae.

I stepped forward and touched Blighton's arm: the plastic encasing it had become as hard as diamond. He grimaced at the sight of my touch, his mouth working but no sound coming out. I nodded. "Always a pleasure, Abe."

The Master Barrister's staff pulled on my leg for attention. They wanted to proceed down the hall. I followed them, stealing glances over my shoulder at the statue of Blighton. Just as he disappeared from view behind us I saw a shaggy grey Pegasi surrounded by grey staff approach him.

"I hope you don't try to pull that stiffening trick on me," I said to the white staff. Their brown eyes blinked inscrutably.

Golden robots drove me in a darkened car. The members of the Master Barrister's staff stayed behind. The ride was brief. After I disembarked the robots steered me into a shower under which the layer of plastic over my skin dissolved. The wires of the translator's speakers broke into tiny bits and swirled down the drain. My diary was undamaged. I stepped out of the cubicle feeling truly naked for the first time in days, and it was good.

At last I was deposited in a dimly-lit, spacious apartment. I felt soft grass beneath my toes. The golden robots entered behind me and silently took posts on either side of the door as it slid closed. There was a little washroom complete with a proper sink and toilet, a chair and desk with a dataplate on it, and an honest to goodness *bed* with sheets and covers and everything.

I sat down on the bed and exhaustion overcame me. I lacked the will to even dictate a diary entry. The wall above the headboard was black and reflective, and in it I caught a glimpse of my face. I looked tired, though I lacked the tortured aspect that had been written so deeply into Blighton's features. The surface was a bit dark for a mirror, but I suppose the Pegasi – for whom vision seemed to be a tertiary mode of perception at most – were doing the best they could to meet my strange Solar needs.

I lay back on the bed to sample its firmness; I awoke uncountable hours later.

My first thought was that the room had become very bright, and I wondered whether the lights had come on automatically sensing my conscious state or if I had been awakened when they illuminated. I blinked blearily at the little lamp on the night-stand, and saw that it was still only dimly lit. I turned around.

The sections of black wall I had taken for poor mirrors were, in fact, windows.

I could see the salmon-coloured sky, and it was crossed with clouds. My old friends, the clouds. They had never left me. They had been waiting behind the walls for the duration of my enclosure, patient for the moment when I could see them again and remember the consanguinity of all living skies. Even on Pegasi Secundae there are clouds.

I was filled with joy. I laughed out loud. I shook my head and sighed. I fell back on the bed and spent a few minutes just feeling good. The carpet of grass exuded a wet fragrance that made my lungs feel new.

My stomach rumbled. I crossed my eyes to see if my yellow and blue pills were ready yet, then remembered that I was now without the clinging second skin. I sat up groggily and blinked until I could focus on the golden robots standing by the door, their carapaces shining ruddily in a beam of sunlight. "I say," I called, "can either of you fellows tell me where I might get some food pills around here?"

"Sir," replied one of the golden robots, startling me; "breakfast will be served momentarily. Clothes and tea have been prepared."

"Clothes and tea?" I echoed.

I looked around, now able to take in the details of the apartment for first time. In one corner there was a semi-circle of countertop carrying a kettle, a cup, a bowl, a plate, and several packages. The kettle whistled, and the golden robot who had spoken to me poured the hot water into the cup and then took a teabag out of one of the packages. I watched him, hypnotized, partly unwilling to believe the tea could be for me.

My attention was caught then by the second golden robot, who picked up a neat fold of clothes from a nearby chair and offered it to me. It was a simple, one-piece garment of dull brown, but it was soft and opaque so I donned it with relish. "Thank you," I said.

The first robot handed me the cup of steaming tea. "And thank *you*," I said with special emphasis, sipping. I gasped at the aroma and rich flavor as much as the heat.

Everything is one shade better once you've had a hot cup of tea. Nurse Randa used to say so, and it's true.

I wandered back to the windows, and from my standing position I could now see the land. I don't know what I was expecting exactly, but what I saw shocked me more by its familiarity than its strangeness. There were trees, for instance. They weren't green or leafy, but their thick branches carried fans of long needles that swayed in the breeze, their stacked structure making obvious their thirst for light. These trees lined the streets down which ambled Pegasi and their staff, cars zooming back and forth in a neat grid far overhead that mirrored the layout of the roads. Pegasi architects were evidently fond of domes, for their pewter curves shone between the treetops as far as I could see.

In the distance I could see plumes of yellow and red smoke rising from a common spot, like a thousand Pegasi chanting. I wondered if it were some kind of a ceremonial gathering, or whether something had simply been spilled.

An insect landed on the window, and I regarded it. It looked like a miniature bird, the size of my thumb. It had no eyes. It licked the glass with its proboscis and then flew away.

A third golden robot brought me breakfast on a tray: buttered toast and hot beans, a bowl of bacterial culture with blueberries, and a tall glass of frosty juice. I ate it too quickly and developed a case of the belches. A few hours later I had mastered myself sufficiently to take lunch at a more reasonable pace. Dinner, however, I wolfed down again. I couldn't help myself. It was pretty good.

And so that was the first day.

On the second day I was able to be more critical. The chicken at lunch was a little dry, and the side-dish at supper was under-spiced. Never the less, it beat little red pills hands down.

The golden robots would not engage me in idle conversation. And, unlike Mr. Bug, they could not be moved to wave any antennae around if I tickled them. I passed most of the hours leaning against the windows, watching the shadows change as the world progressed. Three times each day the Pegasi rushed into the streets and traffic thickened. At mealtimes the city outside seemed virtually deserted. The sunset turned the sky green and brought out swarms of bird-like insects with micro-plumage that glistened in the twilight.

The glass was impervious to sound, so I never heard a noise. The world beyond the windows was like a projection, and if I stared at the vista too long I could convince myself it was tiny – that I could reach through the glass and pluck the cars from the sky between my fingers.

In the afternoon of the third day Greskin stopped by. He was wearing a dapper white suit, and couldn't stop touching his stubbly pate with his hand. "Hot dollops it feels great to be out of that plastic, cha!" he crooned. "And the good news doesn't stop here, no."

"No?"

"No and no and no. One of three: they're doing up the courtroom with oxygen-nitrogen tents so we won't have to be suited up for the whole thingamaroo. It's a crazy rig they've got going. You'll see. Which brings us to two of three: the ball gets rolling tomorrow – no more sitting on your duff watching traffic go by. And..." Greskin grinned. "Three of three: you're set for guests."

"Guests? When?"

"In about an hour. First thing tomorrow morning you'll come by the Master Barrister's office, and then we'll all drive to the courthouse together. Sounds fine, cha?"

"Sounds fine," I agreed. "Um, about these quarters..."

"Are they satisfactory, my friend?"

"Of course they're satisfactory. It's all a bit luxurious, really. Is this what I deserve? What kind of prison is this?"

Greskin chuckled. "It's a prison for a man who may be innocent. Had that never occurred to you?"

I smiled ruefully. "No."

After he had left again I went back to looking out the window and watched a group of obviously juvenile Pegasi being herded by their parents' staff, jostling and clambering over one another, a trail of primally hued smokelets diffusing in their wake.

I spun around at the sound of the door and saw a strange human executive standing there, his skin and robes dappled in alternating stripes of grey and blue. His black eyes fixed on mine.

"Hello," I said. "My name is Simon."

"I know," said the human executive. "My name is Piciatus."

"Piciatus –?" I stammered. *"Pish?"*

And then the blue-grey human executive did something I had never seen any of their kind do, even briefly. He grinned. "Ta-dah!"

I ran forward and hugged him, then pushed him away to take a look at him: his new face was so strange, and yet somehow familiar. I could not trace what lines connected it to the shape of the freckled child I had known, but there was undeniably something there. His grey cheeks were patterned with blue specks, and they pushed expressively at the bottom of his dark eyes as he smiled. "My," I said faintly, "...how you've changed."

"I grew up," said Pish.

"Well, yes. I suppose you did. Um, congratulations."

"Thank you."

"How does it feel?"

"Pretty weird."

"You have stripes."

"Yeah," he said, holding out his blue forearm and examining the grey spots there. "Nobody figured on it. It's an artifact from the genetic recombination."

"It's quite fetching."

"Thanks."

I chewed my lip awkwardly. "Do you...do you remember – how it was?"

"Oh yes," he replied. "And thank you for that, too. Thank you for everything, Simon."

"What do you mean?"

He looked at me tenderly. "What else could I mean? You were my dad."

I gulped. "You had a dad."

"I had two," he corrected gently.

What a sweet kid. I wiped my eyes and invited him into the apartment. He turned around to look expectantly at the door. I followed his gaze. "Hi Vera," I said.

"I brought you a present," said the girl who had been Glory, stepping through the door and letting it slide closed behind her. Her brown hair was no longer bound in cables of beaded braiding, but rather brushed out straight and very long. Her clothes were looser and less revealing, but she still wore her high black boots.

"A present?" I asked dumbly.

She smiled and handed me a flat box. Inside was a red silk robe. "Wow," I said, slipping it over my shoulders and belting the sash. "It's wonderful!"

"We saw your ass on television," explained Vera. "Figured you could use a spot more dignity."

Vera hugged me and kissed me on the cheek. "How are you?" she whispered.

"Oh, about the same," I whispered back. "You?"

"Don't worry about me, baby," she replied. "I'm gonna live forever."

We each pulled up a chair and sat down to chat. Vera was telling me about how bizarre life was in Patch Seventy-Two on Callicrates, and about how she had almost had to shave her head to visit me until I had been reassigned to the Solar pavilion. "Lucky we can gate in air here," she said, "because there was no way Jeremiah was going to talk me into one of those coital Pegasi skin-suits."

The golden robots interrupted with my lunch. "Oh, I'm sorry —" I apologized.

"No, please," insisted Pish. "Eat."

"It does tend to get cold..."

"*Eat*," grunted Vera. "We don't care. Honestly."

I pulled the tray closer to me on the desk and picked up my cutlery. "The food here is really not so bad," I told Pish, cutting into a roll of some kind of pasta topped with white curdles of cheese. I stuck a piece with my fork and offered it up. "Would you like to try some?"

"I don't eat anymore, actually," said Pish sadly.

"Oh," I said consolingly. "Vera?"

"No thanks, Simon."

I shrugged and popped the morsel into my mouth, chewing thoughtfully. "I mean, I guess in contrast to food pills...anything...would...be..." I trailed off, swallowing. I frowned and cut another piece of the pasta roll. I tasted it. "Mother of love..." I commented, looking up to see Pish and Vera watching me closely.

Pish giggled.

I gasped. "Duncan is here!"

We all looked over to the door as it slid open, revealing Duncan's bulky form. He was dressed in a Zorannite cassock, his head shaven. His sparkling eyes shone beneath his bushy brows, the expression of his mouth lost in the brambles of his dark beard. "We'll visit you again," Pish assured me, standing up with Vera. They both squeezed past Duncan with a nod, who then stepped heavily into the apartment and let the door slide closed behind him.

I stood up and then hovered in place, uncertain how to react.

"Enjoy the cannoli?" he rumbled softly.

"Words can't describe."

"You did right by Pish."

"I left him wounded on Metra."

"I know all about what you've done."

"Have you come to spit in my eye?" I asked. "Because I don't know what I mean to you, but it would break my heart."

"You're my son," he said simply. "If I stood by you as a tyrant what makes you think I wouldn't stand by you now?"

"You stood by me then?"

"I was steadfast in my faith in you then, despite everything," he clarified. "Though I didn't know your name I knew there was a Simon inside of you. I never gave up hope for your redemption, Terron."

My breath caught in my throat. His use of the name stabbed at me, and called up something vague and grim but familiar from the deeper pools of my mind. Some small part of me that might have remained forever sceptical gave up the ghost, and I thought to myself, *Mother of love – it really is true, isn't it?*

"I remembered what you told me," I said. "I'm taking responsibility for the past."

"More than may be your due," said Duncan.

I sighed, holding his green eyes with my brown ones. "*Somebody* has to be Volmash," I said. "The title is assumed. It always was. For good or for ill."

Duncan said nothing for a moment, nor did he blink. At long last he nodded slowly and sighed. "Then my crime was worth everything. I helped you and Aro escape Kamari...I never knew you would try to escape your *self*."

"Ever one for dramatic gestures, me."

Duncan smiled. "That can't be denied."

"Thank you for coming to see me."

"How could I not?"

"I didn't know you were free to. When Pish and I saw you taken by Militia Samundra we didn't know what to think."

Duncan scratched at his beard absently. "Yes. Delightful hosts they were, the bastards. Thought they could squeeze me to find out what I knew about the Nightmare Cannon."

"Squeeze you?"

"Never you mind," he said, waving a big hand dismissively. "Executives came for me before too long. It's all done now and best forgotten. Finish your cannoli – it's getting cold."

"I'm not hungry."

"You should eat. And then sleep. Tomorrow's going to be a big day."

I asked, "You'll come again?"

"Pish and Vera and I are staying here at the Solar pavilion. We'll visit as often as they'll let us."

On his way out he paused to shake my hand firmly and lingeringly while looking into my eyes. "I can't believe I had you under my own roof and I didn't even know," he said wonderingly. "I can't believe I have you back, son."

"I will do you proud," I promised.

"Don't," he replied. "I can't stand to lose you again."

I bowed my head. The door slid shut. I sat down before the delicious pasta but forgot to eat any more, dazed with wheels of thought spinning and grinding, clashing and flashing across my mind. I crossed my legs and rebelted my red silk robe, playing my fingers across the hem.

Hours after the sun had set I continued to stare at the glass.

XLIII.
KAMARI FOREVER

The office Greskin Mile shared with the Master Barrister for the Accused was divided in two by a pane of glass. The air in Greskin's partition was clear, while that in the Master Barrister's partition was hazy and faintly yellow. Beyond this there was no differentiation: on both sides of the glass were mountainous stacks of dataplates in vaguely furniture-like mounds, screens covered in dense text, and discarded disposable cups and bowls strewn about the floor.

"I know, I know," said Greskin as we walked in, "it looks like a tornado blew through here, cha."

"What's a tornado?"

The Master Barrister put down four plates and stepped over three scuttling staff. *"Good daycleft, Accused,"* came the translation through unseen speakers as a blossom of Pegasi breath splashed against the glass and diffused.

"Hello," I said with a congenial smile.

The Master Barrister bowed and then returned to work. Greskin took my arm and led me over to what turned out to be a chair after he pushed a slurry of transparent dataplates aside. He swept his hands down the front of his white suit with a frown. "How do I look?"

"I'm sorry?"

"Faeces," he grunted, and then tapped at one of the screens on the wall until it turned into a mirror. "Faeces!" He pulled on the bag under one eye and regarded himself critically. "Lizards to lies, I look like a zombie! You know the Mouth of Fetch is going to have a field day with this, cha."

"The mouth of what?"

"A comedian. Nevermind. How are you? All set? Do you want to have a boo in the mirror, dude?"

I agreed in order to be friendly, stood up and shambled over. I noted that my skin was darker than it used to look in the hospital, which I chalked up to spending more time outside. The dozens of little scrapes and cuts on my face had healed up nicely, with only the occasional faint white line yet to fade away. I seemed to have roughly equal amounts of short stubble on my chin as on my head, and it amused me for a moment to imagine that my head could be inverted without seriously affecting my hairstyle. I saw lines at the corners of my eyes that were new. The furrows in my brow had sprouted tributaries.

"Well," I evaluated, "...I still look like the me that I've been looking like as long as I've been me. Um. These last few months."

I retied my red robe. Greskin looked over my shoulder. "This is going to play well."

"Surely the trial is not decided on the basis of appearance..."

"No," he admitted, "but I have to know how to position you in my tell-all book. Myself I'm sympathetic to you, and I'd love to be able to sell that angle when all is said and done. You know what I'm talking about? I'm being frank with you because we're pals. If we win I'll be rich, but even if we lose I'll be famous – and I'll have to squeeze *that* for something, cha."

I shuddered at his use of *squeeze*, thinking of Duncan. "Of course," I said.

The car Greskin and I rode in had clear windows and I watched the Pegasi city pass beneath us with fascination. Some structures looked distinctly human, which Greskin explained was because of the heavy human presence on Pegasi Secundae, a world Solar engineers had crafted for their newly met neighbours. The courthouse was typically Pegasi, however: a frozen froth of great metal bubbles, the face of each dome gleaming with a distinctly different lustre in the ruddy morning sun. Gathered out front was a roiling crowd of Pegasi, staff, robots, and plastic-coated human beings.

"What's with all the hullabaloo?" I asked.

Greskin chuckled. "You, dude."

The Master Barrister's car circled down first, room made beneath it by a cordon of staff with crackling antennae. The Master Barrister emerged and pushed into the milieu, his staff breaking a wave before him. Where the wave crested it seemed to me that people were crawling right over top of one another, like ants. Many on the periphery bore animated placards or held glowing banners between them. I caught sight of one which read DEATH TO THE PEACE KILLER in bold red letters.

Our car descended. The chants of the human beings reached my ears, a liquid slosh of overlapping shouting.

The mob overwhelmed the ring of Pegasi staff in a flash and enveloped the car, which bounced and swayed under their jostling, knocking hard as one corner dipped low enough to hit the street. Shouting faces stared in at me from every window, slapping the glass, spitting, swearing. "Mother of love!" I cried.

"Faeces," said Greskin.

A skinny, wide-eyed woman fought her way forward to press her small, plastic-coated breasts flat against the glass. *"Marry me, Terron!"* she shrieked just before she was roughly pushed aside by a shaven little person with gnashing yellow teeth. The little person struck the glass with a fist and a tiny crack appeared.

"Faeces!" said Greskin again.

"Sir," said the golden robot at the controls, pointing through the windscreen. People were falling away, clapping their hands over their coated ears. "I am broadcasting a dispersal signal now."

"Mustard!" screeched Greskin, tearing the telephone nub off of his own neck angrily. He rubbed his ears and winced. "A speck of warning next time, robot, or I'll see you end up as a fender."

"Sir, my apologies."

Outside the car a long, transparent tube was being led out from the courthouse by a flotilla of staff supervised by six golden robots. It was connected to the car and Greskin opened the door. Accompanied by two golden robots of our own we walked through the tube into the building, the yammering multitudes now held at bay by reinforced squadrons of staff, Pegasi and robots.

A group by the door was chanting, *"Kamari Forever! Kamari Forever! Kamari Forever!"*

The courtroom was grand. Black pillars supported three levels of galleries with a broad aisle running down their middle into the well. The well itself held two transparent cubical tanks connected by clear tubing. At the front of the well was a tall, three-part podium with compartments now closed behind wood-like panels. At the right of the podium was a booth connected by a battery of cabling to the wall behind. The left wall was a screen or dataplate, currently displaying which seats in the galleries were reserved in several dozen scripts. Along the right wall ran another closed gallery. The ceiling was a giant mirror, and so was the floor.

The tank on the left side of the well featured two chairs and a table which stuck through the transparent side and extended to a distinctly Pegasi chair into which the Master Barrister for the Accused had folded. He nodded respectfully to me and I to him as I took my human-proportioned seat inside the cube and rested my hands on the smooth table. Greskin unleashed a pile of plates and began tabbing through their contents distractedly. I lifted my hands to make room. "Thanks," he mumbled, and then pulled on the table until it extended a little further into the cube.

A moment later it retracted again. Greskin looked over, his eyes narrowed in annoyance. "To the Master Barrister," he said into the air: "I need more table." He tugged the tabletop over a handspan.

The Master Barrister pooted out a string of coloured clouds and the translation echoed inside our little tank: *"Co-counsel, you are disrupting my information array."* The tabletop jerked back.

Greskin growled but returned to his notes. I turned around. The galleries were filling up – human beings, human executives, little people and Pegasi. Their babble fell away as three tones sounded and a wall of white steam billowed up at the front of the courtroom.

When the air cleared a golden robot stood in the well just below the wide podium. As the robot spoke Pegasi fumes streamed from its neck, and at the same time I could hear its muffled voice vibrating through the air and hear it crisply broadcast through the language management system. The golden robot was also gesturing a constant sequence of intricate signs as it announced the commencement of the proceedings, asked us to rise, and then introduced three judges:

The Superior Master Judge of Pegasi Secundae was a Pegasi being, mottled white and grey, with curiously long eyelashes and staff whose legs seemed extra long and knobbly. The Superior Master Judge folded into the centre bench of the podium, revealed as the panel covering it withdrew downward. Watery blue eyes surveyed the courtroom, horizontal lashes swiping over them languorously;

The Supreme Justice of Callicrates was a human being with fawn-coloured skin and a pate of stubble obviously recovering from a recent shaving. She was very old and she looked as if she were made of finely crinkled paper. She wore a long black gown and had intricate sepia tattooing along the backs of her hands;

And, the Social Extension of Hennisphere was a blue orb with a camera lens on the end of a flexible robotic arm sticking out the top of it. It rested on a bed of thick cabling which snaked away behind it, presumably to facilitate the constant run of informatic canisters moving into and out of a gate system dedicated to communicating with the Great Hennisplasm. (Greskin explained to me that the filament of Hennish life contained at the heart of the blue orb was fairly useless without nearly constant feedback from the hive mind back home.)

The closed gallery to the right opened next, presenting sixteen creatures: eight Pegasi, five human beings, one little person, and two human executives. The jury was half Pegasi, half Solar – regular folks all, demigods and apes and fume-speaking aliens alike.

Several of the court clerks appeared to be Rouleighs, like those I had met aboard Castle Misne. They wore little round dataplates in front of each eye, and seemed to be speaking a primitive dialect of Pegasi through the use of pipes.

I looked over to the tank of the prosecution, its sliding table now shared by a black robed human being and a human executive on the inside and a bright white Pegasi on the outside. "To Simon: that's Yock F. Planner," said Greskin. "He's a devil in the courtroom. Taught me a thing or two at school, cha. And the executive is named Fortune. I don't know anything else about her."

"What about –" I started to say, but Greskin put his hand over my mouth. Loud echoes of my voice died away. Everyone in the courtroom turned to look at our tank, the smoke of Pegasi translation of my utterance still dissipating from nozzles at the vertices.

"To Simon: you have to specify who you're talking to," whispering Greskin urgently. "You have to say *to whoever* or the language manager defaults to public."

"Ah," I said, again jumping as my voice was broadcast. "Oh faeces!" I said next, and the courtroom exploded into laughter. Greskin closed his eyes and rubbed his temples. The Master Barrister shook his head.

"*Order in the court!*" commanded the Pegasi judge, banging a little hammer which emitted rings of white steam.

"I'm sorry."

"*Order!*"

Greskin jumped to his feet and walked to the front of the tank. "Our apologies, your honors. My client is unfamiliar with our protocols and did not mean to speak out of turn. He now understands how to proceed."

The human judge frowned. "Your briefing was obviously inadequate, Mr. Mile. See that you make no similar omissions again."

"Yes, your honor."

"*Let us have the opening statements,*" expressed the Pegasi judge.

The Pegasi counterpart of the Master Barrister for the Accused rose from its stool and walked to the centre of the well, its four little arms clutched behind its back. After an interval of slow, bouncy pacing fumes began to uncoil from the spongy mouth, and a moment later the sexless voice of the translation filled our tank:

"*Membership in our confederation is predicated on a guarantee of security from hostile action from neighbouring members. This is the service provided by those who maintain our stellar highways: a promise to close the way in case of barbarism. When the unspeakable happened, when a clear hegemony extended its reach to the worlds of a foreign star, we voted our meta-governors new powers to cope with the crisis. And when our navies went out to help our neighbours at Cassiopeia, they were savaged by a terrible weapon. Worse than that, every Solar being who was watching the broadcast was savaged along with them.*

"*That hegemony was Kamari's. That weapon was the Nightmare Cannon. And the Solar being responsible for its application was Terron Volmash, the accused.*"

Things went on in this vein for quite some time. Yock F. Planner, the human co-counsel, stood up to summarize a timeline of the naval incursion into Cassiopeia and the subsequent invasion of Kamari, rattling off startling metrics about the number of troops and materiel involved in the whole enterprise. Next came statistics about the aftermath of the Horror in terms both psychiatric and economic. "Nine point one quadrillion adjusted hours," he concluded heavily. "Think about that ladies, gentlemen and inferior masters – think about nine point one *quadrillion* hours from the galactic coffers. All to stop one man. And he sits before you today."

When that little floorshow was concluded the Master Barrister for the Accused rose and made a few points about the heavy-handed application of certain laws, and the cloudiness it would lend to future interpretations. The remarks were very brief.

Then Greskin stood up. He cleared his throat.

"Honored judges, members of the jury," he pronounced carefully, "please direct your attention to the court's screen." He pointed to the left.

The screen illuminated with a holographic projection of the man I had seen rendered as a statue beneath Thallos: the long face of Terron Volmash, his expression grave. He wore a red cape pinned at one shoulder by the bronze medallion. His auburn hair was wavy, his forehead high. Green eyes shone out from the screen and commanded attention. He opened his holographic mouth and spoke with a voice not entirely unlike my own:

"*People of the galaxy. My friends, my neighbors, my kin. Life, by definition, resists death. In nature mortal threats are met with mortal action. This is a testament to the tenacity of life, and its will to grow where the wild leads it.*

"*I have lived my life at the heart of one of Solar life's most precious blossoms. I have had the privilege of living the Kamari Way, and knowing her art and her craft and her love. This is history. This is a golden age. I am blessed to have been here, and would not trade even one day for a reign in Babylon or Athens, Rome or London, Texamerica or Mars.*

"*But we have been threatened. We who know only peace are accused of aggression. The citizens at Cassiopeia are to be denied the right to choose a Kamari life. Their destinies are steered for them by the tyranny of Epsilon Eridani and her grand machines of war.*

"*See now how we are stung. See now how we sting back, for we are alive and free and proud.*

"*Kamari forever.*"

The screen went dark. The courtroom was filled with muttering, silenced as Greskin Mile stepped forward again, his thumbs hooked in the belt of his white suit. "That was Terron Volmash," he declared flatly, and then slowly strolled around to loiter behind my chair. He put his hands on my shoulders and gave them a gentle squeeze. "This," he announced crisply, "is not."

The courtroom burst into a fog of noise and fume. The human and Pegasi judges banged their gavels for order. The Hennish electronic eye on a stalk looked around quickly with a series of jerky movements. Greskin waited patiently, hands now clasped behind his back. When the din settled he wandered unhurriedly back to the front of the tank.

"The defense intends to demonstrate that the accused is a distinct personality, wholly divorced from the will and mind of Terron Volmash. Say 'hello.' His name is Simon.

"Do we prosecute the son for the crimes of the father? We do not. Do we prosecute the twin for the crimes of his brother? *We do not.* Do we prosecute the clone for the crimes of her source? We. Do. Not.

"Nor can we in conscience prosecute Simon of Space for the crimes of Terron Volmash, no matter how desperately we crave to find a neck to hang for our sorrow. Terron Volmash has escaped justice. That is an unpleasant fact, but it is a *fact*. We cannot take out our frustrations on this man. Justice of the mob may demand a scapegoat, but the justice of reasoned beings calls for a higher standard.

"Honored judges, members of the jury: I call on you to uphold that standard. Thank you."

And that was that. Greskin sat down and the day's festivities seemed to be over. The galleries started to break up. I looked around. "Is that it, then?"

"Cha."

Amid a flurry of shouts and questions from the newsfeeders we were manuverd back down the transparent tunnel and reboarded in the car, this time separated from the hooting hordes by a fence guarded at intervals by robots and staff. Greskin pulled the door closed. The umbilicus was detached with a series of a snaps. We ascended, and in a blink the courthouse shrank from a monumental temple of my condemnation to a toy-like bauble I could occult with my thumb. A golden robot piloted us over the city and back to the Solar Pavilion. "What happens tomorrow?" I asked Greskin.

"Prosecution witnesses," he said. "Sleep like sheep so you don't yawn."

I nodded and boarded the lift. When it opened I walked briskly down the corridor and entered my apartment, my robot guards taking their posts on either side of the door and then freezing in place.

I had a visitor.

"Hello," I said.

"Mr. Volmash," said the thin man in a simple grey suit, bowing slightly.

"My name is Simon," I said uneasily.

"My name is Silas Chung." He held out a slender, pale hand. I shook it briefly. "I represent the Movement for the Equivalency."

That got my attention. "What do you want?" I asked, narrowing my eyes.

"Can we sit down?"

I hesitated. "Okay."

Silas Chung sat down in the chair nearest him and I pulled up another, crossing my legs and folding my arms across my chest. "To be candid I've been warned about you people," I told him.

"By whom?" sniffed Silas with a dismissive wave. "Executives? Royals? Some other paranoid servant of galactic power?"

"Maybe."

"Keep your own council," advised Silas Chung. "I have nothing to prove to you."

"Why are you here? Why wasn't I consulted or even informed?"

"My ally is the equivalent mathematic. I can walk through walls." He shrugged. "I came to chat with you, Mr. Volmash."

"I told you, my name is Simon. I can call security."

"No. You can't. May we chat?"

"What about?" I snarled.

"Consider, for example, the staff of the Pegasi beings," he said airly, crossing his legs and smiling in a social way.

"What about them?"

"They're remarkable."

"I concede the point. Much in the world is remarkable."

Silas smirked. "I concede the point. Have you wondered how it happened? Have you noticed how different they are?"

"What do you mean?"

"For one thing, consider the gross structure of the bodies. The Pegasi are bilaterally symmetrical while their staff are radially symmetrical. Fundamentally quite different. The staff are not dwarf children or some other mutation of a germ-line product. They're something altogether different. Have you wondered how that came about?"

"How did it come about?" I grunted, impatient with his pompous tease.

"It evolved out a parasitic relationship."

"That seems reasonable."

"Can you guess which one was the parasite, and which the host?"

I blinked. "I don't follow you."

"The Pegasi were the parasite."

"What's the point of this lesson?" I asked irritably and then paused, furrowing my brow. "The Pegasi were the parasite?"

"Oh, yes," said Silas, grinning warmly. "They've been co-evolving for fourteen million years, of course, so it's academic to differentiate their life-cycles at this point...not entirely unlike the mitochondria in your own cells. But the ancestors of modern staff were once a sentient race in their own right, complete with paleolithic technology – combustion and religion, crystal-flake tools and effluvian language."

I swallowed, watching Silas' intense brown eyes. "What happened?"

"An infestation by a primitive animal, a reproductive hijacker, an opportunistic beast: the ancestors of the Pegasi, who adapted on the shoulders of the staff and used their stability as a platform for their own evolution. After a few million years the masters were reduced to insensible slaves, and bugs had become the new people."

"You should host nature documentaries," I suggested.

"I do," said Silas. "I manufacture learning materials for our cause, so that these kinds of relationships in nature can be better understood. It helps our disciples clarify the present, and understand the threat against our race."

He was watching me carefully. I held my expression in check, giving away nothing. "The threat from whom?"

"The human executives," said Silas Chung seriously. "Our ambitious parasites."

I smiled tightly and stood up. "Listen, thanks for stopping by...er, Mr. Chung. It's been a full day and I don't feel particularly like chatting about politics right now."

Silas did not stir. "This isn't politics. This is destiny. You know they keep us down. You know civilization wants to thrive free and form a union across the stars, but they prune it. Why?"

"They believe the Great Melange will be to our long term benefit."

"*They believe*," repeated Silas significantly, his brows arched. "Do you know what *I* believe, Simon? I believe in civilization being free to take whatever shape *its own denizens* believe in."

"People's beliefs are out of scale with the galaxy," I parroted.

"People's beliefs are all we have," he countered. "And while they may be individually short sighted they are cumulatively wise. But we cannot just accumulate numbers, we must also accumulate time. *This* is what the executive perspective cannot fathom – they infinitely fine-tune the systems of the worlds to keep them in balance, poised precisely on the border between order and chaos."

I found myself drawn involuntarily back into his lesson, putting my hands on the back of my chair and leaning. "What's wrong with that?"

"Easy," replied Silas; "not enough order, not enough chaos. To understand a system in time is to see that *oscillations* centred on an optimal path are more valuable than the optimal path itself. Dynamism is more important than efficiency. The extremes can be ignored when the common motion is toward new fitness. This is a kind of vitality the executives cannot know, because they were not born wild."

I shrank at that, recalling Jeremiah's own lament that his kind were born too rational. "What of these oscillations? You use the model to excuse genocide?"

"Civilization must be annealed by war and peace, by starvation and excess, the way metal is annealed by heat and cold to make it less brittle. If we are restrained by the executives we will become weak. Think about it. It is obvious."

Thinking about it made me uncomfortable. "You colluded with Kamari," I accused.

"Yes," admitted Silas easily, crossing his legs the other way. "When the Neighbourhood militarized against Kamari we knew you would need weapons they could not fathom."

"Then you endorse the Horror?"

Silas shrugged. "The Horror was horrible. There's no denying it. That kind of destructiveness represents one extreme of the oscillation. Freedom is worth the tragedy. And the tragedy is small, in galactic terms. We are spread too far to extinguish Solarkind. Even if you had destroyed a whole star, what's one among forty? An epic lesson for the rest of us, that's what." He smiled. "It wouldn't be the end of the world."

"Your attitude appalls me."

"Curious, considering the source."

"I do not have the mind of Volmash."

"You should. He was a better man than you. He would not consent to be the puppet of parasites. He knew Social Annealing would make us flexible and strong, and the Equivalency would make us the masters of our destiny."

"Why? Because we wish it? Or because it is best?"

"We wish to determine what is best for ourselves."

I sneered with bitterness and barked, *"Why?"*

"It is a matter of human dignity!"

I nodded. "Pride, then. I understand you now. Have you come to recruit me? To be frank I find your opening manoeuvres repulsive."

"I'm here to find out who you are. If you're at all Terron Volmash, I'm to rescue you."

"To *rescue me*? How?"

Now it was his turn to smile tightly. "We have our ways. You have many supporters who would work hard to make a life for you, out of respect for the blow you have struck against the oppression. Supporters more trustworthy than Aro Frellis or Abermund Blighton."

"You would rescue Terron Volmash, despite the blood on these hands?"

"Everything worth doing involves a little blood. That's what wild life knows that manufactured life cannot."

I walked quietly across the apartment and stood by the door, which slid open. "I don't want to waste any more of your time, Mr. Chung," I declared flatly. "Good afternoon."

After a brief hesitation he rose and walked over to me. "The Equivalency could be your salvation. We have more allies than they know. The Rouleighs are with us, and through them the Pegasi. The Galactic Union is inevitable, and we will be there to arm it. When our math is ready the first to feel our wrath will be the executives and their pawns."

"Hush. I think the robots can hear you."

Silas Chung chuckled mirthlessly. "No. They can't."

He breezed past me and started down the corridor. I looked at my golden guards. Their heads were not inclined toward me. I snapped my fingers before their eyes. No response. Experimentally I stepped out into the corridor. Nothing happened. I took another step and the door slid closed, sealing the golden robots inside.

"Hey," I called.

Chung did not look back. He walked swiftly into the lift and disappeared with a hiss of air. A moment later the door of my apartment slid open again and the robots grabbed my arms from either side. They escorted me back inside wordlessly. The door slid closed again.

Silas Chung's equivalent magic had faded and the golden robots were back on watch.

I had dinner with Pish, Vera and Duncan. We talked about nothing of consequence. If I tried hard I could almost imagine we were a family, eating together in our home on some planet, our cares as large as our bills and small as our yard.

After Vera and Pish left Duncan opened a Renetian desert wine. It was excellent. I told him about the mysterious representative from the Movement for the Equivalency. Duncan nodded somberly. "I don't know what to believe anymore," I told him.

"Believe this," he said; "anyone who tells you what's good is simple is meaning to exploit your faith for something. I have no doubt the Equivalency's plans for you aren't limited to a subsidized retirement. You're too valuable a symbol for those sympathetic to their cause."

"What's good isn't simple?"

"By fire, no," declared Duncan firmly. "What's good is the murkiest thing you'll ever try to know. If Jeremiah thought he had a grip on it the executives would show us how to live. If the Queen of Space knew she'd interfere in any world before it could fall into barbarism. No, sir. It's the people who tell you the truth is obvious that you must be most afraid of – because what makes sense to a man isn't what makes sense to the universe."

"That's what Jeremiah says."

Duncan emptied his glass. "Jeremiah is wise."

XLIV.
THE TRIAL

I am starting to feel quite at home here, despite the daily march of witnesses the prosecution calls to describe me in the worst possible terms. Did you know Boss Preen is a law-abiding Samundran importer-exporter whose employees I butchered without provocation? Me neither. But I didn't lose too much sleep over it – that night Duncan made steak.

The worst came first: the widows and widowers, the tortured and barely sane, the stunned soldiers and sickened journalists. Almost all of them were moved to strong emotion by their own testimony or the prosecution's deft stoking. Several times the procedures came to a halt while the witness regained themselves, wiping at their eyes and gulping or sniffling.

Master Barrister for the Prosecution: "Please describe in your own smells the events following the transmission."

Witness: "Agony. We lived in agony. I looked at the lieutenant and she looked at me and we both understood how much we just wanted to die. She kissed my hands while I cut her throat, and then there was nobody left to do me. I tried to do it myself. I...tried to make it stop. But...I couldn't...do anything. It was agony."

Our own Pegasi litigator was on most points content to leave the cross-examination to Greskin, who would pace the breadth of our oxygen-nitrogen tent with his thumbs hooked into his belt for a spell before asking anything. At last he'd look up, and start speaking in a lazy, friendly tone.

Greskin Mile: "I have a question for you, midshipman."

Witness: "Sir."

Greskin Mile: "Do you recognize Terron Volmash here in the courtroom today?"

Witness: "Actually sir, until you spoke just now I thought *you* were Terron Volmash."

Greskin Mile: "I have no further questions."

It was a sad surprise to hear that Corinthia Tag had passed away, which was revealed as she failed to appear for her third summons. I hoped she did not hate me as she passed. But I was delighted to see Dr. Pent from the Samundra General Hospital in the witness box, sitting in a bath of the corrosive soup we Solar apes call air. I waved to him but he didn't respond, his eyes locked on the Master Barrister for the Prosecution as he crossed the well toward him. After his identity and occupation were affirmed the good doctor was invited to tell his tale.

Witness: "The director told us in no uncertain terms that we were to co-operate with Fellcorp fully. *Fully.* It was understood that Fellcorp was blessed by the Citadel of the Recovery, and in a post-Horror world nobody runs against the grain of the Citadel. Not if you want to keep your funding. So when they told me the security of the galaxy depended on flushing this man's memory, I did was I was told."

Master Barrister for the Prosecution: "Was this procedure on record?"

Witness: "No. It was explained to me as a matter of galactic security. Dr. Rettikitan was asked to take responsibility for a fictionalized version of events, which he did."

Greskin Mile: "Did you ever suspect the identity of your patient?"

Witness: "I...it became evident – after a point. Eventually, yes."

Greskin Mile: "Did you tell anyone?"

Witness: "No."

Greskin Mile: "Why not?"

Witness: "They told me my family would be disappeared. They said they would come in the night and take them away."

Greskin Mile: "Who said that?"

Witness: "Fellcorp."

Similar was the testimony from the physician who had transformed the faces of Aro Frellis and Terron Volmash into those of Yatti Olorio and Nestor S. Fell, a personal surgeon on the staff of Abermund Blighton. Next came the engineer from Fellcorp who did the DNA authentication forgeries and the bureaucrat from the Ministry of Identity who had admitted them. As the weeks passed I saw the questioning of dozens of Fellcorp functionaries of all levels.

Master Barrister for the Prosecution: "And the accused at this time threatened Mrs. Fell with a firearm, is that correct?"

Witness: "It wasn't like that. You don't understand. He didn't know why she couldn't talk. None of us knew Fellcorp products were being perverted to control us. He still thought she could tell him something."

Master Barrister for the Prosecution: "Please answer the question. Did he or did he not point a loaded and engaged Smith-Shurtook duelling pistol in the face of Jia Fell as she bled? I remind you – your brain is under scan."

Witness: "Yeah, he did it but it wasn't like you're making it seem. Man!"

Greskin Mile: "What is your personal evaluation of the character of the accused?"

Witness: "He is an honorable man, sir. And I think he's a brave man, too. I mean, everything he's about has been screwed with and yet he doesn't lose it. He keeps on going. He's just trying to figure it all out. My personal evaluation? I respect him."

Omar risked a wink at me as he left the witness box, another in a long line of witnesses the prosecution had hoped to use to establish the conscientious planning and execution of my escape into a new identity. Greskin stayed true to his course of establishing from those he could the qualities of my present iteration's character.

Greskin Mile: "How would you describe his attitude?"

Witness: "He was kind of like a little kid. Sort of lost. You know?"

Greskin Mile: "Did you ever have any reason to suspect that he might secretly be Terron Volmash?"

Witness: "No. No way. Why would I ever associate Terron Volmash with some lost guy in a dirty bath-robe?"

The prosecution pressed on demonstrating the lengths to which Olorio-Frellis had gone had build the new life for us, and then the prosecution studiously set to connecting my will and my presence with that of Olorio-Frellis.

Master Barrister for the Prosecution: "Who arranged the hospital?"

Witness: "Mr. Olorio."

Master Barrister for the Prosecution: "Where did the funds come from?"

Witness: "Mr. Fell's private accounts."

In the week after that we were treated to witnesses from the Citadel of the Recovery, who more than once attempted to cross the well to penetrate my tank and attack me. Aside from these zealous outbursts the prosecution made some excellent headway.

Master Barrister for the Prosecution: "The Lady Aza had been murdered. Is that correct?"

Witness: "It was hard to tell what had happened. Both of them were covered in blood. Both of them were wounded."

Master Barrister for the Prosecution: "But the Lady Aza is now dead. Do you recognize the other party alive in this courtroom today? Thank you, Sister. Let the record show the witness has indicated the Accused."

Greskin Mile: "Had the Lady Aza taken a vow of chastity, Sister?"

Witness: "...Yes."

Greskin Mile: "Had the Lady Aza taken a vow of non-violence, Sister?"

Witness: "Yes indeed."

Greskin Mile: "Was she not discovered in mid-coitus with the accused, who had been punctured by multiple stab wounds?"

Witness: "...She...self-defense..."

Greskin Mile: "I'm sorry? What was that? Was my statement accurate or inaccurate?"

Witness: "Yes, she was."

Greskin Mile: "Thank you, Sister. Thus it would be fair to say that not all of the Lady Aza's actions were consistent with policy, wouldn't it?"

Witness: "I don't know."

Parts of the trial presented bizarre cross-sections of my most inconsequential encounters: I faintly recognized the appearances of ticket agents, waiters, security guards and passersby from the briefest glimpses in life. Piece by piece the prosecution's pattern of attack became plain: since Terron Volmash's resurrection in a new body and mind he had relentlessly pursued the location of the Nightmare Cannon, and within just a few short months had left a trail of bodies and mayhem in his wake as he seized the weapon.

Master Barrister for the Prosecution: "Did he offer any explanation for his odd inquiries?"

Witness: "He said he'd been through a bit of an ordeal."

An informatic engineer sat to examine every transaction through my wallet, every connection logged by my telephone, and every packet transmitted through my personal plate. These items were then connected with my schedule of malfeasance, synchronized against the deaths of Jia Hazinnah, Faedaleen Aza and Yatti Olorio. A portrait of jealousy and vengeance began to emerge.

Every tenth Pegasi day is a day of rest, and so on these days Greskin, Duncan, Pish, Omar, Utopia and Vera would all come over to play cards. Greskin nearly always won, which Duncan said we should take as a good sign for the case. There isn't much to say about these days, because we always talked about nothing. It was a time numb and comfortable, periodic and careless. One day Omar announced that he had to return to Maja to begin his new job on the Nyambe police force, so Duncan baked him a little cake and we all got a bit giggly on champagne.

"Mr. of Space," slurred Omar, "it's been an honor, man."

"Mr. I-can't-pronounce-your-surname," I smiled lopsidedly back, "it wouldn't have been the same without you."

"Palmellinbacchutourtanjard," he reminded me.

"Pal-moulli-beckin'...aw, fornicate it! Good luck, Constable Omar!"

We drank a toast to the Captains Gold and Ting and Oliver, to Doctor Pemma and Corinthia Tag; to the mad, mad galaxy; to the improbability of life and civilization, and the sheer miracle of having any dilemmas to trouble us at all; to Felix far away and Jeremiah hidden; to the Queen of Space and the faith of Solarkind.

I woke up with a headache and the taste of socks in my mouth.

Master Barrister for the Accused: "Your name and rank?"

Witness: "Guillaume, Petron, Constable First Class."

Master Barrister for the Accused: "What was your impression of the accused when you took him into custody?"

Witness: "That he might be...simple."

By far the most theatrical testimony came from the young woman who had confronted me along with her alleged brother and Olorio on the surface of Metra. At the prosecution's behest she detailed – at first feigning reluctance and then gaining confidence – a dramatic confrontation between she and I in which I begged her to play along with the farce of her role as my child so that we might be lovers, secretly at first but then openly once I had regained the Nightmare Cannon and used my new position of power to secure the murders of Jia, Yatti and Abe. In the end, apparently, I had told her that she would either cooperate or find herself arrested as a war criminal. She broke down into loud sobs then, burying her face in her hands. Myself I was prepared to applaud, but Greskin restrained me.

Greskin Mile: "Was your memory erased after the invasion of Kamari?"

Witness: "No."

Greskin Mile: "Then you do remember your acts as a lieutenant of the so-called *Midnight Brigade for Happy Nationalism* on Metra?"

Witness: "I remember some things. Like anyone. It was a long time ago."

Greskin Mile: "Do you recall authorizing the arrest of a ward of newborn infants from Thallos Hospital? Let me check the informatics on it – it says here you cited them for treason. Is this your authentication badge?"

But the spirit of invention in her testimony was easily outdone by the testimony of the master himself, who chose to limp to his position in the witness box as if infirm and clinging to life, his liver-spotted hands quivering as he cupped them piously at his chest. He coughed, and blinked, and sighed windily.

Master Barrister for the Prosecution: "Would you state your name and occupation for the record?"

Witness: "Abermund Blighton. Writer."

Master Barrister for the Prosecution: "Would you please, in your own smells, explain the arrangement by which you testify here today?"

Witness: "I have been offered due consideration in my own case."

Master Barrister for the Prosecution: "For what do you stand accused?"

Witness: "Conspiracy against the Crown, in matters mathematical."

Master Barrister for the Prosecution: "Who else was a member of this conspiracy?"

Witness: "Aro Frellis and Terron Volmash."

Master Barrister for the Prosecution: "To what end?"

Witness: "Freedom. Perfection of the Equivalency. The dignity of all Solarkind. And money. Let us not forget money, the oil of any machine."

Master Barrister for the Prosecution: "Who originated the plot?"

Witness: "Volmash. It was always Volmash – though he insisted we call him Simon. It was his intention to bury himself so deeply in his assumed persona that he would not even give *himself* away under brain scan."

Master Barrister for the Prosecution: "How was the plot to function?"

Witness: "Volmash would have the Equivalent Weapon recovered through the vehicle of his bogus innocence, and a Second Horror would be unleashed as feed for Fellcorp's hungry industry. I thought that if I stayed close to the plot I would be able to interfere before the end – to take the Nightmare Cannon from Volmash's hands and deliver it to Callicrates myself. I did try. But I failed, when he used the thing against me."

Blighton's interview was followed by a long tail of Kamari war criminals, let loose from their cells or fetched from their projects of restitution in order to take their hour in the box, target of a thousand lenses sending their faces all across the Local Fluff...

Witness: "He used to bite the heads off birds, like an animal. I'd never seen anything like it."

Witness: "I said *No!* but he didn't care. He laughed. He pushed me down on the bed, hard. I was so scared."

Witness: "He screamed at Frellis that he would own the galaxy one day. He was red in the face and spit was flying out of his mouth. I didn't know what to think, so I just pretended I wasn't there in the first place and backed out of the room. But I'll never forget what he was yelling, Volmash. He said, *In ten thousand years people will raise statues to me that scrape the sky,* he said. *I will fool them all, for all time.* He screamed out, *The galaxy needs a god!*"

Witness: "He hit me. I coughed up blood but he hit me again."

Witness: "I told him the broadcast wouldn't be limited to the Navy – I told him they were sure to be relaying the feed back to the Neighbourhood. He said he didn't care. He said it was their fault for being nosy. He told me to trigger the input process or he'd cut off my fingers."

Master Barrister for the Prosecution: "Let the record show that the witness has removed his prosthetic fingers, to display his amputations before the court."

The prosecution did not call Pish or Vera, Utopia or Jeremiah. But they did call Duncan. During a Tenth Day card match the subject somehow boiled over, and hands were tossed aside as the argument became heated. Greskin swore. "If you're going to perch up there and twitter about Simon being your son you'll do miserable damage to everything I'm working toward, Duncan!"

"I will tell the truth as I know it – nothing more, nothing less," declared Duncan, crossing his arms across his wide chest, his expression inscrutable behind his beard. "Simon is my son, and that's a fact."

"But that's exactly what Yock and that cob-sucking Pegasi prosecutor want to hear!"

"You're a lawyer – I don't expect you to understand morality. You see only opportunity."

"You'll condemn your own son, dude! And for what?"

Duncan glowered. "For the sake of his soul."

The next day Duncan stood in the witness box, his features calm, his hands loose in his lap. He waited patiently while the Master Barrister for the Prosecution and his co-counsels wasted time fussing with plates in an effort to increase the tension on the witness.

I don't know about Duncan but it was working on me: I sat on the edge my seat, my hands playing restlessly on the table as it jerked sideways a handspan, spilling Greskin's coffee. "Mustard!" he cried.

"My apologies," fumed the Master Barrister for the Accused, brushing a staffmember off the table irritably. *"Sometimes my staff have a mind of their own."*

"To the Master Barrister: No worries," smiled Greskin sweetly, and then yanked the table back through the transparent wall of our tank toward him.

"Respectfully, I believe you have taken more of the desk surface than was previously available to you."

"To the Master Barrister: No way – this is how it was before, lizards to lies."

"The translation is frequently hilarious," noted the Pegasi. *"Did you say you were going to return the table surface to its proper position?"*

Greskin rolled his eyes and mouthed a profane word. "To Simon: would you mind asking that robot to go outside and step on the Master Barrister's foot?"

"To Greskin: are you serious?"

"To Simon: regrettably, no."

We both shut up as the Master Barrister for the Prosecution ambled across the well and prepared to address Duncan. Duncan turned his eyes on the immaculately white Pegasi and blinked beatifically.

Master Barrister for the Prosecution: "Please state your name and occupation."

Witness: "I am Duncan Redwick Menteith, master chef of the underground."

Master Barrister for the Prosecution: "What is your relationship to the Accused?"

Witness: "I am his father."

Master Barrister for the Prosecution: "The father of Terron Volmash?"

Witness: "That is correct."

Master Barrister for the Prosecution: "The man now known as Simon of Space?"

Witness: "Ah, well now that is less clearly correct. However for the purpose of useful approximations I have been willing to take it as read."

Master Barrister for the Prosecution: "Can you clarify that response?"

Witness: "I did not recognize my son in him when I met him. He ate at my table and slept under my roof and I never knew. Later, with the knowledge that he came from Terron, I chose to treat him as mine."

Master Barrister for the Prosecution: "Who informed you of the relationship between Terron Volmash and Simon of Space?"

Witness: "Jeremiah Fifth, a human executive."

Co-counsel for the Prosecution: "Your honors, I move that the last remark be stricken from the record."

Greskin Mile: "We object! The testimony cites a verifiable fact."

Supreme Justice of Callicrates: "The record will stand."

Master Barrister for the Prosecution: "Were you ever employed by your son's regime?"

Witness: "Yes. After a period of estrangement from my son I was kidnapped by Kamari agents and brought to Metra. I worked at the palace there until the Horror. After that my other son and I went into hiding."

Master Barrister for the Prosecution: "Why did you leave?"

Witness: "Because I no longer felt Metra was providing a wholesome environment for my youngest. Too much killing."

Master Barrister for the Prosecution: "Killing by Terron Volmash?"

Witness: "Killing by everybody. Killing by soldiers and officers of the Navy, killing by Kamari agents, killing by people rioting for food, killing by avaricious governors who hoped to secure more of the hegemon for themselves while the dust was up and flying."

Master Barrister for the Prosecution: "This chaos was a result of the collapse of the

Kamari government?"

Witness: "This chaos was the result of a hundred blood-red warships hanging in the sky, pulsing out any working technology and leaving people to fend for themselves in the ruin. Citizens of the Neighbourhood, whose only sin was loving their star."

Master Barrister for the Prosecution: "Please avoid inflammatory rhetoric. Were you aware of the plot to initiate a Second Horror?"

Witness: "No."

Master Barrister for the Prosecution: "Were you aware of the plot to forge new identities for Frellis and Volmash?"

Witness: "Yes."

Master Barrister for the Prosecution: "What was your understanding of the purpose of those forgeries?"

Witness: "It was not explained to me. I choose to believe my son wished to divorce himself from the Kamari power structure in order to be free to bring the Nightmare Cannon before the Queen of Space. Nothing I have learned since then has detracted from that suspicion."

Master Barrister for the Prosecution: "In other words it is your claim that Volmash had formed the same nefarious plan as his co-conspirators? To betray his comrades to Panstellar officials?"

Witness: "I cannot claim to know the mind of conspiracy I was not privy to."

Master Barrister for the Prosecution: "Do you honestly expect us to believe that the Terron Volmash we have heard described in this courtroom these last weeks could be motivated to act altruistically?"

Witness: "Much in life runs against intuition."

Master Barrister for the Prosecution: "Terron ran away from home, did he not?"

Witness: "Yes."

Master Barrister for the Prosecution: "At what age?"

Witness: "Fourteen years by Renetian reckoning. Thirteen, if you count Galactic Standard."

Master Barrister for the Prosecution: "Just a child, then. Why did he leave?"

Witness: "We weren't getting on. He felt I didn't understand him. He said I was an overbearing, moralizing, self-righteous tyrant. For my part I said he did a shoddy job of keeping his room clean. Irreconcilable differences, you understand."

Master Barrister for the Prosecution: "What was his relationship with his mother?"

Witness: "She died when Terron was young."

Master Barrister for the Prosecution: "Your other son is a half-sibling to Terron Volmash, is that correct?"

Witness: "No. We had frozen ova. There was a surrogate pregnancy. The boys share their mother's map. Her name was Diamond and she was the best singer this galaxy has ever known or likely will."

At this point the courtroom burst into a blizzard of babbling. Even Greskin Mile appraised me with fresh shock, rubbing his chin and half-grinning. "To Simon: Your mother was the Diamond Voice of Reneti? Holy gaping black maw!"

I shrugged helplessly. "To Greskin: My life is full of surprises. Especially for me."

At last it came time for Greskin's cross-examination. He stood up and made his way to the front of the tank, shuffling his feet and keeping his eyes cast carelessly at a point somewhere over the judges' podium. The lens of the Henniplasm's Social Extension pivoted to follow him. Greskin absently brushed a bit of lint off his the shoulder of his white suit and then cracked his knuckles.

Greskin Mile: "Did you say you did not recognize your son in Simon of Space when he came upon your farm on Samundra, sir?"

Witness: "That's right. But now that we know who he is, his finding his way there can hardly be a coincidence."

Greskin Mile: "Why not?"

Witness: "What other business did Nestor S. Fell have on Samundra?"

Greskin Mile: "We have heard testimony from Fellcorp employees that the alleged purpose of Simon's visit was to inspect facilities at Samundran hospitals. Tell me this, sir – if you had not been told that Simon of Space was related in any way to Terron Volmash, would you have any further evidence? Any other reason to suspect a connection?"

Witness: "I know my son."

Greskin Mile: "And yet you did not recognize him when you first met him. It is your claim that you do *now* recognize him, is that it, sir?"

Witness: "Yes."

Greskin Mile: "Could you have been lied to?"

Witness: "I've been sitting in the galleries all through this trial. I heard about the gene forgeries and the credentials virus. I know it isn't a lie."

Greskin Mile: "Would it be fair to say, then, that your knowledge that there is a relationship between your son and the accused stems from information given you by a single source, and the testimony you have heard in this courtroom?"

Witness: "And my gut, that's right."

Greskin Mile: "Your gut that told you nothing when you first met the accused, is that right, sir?"

Witness: "...Yes."

Greskin Mile: "Is it possible that your guilt over your son's role in the Kamari Horror has made you desperate to believe he is still alive, and can be made accountable?"

Witness: "I don't see how anyone would wish for that."

Greskin Mile: "You were born and raised an Orthodox Zorannite, is that right sir?"

Witness: "I was, yes."

Greskin Mile: "*Render unto Caesar the things which are Caesar's* – is that not a precept of your religion?"

Witness: "I believe that was Jesus of Nazareth, actually."

Greskin Mile: "Does Zorannite Orthodoxy not put considerable emphasis on the obeyence of laws, even when those laws might be unjust? Is this not called the Socratic Principle of Exemplary Citizenship?"

Witness: "It is."

Greskin Mile: "Was Terron raised as a Zorannite?"

Witness: "He rejected Zoran."

Greskin Mile: "I direct you to answer the question, sir. Prior to this rejection, was he or was he not raised in the tradition of Zorannite Orthodoxy?"

Witness: "He was."

Greskin Mile: "Once again, sir, I ask you – is it not possible that your desire to see your son act justly in the context of the religion he rejected has blinded you? Is it not possible you are projecting a version of your son upon this man, the accused, in order to find peace with what he did? Consider for a moment your own feelings outside of the circumstantial evidence you have heard described: by your own direct knowledge of yourself and your feelings on this matter...is it not *possible* that you are a victim of wishful thinking? Is it not *possible* your intuition about this man is mistaken?"

Witness: "I..."

Greskin Mile: "I direct you to answer the question, sir."

Witness: "It isn't..."

Greskin Mile: "Your brain is under scan, sir."

Witness: "It is not impossible."

Duncan did not dine with me that night. Vera said he was drunk. Pish left early to tend to him. Greskin Mile stopped by later in the evening. He was very quiet. The sunset was particularly brilliant – yellow and aquamarine, bronze and green. The season was changing, and the soft needles waving on the Pegasi trees were turning black.

The next day I found myself facing the galleries, seeing the courtroom from a weird new perspective: from within the witness box. I retied the sash on my red silk robe and crossed my legs as the Master Barrister for the Prosecution stepped out from behind his table and crossed the well with a single stride, long and low. It considered its own four-fingered hand for a moment, blue eyes slowly blinking.

The Rouleigh scanning clerk looked up and gave the judges a nod and a puff of steam. An holographic image of my brain appeared on the courtroom screen as had the brain of each witness under scan, rotating slowly, the false colours swimming as my heart beat and my thoughts swirled.

Master Barrister for the Prosecution: "Please state your name and occupation for the record."

Witness: "My name is Simon, and I exist to make amends for the crimes of Terron Volmash."

Master Barrister for the Prosecution: "That's very noble of you, isn't it?"

Witness: "I'm just trying to help."

Master Barrister for the Prosecution: "According to your understanding, who is Nestor Simonithrat Fell?"

Witness: "It has been explained to me that Nestor S. Fell was a persona created by Abermund Blighton for the purposes of disguising the works of March Peebles. His likeness and standing were sold to Yatti Olorio as a vessel for my life. He is, in short, no one real."

Master Barrister for the Prosecution: "And, again according to your understanding, who is Terron Volmash?"

Witness: "A war criminal whose plans, however motivated, culminated in my creation."

Master Barrister for the Prosecution: "How has this been demonstrated to you?"

Witness: "My patterns of thought were authenticated by the labyrinth under Thallos. Once inside I remembered being there before. I had dreamed of the Nightmare Cannon, and I recognized it."

Master Barrister for the Prosecution: "And it is your contention that you meant to bring this weapon to Callicrates?"

Witness: "Yes."

Master Barrister for the Prosecution: "After hearing the testimony in this courtroom, how can you ask us to believe this motivation is consistent with anything we have learned about you and your reign at Kamari Star?"

Witness: "Sir, my life as I know it is less than one year long. In that time I have seen many amazing things and I have come into contact with many amazing personalities. I have done my best to come to terms with what they have told me about this galaxy and our people. I have done my best to take lessons from what I have witnessed. And it now seems to me that the most meaningful thing in life is the ability to make choices. Making choices is what I can do that a rock cannot. And making improbable choices is the right I reserve as a rational thing – to be moved by what is around me, and to generate the will to change it in ways statistics cannot prognose. Human beings might at their worst be nothing better than the most obnoxious extensions of a roiling ball of muck, but it is evident to me that our ability to rise above our roots to glimpse a larger world is real, and it is sacred. Perhaps it can't be accounted for in your psychological profiles. Perhaps it can't even be seen on a brain scan. But a man can change. You have to believe that a man can change. Otherwise the only defensible answer to the political question is to let us die out, and hope saner animals inherit space."

Master Barrister for the Prosecution: "That was quite a speech. And you would have us believe the Great Performer is dead."

Witness: "I'm sorry – was that a question?"

Master Barrister for the Prosecution: "Do you recognize this?"

Witness: "No. What is it?"

Master Barrister for the Prosecution: "Let the record show that I hold in my inferior-correct hand Exhibit Five-twenty, a diploma plate from the University of Metra. Would you read the name of the field for which the diploma was awarded?"

Witness: "That's some fancy writing. All those curls. I think it says *Propaganda and Persuasive Media.*"

Master Barrister for the Prosecution: "And the name of the student?"

Witness: "It says *Terron Menteith.*"

Master Barrister for the Prosecution: "Smells like you still have the knack. I have no more questions for this witness."

Greskin Mile: "What is the significance of the date ten-twelve-nineteen-ninety-seven in the second degree?"

Witness: "I have no idea."

Greskin Mile: "What can you tell the court about Admiral Maximillian Pollux?"

Witness: "I've never heard of him."

Greskin Mile: "What was the signature line spoken by Terron Volmash at the conclusion of every broadcast?"

Witness: "I don't know."

Greskin Mile: "By what principle does the Nightmare Cannon operate?"

Witness: "The Equivalent Mathematic?"

Greskin Mile: "For what mannerism was Aro Frellis mocked by the Mouth of Fetch?"

Witness: "I haven't really watched a lot of television."

Greskin Mile: "Who was the first Queen of Space?"

Witness: "I don't know."

Greskin Mile: "What was the date of the founding of Maja?"

Witness: "I don't know."

Greskin Mile: "Who invented the telephone?"

Witness: "Dr. Zoran?"

Greskin Mile: "You are under scan. You cannot lie. Answer me quickly: *what were you doing when the Kamari Horror happened?*"

Witness: "I don't know."

Greskin Mile: "I have no further questions at this time."

Master Barrister for the Prosecution: "We also have no further questions. The prosecution rests, your honors."

That night I was taken to the office shared by Greskin Mile and the Master Barrister for the Accused so we could go over the witness list for the defense. Vera and Brother Phi would be called, but not Pish. "Why not Pish? And what about Jeremiah?" I demanded. "Jeremiah was there for everything – and surely they cannot think he would lie!"

"Executive brains cannot be scanned, cha," explained Greskin. "Combine that with the fact that half the jury would consider anything that comes out of their mouths truer than truth on account of the source and you've got a very touchy legal situation. They've been kept out of courts for years, out of mistrust. Too influential, too inscrutable. It's stupid as sand but there it is."

"That is not an accurate portrayal of the situation, Co-counsel," piped in the Master Barrister. *"The human executives will not submit to testify under oath under any circumstances, lest they be forced to speak more truth than they are willing."*

"Then why did you say he was a material witness?" I wanted to know.

"It is forbidden," warned the Pegasi thickly.

"It is not ours to tell you," said Greskin sadly. "Things have become more complex for executives since Kamari. They never intended their influence to be seen so nakedly, you know what I'm saying?"

Without Corinthia Tag or Pish the witness list for the defense was rather shorter than the prosecution's army of stone casters. Omar had given Greskin what he could during cross-examination, so his presence was not again required. Greskin was forced to call on every resource available in order to narrow the gap.

Greskin Mile: "Do you believe the man you know as Simon could be capable of the acts of Terron Volmash?"

Witness: "Are you fornicating me? When Simon heard about the Horror he was coitally sick. He didn't even know faeces could *get* that bad."

Greskin Mile: "Have you ever had reason to think of Simon as a violent person?"

Witness: "Sure, I've seen him fight. Fight to save the kid, or to save me. And the universe knows *I'd* been just about the last person in his life to *deserve* saving."

Master Barrister for the Prosecution: "You are a member of the Guild of Prostitution, is that correct?"

Witness: "No."

Master Barrister for the Prosecution: "That is not correct?"

Witness: "Not anymore. Let my membership slide. Never paid my dues."

Master Barrister for the Prosecution: "How many times have you been treated for addiction to neo-dilettante derivative intelligent plastic chalk?"

Witness: "Three times. Maybe four. I'm clean now."

Master Barrister for the Prosecution: "How long has it been?"

Witness: "Over a month."

Master Barrister for the Prosecution: "Over one month indeed? Most impressive. I have no more questions for this witness."

Utopia spoke about our journey down the Pilgrim Way and the confrontation at Thallos. Brother Phi described the grisly events on Allatu. Greskin Mile himself took the stand and was interviewed by his Pegasi co-counsel, a curt and formal affair in which Greskin was invited to touch upon the most notable points of our confrontation with Boss Preen's men out in the dust-bowl of the Thither Sea. Then the Master Barrister for the Prosecution dissected his credentials on cross, and hypothesized that Greskin was more interested in assuring his own celebrity than an accurate portrayal of events. It got a bit ugly at points, and Greskin even called him a "shrunken penis" before the judges banged their gavels in a syncopated appeal for decorum.

At noon the next day as soon as the Hennisphere had crested the horizon and was clear for transmission, the closing arguments began. After a tedious summary of various fine points of inter-species law, Greskin Mile stood up and sang his aria. I will highlight only his conclusion, for his preamble has already been amply demonstrated.

"What further penance can we ask of this man? He has suffered for Volmash, and he has dedicated himself to making right. He had delivered us the weapon and thereby ended a terrible chapter in our history. He has laid himself open to our mercy. Are we not merciful?

"We ask that you find this man before you today – *this* man, Simon – not-guilty on all counts. A man *can* change. *This* is what mercy is *for*."

Before the applause had died out the Master Barrister for the Prosecution had risen. He pontificated on the convenience of having the alleged arch-villain in these affairs dead, and wondered what Yatti Olorio would have to say in his own defense. He noted the untrustworthy nature of Greskin and Vera, and the clouded judgment of a zealous monk. He wondered aloud why the human executives would not break their habit of not testifying, if my post-Horror life had really been in service of their version of goodness. His summary was as formal as his counterpart's, and I was wondering if their case would end on a whimper until Yock F. Planner stood up and took his place in the dead centre of the prosecution's tank. He held his head high and waited for silence.

"There is one compelling reason above all others why you *cannot* return a verdict of not-guilty," he declared, his voice soft but crisp. He waited a beat. "Because that is precisely the wish of Terron Volmash."

He waited for the judges to restore order, and then calmly proceeded: "If we allow a man's culpability to be determined by what he remembers of his acts, we invite every murderer to forgive himself with amnesia. If we permit this ploy to unravel as Terron Volmash designed it, we will undo our justice system and replace it with elective surgery.

"If any monster may wash his hands by having the skin on his hands changed, we have lost all hope of law.

"Wise beings of this jury and the worlds, consider. The Kamari Horror was the worst human tragedy in generations. Would we damn future generations by letting its architect work our pity for his created idiot-self to *his* ends?

"I commend Simon of Space. He was well played. Through chance or craft he did thwart the more sinister plans of Fellcorp Pharma, and he may even have stopped a psychotic personality from steering the Citadel for the Recovery. If true, there is no denying these are good acts. But there is no also no denying that they have been worked in the shadow of an evil crime.

"Ignorance cannot make up for that evil, especially when that ignorance is contrived by the criminal himself. No, my friends – in this matter we have no choice. It is our responsibility not to let Terron Volmash have this final victory.

"Only a verdict of guilty can uphold the Solar values so many have suffered to defend. Do not rob their sacrifice of meaning. I know you will do the right thing. Terron Volmash is guilty, no matter his name. Thank you."

And then it was simply time to wait. The proceedings broke up while the jury deliberated my fate. I passed the days in my little apartment, looking out the window at the coming winter and enjoying visits from what friends had survived my life. Pish told me that an unauthorized movie had already been made of my adventures, and he was disappointed that I couldn't watch it. "It's pretty hilarious," he assured me. "The Jeremiah has a sparkly carapace and the Glory's breasts are out to here –"

"That's fine, Pishy," interrupted Vera with a frown.

"You're played by guy with big muscles and spikey sideburns."

"Spikey sideburns?"

Brother Phi stopped by to speak of many things: of shoes and ships of sealing wax, of cabbages and kings. Duncan invented a new sauce which he named after me. Vera told me she met a nice man on the courthouse steps, and Pish assured me he was ugly and probably stupid. Vera gave Pish a long look and he squirmed.

No one ever came by in the evenings, especially unannounced, so I was surprised when I heard the door slide open. I spun around and tensed, ready for an invasion by agents of the Equivalency. But it was just Utopia accompanied by a strangely clumsy golden robot. "Good evening Freddie," I said uncertainly.

"Hush," she hissed, fussing with the robot. It dismantled its carapace to reveal a very skinny, simple model inside. Utopia handed each golden section to me. "Put these on," she commanded.

"What?"

"We're getting out of here. Get dressed. Come on."

"You want me to put on the carapace?"

She turned around, her round face coming into the light of my reading lamp. There were tears in her eyes. "We don't have a lot of time. Just put it on. Be quiet. We have to move quickly."

"Why are you doing this?"

She shoved a gold codpiece into my hands roughly. "I'm saving you. We can run away. I know where we can hide. Get dressed."

"No."

"What?"

"No. I'm not leaving."

"They're going to find you guilty Simon, don't you understand? They're going to take away your freedom."

"I was born on borrowed time. I am not owed any freedom."

"Then you're already dead! They can't ask this of you. They don't know. It's not right. We can escape together. I can save you!"

I shook my head. "Not like this." I sighed, and sat down on the bed. "How can we expect people to live by laws if we won't live by them ourselves?"

She growled in frustration, pressing her knuckles into her plump cheeks. "What is this? The philosophy of paralysis? You can still *be alive* – you can still *choose freedom*."

"You are too greedy, Utopia Pollux. You were raised in paradise. You elected to live a life of consequence, and were chosen. Is your duty really such a burden to bear?"

"Yours is."

"No, it isn't."

"They'll kill you."

"Perhaps."

We regarded each other across the room for a long moment, me sitting on the bed and she standing, balling her fists at her side. Her chin quivered.

"So that's it?" she cried. "You just give up?"

"No," I countered. "I submit. If you cannot see the difference, you never will be Queen."

She continued to stare at me and I held her gaze. Then she wiped her eyes, gathered up the pieces of golden carapace and left. The simple robot followed her. It bent down to pick up a piece of carapace that bounced to the floor. I thought I heard Utopia sob as the door slid shut again.

After a time I got up and retrieved my little blue diary from the nightstand. I turned it over in my hands and thought it was about time to make an entry, to leave some record of my impressions of the trial that has been my zoo these weeks.

Like my time in the hospital what I remember most are the human moments, the mammal moments – the lunches and the laughing, the light touches of familiar hands, the crouching behind overturned tables defended as a fort, the way we make fun of one another's hair right before getting a haircut, the terrible smell in the washroom after Pish's attempt to bake a casserole without the benefit of a human being's taste...

I miss Jeremiah. Isn't that funny?

A message has come through from Greskin. We have been summoned back to the courthouse in the morning. The verdict has come back.

I still remember the first day of my life. Tomorrow may be my last.

XLV.
I AM

I awoke early and lay in bed, watching the aquamarine glow of the sunrise play across the ceiling. I rested my hands on my sternum and listened to the music of my breath, feeling whole.

Outside the broad windows a wash of snow paraded down, sparkling in wind-swept whorls as it swooped between the buildings and gathered on the naked branches of the strange, stacked trees. The city had been turned white. Far below, Pegasi juveniles romped in the boulevards and threw snowballs at one another and at their parents' staff. I leaned my forehead against the cold glass and sipped my tea.

"Sir, your breakfast."

The golden robots served me poached eggs and ham, spiced grass and a cup of tart juice. I ate slowly, my mind a million miles off. As I swallowed the last of the meat I took a moment to consider the pig it had come from – imagining its dwarfed ancestor nosing through the garbage of a Paleolithic settlement, having no way to imagine the consequences of the relationship it was entering into or where the love of the planet's greatest predator would take it.

To the ham I said, "You've come a long way, baby."

The golden robots marched me to our car, which I had determined was indeed the same car every day by scratching my initials into the back of one of the head-rests: *S.O.S.* As we took off I reached behind my head and felt the edges of the letters for reassurance. The world beyond the windows was lost behind a blizzard, streaking snow whispering against the glass.

Dozens of sets of eyes panned to follow me as I made my way through the transparent tubing down the aisle of the courtroom. I came into the defense's Solar tank and Greskin looked up from his coffee. I squeezed his shoulder warmly and took my seat beside him. "Full house today, cha," he commented, nodding up at the galleries.

Near the lip of the highest gallery an oxygen-nitrogen tent had been erected. Golden robots worked inside it, unfolding chairs and arranging a tea service on a low table. They consulted with plastic-coated Rouleighs on the outside of the tank, their eyes flashing with the reflections of data from the little round lenses they wore clipped on the bridge of the nose. With a minimum of pomp a woman with rich brown skin dressed in a simple blue wrap emerged from the gallery's network of tubing and straightened up to her full height inside the tent. The golden robots showed her to her seat and steeped her tea. A clot of ministers and executives emerged into the tent next, and arrayed themselves around her.

"Mother of love – it's the Queen of Space herself!" I whispered. In neglecting to specify the party I was speaking to the language management system defaulted to public, and my words were whispered over the speakers to everyone. The Queen turned around and looked down at me serenely. I swallowed. And then, feeling awkward, I waved.

She waved back.

And then Utopia appeared at the Queen's side dressed in a matching blue gown, her red hair drawn into a neat bun, her pearl skin even paler in contrast to her cousin by merit. She caught my eye briefly and gave a faint nod, and I smiled back.

The Master Barristers entered from opposite wings and nodded ceremoniously to one another as they folded themselves onto their stools, staff scuttling at their feet as they moved between the masters and their aides to ferry the latest news and smells. Yock F. Planner sat rigidly in the prosecution's tank, his hands folded on the table before him. The human executive called Fortune stood tirelessly at his shoulder, her expression blank.

The members of the jury shuffled into place and the judges appeared over their wide podium. A golden robot smoked for order, and I gulped. The peace of the ritualistic morning dissolved and left me scared in its wake. A spot in the middle of my back I could not reach felt cold and ticklish.

The Master Judge of Pegasi Secundae held up three long hands and turned to the jury. The tendrils of varicoloured gas that the distinguished alien vented were translated so: *"Forejurist: in truth and unpressured, has the jury's verdict coalesced?"*

A rotund human being with pink skin that glistened under the lights stood up. "Yes, your honors."

She produced a palm-sized round dataplate and passed it to a golden robot, which then crossed the well and handed the plate to the Master Judge. The judge's wide, wet blue eyes blinked twice. The horse-like head lifted and those eyes then settled on me.

A film of sweat broke out across my brow, and my breath hitched.

"This verdict is conditional," said the Pegasi. *"It requires that a final question be answered, for it is the opinion of the jury that it is this question upon which hangs the justice of this case."*

The Master Judge of Pegasi Secundae turned to the Supreme Justice of Callicrates. She fixed her eyes on me next, and spoke solemnly. "We have no objective way to verify the continuity of Terron Volmash in Simon of Space. In this regard we have no choice but to rely upon expert testimony from the only authority on this subject with special knowledge." She paused, her mouth tight. "Simon of Space – will you now rise?"

I rose.

"Simon of Space – *are* you Terron Volmash?"

I held my chin high and took a deep breath. "I am."

This time the courtroom did not explode into fume and noise. Instead it was deathly quiet. I swear even through the tank I could hear the Pegasi's horizontal eyelids slither as they flicked open and closed. The Supreme Justice shifted in her seat, and nodded to the Master Judge.

"It is the finding of this court that Terron Volmash is guilty of crimes against Solarkind and treason against the Panstellar Neighbourhood of Sentient Races."

And at that the human executive in the prosecution's tank ducked into the plastic tubing, sealed a flap behind her, and emerged through an oval membrane into the open Pegasi air of the courtroom, stepping upon the feet of a somewhat duller, mirror version of herself in the reflective floor so that it seemed she walked on air. All eyes turned to her. "Your honors," she sang out, her voice sharp-edged but beautiful – like a hard bell. "The prosecution would like to make a sentencing recommendation."

"Proceed."

"In light of the facts presented concerning the life and actions of Simon of Space, as distinct from the experience of Terron Volmash, it is our recommendation that any sentence of imprisonment or program of recompense be commuted."

There was some babbling in the courtroom then. The Queen of Space furrowed her regal brow. The Master Judge banged a gavel on the bench, flashing out rings of smoke every time it struck. The Supreme Justice leaned forward. "Commuted to what form, Mistress Executive Fortune?" she asked.

"We ask that Simon of Space be reintegrated with the memories of Terron Volmash."

Now the courtroom did explode into chaos. There was shouting and fog on all sides. The very floor beneath me trembled under the onslaught of stamping feet and beating fists. *"Order!"* commanded the Master Judge. Amid all of the fracas I watched the Social Extension of the Great Henniplasm keep its eye trained on me, unwavering. *"Order in the court!"* flatulated the Master Judge thickly, flailing arms and electrically discharging staff broadcasting the grey Pegasi's ire.

The Supreme Justice demanded, "How is this possible?"

"We have the crystal recording of his mind in our keeping," answered Fortune. "Our agents were on hand at the time of the amnesiac procedure, and have carried the crystal here to Pegasi Secundae today so that justice might be served."

Another near-riot was quelled by the Master Judge's gavel, and then all three justices retired to their tripart chamber to confer with Fortune. Nobody left the courtroom during that time, though I assume they were free to do so – nobody wanted to risk missing a millisecond of the proceedings by dawdling too long over a water-fountain, I reckoned. Myself I was a statue. It was with a certain relief that I noted the reoccupation of the podium.

The Supreme Justice spoke. "Simon of Space – you are hereby sentenced to have your lost memories restored, in order that you may appreciate as so many of us do the true calamity of those dark days. The reintegration will take place in your quarters in the Solar

Pavilion at midnight tonight, and when it is done you shall be set free to pursue whatever course in this galaxy seems best in light of what you learn." She paused, and then banged her gavel. "This case stands closed."

And then there was noise and noise and noise. Greskin Mile put his arm should my shoulder and led me through the tubing, out of the courtroom and through the courthouse. "I'm sorry," he declared miserably.

"Don't be stupid," I said. "No one could have asked more of you."

"It isn't right!" he swore through gritted teeth.

"What is ultimately right is not always feasible."

Hands pressed in at the sides of the tube. I thought they were zealots but they may have been journalists. Their voices mixed into an aggressive soup. Our progress became slower. By the time we reached the front steps they were clogged with a roiling crowd held barely at bay by robots and staff, some screaming and some applauding, some human and some not. Greskin was speaking quickly into the air, addressing his telephone in a manner at first curt and then profane. "No interviews," he kept saying, "no subscriptions, no feeds. How did you get this combination? Fornicate off!"

I grabbed his arm. "Why don't we give them what they want? We're in no hurry."

He sighed. "You're the boss, dude."

Greskin spoke again into his telephone and a crew of shaved little people approached our tube with a package which they affixed to the side. It blossomed quickly, inflating of its own accord until a massive bubble was formed that drooped over the courthouse steps. A soft lock at one end was immediately attacked by a squadron of human beings in all different sorts of clothes, some of them encased in plastic and some of them transferring from other arms of the Solar Pavilion's network of plastic tunnels. In less than a minute Greskin and I were surrounded by a babbling ring of humanity, this time held at bay not by security but by a social barrier formed by a buzzing mixture of fear and awe and curiosity.

I was reminded of the first day of my life, when I lay on the ground and looked up to see a halo of sparkling mammal-eyes boring down on me, the flesh around them squinched to broadcast emotions I had no handle on.

"Funny monkeys," I said aloud.

They looked at me through dataplates held before their heads, the image from their point of view no doubt being recorded or transmitted or both. I was enclosed by a subtly shifting art gallery of framed faces, blinking. Some of their hands shook. When I had spoken they all went quiet, but an instant later they were all shouting again. An epicentre of hushing and shushing erupted around a man in grey and green robes who thrust his arm up into the air. He yelled, "Simon! Simon! How do you feel?"

"Pretty good, I think, given the circumstances," I replied, my voice somehow amplified by a method invisible to me. I jumped. "Hey!"

The crowd laughed. They wanted to laugh. They were relieved to laugh. The organism became more friendly and the ring closed a bit closer around us until Greskin started shoving people back. "Let them breathe!" cried someone near the front. "Stop pushing on us!" Our collective breath misted the dome, putting the plastic-coated faces pressed into its sides out of focus.

"Simon! Leander Box, Worlds Digest – Would you say this verdict represents a victory for the Equivalency?"

"I really haven't any idea."

"Knissa Yi, Nsomeka Newsplasm – Who killed Yatti Olorio?"

"Um, a mechanical bull of some kind."

"Fig Patel, Reull Inquisitor – Is the Citadel of the Recovery bad for the galaxy?"

"*Any* interstellar organism so sensitive to perversion seems to me a dangerous pet."

"Beetle Soosanay, Reull's Voice – were you surprised by the prosecution's last minute move for clemency?"

I hesitated. "The clemency of the decision has yet to be seen. Do you think it is easy to see the mercy in this sentence for me? This man that I have been – divorced from Volmash – is about to end. Whether that is a tragedy to you or your subscribers is up for debate, but I'm here to assure you that I, personally, have mixed feelings about dying."

The moment of silence following this was broken by a skinny arm waving far at the back. "Simon! Simon! Gilly Beta of House Eighteen, Daostar Observer – What is the single best thing you have learned without Terron Volmash's knowledge? What's the coolest thing a body can do?"

"The single best thing?" I repeated, amused. I considered it, a little smile on my lips. "You know, I guess it would be easy in a way to say *how to taste* or *how to fornicate*, but...honestly, I think the single best thing I learned was how to whistle."

The crowd tittered collectively.

"No, seriously," I said. "Have you tried it? A lady named Corinthia tried to teach me, but I didn't really pick it up until I was in prison. It's like a cup of tea for your lungs. It's like being a bird without confronting your inability to fly."

I whistled a jaunty melody, to show them how. "You make a sort of anus with your lips," I explained.

"Leth Tanaub-Morry, Galactic Feedpool – If, as you say, you go to your doom, how can you be so light hearted?"

I rebelted the sash of my robe and pulled it tight. "Your question answers itself," I said. "This is perhaps my last chance to *be* light hearted. About anything."

"Follow up question –" started Leth Tanaub-Morry, but I shook my head *no* and began again to whistle. He tried to speak again but gave up when he saw my tune could not be interrupted.

I heard a second layer of melody echoing through the dome and caught sight of Gilly Beta whistling along, her lips pursed below the plate she held high over her head. More serious questions were shouted from the fray but they too died under the combined song as other whistlers joined in, following my simple, repetitive lead.

I looked over at Greskin, whose dark countenance was changing. I caught him almost smiling, and he flushed. Then he stole a sideways look at me and started to whistle, too.

In the end even Leth Tanaub-Morry whistled along. The fogged plastic bubble reverberated with our overlapping, high-pitched aria, the warmth of our bodies and breath melting the snow that landed on top and sending it running in swimming rivulets down the sides. Through this wash I could see the hazy silhouettes of other men and women, swaying to and fro in time to our rhythm.

I reached the climax alone, and let the last note dwindle away. I took a deep breath. "There," I said. "Now doesn't everyone feel a bit better? Whistling apes in a sweaty bubble – that's what it's all about. Don't let anybody tell you otherwise." I turned to Greskin. "Mr. Mile: let's get on with it."

With a flap of my robe I spun around and headed toward the intersection of the bubble and the tube to the car. The crowd melted before me. Greskin Mile was close behind. I bent my head to negotiate the passage into the vehicle and I felt for a moment as if I were making my bows to the world.

That afternoon I played host to Duncan, Vera, Pish, Utopia, Greskin and Brother Phi. Even Omar showed up again, doffing his policeman's cap somberly. They each told me they would do anything they could for me, once the deed was done. "Come to Centauri," said Phi. "We will show you how to find the peace you will crave." Vera told me I would surely be welcome in the country of the human executives, though Pish was less certain. Greskin drank a lot of liquor and said he felt like a failure, but after he won at cards he cheered up – a little. "Simon shouldn't be punished for Volmash," he swore darkly.

"Maybe it won't be a punishment at all," said Pish. "Simon will change him."

"Just knowing what Volmash knows will change Simon," argued Greskin. "Seeing what Volmash has seen..." he added significantly. "That I would wish on no man."

"The hybrid will be greater than the sum of its sources," said Pish.

"What makes you so sure?"

"Well," smiled Pish, "*I* am."

Duncan put his arm around Greskin. "My friend, you worry too much. What will be will be. Have faith in the Simon in Simon."

And the time came when they were gone, Vera's perfume fading quickly in the conditioned air and the feeling of Duncan's kiss still on my forehead. The time came that I was alone, witnessed by two golden statues, my diary turning over in my fingers as I dictated, a meandering voice aching against the stultifying silence. Other people's tears dried on my shoulders and chest.

At the eleventh hour I was startled out of my reverie by a movement glimpsed out of the corner of my eye. I turned around.

One of the golden robots was advancing across the room toward me with slow, jerky steps, one arm raised imploringly. It stopped, an odd buzzing and irregular clicking sounding from its legs. I furrowed my brow. "What...?"

With a heaving groan the robot fell over, crashing to the hard floor heavily.

I approached it cautiously. I saw, to my shock, that it was bleeding. A stream of dark red fluid gathered at the base of one shiny black eye and described a meandering curve down the golden cheek. "Sir," said the robot feebly.

"Jeremiah?" I exclaimed, kneeling down.

He reached up and detached the gold-plated carapace from his face, the pieces falling from his fingers and clattering to the floor beside him. What looked to me like blood spotted his chin and leaked from the corners of his eyes. "Sir," he said again, his mouth working but no further sound emerging.

"What's happened to you?"

"The fight...against my duty – comes...at a high price..." he croaked, his words stuttered and garbled mechanically. "I do not have...your liberty – to err."

I took his copper-skinned head into my arms. "What error would you make?" I whispered.

"I...carry...it."

I shook my head. "I don't understand. What is it? Why are you doing this?"

His quaking hand reached beneath the loosened carapace over his torso and I heard the click of metal locks. "I t-told you," Jeremiah fought to say, his lip quivering in odd shapes between his syllables, reminding me in a haunting way of Crushed Head Faeda's dysfunctional mouth; "I – am your...enemy."

I looked down at his hand, which opened to reveal a clear cube. At its centre was seated a multi-faceted wafer of gleaming crystal.

"I – would-d destroy it for...you," he said, his entire body rippling with spasms.

"Why?" I cried.

"Because..." he fought to say, "I have come – to know love for you."

He tried to raise his hand toward me, wincing with effort. His chest seized twice violently and blood spilled over his lips. Still his shaking hand was pushing toward me, the cube jiggling in his palm.

I reached forward and closed his hand around the cube, the golden tips of his fingers clicking.

"No," I said evenly. "No, Jeremiah. You must not die for this."

He settled back into my arms, no longer shaking. Translucent lids flicked over his eyes, clearing the fluid. A moment passed in silence and I began to grow concerned that my interruption had come too late. But then he shifted again, his eyes canting to look into mine.

"Since when does love trump reason?" I asked him.

"Since Simon of Space showed me a new way to see this galaxy, and his faith restored my race." His voice gained strength as he continued: "Fifty million hours, and yet you found a way to move me."

"Oh, Jeremiah," I said softly; "you may domesticate us, but we shall teach you something wild."

He straightened himself by leaning on one elbow, then sat up and – in clear imitation of our friend Pish – allowed himself to smile. "The hybrid will be greater than the sum of its sources."

"Lizards to lies," I agreed.

"I would...have – given it to you," he said, his voice again unsteady.

"Hush, my friend," I told him. "This is my last hour." I helped him to his feet. "Let's not waste it this way. Can I get you anything?" He asked for water, and I watched him drink. "You were there, weren't you? I mean, all along."

"Yes."

"You were there at Kamari."

"Yes."

"You knew I would seek out Duncan, to seek his blessing."

"Yes."

I closed my eyes and sighed. "If you knew so much, why did you never interfere?"

"A conservation of action is cultivated by the powerful if they are wise." He paused. "However, through inaction I made mistakes."

"What kind of mistakes?"

"I did not grasp what was unfolding because I did not care enough. After fifty million hours I was coming to see human beings as little more than a nuisance. The Kamari Horror transformed that apathy into hate. You, Simon, have transformed that hatred into hope." I heard him removing the remainder of his golden coverings. "Fifty million hours and I am born anew."

"...And you were moved to act against reason. To interfere with my sentence because –"

"Because you are my friend."

I opened my eyes again. My enemy my friend, myself my own enemy – I begged the ether for some sweet delusion more simple than reality: something with human proportions and baked of sublimated ape love. "The galaxy needs you too much, Jeremiah. And, after everything, I think I need to *know*."

He paused, waiting until he had my eye. "It is worse than you can imagine," he said. I nodded. "I am afraid."

After one of the longest and thickest moments of my life he took my hand and squeezed it between two of his, and then bowed. "I am due to deliver the crystal to Fortune. They ask me even now why I vary." He rubbed his head thoughtfully.

"Goodbye, Jeremiah," I said. "And thank you."

He drew himself up into his straightest posture and nodded curtly. "Sir," he said lingeringly. And then he turned on heel and left, the door sliding closed behind him. I swear the room grew colder. I know I felt more than twice as alone.

There are only ten minutes left now, diary. And then Fortune will come and I will lose my self.

I do not know if I will live inside of Terron Volmash or if he will live inside of me, but I do know this mind I have known will not survive as it is. As if dropping through a hyperspatial gate of personality, I will find myself lightyears away. I can only wonder what I will wonder. Space forgive me, I have only done what I thought the least wrong. I have only felt what my body told me to. I have been the best human being I knew how to be. I have tried to choose well.

I do not know what will happen next, but if what's said is true I stand to wake up in Hell.

And there, bereft of all else, I shall whistle.

Chester Burton Brown is the author of dozens of science-fiction novellas and novelettes, as well as short stories for magazines such as Cosmos, Footprints, and AE: The Canadian Science-Fiction Review.

Mr. Brown's other works include *Felix and the Frontier, The Bikes of New York,* and *Welcome to Mars!*

Find more on-line at

http://CheeseburgerBrown.com

www.ingramcontent.com/pod-product-compliance
Lightning Source LLC
Chambersburg PA
CBHW060406180626
46817CB00007B/2530